Yankee Bride /
Rebel Bride:
Montclair Divided

*Also by Jane Peart
in Large Print:*

Ransomed Bride
Valiant Bride
Scent of Heather
A Sinister Silence
Love Takes Flight
Autumn Encore
Sign of the Carousel
Circle of Love
Undaunted Spirit
A Distant Dawn
Where Tomorrow Waits

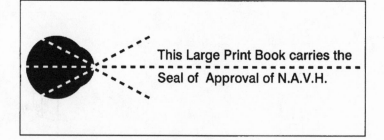

Yankee Bride / Rebel Bride: Montclair Divided

Book Five
of the
Brides of Montclair series

JANE PEART

Thorndike Press • Waterville, Maine

Copyright © 1990, 1985 by Jane Peart

Published in 2004 by arrangement with Natasha Kern Literary Agency, Inc.

Thorndike Press® Large Print Christian Romance.

The tree indicium is a trademark of Thorndike Press.

The text of this Large Print edition is unabridged.
Other aspects of the book may vary from the original edition.

Set in 16 pt. Plantin by Liana M. Walker.

Printed in the United States on permanent paper.

Library of Congress Cataloging-in-Publication Data

Peart, Jane.
    Yankee bride/rebel bride : Montclair divided / Jane Peart.
        p. cm.— (The brides of Montclair series ; bk. 5)
    ISBN 0-7862-6897-2 (lg. print : hc : alk. paper)
    1. Plantation owners' spouses — Fiction. 2. Williamsburg
Region (Va.) — Fiction. 3. Plantation life — Fiction.
4. Large type books. I. Title.
PS3566.E238Y36 2004
    813´.54—dc22   2004053013

Yankee Bride /
Rebel Bride:
Montclair Divided

As the Founder/CEO of NAVH, the only national health agency solely devoted to those who, although not totally blind, have an eye disease which could lead to serious visual impairment, I am pleased to recognize Thorndike Press★ as one of the leading publishers in the large print field.

Founded in 1954 in San Francisco to prepare large print textbooks for partially seeing children, NAVH became the pioneer and standard setting agency in the preparation of large type.

Today, those publishers who meet our standards carry the prestigious "Seal of Approval" indicating high quality large print. We are delighted that Thorndike Press is one of the publishers whose titles meet these standards. We are also pleased to recognize the significant contribution Thorndike Press is making in this important and growing field.

Lorraine H. Marchi, L.H.D.
Founder/CEO
NAVH

★ Thorndike Press encompasses the following imprints: Thorndike, Wheeler, Walker and Large Print Press.

PART I

Yankee Bride

Milford, Massachusetts
Spring 1857

chapter

1

"No, Rose, you can't!" The urgency in Kendall Carpenter's voice gave it a harsh edge. "You can't mean you intend to marry Malcolm Montrose!"

"But I do and I am!" retorted the girl facing him, her dark eyes flashing with indignation.

Framed by the trellised arch in her father's New England garden, Rose Meredith had never seemed more beautiful to the distraught young man — the rosy coloring in her rounded oval face heightened by emotion; the sweetly curved mouth; the rich brown hair falling from a center part and tumbling in ringlets about her shoulders rising from the ruffled bodice of the wide-hooped muslin dress. Perhaps the fact that he knew now he had lost her, made him more keenly aware of her beauty today.

As soon as Kendall heard the news of her engagement from his classmate, her brother John, he had rushed over to Milford from Harvard only to hear the truth from her own lips. His hopes of winning Rose himself lent desperation to his argument.

Her initial indignation softened as Rose saw the genuine distress in Kendall's expression, the hurt in his eyes. She put out one delicate hand and touched his arm. "Please, Kendall, try to understand."

"*Understand?* It's *you* who doesn't understand, Rose."

Rose sighed. She knew Kendall would use all the skills at his command as a law student to dissuade her. She had tried arguing with him before to no avail. She would just have to hear him out.

"Has your father given his approval?" he demanded.

Rose smiled slightly. "Why, Kendall, that you should ask such a question!" Her tone implied a gentle reproof. "After all, this is 1857. Even my father thinks a woman has a right to make her own decisions."

Undaunted, Kendall continued. "But you can't, Rose. You don't realize what you're getting into. The South has a different culture, a different outlook on life.

10

For someone like you, Rose, that kind of life would be slow death."

"What are you talking about, Kendall?"

"Their attitude toward women, for example, is almost medieval. Women are merely pampered little girls who never grow up because the men they marry won't let them. They are desired for decorative purposes and, well, for other reasons, of course. But Southern men certainly don't consider women their equals, any more than they do blacks. And that's another point —"

"Kendall," she interrupted, "I won't hear any more. I love Malcolm Montrose and he loves me. It's disloyal for me even to listen to what you're saying. Malcolm isn't like the men you're describing. I know him and —"

"I know him, too, Rose! I sat around debating with him often about the very things we're discussing now. Southerners are *not* like us. It's a different country down there."

"You're talking pure nonsense. A different country, indeed! Aren't we all one United States? Didn't our grandfathers all fight for the same freedom less than one hundred years ago?"

"No, Rose, you're wrong." Kendall

shook his head. "Even then we were fighting for different reasons. Remember, I've been down South visiting just recently, and I know what I'm talking about. It *is* a different country with different ideas, accepted rules, traditions," he continued. "You'll find — if you're headstrong enough to go through with this ridiculous notion — that it will be like living in a place where no one speaks your language. Mark my words, Rose, it's not just that I don't want to lose you. I don't want to see you lose *yourself.* If you marry Malcolm Montrose — you'll live to regret it!"

Rose was startled by Kendall's vehemence. John had warned her that it might be difficult to explain her decision to the enamored young man, but Rose had confidently replied, "Oh, Kendall will understand." Still, Kendall obviously did *not* understand. For the first time Rose became aware that what she had considered only a pleasant friendship had meant more, gone much deeper with him. She had liked Kendall more than any of John's Harvard friends. That is, until the weekend her brother brought Malcolm Montrose home for a visit.

Almost from the beginning Rose had felt a strong attraction for the tall, soft-spoken

12

Virginian. It was mutual, and had moved quickly from interest to affection to love, the kind of love Rose had often dreamed of but had never dared to believe would be hers.

They had learned almost at once that they shared many interests in common — a love of nature, philosophy, and literature. They had taken long walks together, held lengthy discussions on every subject, watched sunsets, and strolled through the quiet, winding country lanes around Milford — more and more absorbed in each other's company, lost in each other's words, eventually completely in love.

Malcolm was quite the handsomest man Rose had ever known, but it was his gracious manners, gentle humor, and more than that, his poet's soul that endeared him most to Rose.

For his part, Rose knew that Malcolm not only considered her beautiful, but also often commented that her keen mind, her vivid imagination, and unconscious charm both awed and delighted him. That she could articulately discourse on the subjects that intrigued him was a cause for endless pleasure. Indeed, they often explored the new philosophies together — transcendentalism, pantheism, the essays of Emerson and other noted preachers of the day.

Rose had been well educated in a private academy that offered a curriculum for young women comparable to Malcolm's at Harvard. She had, therefore, studied French, Latin, history, botany, and even geometry and astronomy.

Theirs was, Rose was positive, a match made in heaven. She and Malcolm, in spite of misgivings others might have, were absolutely sure they were destined for each other, and nothing this passionate young legal student could say could convince her otherwise.

"Rose, I beg you to reconsider," Kendall pleaded.

"There is nothing to reconsider," she said gently. "I love Malcolm. None of your arguments can change my mind on that."

"Then, nothing matters," he said dejectedly. "There is nothing left for me."

"Oh, Kendall — my dear, dear friend — at least wish me happiness."

Kendall shook his head, the firm lips compressed. "I can't! I won't!" He struggled before he burst out impulsively. "I can't because . . . I love you! I want you for myself!"

With that, Kendall stepped forward. Taking Rose's face between his hands, he kissed her on the mouth — at first gently, almost sorrowfully, then with a firmer pressure, and finally with a fierce intensity.

Rose pushed her small hands against his chest, forcing him to release her. Breathless and shaken by this unexpected display of emotion, she gazed at him, speechless.

Kendall dropped his head, saying brokenly, "Forgive me, Rose. I shouldn't have done that." Then he turned and walked hurriedly down the path, letting the garden gate slam behind him.

It took Rose several minutes to regain her composure. She had never dreamed Kendall felt so deeply about her. But with just a few weeks remaining until her marriage to Malcolm, nothing could mar Rose's happiness for long.

She spun around, gathering up her skirts, and ran lightly up the steps into the house. Inside she paused for a moment, listening, but the household was still. Her Aunt Vanessa must be napping. From her father's study came the low murmur of voices. He must still be visiting with some of his friends.

Rose tiptoed up the broad front stairway to the second floor. Moving down the hall, she came to the spare bedroom. Opening the door carefully, she stepped inside. In

15

the dim light she searched out the dress form on which her wedding gown hung, awaiting only the final fitting before Aunt Van, an accomplished seamstress, would pronounce it perfection.

The gown was of ivory watered silk; the bodice, with its tiny tucks, tapered into a V and was edged with Brussels lace taken from Rose's mother's wedding gown. That dress had been too small in every way for her tall, willowy daughter. Rose's eyes misted as she touched the beautiful lace. How sad it was that Ellen Meredith had not lived to see her daughter a bride.

Rose's gaze fell on the wispy froth of veil secured to a circlet of tiny silk roses and spread out on the quilted coverlet of the four-poster. Beside it were the white silk stockings and satin slippers she would wear.

Excitement tremored through her as she lifted the wreath and tentatively tried it on. Rose smiled at her image, noticing the dimples that hovered at the corners of her mouth. Malcolm had teased her about her dimples and often kissed them when he told her how pretty she was.

"What a vain creature you are, Rose Meredith soon-to-be Montrose!" Rose scolded herself with a mock severity, taking off the veil and placing it carefully beside the slippers.

"Beauty, after all, is in the eye of the beholder. If Malcolm thinks so, that's all that matters," she told herself. Aunt Vanessa would have likely added, "Beauty is as beauty does," and directed Rose to look up the scriptural description of a virtuous woman whose price was above rubies.

With a final, satisfied look at her wedding finery, Rose left the room, closing the door quietly behind her, and tiptoed down the hall to her own bedroom.

She had always loved this room with its slanted ceiling, its windows that looked out on the lovely orchard where she and Malcolm had often walked and where he had proposed. This room had always been her place of refuge from childhood hurts and schoolgirl sorrows. Here she kept her favorite books, her old dolls; here, at her little maple desk, she had written poetry. She looked around now with a certain poignancy, knowing that within a few weeks she would be leaving it forever.

Of course, she wanted to go, to become Malcolm's bride. Still, there was a nostalgic clinging to all that would be left behind.

Everything had changed for Rose since

Malcolm had come into her life. Even the things Kendall had spoken of ceased to make a difference. She loved her home, the town where she had grown up, but she loved Malcolm more. It was all well and good to point out the importance of a husband and wife having the same roots, the same background, but that did not allow for the unexpectedness of love.

Sometimes, Rose had discovered, love enters unawares, kindling a spark one did not even know existed until it is set aflame. One does not question it when it happens. As with her and Malcolm, love held all the exciting possibilities, the lovely surprises, the mystery one dreams about and hopes to find.

For all Kendall's arguments, even her father's suggestion that perhaps she and Malcolm should put off their marriage for another year to test their feelings for each other, Rose knew she did not want to wait a moment longer than necessary.

She held out her left hand and gazed at the third finger. The engagement ring Malcolm had placed there a few weeks ago glistened in the late afternoon sunlight.

The ring had been especially designed for her. It was crafted of mellow gold with a sculptured rose and cradled in its center like a dewdrop, one perfect diamond. Rose twisted the lovely jewel to allow the facets to glitter in the ray of sun streaming through the window.

Malcolm was a superior man, sensitive and romantic. How blessed she was to be loved by such a man. His thoughtfulness never failed to astonish her.

She picked up a blue leather book from her desk, its soft cover emblazoned with a tooled rose, delicately detailed even to tiny thorns on its graceful stem. She opened the volume and its empty pages fluttered. It was a journal, Malcolm had explained, for her to begin keeping when their new life together began. It would be a record of their lives, beginning with the European honeymoon they would take following their wedding. On the first page, in his handsome script, Malcolm had written: "To my darling Rose," then the quotation after:

Rose, thou art the sweetest flower
  That ever drank the amber shower;
Rose, thou art the fondest child
  Of dimpled Spring,
    the wood-nymph wild.
                — Thomas Moore

19

She lifted her eyes from the writing on the page to the small, framed daguerreotype of Malcolm on her desk. She felt her heart contract with unconscious joy and wonder that this noble-looking young man was soon to be her husband. The high-cheekboned face with the large, serious eyes, the dark, wavy hair falling upon the broad forehead and curling around his ears, the winged collar and wide cravat, his chin resting on his hand gave him a scholarly appearance, yet the mouth, so sensitive and gentle, held just a hint of a smile that bespoke the subtle sense of humor that so delighted Rose.

She picked up the picture, kissed it, and held it for a long moment against her heart.

Almost at the same time she felt an odd chill, and she shuddered slightly as Kendall's words lingered like a troublesome specter clouding her happiness:

"If you marry Malcolm Montrose, you'll live to regret it!"

chapter

2

Garnet Cameron, cantering happily home on an April afternoon, had no idea that within the hour her safe world would be shattered, her life unalterably changed. She was aware only of the soft wind in her face, the warm Virginia sun on her back, the exhilaration of riding her favorite horse through the shadowy woods bordering Cameron Hall, the family plantation.

Jumping the fence at the edge of the pasture, she galloped under the leafy arch of elms lining the road that led to the stately white-columned mansion. The clatter of hooves on the brick drive startled three peacocks strutting on the lawn and sent them scattering, as a golden flash of flying mane streaked by them.

In front of the portico Garnet slid from her sidesaddle and tossed the reins to the stableboy who ran out from the shade of the giant lilac bushes where he had been waiting for her return. Giving the chestnut mare an affectionate pat on her arched neck, Garnet swept her long skirt over one arm, ran up the steps and into the house.

Just inside the cool vaulted hall Garnet paused, hearing the sound of voices coming from the parlor. Guiltily she recalled that her mother was having guests for dinner and had asked her to be home early to help receive them. If the guests had already arrived, she was certain to be in for a scolding.

Tiptoeing over to the gold-framed mirror, she made a quick appraisal of her appearance should she be caught before she could slip unseen upstairs to her room. The sun slanting in from the fanlight above the front door shone on her gold-bronze hair, sending shimmering lights through the cascade of curls that had escaped their confining snood. She tucked them back under, then tilted the jaunty brim of her brown velvet riding hat with its long, red-tipped feather.

She took a minute more to straighten the jacket of her biscuit-colored riding habit, smoothed its cinnamon velvet collar and cuffs and adjusted the creamy silk stock at her throat. Turning sideways, she admired her pleasing image.

At eighteen Garnet could not be considered beautiful. Her features were pert rather than classical, but her coloring was vivid and her enormous eyes, fringed with thick dark lashes, were unusual — like clear topaz. She was taller than average with a slim, rounded figure. If not the prettiest, Garnet was one of the most popular belles in Mayfield County, envied by other girls who gossiped that she was vain and an incorrigible flirt, none of which concerned her in the least.

Satisfied that she would pass inspection even by her mother's sharp eye, Garnet moved quietly across the hall. However, passing the parlor at the stairway, she heard a name spoken that never ceased to cause a strange little throb under her heart. *Malcolm. Malcolm Montrose.* They were talking about Malcolm!

With one booted foot on the bottom step, Garnet stopped to hear what was being said about him. The voice belonged to one of her twin brothers, either Rod or Stewart. They sounded so much alike she was not sure which was speaking. But if it were Malcolm they were discussing, it was worth the risk of her mother's displeasure to go in and hear for herself.

Tossing aside her gloves and riding crop, Garnet turned and hurried to the parlor. Standing in the curved doorway, she surveyed the room and was relieved to see that only family was present. No guests yet.

"Hello, everyone!" she called out merrily.

All four of the room's occupants looked in her direction and all smiled fondly, even though her mother shook her head slightly and glanced at the ormolu clock on the marble mantlepiece.

Ignoring the implied reproach, Garnet cast a dimpled smile at her father and, moving toward the abundantly laden tea table, stopped at his chair to drop a kiss on his cheek. Her tall, russet-haired brothers exchanged a knowing look, but watched indulgently as Garnet helped herself to some cake.

"Garnet, dear, you're late. The Maynards will be here very soon," her mother admonished her gently.

"I know, Mama, and I'm sorry, truly I am. But I'm simply famished. Just a bite and I'll go get ready. It won't take me long to —"

"To make yourself beautiful enough to

dazzle poor Francis Maynard?" teased her brother Rod.

Garnet gave an exaggerated shrug. "Oh, *Francis*," she scoffed. "It doesn't take much to dazzle *him*."

"So, missy, you can do it without half-trying, eh?" asked her other brother Stewart with a lift of his eyebrow.

Garnet chose to disregard the question, merely smiled archly and nibbled on her cake.

"Now, boys!" Mrs. Cameron chided her sons, "how can I ever hope to make a proper lady of Garnet when you two laugh at everything she does? And you're every bit as bad, Douglas," she addressed her husband, trying to look severe.

With the confidence of an adored only daughter, one treasured by her brothers, Garnet laughed along with the others at her mother's mild reprimand. Then, looking at Rod and Stewart, she demanded, "So, what have you two 'double-troubles' been up to this afternoon?"

"The same as you, little gypsy," Stewart retorted. "Riding all over the countryside. We did, however, manage to honor our dear mother's request to be home early, dressed, and ready to receive our guests. A point, I might suggest, that you would have been wise to make as well."

"But we also made a call at Montclair and paid our respects to the Montroses," added Rod.

So they had been to Malcolm's house, thought Garnet, with a small stirring of excitement. In June after his graduation from Harvard, Malcolm would be back at Montclair for good. How she had missed him, longed for the day when he would not be going to Massachusetts each fall. It seemed ages since Christmas, the last time she had seen Malcolm.

His dear image flashed into her mind, all six spendid feet of him, with his dark, silky hair, deep blue eyes, his high coloring, and aristocratic features. He was a few years older than the twins, which meant he was nearly six years older than Garnet, and had always treated her as a beloved younger sister, just as her brothers did. At least, until last Christmas. . . . *Last Christmas had been different,* Garnet thought dreamily.

But at her brother's next statement she was jolted out of her daydreams.

"You'll never guess what news is flying at Montclair," Rod announced with the air of one about to spring a spectacular surprise. "Malcolm is engaged to be married."

Startled, Garnet gripped the delicate

handle of her teacup. She heard her mother's soft voice phrase her own agonized question.

"Who is the girl?"

"A sister of one of his classmates. Rose Meredith is her name."

The parlor seemed to spin crazily and Garnet's ears rang with the words that were reverberating in her brain. *Malcolm engaged to be married? It can't be true!*

"She's the daughter of a professor, I believe," Stewart continued. There was a trace of amusement in his voice as he added this bit of information.

"A Northern girl, then," Kate Cameron said with a hint of bewilderment.

"That's what comes of sending your sons up north to school. Never did understand Clay's reasoning when we have the University as well as Washington College right here in Virginia," commented Judge Cameron tersely.

Garnet finally found her voice. Struggling to sound natural, she asked, "Rod, how did you find out?"

"Apparently they had just gotten the news. Seems it's a bit of a surprise to all of them, too. We were visiting when Bryce showed us a picture Malcolm had just sent home."

"Is she pretty?" Garnet asked sharply.

Rod turned to his twin. "I'd say so, wouldn't you?"

"If you like them dark and demure." Stewart grinned.

"She's probably a terrible 'blue stocking'," remarked Mrs. Cameron. "Most Northern girls are."

"If you mean by that 'well-educated,' Mama, I believe Miss Meredith is, indeed. Mr. Montrose read us part of Malcolm's letter. His fiancée is 'as intelligent as she is beautiful.' Those were his words, if I'm not mistaken."

Trying to conceal the shock of this news, Garnet bit her lip and concentrated on the contents of her teacup. If she could just manage to control herself until she could escape to her own room, she thought desperately. The thought of attracting her mother's anxious attention or exposing herself to possible teasing by her brothers was unbearable. She attempted to appear as usual while the conversation flowed unheard around her.

Unknowingly her mother came to the rescue. "Garnet, dear, you really must go up and get ready. . . . It's getting late."

Gratefully Garnet stood up with a great show of reluctance.

"Oh, bother, I'd much rather eat supper like this . . . not have to fuss —"

But even as she spoke, she was moving toward the parlor door. Once out in the hallway, out of sight, she picked up her skirt and flew up the curved staircase, her little leather boots tapping on the polished steps.

Safely in her bedroom, Garnet's composure crumpled. Malcolm to marry someone else? Harsh sobs choked her as she pressed her fists against her mouth to stifle the sound. It couldn't be true! It just couldn't! Why, she had been in love with Malcolm Montrose forever! Or at least ever since she was twelve.

She had dreamed of marrying Malcolm someday — believing that he was only waiting for her to grow up. And last Christmas, at Mamie Milton's wedding, he had looked at her differently, had treated her differently, and Garnet had been convinced he had thought of her differently. Her mind raced back to that crisp December afternoon at Oak Haven. Decorated for Christmas, the house had been transformed into a fairyland. Garlands of fresh greens entwined through the banisters of the central circular staircase and holly tied with red ribbon suspended from

29

the sparkling chandelier, made it an enchanting setting for a holiday wedding.

Garnet, one of the ten bridesmaids, was particularly pleased that Mamie had chosen emerald velvet for the gowns, which set off her hair gloriously.

She recalled coming into the house in a flurry of cold wind and drifting snowflakes, and Malcolm, handsome in a dark waistcoat and ruffled shirt, was the first person she had seen.

"Why, Garnet, I declare you look too pretty to be real!" he greeted her.

At his words her heart had turned over with happiness to have Malcolm gaze at her like that.

After the wedding ceremony they had danced nearly every dance together as Malcolm, in a teasing, reckless gesture, had torn up her dance card. Later they had eaten supper on the staircase by themselves, out of range of Garnet's ever-watchful mammy-nurse who had always accompanied her to social events and held it as her sole purpose in life to "be sure Miss Garnet ax lak a lady and doan disgrace her mama."

When at last it was time to leave, Malcolm had slipped one of her small, white kid gloves into his sleeve, and Garnet had floated home in a daze.

Could it be possible that he had known Rose Meredith at Christmas? No! Malcolm was too honorable to pretend an affection he did not feel.

"I know Malcolm still cares for me! I know it!" Garnet railed. "I saw something special in his eyes! I know I did!"

Feeling betrayed, abandoned, Garnet smothered her anguished screams in the pillows, kicking her feet in frustrated fury. Gradually the sobbing lessened, but her fists remained clenched, her heart broken.

But it had been months since Christmas, since Malcolm had returned to Harvard to complete his studies, and while she had been counting the days until summer when he would come home to Montclair and to her, had Malcolm fallen in love with someone else?

Suddenly the bedroom door opened and Mawdee, her mammy-nurse, came in demanding, "What you doin' here mopin' lak dat for when dey is company downstairs waitin' fo' yo'?"

Garnet sat up quickly on the bed where she had flung herself in her first burst of bewildered grief. Keeping her head averted from Mawdee's eagle eye, she surreptitiously wiped away the telltale traces of

31

tears. But Mawdee unnoticing, bustled over to the big armoire to get out Garnet's dress for the evening.

While Mawdee's back was turned, Garnet jumped off the bed and hurried over to the marble-topped washstand. Picking up a pitcher of water, she poured it into the porcelain bowl and, leaning over, splashed her hot face.

Somehow she would get through this evening. Then when she was alone again, she would think of something — some way to pay Malcolm back for what he had done to her!

chapter

3

As if in benediction, a shaft of May sunshine, streaming in through the narrow, arched windows of the church, enveloped the couple standing at the altar rail in its golden light. To those attending the wedding ceremony of Rose Meredith and Malcolm Montrose, it seemed to hold special significance.

Vanessa Howard beheld the scene through a blur of unaccustomed tears. Usually not a woman prone to a show of emotion nor given to displays of affection, she dabbed at her eyes discreetly. Her niece was very dear to her. She sincerely hoped Malcolm would understand how sensitive she was, how easily hurt, how loyal and loving.

Rose had been such an interesting child — bright, lively, and with a vivid imagination. She had given to Vanessa, then a spinster past thirty, the gift of a relationship she would never have known otherwise. When Vanessa had come into that motherless home fifteen years ago to take care of John and Rose, it might have seemed to others that she was making a sacrifice. But her sojourn in the Meredith household had proved to be quite the opposite. Helping rear those children had brought her unprecedented joy and fulfillment. This day marked the end of her task.

She was handing over her precious charge to the young stranger from the South who would take Rose away to another life. Vanessa prayed with all her heart that he would treat his bride tenderly, keep all those promises he was making today. But who could say what lay ahead of them? They were so young and so gloriously in love that it made the heart ache to see them.

Taking his place at the altar, the Reverend Amos Brandon looked at the two young people in front of him and felt a sudden tightening in his chest. Though he had performed hundreds of marriage ceremonies, this one had added meaning. Perhaps it was because he had known Rose's mother, Ellen, had married her in this same church, and had buried her not five years later.

But no. There was something else, something particularly touching about this wedding, about these two people. It was as if a mantle of sadness hovered above the beautiful couple — as though this day were an ending, not a beginning. He tried to dismiss the pervasive melancholy as he cleared his throat and began the time-honored words.

"Dearly beloved, we are gathered here today to join this man and this woman in the bonds of holy matrimony, a state instituted by God and blessed by Him as an honorable estate —"

Seeing his daughter's enchanting profile turned toward her bridegroom, Thomas Meredith was conscious of an ache in his throat. Rose was very like her mother, his own Ellen, hardly more than a bride when he lost her. Yet Rose was very different. While Ellen had been gentle, submissive, quiet, Rose was intense and intelligent, with a strength of mind and a clear individuality — qualities not often appreciated by men. Perhaps it had been unwise to educate her as highly as her brother. Still, Malcolm had not found this unappealing. In fact, he seemed drawn to Rose by those very traits. That these gifts would blend with her sweet nature and femininity was devoutly to be hoped, her father sighed.

"These vows you are about to exchange should not be taken without full understanding of their importance, their mutual binding, and without any mental reservations whatsoever, as you shall answer on the dreadful day of judgment —"

Clayborn Montrose, Malcolm's father, the silver-haired, impeccably tailored gentleman in the front pew, shifted uneasily. As opinionated as he was strong-featured, he did not take to this kind of pious threat. Of course his son knew marriage was a serious step! Malcolm was a serious young man — thoughtful, reserved, not given to foolishness or flirting like his brothers, Bryce and Leighton. Malcolm was the intellectual one. Yet he could sit a horse as well as any other Virginian, even if he did not spend every waking hour in the saddle — riding, hunting, courting every pretty girl in the county. Clay might have wished his eldest son had chosen a bride from among the many eligible young ladies in Virginia, daughters of his lifelong planter friends.

But he had to concede that Rose Meredith was graceful and charming. A real beauty, as well. And her background was as prestigious and proud as his own. Her family, wealthy and well-born, her dignified father and refined aunt all spoke well of Malcolm's choice of brides. Clay had been equally impressed with the stately pink-bricked Federal house facing the well-kept common in the historic town of Milford as well as with the elegance of its furnishings, the gracious hospitality accorded by his host, and the well-trained servants in the household. Now, if only this present unpleasantness between the northern and southern states of the nation would get settled quickly — a subject that no one in this well-bred gathering had mentioned over the last few days — things would be fine.

Of course, there was Sara.

Ah, Sara, Clay sighed, remembering his own beautiful bride. Tall, slender, as graceful on horseback as on a dance floor, Sara had ridden daily until the terrible day of her accident. Clay closed his eyes, recalling the scene with an awful clarity.

He and Malcolm, then only a little boy, were watching her from the fence along the pasture as she practiced her jumps. The sun was shining that day on the slim figure in royal blue velvet, with dark hair tightly netted into a chignon under the plumed hat. Then suddenly the magnificent bay shied and turned at a stone hurdle, throwing Sara to the ground. When Clay reached her, she was lying motionless, the lovely dark hair loosened and spread on the grass, the lithe body broken. Malcolm had seen it all.

When even the finest doctors in Richmond could not promise that Sara would ever walk again, Malcolm had kept his mother's hope alive, staying by her bedside constantly. From that time a deep bond had been forged between mother and son, deeper and stronger than Sara had with either of her other sons — or with anyone else, Clay thought ruefully.

From that time on Sara had lived the life of a semi-invalid. Since he could not give her back the active life she had once enjoyed, adoring her as he did, Clay had tried to give her everything else.

The one exception was in Clay's choice of schools for their eldest son. Sara had not wanted Malcolm sent north to be educated, had argued hotly against it, but Clay had insisted, secretly believing Sara's possessive love for Malcolm to be unhealthy. Now, of course, Sara blamed him for Malcolm's choice of a Yankee bride.

". . . and should not be entered into ill-advisedly without prayerful consideration —"

Clay Montrose changed his position again, mentally decrying the fact that New England churches had such hard benches. *Probably a leftover Puritanical belief that there is some virtue in being as uncomfortable as possible,* he thought and chuckled inwardly, recalling with some longing the cushioned comfort of the Montrose family's private pew in the church they occasionally attended in Williamsburg.

"So, now I do ask you both to search your hearts and consciences that you may freely agree to the questions I will now put to you —"

John Meredith regarded his sister with eyes both affectionate and thoughtful. He had spent long hours with a deeply distressed and disappointed Kendall Carpenter in their lodgings at Harvard, talking about Rose's planned marriage to Malcolm.

Although he entertained some of the same misgivings about the match, John also admired and respected the Virginian. He had found Malcolm to be unusually intelligent, cultured, compassionate. Besides, Malcolm had spoken so convincingly of his love for Rose, his intention to devote his life to making her happy that John had no reason to doubt him. No, it wasn't the man she had chosen that struck some fear into his heart; it was the way of life to which Rose must become accustomed, a way of life so diverse and foreign to her that he could not help wondering if her happiness was really assured. Or if, once the newness of their mutual passion faded, the differences in upbringing and outlook would become more apparent.

John sighed heavily. There was nothing he could say or do that would have changed either of their minds, he realized. Rose, for all her soft sweetness, was strong-willed and stubborn, and Malcolm had been quietly determined.

"If there be anyone present who knows any reason why these two should not be joined together as man and wife, let him now speak or forever hold his peace —"

Kendall Carpenter, arms folded across his chest, sitting in the very last row, swallowed hard. He had not wanted to come to this wedding. It had taken every ounce of his strength and will power to bring himself here to witness another man marrying the girl he had dreamed and hoped and longed to have for his own. He set his jaw and clenched his teeth together, willing himself not to leap to his feet and stop the ceremony, shouting, "Yes, I do! It's wrong! It's a terrible mistake!"

He recalled clearly, with every detail distinct, the first day he had set eyes on John Meredith's sister. It was their first year at Harvard and John had invited him home for the Thanksgiving weekend. He remembered his thoughts when John had introduced him, saying, "This is my sister, Rose." *Of course, what other name could this delightful creature be called? The slender figure, the graceful bearing, the petal-soft mouth, the delicate rosy coloring . . . what, but Rose?*

He had fallen in love with her at once and had loved her every day since . . . and today he was losing her forever.

"Do you then, Malcolm, take Rose — to love, honor, and cherish in sickness and in health, for better or for worse?"

Malcolm had experienced a feeling of unreality ever since he had awakened that morning and realized with his first moment of awareness that this was the day Rose would become his bride.

Every miserable moment of his years at Harvard faded away after he met her. Now, as he looked down into her upturned face, her eyes radiating such warmth that his heart pounded, roaring in his ears, he thought of his happiness the day he had asked her to marry him and how she answered almost before he had gotten the words out of his mouth.

"Oh, my dearest, yes!" she had whispered and her voice was husky and tremulous with emotion. She went into his arms then as trustfully as a child, and he was overwhelmed with the sweetness and ardor of her surrender.

As Malcolm repeated the vows the minister was reciting, he prayed that God would help him to keep them, that he would never fail Rose nor do anything to take away the happy bright shining in those love-filled eyes.

"Do you, Rose Ellen, take Malcolm for your lawful husband, to live together in God's ordinance as his wife, to love, honor and obey him —"

"I do," Rose replied in a tone so light, so soft it had an almost childlike breathlessness.

At last it was here. . . . She was standing "in the presence of God and this company," as Pastor Brandon had said, taking the most solemn vow of her life, making the most binding promises, blending her life — past, present, and future — with this man whom she loved with a blinding, blazing emotion beyond anything she could ever imagine or had ever known. . . ."From this day forward" . . . for all her life on down all the years to come, into eternity, she and Malcolm would be one soul, one spirit, one body . . . before the Creator — one — enduring, exclusive, encompassing all they had been, were, or would become. It was happening! Now! *I love you, Malcolm!* her heart sang as his voice quietly spoke the words of the traditional service.

"And with the giving and receiving of this ring, pledging your troth one to the other, I now pronounce you husband and wife —"

Malcolm took Rose's hand and she felt a quicksilver tingle as he slipped the wide gold band on her finger.

Reverend Brandon took their clasped hands and, placing his own upon their joined ones, said, "Henceforth you will belong entirely to each other. You will be one in mind, one in heart, one in affections."

As if from a long distance, Rose heard the deep tones of the organ begin to play the familiar recessional hymn. Malcolm was smiling, offering her his arm as they turned to face the congregation. She slipped her hand through it, and with his other hand he pressed hers and said in a low voice intended only for her ears, "My darling wife . . . *Mrs. Montrose!*"

The radiance in Rose's face brought tears to the eyes of the observers as the couple started down the aisle. *If wishes and prayers could ensure their future happiness, it is a certain thing,* Vanessa thought, turning to watch their departure for the reception area and the European honeymoon to follow. Unfortunately, that was sometimes not enough. Life, after all, was as the minister had said, "a vale of tears." She only hoped that *this* day would always remain in their hearts and minds as completely and blissfully happy, no matter what came afterward.

PART II

Rebel Bride

Mayfield, Virginia
Summer 1857

chapter
4

Garnet awoke the next morning to a roomful of spring sunshine. At first she did not remember the terrible shock she had suffered the night before. Then as she awakened fully, remembrance came, and she felt the bewildering despair assail her once more.

Not daring to be around the house under the watchful eye of her mother or the suspicious Mawdee who was expert at ferreting out Garnet's best-kept secrets, she decided to go riding. On horseback she was always happiest, clearest-headed, at her best. There she could think, plan, decide what she should do.

In the golden light of the morning some of the tension, confusion, and pent-up emotion began to ebb in the exhilaration she always felt seated on Trojan Lady, a sixteenth-birthday present from her father. The fine horse beneath her responded to her slightest touch on the reins and moved forward with a buoyant step. Through the sun-dappled woods they went, horse and rider finding release in an easy trot along familiar bridle paths.

Slowly Garnet grew calmer, the woods seeming to enfold her in its peace; the only sounds, those of hoofbeats on a carpet of pine needles. When she stopped to let Lady drink from the rushing stream midway through the woods, Garnet lifted her head and looked about. Through a curtain of lacy white dogwood she could see the outline of the little house called Eden Cottage, and she knew she had reached the dividing line between Cameron and Montrose land.

Eden Cottage! Garnet caught her breath. Traditionally, the "honeymoon house" to which Montrose men brought their brides for the first year of marriage was the architect's model for the big house, a miniature Montclair, built on the site of the original log cabin occupied by the first settlers on their land. As she looked, Garnet was filled with renewed distress.

How often she had ridden by this very place and thought in passing that one day she would spend her honeymoon year inside that charming little house — with

Malcolm. Was it really possible to have dreamed such a dream? A dream with no foundation?

Again she felt that wild rush of defiance rising within her, the irrational hatred for the clever Yankee girl who had somehow "tricked" Malcolm into marriage.

Garnet's hands on the reins tightened convulsively and the startled mare jerked her head upward, shaking it and whinnying in protest at the sudden pull on her tender mouth. Garnet leaned forward to pat the horse's neck soothingly. Her anger was for Malcolm, and the fiery energy of it coursed through her. She gave Lady a gentle kick with her heels, urging her forward. They splashed through the creek beside the rustic bridge and clambered up the other side and onward to the ridge of the hill. Here she had an almost unobstructed view of Montclair gleaming in the April sunshine.

Garnet dismounted and loosely tied the mare's reins to a nearby tree. Then, walking over to the edge of the little rise, she gazed down on the house, the source of all her plans and dreams.

What was it about Montclair that gave it such a magical quality? she wondered. It was not as magnificent as her own home, which had been designed by a famous English architect and embellished with elaborate formal gardens and Italian statuary. There were terraced lawns and rooms filled with fine French furniture. In contrast, Montclair, built with white oak felled and milled right on the plantation, and bricks made by their own people, had a simple dignity that was at once austere and appealing. Garnet could not explain why she had always been drawn to it. Maybe it was because Montclair was so like Malcolm himself, who was sometimes thoughtful and serene and at other times, lighthearted and laughing.

Everything about these surroundings reminded Garnet poignantly of Malcolm. She had often met him on this very same bridle path when he, too, was riding. She remembered particularly the day before he was to leave for Harvard for his first year. She had been a skinny twelve-year-old; Malcolm was already a young man of eighteen. They had both dismounted and walked along the creek. Garnet remembered every word of that conversation —

"I wish you weren't going, Malcolm. Papa says it's nonsense to send Virginia boys up north to school."

"Well, my father feels differently. He

thinks it's important for Southerners to learn how people in other parts of this country think, feel and live. Maybe it will be good for me to get out of my own little world for a time. Anyway, I'm curious."

Garnet had tossed her long tangled mane impatiently and had pushed her rosy underlip into a pout. "But I don't see why you have to go so far away. Papa says Virginians should know their own state, their own people. Our ways are good enough — better, Papa says. After all, you're going to live the rest of your life in Virginia anyway."

Malcolm laughed. "Well, I'll be home for Christmas and all during the summers. Besides, you'll be going away to school yourself before long, little one."

"No, I won't. Mama wanted me to go to the Academy where she and your mother went, where my cousin Dove Arundell is going, but Papa put his foot down. He doesn't want me to be away from home. So, I'm to have a tutor instead." Here Garnet had made a face. "But she's a *Yankee* from *Philadelphia!*"

"And that's a problem, is it?" Malcolm had teased. "I'll wager you'll lead her a merry chase."

And she had, Garnet recalled wryly. She

could easily reduce the hapless Miss Simmons to tears, then run out of the house, get on her horse, and ride off for the afternoon. She had managed to get away with it, too. Over her mother's protestations, her father had just called her "a little dickens" and pacified the governess with a new shawl. Garnet was his darling and he could never punish her nor deprive her of anything. He would have moved heaven and earth to make her happy, Garnet knew.

With aching heart she remembered another conversation with Malcolm that had taken place when she was about fifteen, not yet "come out." On the evening of the Bachelors Ball, which she was considered too young to attend, Malcolm had come by Cameron Hall to ride over with Rod and Stewart. Garnet had poured out her pique about it to him while he was waiting for her brothers.

"It's always *when I'm older*," she complained. "I'm tired of hearing it! Everything nice is going to happen *when I'm older!* Nothing *now!*"

"Garnet, that's not true. Lots of nice things happen now. Like your birthday. *That's* going to happen very soon — with presents, a party, all sorts of nice surprises."

"But it's my *sixteenth* birthday that counts!" she insisted. "People are still telling me 'wait until you're older.' I don't want to wait! I want what I want *now!*"

Malcolm had studied the young girl who no doubt would grow up to be quite irresistible.

"Listen, Garnet, the best is yet to come, believe me," he had told her very seriously. "You'll see. In another year or two you'll have so many beaux you'll be like a princess with knights riding up to your doorstep, begging your papa for your hand in marriage."

"I already know whom I want to marry," she told him tartly, looking up at him from beneath long lashes.

"If you were six years older, I'd marry you myself," Malcolm had said laughingly.

"Then I wish I *were* six years older," she had declared. But at that moment her older brothers had come clattering down the steps, drowning out her reply.

All at once the impact of his engagement, the crushing end to her long-held dream, struck her full force. She began to sob. With all the violence of a thwarted child, Garnet cried wildly, bitterly.

Finally with a last shuddering sob, she dug her fists into her eyes, swallowed hard, and flung back her head.

A lifetime of having every wish fulfilled had given Garnet an unrealistic expectation, had instilled in her false confidence that such an existence would continue unabated.

Before her lay the serenely beautiful house where she had expected to live as Malcolm's bride. Now the man who could have made that possible was marrying someone else.

From somewhere deep within Garnet came a taunting suggestion: *You may not marry Malcolm . . . but you could still be Mistress of Montclair.*

The desire for revenge activated in Garnet a dark, devious part of her, heretofore undetected — unplumbed because there had never yet been anything she truly wanted that she had been unable to attain. Now, an insidious plan, seemingly simple, hovered tantalizingly before her. If she could not have the man she loved, Malcolm, she *could* have his brother — Bryson Montrose! What delicious irony to be already ensconced at Montclair as its potential mistress when Malcolm brought home his Yankee bride.

Suddenly what had appeared hopeless seemed within easy reach, and the seductive sweetness of revenge filled Garnet's heart. She did not know that once the impossible seems attainable, all obstacles of honesty and decency are sometimes swept away in the lust to grasp the dream. So she fixed her sights on Bryson Montrose.

Bryce was a direct contrast to Malcolm in both appearance and character. Ruggedly handsome, with an air of nonchalance, Bryce cared little for the knowledge gained from books. He was content to spend his days astride the horses he rode like an Arabian prince. Bryce possessed all the careless charm, the good-natured personality, the well-bred manners expected of a Southern gentleman. He was, however, the dismay of every hopeful mother of marriageable daughters in Mayfield County, for although any of the three Montrose sons would have been considered more than eligible, this one seemed most unattainable. It was said he cared more for horses, dogs, and hunting than for the company of young ladies. This fact had discouraged most of the matchmaking mamas.

But thus far in her short life as a belle, Garnet Cameron had never failed to snare any beau she pleased in her butterfly net of coquettish smiles, flattery, and winsomeness. Bryce might present more than the usual challenge, but Garnet had every confidence she could claim her prize in due time. With bitter relish she imagined the satisfaction she would feel at greeting Malcolm and his Yankee bride from the steps of Montclair.

Her frenzied thoughts were interrupted by the sound of rain pelting the leaves of the overarching trees. Feeling them on her face, Garnet realized that the sky had darkened and become heavy with clouds scudding across at an angry pace. A loud clap of thunder startled Lady, and Garnet had to speak soothingly before the mare allowed her to mount and start back down the path heading homeward.

By now the rain was falling steadily. It wasn't the first time she had been caught in one of the April showers prevalent in this part of Virginia. They came almost without warning and, although of short duration, they were drenching.

By the time Garnet emerged from the woods, galloped along the meadow, and cleared two fences taking a shortcut back to the stable, she was wet clear through. As she cantered into the slick cobblestone stable yard, she saw Tully, one of the grooms, saddled up and starting out, confirming her suspicion she had already been missed. Obviously he was being sent out in search of her.

Garnet frowned. Sometimes it was a real nuisance to be the object of so much affectionate care. She had hoped to avoid her mother's reproach, then she saw Mawdee, arms folded over her ample bosom, standing at the top of the stairs, and she knew she was in for her sharp upbraiding.

As Mawdee helped her out of her sodden riding habit, Garnet sneezed twice.

"See there, missy, what yo' foolishness done got yo'?" she glared at Garnet, her face fierce with indignation. "Yo' done ketched yo' death of cold, iffen I ain't mistook!" She then turned to the little maid, Bessie, and ordered, "You, gal, fetch some hot water up to Miss Garnet's room direckly. Doan' jes' stand there gawkin'! Git movin'!"

Within minutes Garnet's rain-soaked clothing was removed and she was wrapped in a blanket until the younger maid could pour pails of boiling water into the iron tub Mawdee had placed before the bedroom fireplace. In a way, Mawdee's grumbling ministrations were soothing to Garnet's bruised emotions. After a brisk rub-down at the black woman's none-too-gentle hands, Garnet was tucked into her high poster bed, in a nightgown that had been warmed, and with a heated brick folded in flannel at her feet. Later, a hot lemon and honey drink was brought in for her to sip in the soft luxury of her fluffy pillows.

"Now, missy, yo' hab yo'sef a good res' and doan' think 'bout doin' no sech foolishness agin. I'll tell Miss Kate yo'll be havin' supper on a tray 'stead of comin' to de table dis ebenin'," Mawdee announced before waddling out of the room and leaving Garnet to the dubious comfort of her newly hatched scheme.

Garnet was relieved to be left alone, dismissed from dinner with her family and the ever-present guests. Usually she enjoyed the sociability of her home, its constant flow of company, but tonight she had so much to think about she needed uninterrupted time to herself.

Since Bryson Montrose had never shown the slightest romantic interest in Garnet, she knew this would have to be a carefully orchestrated campaign, executed with great finesse. Bryce was known to have resisted the charms of the prettiest girls in Mayfield. So, as the unsuspecting pawn in the game Garnet was preparing to play, his reluctance must be overcome.

Garnet heard the whisper of rustling taffeta on the polished floor outside her bedroom door, scooted further down into her quilt, and closed her eyes. She knew by the subtle wafting scent of lilac that her mother had quietly opened the door to look in on her. Thinking Garnet was asleep, she closed the door softly.

With a belated prick of a dormant conscience, Garnet realized that her mother, whom she loved dearly, must never suspect the motives behind her daughter's sudden interest in Bryson Montrose.

chapter
5

"Two sons married within weeks of each other!" Mr. Montrose declared when he dropped in at Cameron Hall to exchange congratulations with his neighbors.

"I was barely back from Massachusetts, seeing Malcolm and his bride off to Europe, when Bryson announced that he, too, will be a bridegroom. Well, Sara and I could not be more pleased that Bryce, at least, is choosing a Southern girl for his wife — and the daughter of our dearest friends as well!" He beamed. "Sara is especially touched that Garnet wants to be married at Montclair. Very considerate of her, knowing how grieved Sara was not to be able to attend Malcolm's wedding. Now she will be able to see one of her sons married properly."

The engagement of their daughter to Bryce Montrose had come as much of a surprise to the Camerons as to the rest of the community. But it was Garnet's insistence on being a June bride that bothered Kate most. She would like to have planned the wedding of her only daughter at a much more leisurely pace. As it was, there had not been time to have all her linens monogrammed, her silver engraved, or for a complete set of Belleek china ordered from England to arrive. Invitations to relatives and friends were rushed out, but not all had responded yet, making it difficult to anticipate the number of guests who would be attending the reception after the ceremony.

"Can't we hurry up? I'd like to go riding!" complained Garnet petulantly, tired of standing for what seemed like hours on a footstool while her mother measured the skirt of the ivory satin wedding gown that still needed hemming.

"Only a few more minutes, dear," Kate replied patiently.

Garnet sighed and studied her reflection in the oval mirror.

My dress for my sixteenth birthday was white, too. A white embroidered dimity with little blue forget-me-nots, she remembered, and narrow blue ribbon threaded through the shirred bodice, and small puffed sleeves. It had been a warm summer evening and the August moon rising like a huge, yellow balloon over the treetops made the lawn as bright as day. There had been a barbecue in the afternoon, then the ball. All the young men had clustered around the birthday girl, clamoring for dances. But it was Malcolm for whom Garnet saved the special dances, especially the one before supper so they could eat together on the cool veranda. She would have him all to herself at least for a little while. When he came to claim his dance, she had moved eagerly into his arms and gracefully out onto the polished floor.

She had smiled up at him and asked with pretty coquetry, "I'm sixteen today, Malcolm. Am I grown up enough for you now?"

"Garnet, you certainly look all grown up and very beautiful. But I still see a mischievous little girl lurking behind that lovely façade." He had looked down at her, half-seriously, half-teasingly.

Garnet frowned. "I wish you wouldn't always use such big words, Malcolm. I declare, seems like you're showing off!"

Malcolm threw back his head and laughed.

"That's what comes of going up north to school. You begin to talk so no one down here can understand a word you say!" Garnet pouted. "Papa was right, you know. The schools here in Virginia are every bit as fine as the ones in Massachusetts. All you learn up there is Yankee ideas and fancy words!"

Malcolm laughed again, the laughter sending sparkles into his usually grave eyes and little crinkles around them.

"Ah, Garnet, you're precious. Don't ever change!"

"But I want to change! I want you to think of me as a proper grown-up young lady!"

"I may someday think of you as a young lady, but never a *proper* one!" he teased. "Besides, no matter how old you become, I'll always think of you as a 'little sister'."

The music stopped and Garnet, still in the light circle of Malcolm's arms, felt helpless fury at his words. How would she ever make him see her any other way? "Little sister," indeed! How infuriating when she wanted him to think of her as someone with whom he could fall in love, marry, and bear his children!

Memories of that long-ago night came back to Garnet now, overwhelming her with unbearable longing. If it were only possible to bring it back, she knew what she would say to Malcolm. She would be done with all those silly games that girls were taught to play. She would tell him straight out that she loved him. Garnet closed her eyes and swayed slightly.

"You can get down now, dear," came her mother's voice, breaking her reverie. "I know you're tired with all these fittings and trying on and such, but we did have so little time to get your trousseau ready —"

Garnet stepped down off the stool, knowing that it wasn't fatigue that dazed her, only that she was heartsick, remembering that moment on her birthday when she had had the chance to tell Malcolm and maybe make the difference in her destiny and his. What was it he had said to her?

"You have more charm than anyone should be allowed, Garnet. Too much, maybe. It won't win you any friends among the ladies, I'm afraid, and it's going to bring unhappiness to a mighty number of young men, I'd wager."

His remark had flattered Garnet. She had wanted to say, "But it's *you* I want to charm — it's *you* I want to please!" But she had let the moment slip away.

Then Francis Maynard had come to claim his dance and there had not been another opportunity to be alone with Malcolm. Now it was too late. Would she go her whole life long, regretting a moon-drenched night and the lost opportunity to speak of her love?

"Aren't you feeling well, Garnet?" Again it was her mother's voice, soft with concern, that brought Garnet back to the present.

She stared blankly at Kate and shook her head. She was remembering what her mother had said to her after she and Bryce had announced their engagement and wish to be married as soon as possible. Kate had come to her bedroom and, in her own tactful way, had questioned Garnet about the suddenness of her decision.

"If you're sure —" Kate had begun. "If you have searched your heart and soul, and know beyond a doubt that you love him. . . . We just don't want you to make a mistake, darling. Your happiness is our primary concern. Bryce obviously adores you. But marriage is for a lifetime and you are very young. I wouldn't want you to persuade yourself that you love a man, only to find out too late it was not really love at all."

It was as if her mother could read her thoughts, Garnet fretted, turning away from that too-perceptive gaze. Had Kate seen in her eyes the stirring of an uneasy conscience?

Mesmerized by her inner turmoil, Garnet watched her mother's long, slender fingers making the fine stitches characteristic of any properly trained Southern gentlewoman, and wondered.

How do you stop loving someone? Garnet stormed within herself. How could she stop thinking about Malcolm? How could she stop seeing his haunting smile, his thoughtful gaze every time she closed her eyes? How could she free herself when Malcolm held her heart and mind and emotions captive?

"I can't! I've tried and I can't!" she exclaimed — then gasped, clapping her hand to her mouth.

Startled by her daughter's outburst, Kate pricked her finger and a tiny spot of blood stained the white satin hem, but Kate was too startled to notice. But the superstitious Mawdee saw and took it as an evil omen, one more reason Garnet should not marry in such haste.

The old woman had been stubbornly silent on the subject of Garnet's engagement and wedding plans. Usually, she had plenty to say and said it boldly. Garnet thought Mawdee might be upset because she was not taking her along with her to Montclair, where there were already twenty house servants. She was only taking Bessie as her personal maid so as not to cause any trouble in the new household. But when she explained this, Mawdee just shook her head. "Didn't 'spect to go wid yo' " was all she would say.

Garnet knew that when Mawdee wouldn't talk, there was no way of making her. So she tried to ignore this unusual behavior. But on the morning of Garnet's wedding, Mawdee at last became vocal with her opinions.

Garnet, in camisole and pantaloons, stood holding on to the bedposts while Mawdee tugged at the lacings of her boned corselet.

"That's enough! Don't you want me to be able to breathe?" gasped Garnet. "If you lace me any tighter, I'll faint dead away during the ceremony!"

"All yo' has to do is to say 'I do'," mumbled Mawdee.

"What do you keep mumbling about? You'd think I was going to a funeral, not a wedding!" declared Garnet crossly. She was feeling nervous enough without this old woman giving her more trouble.

"Jes' all dis hurryin' up ain' proper," Mawdee insisted. "No time to finish wid yo' hope chest belongin's — no time a'tall! Iffen yo' cousin Elvira ain' done loan us her weddin' dress and us hab your mama's own weddin' veil, we couldn't of had a proper weddin' day outfit or nuthin'." Her tone was outraged indignation.

"Two months is plenty long enough for an engagement, Mawdee. I declare, I never heard anything so silly," retorted Garnet haughtily. "It isn't like the olden days. Young ladies don't have to be engaged for two years like they did in Mama's day. Besides, Bryce and I wanted to be married and back from our honeymoon in New Orleans before the beginning of fox hunting season."

"Huntin' or no huntin' doan hav nuthin' to do wid bein' proper," grumbled Mawdee.

"Yes it does! Bryce *has* to ride. His father has always been Hunt Master and, if you talk about being *proper,* we wouldn't have time for a *proper* wedding trip and do all our visiting to relatives as newlywed couples are expected to do, and still be back in time to get settled at Montclair. So stop your fussing, Mawdee!"

"Jes' too much hurryin' up is all I have to say," Mawdee insisted.

Garnet whirled around with her hands on her hips. "I declare, Mawdee, I should think you'd be glad and proud instead of acting so uppity. All you and Mama have talked about ever since I can remember is how important it was for me to find a suitable husband. *You* especially!" Garnet pushed out her lower lip in exact imitation of the plump old woman. " 'Act lak a lady, Miss Garnet. . . . Doan' do dis and doan' do dat, Miss Garnet . . . so's yo' kin ketch you'sef a husbin'!' *Now* all you do is complain about all this 'hurryin.' I'm eighteen — nearly nineteen! Do you want me to be an *old maid?*" she demanded.

"Some chanct of thet!" Mawdee would not relent, just lifted her fat chins higher.

"You are an old mule, Mawdee." Garnet's eyes flashed angrily. "Now that I've 'ketched' myself a fine husband from one of the best families and biggest plantations in the entire county, and good-looking and sweet-tempered besides, you're scolding me for wanting to marry him before some other girl gets him!"

In spite of herself Mawdee's lips twitched in an effort not to smile. Instead

69

she pursed them primly and said loftily, "Well, mebbe I'm some surprised myself."

"Oh, Mawdee!" Garnet sighed, half in irritation, half in affection, knowing that regardless of her criticism Mawdee loved her dearly and was feeling a sense of pride in Garnet's good match.

Reluctantly she admitted, "Yes'm, I'm sho' enuf proud. Mr. Bryce is mighty fine and I is happy yo' done ketched such a nice gen'leman."

With that, Mawdee turned, picked up the length of ivory satin that was spread carefully on the bed and dropped it over Garnet's head. It slithered over the tiered hoop and starched crinoline petticoats, and fell in graceful gathered scallops, each loop caught into a velvet bow all around.

"My, my," Mawdee hummed with satisfaction as Garnet slowly pivoted before the mirror. "Nebber seen yo' look so pretty!"

The dress *was* becoming, as if it had been especially designed to show off her figure to full advantage, her creamy shoulders and rounded bosom. But for some reason, no dress in her life had ever seemed less suited to her. Just then, however, the bedroom door opened and Kate

Cameron, elegant in mauve taffeta, entered.

"What a beautiful day for a wedding!" she said as she came over to view her daughter. "And what a beautiful bride." Cupping Garnet's chin with one cool hand, she smiled, quoting softly, " 'Happy is the bride the sun shines on!' I wonder if Bryce Montrose knows what a lucky man he is?"

Lucky? Bryce? Garnet controlled a shudder. Her pursuit of Malcolm's brother had been subtle, yet relentless. He had never known how deliberately his ultimate surrender had been planned.

After Garnet had first devised the plan of marrying Bryce Montrose, it became a kind of obsession, controlling every waking moment, motivating every action. With reckless abandon she pursued the unsuspecting Bryce, her ruthless intensity masked in charming flirtatiousness. Since spring brought a flurry of social activities for the young people of Mayfield, Garnet had lost no opportunity in showering Bryce with flattering attention.

The once indifferent young man was first astonished to be the focus of the pretty and popular belle whom he had known all his life as his friends' "little sister," then stunned by his vulnerability to her charms. For the first time in his rather uncomplicated life Bryce found himself confused, dazed, enamored. With every day that passed Garnet Cameron became more and more the reason for his existence.

His was a lost cause. By the time he finally got up the courage to speak to his father about his desire to marry Garnet and was given permission to speak to Judge Cameron, Garnet's conquest was complete.

Now, at her mother's words, Garnet felt a tiny pang of conscience. *Lucky?* Garnet wondered with a small stirring of panic. Would Bryce consider himself lucky if he knew his bride was not in love with *him,* after all, but with his *brother?*

"Here comes Bessie with your bouquet, dear." Mrs. Cameron took the spray of white lilacs from the little maid.

Numbly Garnet received it into her own clammy hands. She gave her head a small, impatient shake as Kate adjusted her veil. She felt chilled yet flushed and warm. She tried to swallow, but her throat was bone dry.

In sudden frightened awareness of what she was about to do, she spun around to confront her mother. "Mama, there's something I must —"

But Garnet never finished, for there was a knock at the door and Judge Cameron's voice called to them.

"The carriage is out front, my dear. Is Garnet ready?"

"We'll be right along!" Kate replied gaily. "Come, darling, it's time to go."

Garnet knew she could delay no longer. The time had come. The day she had schemed for was here. All her devious plans were coming to pass. Her heart thudded heavily. Turning her head quickly, she felt something catch as she raised her free hand to her coronet of orange blossoms. Then there was a strong tug, then the sound of ripping fabric.

"Oh, my goodness, your veil!" There was a note of genuine distress in Mrs. Cameron's voice.

Horrified, Garnet looked at an ugly tear marring the delicate tracery of butterflies and flowers in the gossamer lace. Though her mother tried to conceal it, she saw, too, the anxiety in Kate's face as she moved swiftly, followed by Mawdee, to examine the damage. Garnet saw the two women exchange a glance. Their expressions reflected in the mirror were inscrutable, but she felt a twinge of fear.

"Don't worry, dear," her mother was saying reassuringly. "It's only a small rip. I don't think it will show. This lace is very old and fragile and it caught on the bureau handle. It will be just fine. . . . Now, we really must go, or we shall be late."

Kate hurried to the door, waiting for Garnet to follow. But Garnet moved stiffly, feeling the weight of her heavy satin train, the stab of pins securing her headdress.

At the door she hesitated as if uncertain. Again she turned toward Kate, trembling visibly. Quickly Mrs. Cameron touched her daughter's arm. "There, there, dear, it can be fixed," she assured her calmly. "It's not the end of the world, you know. Hurry now. Your father is waiting — and your bridegroom."

With a kind of despairing bravado Garnet swept through the doorway, knowing it was indeed the end of the world — at least, it was the end of the dream world she had cherished for so long.

chapter
6

Garnet would have dearly loved a European honeymoon, but Bryce had no such inclination. He had no desire to see foreign countries nor deal with strange languages or unfamiliar customs. So a compromise was struck when they left by riverboat for New Orleans three days after the wedding.

Denied the delights of sightseeing in London and shopping in Paris, Garnet indulged her extravagance in the many luxurious stores of this sophisticated and fascinating city. Bryce accompanied her and waited patiently while she spent hours trying on dresses and bonnets and making decisions on her purchases. She ordered new furniture in the ornate modern style for their wing of Montclair, as well as elegant accessories.

Garnet was finding her first taste of life

as a grown-up married woman to be enormously satisfying.

Bryce, who was out of his element in these surroundings, merely allowed his vivacious bride to satisfy her whims, content only to see her happy. His compliance with her every wish intensified Garnet's sense of guilt — a guilt she released, ironically, through frequent outbursts of temper. Bryce, who beneath his rugged masculinity was shy and gentle, reacted awkwardly, bewildered by his new wife's rapid mood swings. When she snapped at him over some incidental matter, Garnet was just as likely to turn around and make him laugh with a bit of mimicry, an amusing observation, a witty remark.

They had only been married a few weeks when Garnet made the surprising discovery that no matter how willful she was, how easily irritated and how often cross, Bryce put up with all her faults. She had a feeling, which she failed to explore, that he loved her unconditionally and saw something in her she did not even know about herself.

For Garnet their stay in New Orleans with its lavish attractions, new people, and new experiences could have lasted much longer. Away from Mawdee's stern eye and her mother's gentle but inflexible code of behavior, Garnet found her new freedom intoxicating.

But Bryce had been away from the fields and streams and meadows of his beloved Montclair long enough. He missed his daily horseback rides, his hunting dogs, and the outdoor life he lived there. He had had his fill of touring and shopping. He was anxious to go home.

On their way back to Virginia, as was the custom, they visited relatives on both sides of the family. Although the couple was royally entertained and urged to stay longer, Bryce would not delay his return to Montclair another day.

It was different for Garnet. Returning to Virginia and her new home, the one where she had dreamed of being mistress, was a jolting letdown. Montclair was magnificent, everything she had ever remembered it to be, but living there was not at all as she had imagined it.

Ordinarily a young woman marrying into the family of a large plantation owner would have moved into a complex, demanding role. But even though Sara Montrose was an invalid, still it was she who ruled from her "ivory tower." Her personal maid Lizzie, trained expertly to

77

relay Sara's orders to the twenty or more house servants, kept the household running smoothly. As a result there was very little for Garnet to do. She had no duties, no responsibilities — no authority.

Since its early days Montclair had developed into one of the most beautiful plantation homes along the James River. The stark simplicity of its original design lent itself well to structural changes, additions, ornamentation, and enhancements that had been made through the years by its subsequent masters and mistresses.

The house had been constructed to last for centuries to shelter the dynasty the first master had envisioned would follow him. Built on an original King's Grant when this part of Virginia was still wilderness, a network of tunnels for refuge and food storage had been built underneath the superstructure of the house — a necessary precaution in time of Indian attacks. Now, of course, such a threat was a thing of the past.

For the first few days Garnet explored the splendid mansion. On previous visits she had seen only the first floor of the three-story house — the drawing room, the parlor, the dining room, music rooms, the veranda encircling the downstairs area.

Now it was a delight to survey all the other rooms.

The newlyweds were given their choice of one of the new wings on the second floor. Garnet chose a front suite overlooking the sweeping drive. Every window in each room commanded a view of orchards, meadow, and the woods banding the terraced lawns.

When the furniture Garnet had chosen in New Orleans began to arrive, along with other pieces ordered through catalogs from northern furniture factories, she spent a few happy weeks supervising the arrangements. A bedroom, two dressing rooms, and their own sitting room were soon lavishly appointed in the elaborate style Garnet admired. Once this was achieved, however, she found time heavy on her hands. Since there was nothing to complain of in the luxurious circumstances into which she had moved, Garnet found other things with which to find fault.

The easygoing Bryce, who once back at Montclair reverted to his old bachelor habits of rising early to be out with his horses most of the day, found it an escape from his bride's petulance and frequently left her to her own devices. He had decided the best way was one of least resistance and habitually gave in to her in most things.

Garnet quickly acquired a defiant attitude. Ignoring the set pattern of life at Montclair, she slept late, had breakfast served in her room, then often went riding over to Cameron Hall, often choosing to stay overnight if there were guests whom she enjoyed. If Bryce minded his bride's unconventional behavior, he did not say. Mr. Montrose liked order but prized peace more, so said nothing. If Sara was annoyed — well, no one stayed angry with Garnet for long. She was so delightful, amusing, and playful — when she wanted to be.

Within a few weeks Garnet found herself restless and vaguely discontented. In spite of her indulgent husband and a life of luxurious ease, marriage had proved to be a great disappointment. Instead of the freedom she had expected to enjoy out from under the strict rules of decorum for young girls, she discovered all sorts of restrictions imposed by society on "married ladies."

Besides forfeiting the fun, flattery, and gaiety of her life as a belle with many beaux, Garnet's disenchantment was tinged with deep regret. The underlying reason for her unhappiness, for which there was no remedy, was the unalterable fact that she had married the wrong man.

In her way, Garnet had become very fond of Bryce. How could she help it? He was good-natured, amiable, fun-loving, and he adored her. His only fault was that he was not Malcolm.

And there was something more that Garnet had not counted on when she had forged her plan for marrying Bryce and being established at Montclair before Malcolm brought home his Yankee bride. It was the painful fact that she faced each day as she walked through the rooms of the house where Malcolm had lived most of his life, sitting at the table in the high-ceilinged dining room where he had taken his meals. All — daily reminders of the man she loved and had lost to a stranger.

When letters arrived bearing European stamps and postmarks, Garnet felt the ache of imagining Malcolm with Rose, honeymooning in Italy. And as the October date for their return grew near, Garnet's tension increased beneath her frenetic activity.

Malcolm sent a telegram from New York, stating that he and Rose would be taking a steamboat to Norfolk, the train from Richmond, on to Mayfield and Montclair.

"I want the whole family here to welcome Rose when they arrive," Mr. Montrose said at dinner the night before. "Since this is her first trip south, we want to show her what real Southern hospitality is like."

His words seemed directed to Garnet, whose unexpected comings and goings were a source of irritation to a man accustomed to promptness and order.

But Garnet found it impossible to comply with her father-in-law's request and on the day of Malcolm and Rose's expected arrival she rose early, slipped out of the house, and galloped through the morning mist to Cameron Hall, where she stayed until Bryce was sent to fetch her back. Even then she fussed, procrastinated, and delayed to the last possible moment her first encounter with Rose and the reality of her own shattered dream.

PART III

North and South

Montclair
1857–1858

chapter
7

Rose Meredith Montrose sat holding the hatbox containing her extravagant Paris bonnet as their carriage rolled up the winding road to Montclair. Though she looked properly demure as befitted a young matron, her cheeks were flushed with excitement and her eyes danced with anticipation. She glanced anxiously over at her husband of five months.

"Oh, Malcolm, I hope your family likes me!" she said anxiously.

"They'll adore you!" Malcolm assured her fondly, putting his hand over her small gloved one and giving it a gentle squeeze.

"Especially your mother. I want to be a *real* daughter to her. You said she has always wanted a daughter." Rose sighed. "And I have always wanted a real mother. Oh, not that Auntie Van hasn't been kind and caring and wonderful . . . but, well, you know, it's not really the same."

"Now, Mama will have *two* daughters," Malcolm reminded her.

"Yes, that's true."

Rose nodded, remembering Malcolm's surprise when his father's letter had reached them in Rome, telling of his brother Bryce's marriage. They had been sitting on the sunny terrace of their rented villa, overlooking the cypress-dotted hills, reading their mail after breakfast. She recalled Malcolm's bemused expression as he handed Rose the letter to read for herself, remarking, "*Garnet!* I would never have guessed *those* two —"

"Who is Garnet?" Rose had asked.

Malcolm had laughed softly. "Garnet Cameron was a spoiled little scamp who grew up to be the belle of Mayfield County."

Ever since that enigmatic description, Rose had been curious to meet her new sister-in-law. But the honeymooners had extended their romantic European idyll two months longer than planned, lingering in the lovely Italian countryside, taking side trips to Naples, Venice, and Florence. When at last they were ready to depart for America, Rose was reluctant to leave this place where they had been so happy.

"But no place is as beautiful as Virginia

in the autumn," Malcolm assured Rose.

When Rose first saw the Virginia hills, brilliant with fall colors, she had to agree.

Their train from Richmond had been met at the small Mayfield station by the Montrose carriage, whose driver, Mordecai, greeted Malcolm heartily and swept Rose a bow that would have been acceptable in the court of the young British Queen Victoria, she thought with secret amusement. Mordecai, handsomely black with gray hair and sideburns, then donned a top hat and, after settling them inside the carriage, oversaw the loading of their luggage. He then mounted the driver's seat alongside the coachman, also attired in bright blue jacket trimmed with braid. With a smart snap of his whip, the four matched horses started up.

"We'll soon be home, darling," Malcolm said. "Home to Montclair."

Rose found Malcolm's excitement contagious, although hers was mixed with a kind of nervous exhilaration.

After leaving the main road, they took a less-traveled path through a wooded section, lined on either side by dark pines slashed here and there with glimpses of crimson maples, scarlet redbud trees, and golden oaks. All along the road Rose noticed bushes bright with dazzling yellow flowers.

"What are those brilliant blossoms?"

"Scotch broom," he replied. "It grows wild here. Well, almost wild. You see, there's a legend about its start in this part of Virginia. It seems Cornwallis's retreating army used dried stalks for cannon-ball packing, dropping the seeds inadvertently as they pushed back to Yorktown and the sea. The seeds germinated and — well, the result is a reminder of how the Virginians defeated the British! We take great pride in that fact, so the weed is allowed to grow and flourish as a talisman of how much we value our freedom." Malcolm smiled.

"It seems that Massachusetts and Virginia have much in common." Rose raised her eyebrows and inclined her head.

"A very happy coalition, I agree," he said softly, leaning over and kissing her tenderly on her rosy lips. "Did I tell you today how much I love you?"

"And I, you, my darling," she murmured.

As they continued, every once in a while Malcolm would point out an ornate gate or a narrow road seeming to lead nowhere except into denser woods. "That's Oak Haven," he would say. Or, "Just there is

Fairwoods, where our friends the Tollivers live," or, "The Grahams' place is over that ridge."

To Rose, all seemed such surprising distances from each other to be spoken of as "neighbors." In Milford, neighbors lived just down the road or across the Common. When her husband gestured to a particularly high wrought-iron gate flanked by stone pillars and said, "That's Cameron Hall, the home of our nearest neighbors and oldest friends," Rose was particularly interested. That would be the home of Garnet, Bryce's wife, whom she was soon to meet.

Still, "nearest neighbor" seemed an understatement, because it was quite some time before Malcolm sat forward, leaning eagerly out the carriage window and said, "We're almost there. Around another bend and you may be able to see the house."

Rose sat up, looking in the direction he was pointing, but could not see anything through the thick foliage. A little farther on and then she did see it — the ancestral home of the Montrose family, Montclair.

As often as Malcolm had affectionately and proudly described it to Rose, nothing had prepared her for its magnificence.

As the carriage rounded the final curve,

she saw the house bathed in the October sunlight that gilded the roof and turned the long windows into flaming rectangles as if from some inner fire. This first impression was so startling it caused a quick intake of breath and a sudden, irrational sense of fear. The sensation of foreboding came and went so swiftly Rose barely noted its passing, for at this moment Malcolm reached for her hand and held it tightly.

"There's your new home, Rose. What do you think of it?"

Rose's eyes widened. She had not imagined Montclair to be so large, so imposing. It stood on a rise of sloping, terraced lawn sheltered by elm trees. The house of white-washed brick and clapboard rose three stories, built in a U-shape with wings like embracing arms on either side, and a circling veranda. Six fluted columns paced the deep porch, broken only by a center doorway flanked by tall, blue-shuttered windows running the length of the house.

When the carriage drew to a stop in front, the door opened immediately and Malcolm's father stepped out to greet them. As he strode to the edge of the porch, he was waving his gold-headed cane and issuing brisk orders to someone invisible to Rose. In another minute, as if by magic, several Negro servants appeared in the doorway — women in blue homespun dresses with starched aprons and turbans. At the same time a group of Negro men and clusters of small black children gathered around the perimeter of the yard. The children's eyes were big with curiosity, and they pressed their hands to their mouths as if to suppress their giggles.

"How cunning they are," said Rose.

"They're all anxious to get a peek at the new bride." Malcolm smiled indulgently.

The carriage door was opened by Mordecai, very conscious of his role. He stood at attention while Mr. Montrose came down the steps, holding out both his hands and calling heartily, "Welcome home, Malcolm! And welcome to Montclair, Rose!"

A little shy in the face of all the attention she was receiving, Rose accepted the arm Mr. Montrose offered and alighted from the carriage. They mounted the steps together.

Rose's new father-in-law was a commanding figure with a leonine head of silvery gray hair, a well-trimmed mustache and beard. His eyes were deepset and fiery, his features nobly sculpted, his voice thundering. At a word from him the servants went scurrying like leaves before the wind in all directions, forming a double line all the way back to the hall. Rose vaguely counted fifteen or more as she passed by on his arm, Malcolm following close behind.

In the center hall she looked about her in awed admiration. From the high ceiling hung a splendid, many-prismed chandelier and, rising in front of her, was a curved twin staircase leading to the second floor, its balcony circling the foyer. The interior of the house was all elegance, warmth, and graciousness, and smelled of lemon wax, candles, and the pungent aroma from masses of fall flowers arranged in two blue-and-white Meissen vases resting on a highly polished Sheraton table.

All along the paneled walls hung family portraits. From where she stood Rose could look into one of the parlors, where a glowing fire burned cheerfully in the grate of a white marble fireplace. Suspended above it was a huge gilt-framed mirror. In it she could see herself, Malcolm, and Mr. Montrose, reflected like figures in a painting.

"Come along, my dear," the older man said tersely. "Malcolm's mother has been waiting all day to meet you. Bryson and Garnet will be along later. They rode over to Cameron Hall earlier and have not yet returned, although I expected them to be here when you arrived." A fierce scowl pulled Mr. Montrose's heavy brows together, and Rose was instantly aware that he was barely controlling his annoyance.

"I'll go on ahead," Malcolm said and preceded them, taking the steps two at a time.

"It is only fair to tell you that Malcolm's his mother's favorite," Mr. Montrose told Rose in a confidential tone as they followed several steps behind Malcolm. "It's a family secret, though an open one . . . if you get my meaning. I suppose the first-born in any family has a special place, and the younger boys have never seemed to mind."

"Are these portraits of Malcolm's ancestors?" Rose asked, pausing on the landing before an especially appealing one of a young girl dressed in the fashion of the eighteenth century. Gowned in scarlet velvet, she was holding a fan, and her jewelry was so realistically painted that the rubies and diamonds of her earrings and pendant seemed to sparkle.

"That is Noramary, the *first* bride of Montclair," Mr. Montrose explained. "She was the wife of my great-great-great grandfather, Duncan Montrose, who settled here when the part of Virginia you have just driven through was still considered wilderness, mostly unexplored territory."

"She was very beautiful."

"All Montrose brides are beautiful." Mr. Montrose gave Rose a sidelong glance. "We must have you sit for *your* portrait soon, my dear."

They proceeded up the steps, Rose thinking with some trepidation that she had surely married into a family steeped in tradition. In some ways it would be a considerable task to live up to all these former brides.

When they reached the second floor, Rose saw that from the wide, spacious center hall, several other narrower walkways fanned out into the various wings of the large house.

As they started down the hallway, they could hear the sound of conversation and light laughter coming from the other end.

"My wife's suite is just off here. It is over the garden and has a view of the drive so she can see people coming and going." He lowered his voice. "I suppose Malcolm has informed you that his mother is an invalid and rarely leaves her rooms. She does take the waters at White Sulphur Springs in the springtime. We find this extremely beneficial to her health. She seems to recover some of the strength sapped by the long, confining winters."

At the archway leading into the suite Mr. Montrose stepped aside, and Rose found herself standing at the door of Sara Montrose's sitting room, witness to a tender scene. Malcolm was down on one knee beside the French chaise on which reclined a fragile, dark-haired woman with a cameo profile. As they conversed in hushed tones, she was gazing raptly into his face, brushing back his thick curly hair with one hand.

Feeling like an intruder, Rose stood there uncertainly until some small sound or movement caused Malcolm to turn his head in her direction. Smiling, he got to his feet. Still holding his mother's hand, he invited, "Come in, darling. Mama, this is Rose. Rose, my mother, Sara Montrose."

Rose was struck at once by the strong resemblance of mother to son. Mrs. Montrose's features, although cast in a feminine mold, were remarkably like Malcolm's, especially the eyes and mouth. Her hair, drawn back from a pale face, showed not a trace of gray in its dark waves. She was exquisitely attired in lavender taffeta. The skirt, which spread over the end of the settee, was scalloped in layers, caught here and there with tiny purple velvet bows, and there were deep ruffles of ecru lace at her throat and falling over her wrists.

Sara Montrose turned her head slowly. The dark-lashed, deep-blue eyes that Rose had first thought were so like Malcolm's, seemed to change into a gray-blue, the color of a winter sea — and as cold. The impression stunned Rose and she had difficulty masking her reaction. Then in sharp contrast came a low, melodious voice.

"Why, Rose, come in so I can see you better. See for myself if all Malcolm's extravagant praise is true."

The gentlemen laughed appreciatively as Rose moved hesitantly toward her mother-in-law. Only Rose was aware that the faint smile that touched Sara's mouth was not echoed in her eyes.

The woman's thin hand, when she held it up, was studded with rings, and Rose was momentarily at a loss as to whether to shake it or kiss it. Gathered as they were around Mrs. Montrose's chaise, like courtiers in the throne room of a queen, there seemed some unspoken code that rankled Rose. The light touch of Sara's hand gave no indication of warmth, and Rose was not surprised when Sara turned to her son, the interview apparently at an end.

"Now I want to hear everything," she demanded in the tone of a coquette.

Malcolm obediently launched into a descriptive narrative of their European travels, with Sara interrupting now and then to ask animated questions, giving him flattering attention and virtually ignoring Rose. Watching the interplay between mother and son, Rose was puzzled. It was, she thought, rather like watching the performance of a consummate actress.

"How I envy you, Rose!" Mrs. Montrose turned to her at last, placing a possessive hand on Malcolm's arm. "To have seen all those glorious sights! It was my dream that when Malcolm finished at Harvard, the two of *us* would make the grand tour." She gave a small deprecating laugh. "But, alas, that was not to be!"

"Your health, my dear, would have made that quite impossible," Mr. Montrose interjected, glancing at Rose half-apologetically.

Rose smiled, but she had not taken the wrong impression from Mrs. Montrose's lightly spoken words. She had received *exactly* the message Mrs. Montrose intended to convey. There was no mistake. She deeply resented her son's marriage, the fact of his European honeymoon, and most of all, his bride.

Rose was too intelligent and insightful not to have realized from their first meeting that Mrs. Montrose was jealous of anything and anyone who came between her and her son, and too sensitive not to be hurt by that knowledge.

In those first few moments Rose's own bright hopes of finding in Malcolm's mother a mother for herself were dashed. From now on, reality would be her guide in her relationship with her mother-in-law. There was much resentment to be overcome, but Rose was determined to win Mrs. Montrose — if not her love, then her admiration. Nothing would destroy what she and Malcolm had found together. She was willing to share him, even if his mother was not.

While the conversation turned to people and events, items of local news and gossip that excluded Rose, she let her mind wander, and looked around the beautifully appointed room in which Malcolm's mother spent her days, and, if what her husband had said was true, most of her life.

It is rather like a lovely shell, Rose thought. The walls were pale pink; the furniture, French; the draperies, damask of palest blue. Through another door Rose could see the bedroom. A tall canopied bed of blond wood with pink moiré silk curtains and coverlet dominated the room. Everything around her, like the woman herself, was delicate, dainty, tasteful, of priceless quality — but fragile.

A lull in the easy flow of conversation occurred when they heard the sound of horses' hooves and carriage wheels, the strident bark of dogs, doors banging downstairs, and then footsteps on the stairs.

Mr. Montrose got to his feet, smiling broadly.

"Bryce!" he called, as if the name were explanation enough.

"And Garnet! Back from Cameron Hall!" declared Mrs. Montrose, lifting one elegant brow and shrugging. "That girl rides like a boy still! Yet she is as charming and feminine as can be."

With a little flutter somewhere between anticipation and apprehension, Rose shifted slightly in her chair, awaiting the appearance of this girl who had piqued her curiosity for the last several months.

chapter
8

As Bryson Montrose stepped into the
doorway of his mother's sitting room, filling
it with his tall, broad-shouldered frame,
Rose saw at once that he was as different
from Malcolm as two brothers could be. He
had tawny, windblown hair and the tanned,
healthy complexion of one who spends most
of his time outdoors. His boyish smile ig-
nited clear blue eyes as he greeted everyone,
then stepped back to allow a slim, graceful
girl in a moss-green riding habit to enter before him.

"Garnet!" Malcolm exclaimed, leaping
to his feet, his hands extended. There was
something in the way he said her name
that sent a dart of alarm winging through
Rose's heart. It spoke of affection and intimacy and something else she could not
quite define. It brought her to a tense ri-
gidity and riveted her gaze upon the young

woman framed in the doorway.

For someone who could not be considered classically beautiful, Garnet Cameron Montrose was arrestingly attractive, Rose thought. Hers was an unforgettable face with its vivid coloring, enormous amber eyes, small nose with delicate, flaring nostrils, and full, red mouth.

Garnet stood poised for a moment, surveying the room as if evaluating an audience, completely aware of the drama of her entrance, the impact of her presence.

Then with a careless gesture, she swept off the jaunty little tricorn hat so that her hair was loosened from its confining net and fell in a shimmering red-gold mane nearly to her waist.

She moved lightly, gliding across the room to Sara's couch and swooping down to kiss her mother-in-law. Sara reached up in turn and patted Garnet's rosy cheek affectionately. "And here's our girl now. See? Our Malcolm is home at last!"

Garnet pirouetted toward Malcolm, the movement adroitly showing her high-breasted, narrow-waisted figure to full advantage. A mischievous sparkle lighted her eyes and a teasing smile hovered on her lips as she said, "Well, Malcolm, now that we're *kin*, you can kiss me hello!"

There was a subtlety in Garnet's tone that rather bewildered Rose and a disturbing quality in Malcolm's answering laugh as he took Garnet's hands and leaned toward her. Just then Rose's attention was diverted by Bryson's bantering suggestion.

"Then, may I not claim the same privilege with my new sister?"

Startled, Rose turned as Bryson bent and kissed her lightly on the cheek, causing her to blush hotly and at the same time to miss whether or not Malcolm had accepted Garnet's challenge.

The next few minutes were a blur of movement and confusion. Bryson greeted his brother and there was a lively exchange of comments and questions. In the general hubbub no one seemed to notice that Rose had not been properly introduced to Garnet, but she felt immensely uncomfortable. She had seen the girl's eyes sweep over her and away without a glimmer of acknowledgment. But even the considerate Malcolm had been unaware of this oversight, and Rose tried to appear poised and calm in spite of it.

She was glad, however, for the entrance of a maid bearing a tray with a silver coffee service and a frosted fruit cake. Since this woman wore a gray muslin dress, white ruffled apron and cap instead of the turbans worn by the other Negro servants, Rose wondered if she held a privileged position in the household. This was soon established when the woman moved behind Mrs. Montrose, and, with a slightly proprietary air, adjusted her pillows. When Mrs. Montrose whispered something, the woman went quickly into the other room, bringing back a lacy shawl which she gently placed around her mistress's shoulders.

The tall, light-skinned servant must be her mother-in-law's personal maid, Rose decided.

Rose had little time to pursue her puzzling thoughts before Mrs. Montrose announced dramatically, "I am coming down to dinner tonight in honor of Malcolm's homecoming!"

"Then it will *really* be a celebration, my dear!" Mr. Montrose said heartily.

"And Malcolm shall have the honor of carrying me down since it is his first night home after such a long absence." The worshipful look Sara bestowed on her son was so obvious that Rose glanced to see if Bryson registered any resentment. But he was deep in discussion with his father and seemed oblivious to any undercurrent.

It was Garnet who broke up the gathering. Jumping to her feet, she gave her head a little toss. "Well, if dinner is going to be such a *special occasion,* I must be off to make myself presentable."

As she started out of the room, Bryson reached up and grabbed her wrist, saying with a deep-throated chuckle, "But, honey, you *always* look beautiful."

"Spoken like a true Southern gentleman!" roared Mr. Montrose. "Why, Bryson, I do believe marriage is taming you. You'll soon be a real poet!"

Garnet dropped a light kiss on the top of Bryce's head, but Rose saw with dismay, her knowing look was for Malcolm. "Marriage has strange and mystical powers to change people."

"For the better, I hope!" Bryce grinned.

"That depends upon where you were when you started," Malcolm remarked enigmatically.

When Garnet was at last out of sight and safely in her dressing room, she pressed both hands against her mouth to stifle the dry sobs that rushed to choke her, then closed her eyes against her white-faced image reflected in the full-length mirror.

She had not imagined it would be so hard. To see Malcolm again — to be in the same room with him — *and* the woman he loved!

Garnet saw now that her childish scheme to make Malcolm regret that he had rejected her was like a knife flung in anger. It had turned, instead, to inflict deeper pain on the one who had hurled it.

Nor was she prepared for Rose to be so beautiful. It would have been easier for her to believe that Malcolm had been drawn to his Yankee bride by her intellect. It was more painful to see that he may have been dazzled by her exquisite beauty as well.

In a single glance Garnet had taken in everything she needed to know about Rose. Here was obviously a young woman of elegance and poise. Her traveling costume must have been bought in Paris, Garnet surmised. Of sage green serge appliqued with dark green cording, both its cut and style were flawless. And Rose was wearing her abundant dark hair in the new French chignon. Her enormous brown eyes were heavily lashed; her features, delicate; her complexion, translucent.

It was easy to see how any man might fall prey to such beguiling beauty and charm, but it was galling for Garnet to meet in person the girl Malcolm had preferred to her.

For all her gay façade upon entering Sara's room where everyone had gathered to greet the newlyweds, Garnet had been seething on the inside. All the old wounds of unrequited love were opened at seeing Malcolm again. *He is more handsome than ever,* she thought with anguish. His new status and the experience of travel had given him a maturity and polish that only enhanced his dark good looks. He seemed more at ease, laughed more readily, conversed with his parents with new assurance.

As Garnet listened, almost ill with envy, the only thing she could find immediately to criticize about Rose was her New England accent. Rose's voice, though low and refined, still held a brisk clarity that sounded strange in a room filled with softly slurred syllables.

But Rose's replies to Sara's eager queries about Paris fashion and the plays they had seen in London were gracious and lively. And she answered Mr. Montrose's questions with intelligence and respect. Garnet could see that Rose was making a favorable impression on her new relatives.

Just then the door to the dressing room opened, and Bessie entered, all grins and chatter.

"Oh, ma'am, isn't Mr. Malcolm's lady the purties' little thing? She so dainty and talk so sweet! I do declare I wuz sayin' to Tilda, I doan know when I seen a lady so —"

Garnet whirled about furiously. The last thing she needed right now was to hear anyone else singing Rose's praises. Bessie's entrance was ill-timed, and the little maid's thoughtless ramblings further fired Garnet's anger. Jealousy rose within her, obscuring everything else.

"Oh, hush up, Bessie!" she snapped. "Go fetch my hot water. I have to bathe and change for dinner. And hurry up about it, too!"

Everything vanished from Garnet's mind except the desire to outshine Rose. Determinedly she chose the most flamboyant of the extravagant gowns she had bought in New Orleans on her honeymoon. Of peacock blue peau-de-soie, the gown was designed with a fitted basque, sashed in wide grosgrain ribbons, tied in back and falling in long streamers over the flounced skirt. The Vandyke neckline revealed her gardenia-white skin.

Regarding her image with narrowed eyes, Garnet tried to picture herself as Malcolm would see her. She wished she could wear the Montrose rubies, the legendary bridal set of pendant earrings and necklace. But, of course, as long as Sara was living, no other Montrose wife would wear them. Instead, Garnet fastened on the pearl necklace with its coral medallion Bryce had given her as a wedding gift.

With a final pat to her coiffured hair drawn up to show off her small, flat ears, and swirled into a figure eight in back, Garnet felt ready to go downstairs and face the events of the evening.

But even knowing she looked her best and that her spritely conversation had captured its usual appreciative audience, Garnet found that the effort required to sustain it soon produced a pounding headache.

Sitting across the table from Malcolm was unbearable. Even though he laughed at her witticisms and bantered with her in teasing affection, it was Rose, sitting at the opposite end of the table, to whom his attention was drawn most often, his eyes resting upon her ardently in the softness of the candlelight.

Garnet struggled to keep her bright

smile in place. It was difficult to keep from staring at Rose. Some inner magnet kept pulling her to the radiant face of her victorious rival. On two such occasions Rose met her glance and Garnet felt her face flush. That delicate, intelligent face — those grave, penetrating eyes sent a dart of conviction into Garnet's innermost being. *Could Rose guess what she was thinking?* she wondered in consternation.

After dinner when they were all sitting in the parlor having coffee, Garnet punished herself further by watching the touching tableau — Malcolm hovering solicitously over Rose, making sure she had her coffee with just the right amount of cream; lingering by her side even as he responded to his father's questions about England. When at length Malcolm suggested Rose might be weary after the long day of travel and the excitement of their homecoming, they said their goodnights before taking the woodland path over the bridge to Eden Cottage.

Rose came to Garnet then, both hands extended, and said, "I've been looking forward so much to meeting you, Garnet. I've always wanted a sister."

Taken off guard, Garnet said the first thing that popped into her head. "How odd! I have never felt the slightest need of one!"

The moment the words were uttered, Garnet could have bitten her tongue. The expression on Rose's face was so startled, her dark eyes widening at the rebuff. Garnet was instantly penitent. But it was too late.

Bryce cast her a quick look, then immediately stepped up saying smoothly, "Well, *I* have, Rose. Garnet's never had to share the spotlight with anyone before, so she hasn't missed having a sister. But I can't tell you how pleased I am that Malcolm's marrying you has given me one at last!"

His gallant remark removed the sting from Garnet's careless words, and some of the color that had drained out of Rose's face returned. Under Bryce's obvious admiration, she even blushed a little.

Garnet squirmed inwardly. Never before had Bryce given her such a cold, disapproving look. It was not until later, when she was brushing her hair at her dressing table, that he put his head in the door and mentioned the incident.

"I think you hurt Rose's feelings tonight, honey," he began.

A look of honest contrition briefly crossed Garnet's face, but she quickly affected an airy nonchalance. "I say what I feel! If people get their feelings hurt —" She shrugged indifferently.

"Well, it's not a very charming trait, honey." Bryce's voice was gentle, but it held a note of warning. "Rose is family now. We want her to feel . . . welcome, don't we?"

Bryce came fully into the room, walked over behind her, then placing both hands on Garnet's shoulders, leaned down and kissed her cheek. "It's just that I don't want Rose to get the wrong impression of you, darling. I want everyone to love you as I do, that's all."

Garnet endured his embrace as she had all the others. Bryce was a dear and so undemanding in every way she did not want to offend him unnecessarily. So she checked the defensive words that sprang to her mind, but she stiffened. With a half-sigh, Bryce left to go into his own dressing room.

Alone, Garnet flung down her silver-handled hairbrush. Bryce couldn't possibly understand what she was going through! How *could* he?

She shuddered as a cold fear clutched at her heart. If tonight was any example of what lay ahead of her, how could she endure it? To go on pretending for the rest of her life that she was happily married to one brother — when all the time she was dying of love for the other?

Pulling her velvet peignoir about her shivering shoulders, Garnet rose and went quickly into the bedroom. She wanted to be in bed, pretend to be asleep before Bryce joined her.

She was trembling as she slipped into the massive mahogany bed with its arched, ornately carved headboard. It was torture to see Malcolm with Rose, to know that at this very moment they were probably in each other's arms. She squeezed her eyes shut tight, willing herself not to weep and cry out in her desperate longing to be in Rose's place.

Garnet pounded her pillow with a clenched fist. If only she could bring back yesterday when she had ridden with Malcolm through the woods between their plantations, when they had laughed together, long before he had gone north to school — before there was anyone else! Before there was a Rose! *I could have made him love me! I know I could have!*

Rose's thoughts were troubled as she sat in front of her dressing table later that night while her newly acquired maid, Tilda, brushed her hair with practiced strokes.

Not only that, she was exhausted. The day had been fraught with anxiety and excitement. The arrival at Montclair, meeting Malcolm's mother for the first time, reacting appropriately to her new surroundings — all had proved a draining experience for Rose.

Rose's image in the mirror reflected the toll of the day's activities. There were shadows under eyes glazed with weariness. The effort of maintaining alertness throughout the long dinner hour, pretending an interest in the discussion of subjects she neither understood nor had enough knowledge of to participate in, was wearing. Toward the end of it she felt herself becoming numb, visibly drooping.

Now she found the quiet though unaccustomed attentions of Tilda immensely soothing.

All through dinner she had felt herself scrutinized by Malcolm's mother, whose initial appraising stare had severely shocked Rose and still lingered like a small bruise in her heart. Her expectations of a motherly welcome had been shattered by the reality of the hard coldness in those beautiful eyes.

And then there was the matter of Garnet, whose relationship with Malcolm puzzled Rose. What part would she play in their lives?

Granted, they would live separately from the big house in this small, exquisite cottage. Still, they would take their meals with the family, and most of the activities would involve constant contact with Malcolm's parents and brothers. This, of course, would also include Garnet.

Malcolm, caught up in the excitement of his homecoming, had seemed unaware of Rose's growing feeling of isolation. Seated down the length of the dinner table from her, he could not know how their easy conversation excluded her. He did not seem to realize that she was not yet a part of his world. The world that was so familiar to Garnet, for instance.

The picture of Garnet tonight thrust itself into Rose's consciousness. In the soft glow of the candles she looked particularly appealing — the satin sheen of her skin, the curls bobbing around her heart-shaped face, her white teeth gleaming and eyes shining with youthful mirth as she laughed at some witty remark made by Malcolm.

Garnet was so fresh and alive that she made Rose feel dull by comparison — a feeling Rose had never experienced before in the company of others.

Rose felt a twinge of jealousy, thinking of the intimate way Garnet had leaned toward Malcolm, hearing the intimate laughter that came from their end of the table where they sat across from each other, on either side of Sara.

Immediately Rose was repentant. It was wrong to feel jealous. Garnet was her sister-in-law, as well as Malcolm's, not a rival! Rose wanted to love her, if that were possible, yet Rose was not sure Garnet cared one whit whether she did or not.

Just then Tilda's soft, shy voice interrupted Rose's confused thoughts. "My! Missus, you has de mos' pretties' hair I ever did see. Us all thinks Marse Malcolm done bring hisself home some pretty bride!" she chuckled.

"Well, thank you, Tilda." Rose was surprised and touched.

"Yes'm. Us all worried some when we heard he wuz bringin' home a lady from the No'th. Yes'm, we wuz."

The click of the door in the adjoining room cut short any further opinions Tilda might have given her new mistress about the rumors and speculations that had taken place among the people at Montclair before her arrival. Tilda leaned down and whispered, "Dat be Marse Malcolm. So I be done now." She put down Rose's brush and slipped quietly out of the room.

As Rose looked into the mirror, she saw Malcolm's handsome face in the place of Tilda's round, black one. Their eyes met. He put his hands on her shoulders. Smiling, he leaned forward, gathering a handful of her shining hair and burying his face in it. Then with a gesture like a caress, he lifted it away from her neck and kissed the soft nape. At the touch of his warm lips on her bare skin, a deliciously sensuous shiver trembled through Rose.

She raised her arms, capturing his face in her hands, and turned her head slightly so that he could kiss her cheek, the lobe of her ear. She closed her eyes and sighed as he murmured her name.

Before Malcolm, Rose had never understood the overwhelming love that could exist between a man and woman. To her, marriage had been wrapped in mystery, in romantic symbolism. Since he had gently introduced her to the glorious completeness of married love, she had discovered in herself a depth of feeling she had not thought possible.

"My darling," Malcolm whispered. "Our first night in our new home, our first night at Montclair —"

She laughed softly. "Our first night in 'Eden'."

"Come," he said gently, getting to his feet and lifting her by her hand to stand beside him. Over his shoulder she could see into the bedroom, the one they would share here in this perfect gem of a little house — see the high tester bed with its filmy curtains, its ruffled coverlet, and mounds of lacy pillows.

As she started to follow him, she glanced back at the dressing table into the mirror and saw the two of them reflected there. Then her eyes went to the silver brush, comb, and hand mirror, a wedding gift from Malcolm, engraved with her new initials, "R. M." Oddly enough, she thought, they were the same as before — R. M., Rose Meredith; R. M., Rose Montrose. Yet everything else had become new.

"Come, darling," Malcolm repeated, giving her hand a gentle tug.

Was she mistaken or was Malcolm's Virginia accent more pronounced now than it had been a few hours ago? Had being home at Montclair already begun to change him?

Quickly Rose brushed away the tiny flicker of fear that flashed through her mind. Moving into Malcolm's embrace, she promised herself to stop imagining things, putting significance on every glance, every word, every nuance in this strange new world she had entered. It was Malcolm's world and she wanted to be a part of it.

The minister's words spoken to them on their wedding day sprang to remembrance as, arms around each other's waist, she and Malcolm walked into their bedroom. "Henceforth, you will belong entirely to each other — one in mind, one in heart, and one in affection."

That's how she wanted it to be for them. With God's help, it would be.

chapter

9

"Chris'mas gif'! Chris'mas gif', Miss Rose!"

Tilda's voice sang out the traditional Virginia Christmas greeting, awakening Rose on the Christmas morning of 1857. She opened her eyes, raised herself on her elbows, and saw her maid standing at the foot of her bed, her wide grin making a white crescent in her shiny black face.

Christmas day! Rose thought. *My first in Virginia, my first at Montclair, my first as a married lady! And,* she added wistfully, *my first away from home.*

She turned and saw that the other side of the bed was empty, the pillow still bearing the imprint of Malcolm's dark head. Instinctively Rose wished he had been the one to awaken her with a kiss and "Christmas gift!"

"Time you wuz up and dressed, Miss Rose. The peoples will be gatherin' outside de big house 'fore long fo' dey Chris'mas presents. Ole Marse stands out on the veranda and they allus come up one at a time to present deyselves. You bes' be right dere 'longside Marse Malcolm," Tilda said as she moved about the room, drawing back the curtains and stirring up the fire that was already crackling merrily in the small fireplace.

"Where *is* Mr. Malcolm?" Rose asked.

"He and Mr. Leighton went out ridin' early, early!" Tilda told her as she brought Rose's coral-colored velvet morning robe and set her slippers on the top step of the wooden stairsteps on the side of the bed. "Dat Mr. Leighton couldn't wait to try out dat new horse Old Marse done gib him fo' Chris'mas." Tilda shook her head. "Horses, horses, seems like dat's all dat young man lib for. Don't it beat all?"

Leighton, Malcolm's other brother, was home for the holidays from Virginia Military Institute. He was as big, blond, and brawny as Bryce, with the same graceful manners and easygoing personality.

Tilda held out the robe for Rose to put on. "I set yo' tray of tea and biscuits on de table in front of de fire, so you'd be nice and warm. Big breakfus later, but I thought yo' might need a bite aforehand."

Rose pushed aside the covers, swung her legs over the edge, then started to stand to get into her robe. As she did so, she swayed slightly. Tilda caught her elbow to steady her.

"What's de matter, Miss Rose? You feelin' po'ly?" She shot Rose a suspicious look.

"No, I'm fine. Just felt a little dizzy for a minute. Probably got up too quick."

"You sure?"

"Yes, I'm sure, Tilda," Rose spoke sharply. Sometimes Tildes surveillance of her every move got on Rose's nerves. But when she saw the instant hurt in the girl's eyes at her tone, she gave her a reassuring smile. "Really, I'm fine. And thank you for fixing such a nice place for me."

"Yes'm." Tilda was all smiles again.

Rose seated herself in the wing chair and poured the steaming, fragrant tea from the small silver pot into a fragile china cup. She sat sipping her tea as Tilda shook the quilt, plumped the pillows, and straightened the covers on the bed, chattering away like a magpie.

Rose had grown fond of the girl even though there were times when her constant presence in the little house was tiresome. The same could be said for Malcolm's manservant, Joseph. Rose simply could not treat them the way she saw some Southerners treating them — as pieces of furniture, or inanimate objects.

It seemed ironic to Rose that the purpose of allowing newlyweds to live at Eden Cottage was to ensure prolonging their honeymoon privacy when, in truth, they were never alone. But that confirmed her argument that Negroes were not considered *people* here, merely *property*.

"What is you wearin' dis mawnin', Miss Rose?" Tilda asked, standing in front of the armoire.

"Something bright, I think," Rose said. "My red merino would be nice."

While Tilda fetched hot water for her bath, Rose finished her breakfast, contemplating the day ahead. Malcolm had forewarned her of some of the traditional rituals at Montclair — giving each servant on the place the gift of a ham, molasses, blankets, and sweets, then the family breakfast and gift exchange in his mother's suite. In the afternoon they would be going over to Cameron Hall to attend the annual open house.

It disturbed Rose to learn there were no plans to drive to Williamsburg to attend church services. It seemed strange to celebrate the birthday of the Christ Child so extravagantly, yet not honor Him in worship.

Rose sighed. It was the one flaw in her otherwise perfect relationship with Malcolm. He was so fine and yet he had never made a formal commitment of his life to the Lord. She remembered the many discussions they had had before their marriage. In spiritual matters Malcolm had said that unless he were convinced, he could not make such a commitment; that he believed with Emerson that "God enters by a private door into every individual." Malcolm could not be persuaded, pressured, or coerced. In any event Rose realized it is only by God's Spirit that one comes to believe and accept. Still, she could wish that she and Malcolm were one in this important area as they were in every other.

Rose tried to conquer her own slight melancholy, remembering Christmases past in Milford with her own family. She was a Montrose now and must participate fully in the festivities of the day with her husband's family, she reminded herself firmly.

"Better we hurry, Miss Rose," Tilda warned as they heard in the distance the resonant sound of the plantation bell summoning the Montrose Negroes from the yard to the house.

Rose finished buttoning the cuffs of the jacket of the raspberry-colored merino dress. The stand-up collar lined with white ruching and fitted bodice were edged with black velvet in a Roman key design.

"You is some handsome dis mawnin', Miss Rose," Tilda exclaimed, giving a final pat to Rose's hair arranged in a chignon secured in a snood tied in a flat velvet bow.

Tilda was holding Rose's short black velvet cape for her when Rose said, "Before I go, I have a Christmas gift for you, Tilda."

Tilda looked surprised. "But Ole Marse is de one to gib me a gif', Miss Rose."

"But this is a special one from me to you." Rose went to the dressing table where she had wrapped and concealed the package Aunt Van had sent. Rose had written her aunt, requesting that she find a children's Bible, one like she herself had had as a child, with pictures in bright colors.

She had not missed the many curious glances Tilda had given Rose's own Bible when dusting and straightening the bedside table. Several times Rose had observed the girl touching the leather-bound volume with a tentative finger, and once Tilda had even opened it and smoothed the pages. It was then Rose had decided that Tilda, who had become quickly devoted to her young mistress, must have a Bible of her own.

Rose had wrapped it in a gaily patterned scarf she knew Tilda would like to wear at gatherings in the quarters. As she handed it to her and watched her unwrap the package, she was shocked to see the girl's happy look of expectation turn to one of sadness. Her big eyes widened and filled with tears. With a small choked cry, Tilda threw her apron over her face and sank to her knees on the rug in front of Rose.

Stunned, Rose stood still, not knowing what was the matter.

"Tilda! What in the world!" she exclaimed. She bent over the huddled figure. "Tell me, for heaven's sake! What is the matter?"

A moan followed by loud sobs shook the small frame.

Rose knelt down beside her, placing one arm around the shaking shoulders.

"Come now, Tilda, I want to know what's wrong." She tugged gently at the apron that covered the weeping girl's face.

"Oh, Missus!" Tilda sobbed. "You is so good to me!"

"Well, that's nothing to cry about, is it? You're good to me, too, Tilda. Don't you like your present? I wanted to give you something to tell you how much I think of you. I wanted you to have your own Bible so you could read about Jesus as I do every day. One that belongs just to you."

The girl sniffed piteously. "Yes'm. But, but . . . I doan' know —"

"Don't know Jesus?" Rose was aghast. "But I hear you singing hymns about Him."

"No'm. I mean, yes'm. I sure do know de Lawd. Preacher Halsey, he come here mos' every summer and teach us all about Moses, Noah and de Flood and about de Lawd Jesus, too. But . . . but I doan' know —" and she burst into fresh tears and shook her head.

"What is it? You *must* say!" Rose insisted.

The girl lifted her face, wiping her tears with a fisted hand like a small child. "I cain't *read*, Miss Rose. I doan' know *how!*" she wailed.

Rose sat back on her heels, relieved.

"Oh, Tilda, is that all? My goodness, I can teach you to read! I used to teach the younger girls at the school I went to back home. Then you can learn more about Noah and Abraham and Moses, and most of all, about the Lord Jesus." She patted the girl's shoulder comfortingly. "Now, dry your tears. We'll start the lessons right after the holidays." Rose got to her feet. "In the meantime, you can look at the pictures."

"Yes'm." Tilda was smiling now as she scrambled to her feet. Then she dropped a little curtsy. "Thankee kindly, Miss Rose. I doan' never had nothin' as nice as this," she said with shining eyes. "Jes' wait till I shows that stuck-up Lizzie!"

Rose looked dubious, but checked her inclination to remonstrate with Tilda just then about the incongruity of trying to make Lizzie envious of her new Bible!

Of course, Rose knew that Tilda and Carrie, as well as some of the other house servants, considered Lizzie "uppity." She had overheard her two maids discussing Lizzie's superior attitude on other occasions. Rose herself was aware that Lizzie carried herself with a kind of arrogant dignity, obviously thinking her status as Mrs. Montrose's personal maid gave her an exalted position.

It seemed strange to Rose that even in

the slave system itself there was a sense of "caste" or "pecking order."

Delayed by the unexpected scene with Tilda over the Bible, Rose realized she had to hurry. She left the cottage with Tilda's voice raised in one of the rhythmic melodies the Negroes often sang as they went about their work. These songs had a uniqueness that she had never heard until coming to Virginia.

As she made her way up to the main house, Rose still felt the day should have begun with church attendance. Maybe she should have asked, even insisted, that Malcolm take her into Williamsburg. She understood there was a beautiful Christmas Eve candelight service there, and she knew the Montroses had cousins in town who would have welcomed them. But Rose had been at Montclair long enough to know old habits and traditions were not easily changed. Next year things might be different. Next year, she thought with a secret smile, *many* things would be different.

By the time Rose reached the main house, some of the black people were already gathered in front of the porch and more were coming up from the quarters. Inside, Mr. Montrose was directing Josh and Ned, two of the menservants, to assemble the boxes and carry them out onto the veranda for distribution.

Malcolm, Bryce, Garnet, and Leighton were in the dining room having coffee when Rose entered. Malcolm got up and came over to her at once, taking both her cold hands in his and kissing her. "Merry Christmas, darling."

As he did, Rose saw Garnet give her a cool stare, and with a toss of the red-gold ringlets, turn away. Rose still could not penetrate Garnet's wall of veiled hostility.

But why Garnet continued to rebuff her attempts at friendship, Rose did not understand. As wives of two brothers, daughters-in-law in the same family, they could at least be friends. In all her relentless honesty, however, Rose had to admit she found it hard to like Garnet whom everyone else seemed to adore.

Most of the time, it seemed to Rose, Garnet acted like a child, demanding attention, flattery, and service without regard for anyone else's convenience or comfort. Oddly enough, this was accepted, even condoned.

As Rose drank her coffee, she could not help observing the Montrose brothers. The three of them were different and interesting. Bryce, with his good-natured acceptance of life and people, especially his casual indulgence of Garnet's mercurial ways, had an easygoing manner that seemed a sharp contrast to his recklessness on horseback. Rose had often watched him take hedges, fences, or stone walls with fearless skill that brought her heart into her throat at his daring.

Leighton, called Lee, whom Rose had just met, charmed her at once. With his sweet nature and endearing personality, one could not help loving him. In his smart VMI cadet's uniform, he was devastatingly handsome, yet seemed totally unaware of it.

He came over to Rose now, smiling, and said, "You're under the mistletoe, Rose!" and leaned down from his great height to kiss her.

Bryce was right behind him. "Move aside, brother. My turn!" He laughed and kissed Rose, too.

Over his shoulder, for the second time that morning, Rose caught a steely glare from Garnet that chilled her to the bone.

But the moment was cut short when Mr. Montrose appeared at the dining room door.

"Come along, everybody. The folks are

gathered outside. Let's not keep them waiting!" He motioned the young people up with both hands.

Malcolm stood immediately and took Rose's hand to follow his father. Garnet took another sip of her coffee while Bryce patiently held her fur-trimmed pelisse to put around her shoulders. Leighton was already in the hall, holding the front door open for the others.

Standing on the veranda in the chilly morning air for almost an hour, Rose was newly aware of the genuine affection that seemed to exist between the master and the servants of Montclair. It certainly did not seem to be the fear-ridden relationship of master-slave depicted in abolitionist literature or the novel by Harriet Beecher Stowe.

As each servant advanced and curtsied or bowed, Mr. Montrose bestowed generous gifts of fabric yardage, jugs of molasses, and blankets. Rose noted that the black faces were bright with happiness. Was the scene she was witnessing the exception or was this the rule of most of the plantation owners and their "people"? Rose had mixed emotions as she watched. Finally when all the presentations had been made, the servants, laughing and chattering, dispersed to the quarters for their own celebration. And the Montrose family went upstairs to theirs in Sara's sitting room.

Although Garnet had always loved Christmas and looked forward to it with a child's eagerness, Christmas of 1857 promised to be quite different from any other, and she did not anticipate it with any of her usual enthusiasm.

She had discovered, however, that she was a fairly good actress and was learning to guard her words and actions lest she ever reveal her true feelings for Malcolm or her resentment of Rose. It was like walking a tightrope daily, and the strain of it often made her cross and sullen.

It was in this dark mood that she approached the family gift-giving in Sara's suite.

A fire had been laid and was glowing cheerfully in the white marble fireplace, and the room was filled with crimson hothouse roses in milk glass vases and decorated with holly and other fresh greens. Sara had her own small fancifully trimmed tree, sparkling with delicate handpainted ornaments, cornucopias of marzipan in the shape of fruits and flowers, tiny candles in fluted tin holders.

A round table near Sara's chaise was piled high with brightly wrapped packages, and everyone took a turn pinching, shaking, and examining them, making exaggerated guesses as to their contents.

Mr. Montrose, in a jovial mood brought on by his feeling of benevolence and the holiday spirit, beamed at the assembled members of his family with a heightened sense of his good fortune. Even his delicate Sara seemed less languid this morning — no doubt happy to have all three sons home at the same time.

Their youngest, Leighton, was handing his mother her coffee. Lee had grown like a reed since fall. The two other boys seemed content and happy. Well they might be, he thought with pleasure, regarding his two attractive daughters-in-law.

Of course, Malcolm's Rose was the undisputed beauty, all demure charm this morning in a cherry red dress. And then there was Garnet, as reckless and headstrong as Bryce, so they were well-matched and would probably settle down in time and have strong, healthy children like themselves.

Surely my cup runneth over! was Clay's thought, which surprised him somewhat, as he was not given to thinking in Scripture verse. But, indeed, he did have much for which to be thankful this year.

"Who is going to play Santa Claus?" asked Sara.

"Lee should do the honors. He's the youngest and still believes in him!" joshed Bryce.

"Look who's talking! I remember someone getting up ten times on Christmas Eve to wake me up, swearing he heard reindeer's hooves on the roof!" teased Malcolm.

"Well, whoever is going to do it, let's get on with it!" exclaimed Garnet impatiently. "Mama's expecting us at Cameron Hall at noon, remember." She was thinking of the traditional open house and buffet held each Christmas afternoon for friends and relatives of the Camerons.

Still, Garnet was particularly anxious to see how Malcolm would react to her present for him — a handsome stickpin, a jade four-leaf clover set in gold. She had bought it in New Orleans on her honeymoon. She had spotted it in the window of a jewelry store and knew at once she wanted to buy it for Malcolm.

Bryce had been puzzled by her urgency. Christmas shop in June? Personally, he had thought the tiny piece of jewelry an insignificant sort of present for his brother.

"Why not wait and get him some riding gloves or a shaving case — something useful?" he had suggested.

Of course Bryce had no idea of its secret meaning for Garnet, that it symbolized a precious memory — a day with Malcolm that lingered bittersweet and unforgettable — one she sincerely hoped this gift would recall to him.

While riding one afternoon, she and Malcolm had dismounted to let their horses drink from the stream that ran by Eden Cottage. Looking for violets on the mossy bank, Malcolm suddenly dropped to his knees and, when he arose, he was holding out a four-leaf clover to Garnet.

"For good luck," he had said. "Not that anyone as pretty or clever as you needs luck!"

But Garnet had taken it gratefully, later pressed it, and had kept it in a small porcelain pillbox on her dressing table ever since. It had been a reminder of that special afternoon — the only thing Malcolm had ever given her and, therefore, priceless.

Perhaps it had meant something to him, too, Garnet had hoped. Lately, she had begun to fantasize that Malcolm's spontaneous feelings for her were complicated by the fact that she was so much younger than he, that he had regarded her through the years as his friends' "little sister," and consequently suppressed any romantic inclinations toward her. But then Rose was only a year older! Garnet recalled indignantly.

She looked over at Malcolm, but he was fingering the smooth leather cover of some book Rose had just given him, touching it with appreciation and embracing Rose with his eyes.

Her moment of anticipatory happiness left as swiftly and completely as if a cold wind had blown across her heart, and she felt quite miserable again.

The little gift exchange over, it was time to leave for Cameron Hall. The moment could not have come too soon for Garnet, who had found it an unbearable burden to continue to chat and act pleased with the many presents that had been showered upon her — none of which meant anything at all.

Downstairs waiting for the carriages to be brought around, Garnet gazed in the mirror and adjusted the satin bow of her bonnet. In spite of her inner disappointment over Malcolm's gracious but perfunctory thanks for his gift, Garnet looked enchanting in her dark blue pelisse trimmed in soft gray squirrel fur, her red-gold curls peeking out from under the shovel brim of her matching blue bonnet and framed by the lighter blue satin lining.

Fretting over the unsatisfactory moment when Malcolm had opened her gift and quickly put it aside for one of Rose's, she recalled the wizen-faced old jeweler in the shop in New Orleans squinting at her through his wire-rimmed spectacles.

"This is especially fine jade, madam," he had told her. "They say when you give jade, you give a part of yourself. Did you know that?"

Garnet had been giving Malcolm a part of herself for years, she thought — all her childish dreams, her impetuous affection, her unrivaled admiration. Then she had given him the most important part of herself — her heart.

Just at that moment Garnet looked up, and over her shoulder she saw reflected in the mirror Malcolm and Rose coming down the staircase, hand in hand, and something cold and hopeless wrenched her soul.

On their way downstairs to get in the

carriage bound for Cameron Hall, Malcolm squeezed the hand he was holding and leaned over to whisper to Rose. "I have a special gift for you — later. I didn't want to give it to you in front of the others. I wanted to wait until we have our own private Christmas alone."

Suddenly the whole world seemed right. Rose felt a warm glow of happiness. In spite of the alienation she sometimes felt in the midst of his family, these were moments that reassured her that she and Malcolm were, after all, bound together uniquely, that they were one. These were the moments she treasured. These were the times that made the difficult ones easier. She barely registered Garnet's scowling face as she and Malcolm reached the bottom of the steps and stepped outside into the sunlight.

By the time they reached Cameron Hall, Rose felt she was in the only place in the world for her now — with Malcolm.

chapter
10

Stepping through the front door of Cameron Hall, Rose felt that she had walked into a beautiful stage setting.

She was greeted by the glow of candles, the smell of evergreens and cedar, the happy sound of music, laughter, and the murmur of cheerful voices.

The company was gathered in both parlors — festively dressed ladies and gentlemen, and children who ran about unchided by the adults. An atmosphere of joyous gaiety prevailed.

Tall and slender as a girl, Mrs. Cameron in rustling blue taffeta came forward.

"Welcome, and Merry Christmas, my dears!" She gave Rose a welcoming hug and kiss.

From their first meeting, Kate Cameron had already been especially kind to Rose, confiding that she had been a stranger from Savannah at the time of her marriage and new to Virginia, and that it had taken her some time to feel comfortable and "at home."

Garnet had inherited her mother's coloring, the glorious bronze-gold hair, but not her beauty, Rose decided. Kate's features were delicate, aristocratic — Garnet's pixyish. The main difference was the air of serenity, an inner peace lacking in the daughter.

Feeling guilty for her uncharitable thoughts, Rose quickly decided that when Garnet was older, she would likely acquire some of her mother's enviable qualities.

"Come, there's someone special I want you to meet, Rose," Kate was saying. "My little cousin, Dove Arundell."

As she gestured to one of the women servants standing by to take Rose's cape, muff, and bonnet, she complimented her, "How charming you look, Rose, and how glowing! Malcolm must be making you very happy."

"I'm trying!" Malcolm laughed.

When Kate led them toward the parlor door, Rose saw Bryson involved in a lively discussion with some of his friends while Garnet circulated gaily among the guests, apparently never without a dance partner.

She wondered briefly if Bryce minded. When Kate beckoned to a petite, dark-haired girl standing in an admiring circle of young men, one of whom was Leighton, the girl excused herself. Her wide-hooped coral dress swung like a bell as she approached them.

"This is our Dove," Kate introduced her.

The name suited her, Rose agreed. Her small-featured face had an expression of infinite sweetness. She was tiny and as exquisitely proportioned as a French doll.

"I hope you and Dove will become friends, Rose. Since you're both newcomers, you should make good companions. You can gossip about all your strange new relatives," Kate said teasingly, then whispered, "Remember, I'm a transplanted Georgian!"

One of the large parlors had been cleared for dancing, the furniture removed, and the floor highly polished. The small Negro band playing at the end of the hallway struck up a tune and couples began moving in the direction of the music.

Leighton came to claim Dove and they departed to dance.

While Mrs. Cameron was still drawing them both into conversation, Rose spotted

Garnet, a look of triumph on her face, making her way toward them. But she had no greeting for Rose, only a pert invitation for Malcolm.

"Is your dance card filled already, or did you save one for me?"

Malcolm seemed amused and answered indulgently, "I will always save a dance for you, Garnet." Then with a little bow to Rose and Kate, he said, "If you ladies will excuse us?"

Rose stiffened imperceptibly, trying to keep her smile steady and her outward composure, while inwardly she felt a rush of indignation at Garnet's boldness. Should not Malcolm's first dance have been with his wife?

Mrs. Cameron seemed disturbed, too, although the only visible sign was her quickly unfurled fan beating rapidly as she said in a conciliatory tone to Rose, "Garnet is such a child! I'm afraid, quite spoiled. Our fault, no doubt. We just wanted her to be happy. She has always had beaux, and she is — so amusing, so lighthearted — so frivolous, I suppose. And yet, I would not have her change. So few people know how to be happy." Here Mrs. Cameron's expression grew thoughtful, "I only hope Garnet recognizes real happiness when she has it."

Rose watched mutely as Malcolm and Garnet moved with the ease of two people who had danced together often, surely, gracefully, and with obvious pleasure. Garnet's face shone as she smiled up at Malcolm, and Rose's stomach tightened with tension. It was an effort of sheer will not to betray herself, so she continued the conversation with Mrs. Cameron afterward, but not a single word could she remember.

The music ended, and Malcolm was again at Rose's side. "Shall we?" he asked, and she moved into his arms. As he whirled her onto the floor, she caught a glimpse of Garnet's face and was momentarily so unnerved by its hostility that she missed a step and Malcolm had to halt until they were once again in rhythm.

That image lingered to trouble Rose deeply, in spite of the cordiality and warmth she met on every side that day from the Camerons and their guests. Why had she not been able to win Garnet as her friend? What did Garnet hold against her?

The afternoon wore on, filled with music, genial chatter, and good food. In the dining room a bountiful feast had been spread on two long tables glistening with crystal and silver on a damask cloth set with elaborate chinaware. There were magnificent turkeys on platters at either end, a huge ham, as well, bowls filled with rice, mashed potatoes, sweet potatoes, vegetables of every variety. On a side table diners could choose from three kinds of pies — apple, apricot, and peach; a tiered Lady Baltimore cake, candied fruit between its frosted layers; and the traditional Virginia favorite — ambrosia, in an exquisite cut-glass bowl.

It was already dark when Malcolm and Rose finally said their good-byes and stepped out onto the porch when their carriage was called.

To Rose's delight, great feathery snowflakes had begun to fall. She clapped her hands like a child and exclaimed, "Look, Malcolm! It's snowing!"

On the ride home, bundled into warm lap robes and snuggled in the curve of Malcolm's arm, Rose was supremely content. It had been a lovely Christmas, after all, she sighed, leaning her head against his shoulder.

Letting themselves into their cottage, they found a fire burning in the grate of the little parlor, and on the gateleg table in front of it, a tray with a pot of chocolate and a plate of wafer-thin cookies.

Malcolm helped Rose remove her cape before they settled themselves cozily on the love seat facing the glowing fire.

"Now I want to give you my gift," Malcolm said, drawing a slim, oblong velvet jewelry case from his pocket and handing it to Rose.

With trembling hands she sprung the little catch and found a pendant shaped like a snowflake, glistening with diamonds.

"Oh, Malcolm!" she whispered.

"You know, it is said there are no two snowflakes exactly alike," he told her as he fastened the delicate gold chain around her neck, lifting her hair to do so. "That's the way I think of you, Rose . . . so special, so different from every other woman in the world, so uniquely lovely . . . so fragile . . . to be treated with gentle, careful love."

Tears blurred Rose's eyes as she saw Malcolm gazing at her so tenderly.

"Merry Christmas, my darling Rose," Malcolm murmured before his lips claimed hers in a deep, sweet kiss.

She nestled in his arms and he held her in the circle of his embrace, his chin resting on her hair.

Rose gave a deep sigh of contentment,

and Malcolm tightened his arms around her. For the second time that evening, he asked, "Happy?"

"Yes," she breathed. "Sublimely."

For a long while they remained quiet, the soft firelight playing on their faces, casting shadows on the wall behind them, in the kind of warm intimacy that needed no words. With Tilda and Joseph dismissed to their own festivities, they basked in the rare delight of being alone together. Their future seemed to stretch before them in endless bliss; their love, so new, was still wrapped in the magic of discovery, full of surprises and unexpected joys. Nothing yet dimmed that first sweetness of belonging only to each other; no shadow of uncertainty or doubt or sorrow threatened.

After some time, Rose stirred in Malcolm's arms and shifted so that she could look up at him. "Malcolm, I, too, have a kind of gift for you that I've been saving until we were by ourselves."

"Oh? Keeping secrets, are you? I thought we weren't going to have any secrets from each other," he teased.

"I wanted to be quite sure before I told you."

"Told me what, darling? You never need hesitate to tell me anything, Rose. Whatever it is, I would try to understand."

"It's not anything you'd have to try to understand, Malcolm." Rose smiled a secret smile, then rushed on. "In fact, it's very . . . natural and normal for two married people. I just hope you'll be as happy as I am about it."

Malcolm struck his forehead with the heel of his hand in mock exasperation. "Rose, will you stop teasing and tell me what it is?"

"I — we — Malcolm, I'm going to have a child."

He stared at her as though he had not heard her, then as comprehension dawned, a smile spread over his face, lighting up his eyes, changing his entire expression.

"Rose, how wonderful! How perfectly splendid!" He drew her slowly into his arms again. Looking down at her with great tenderness, he asked, "And you're quite sure?"

She nodded, the color flowing into her cheeks, delighting in Malcolm's obvious joy, the pride and happiness shining in his eyes.

He leaned down then and kissed her, slowly, then more deeply, possessively. She could feel his heart pounding against hers, aware of his palms on her waist, gathering her even closer. She raised her arms to his shoulders, feeling the strength of him, caressing the back of his neck where the thick hair curled. Then she was aware of nothing but his kiss and her eager response.

Finally they drew apart, smiling into each other's eyes.

"What a fine way to start the New Year," Malcolm said, "bringing a child into the world." He threw back his head and laughed. "Our child will be born in 1858. I feel it's going to be the happiest year of our lives, my darling Rose!"

chapter
11

All day December thirty-first, Montclair hummed with preparations for the annual New Year's Eve party and Midnight Supper. Welcoming the new year was to be especially festive, for it was also the official event honoring the two Montrose brides.

The house was still decorated for Christmas with a tall pine tree in the front hall, its pungent scent mingling with the smell of twinkling wax candles. The house servants were dressed in their best for the occasion — the men, in gray broadcloth coats; the women, in wool dresses worn under white ruffled aprons starched so stiff they crackled as they moved about.

Cut-glass bowls of eggnog and cranberry punch were set at either end of the long table, along with candied fruit; dark spicy fruitcakes on milkglass pedestals, and tiered silver compotes holding nuts, sugared orange peel, and French chocolate bon-bons.

Upstairs in her dressing room Garnet was getting ready, fighting back the cloud of depression that had threatened to descend all day. The thought of celebrating another year at Montclair filled her with dread. She had never thought that being in constant contact with Malcolm and Rose would be so impossible. Suddenly she felt something stirring within her, a longing to be free, like an imprisoned bird impatiently beating its wings against the restraining cage.

Even the sight of her ballgown did not lift her dismal spirits. It was an extravagance of salmon-colored satin and tulle. Its froth circled the low, off-the-shoulder neckline and was gathered in loops all around the wide skirt, caught by silk flower nosegays. She fastened the new coral pendant earrings Bryce had given her for Christmas, matching the medallion on her pearl necklace.

She had heard the recurring sound of carriage wheels on the drive below as the guests arrived, and she could already hear the murmur of conversation and music drifting up from the lower floor of the house. But Garnet felt reluctant to go down. To pretend a gaiety she did not feel seemed absurd. She did not want to start a new year or look into the future. It was the past she clung to — the dream of what might have been. In that dream everything was the way it used to be. Her sorrow was that she knew she could no longer hold onto her dream; yet she hated living in a world so irrevocably changed.

Garnet walked over to the window and leaned her burning forehead against the frosty pane. Montclair, on this winter's night, was bathed in moonlight and glowed with a luminescent beauty. The river in the distance was like a sheet of silver. Since the light snow of Christmas, the temperature had turned very cold, and icicles dangled like crystal prisms from the eaves above the windows.

Sadness suddenly overwhelmed her. As she gazed out into the winter darkness, the lights of the lanterns set along the drive to mark the way for carriages blurred into sparkling diamonds through her tears.

She whisked them away. This sadness she felt was not new. She was experiencing it more and more often. If Garnet had tried to search her heart, she would have discovered the cause. But she rarely explored her own feelings. If they frightened her, as this unexplained sadness did, she ran.

Tonight was no exception. Blocking out the heavy, smothery feeling, she rushed out of the room and down the stairs, toward the lights and the music and the laughter of the party.

The doors to both parlors had been folded back and the floors polished for dancing. As she came down the steps, Garnet could see couples spinning like colorful tops to the newly imported European dance, the waltz.

Garnet stood for a moment on the edge of the floor, tapping her satin-clad foot to the rhythm of the tune, then she was claimed for the next set.

Though Garnet danced every dance throughout the long hours of the evening, only one really counted. The very special one just before midnight she had reserved for Malcolm!

Where was he now? She looked about, searching out the one face among all the others she longed to see. There he was! With Rose, of course.

Garnet knew this dance was traditionally to be danced with one's special beau or spouse. Making the arrangements called for some clever manipulation. But Garnet was never at a loss for long. A few minutes before the midnight hour, she slipped over to the band leader and suggested he announce a Paul Jones. This dance required two circles — the men on the outer circle; the ladies moving counterclockwise in the inner circle. When the music stopped, one's partner was the person facing. Garnet agreed to give the leader a signal so that when she was opposite Malcolm, the musicians would stop playing.

Her ruse worked, and she feigned great surprise to find herself standing opposite Malcolm as the sweeping bars of the waltz began. He bowed, held out his arms, and she moved into them smoothly.

Was ever a man so romantically handsome? Garnet wondered, looking up into his smiling eyes, feeling as if she could drown in their depths. He looked magnificent in his velvet-collared dress jacket, with the tucked, ruffled white shirt. Then she saw with delight that he was wearing the jade four-leaf clover stickpin in his gray silk cravat.

Deliriously happy, Garnet smiled radiantly, seeing her own gladness reflected in Malcolm's face as he guided her in the steps of the new dance.

At the first stroke of the grandfather clock in the hall, the music stopped and the dancers began to count the remaining seconds as they milled about, seeking that special one with whom to share the dawning of the new year. Garnet's fingers tightened on Malcolm's.

"Oh, Malcolm!" she burst out impulsively. "Why did you have to go up north to school? Everything would have been so different if only —"

In the tide of voices, laughter, the swish of skirts, the shuffle of feet, Garnet's words drifted away. Malcolm seemed not to have heard them. Instead, he leaned down and kissed her lightly on the cheek, saying, "Happy New Year, Garnet," then went in search of Rose.

Watching his tall figure move through the crowd, a tide of grief and despair rushed over her in a terrible, choking flood. Mindlessly she turned and pushed her way to the French doors leading out to the veranda.

Outside she took great gulps of the stingingly cold air, then leaned against one of the porch posts. Gradually her hot coursing blood cooled, and she shivered.

As the keen sharpness of the winter air sharpened her spinning thoughts, calmed her clamorous emotions, Garnet knew if she were not to go mad, she would have to quell her longings, force herself to stop thinking of Malcolm. She clenched her teeth, stifling a groan. Even so, she knew the longings were still there lingering behind every thought.

That night the wind rose, blowing in more snow and sending the branches of the trees to finger the windows of Garnet's bedroom.

She had fallen asleep quickly, then awakened with Malcolm's name on her lips. She sat up, her forehead beaded with perspiration, her heart pounding wildly. Had she spoken his name aloud? She glanced over at Bryce who slept on, undisturbed.

Garnet lay back on the pillows, staring into the darkness. It was wrong, she knew, to dream of Malcolm now. Dreadfully wicked! And yet how could she help it? Seeing him every day, seeing Rose.

Rose was the problem! Rose was the root of all her unhappiness, Garnet fumed. Without Rose . . . Malcolm would surely be hers. Then a cold, insidious thought crept into the heat of her turmoil. If Rose were gone . . . if Rose should die! Garnet felt the bitterness rise up in her, seeping through her like a poison. If there were no

Rose, then Malcolm would be free to love her!

Bryce stirred beside her and suddenly Garnet was bathed in cold sweat. How could she be thinking these awful thoughts with her own husband lying beside her? God would surely punish her!

Garnet began to tremble. She hardly ever thought of God. She was afraid of Him. She did not know when the fear had taken root, but as with many things in her life that frightened or confounded her, she had simply ignored it. What disturbed her most was that God was difficult to ignore. With an effort, she now thrust away the thought of God and His justified wrath at her sinful thoughts.

Instead, Garnet's mind turned to the more tangible things she could manage. For her own survival, her own sanity, she knew she must get away from Montclair, go where she wouldn't have to see Malcolm or Rose and be consumed with envy —

Garnet woke up late the next morning. Her head ached but she felt oddly revitalized. She remembered having been awakened before dawn when Bryce rose and went into his dressing room to don his riding clothes. She had lain there in the predawn darkness of the room and thought over the events of the night before. Now she was more determined than ever to leave Montclair. She refused to stay here and eat her heart out in weakening daydreams, frustrated hopes, and frightening, vengeful nightmares.

As soon as she was fully awake, she called for Bessie to send for her little trunk from the attic, and by the time Bryce returned at midday, her plans were made.

In two weeks' time Garnet had left Montclair for a prolonged visit to her mother's relatives in Savannah and Charleston. And none too soon — for it was about that time that Malcolm announced proudly to the family that he and Rose were to have a child in late summer.

PART IV

A House Divided

Montclair
1858–1860

chapter

12

Rose had not written in her diary in months until a growing feeling of emotional separation from Malcolm prompted her to pour out her heart on its pages once more.

April 1858

Spring has come to Virginia early and Montclair is a fairyland of flowers and blossoming trees. But my spirit is as bleak and abandoned as a New England winter beach, wrapped in a melancholy I cannot seem to overcome. It is because of a deepening sense of alienation I feel in these surroundings and most of all a widening distance between me and my beloved Malcolm.

It began when I made an unfortunate remark at the dinner table one night among guests. I had heard through my maid that my father-in-law had sold a young black man, the plantation carpenter, to a friend. The word *sold* always grieves me. How can one treat other human beings as *property* to be bought and sold at will? Perhaps I would not have brought it up at all except for Tilda's sad tale of a black woman who had been hoping to marry the man. The effect of my statement was dreadful, indeed. I knew immediately that both my father-in-law and my husband were incensed at my expressing my opinion on the matter, an expression that they considered inappropriate. But it was not until much later when Malcolm came to our bedroom that I knew how unpardonable they all considered my action.

Here Rose put down her pen and shuddered involuntarily, recalling the wrenching scene with Malcolm.

"Rose," he had begun, "why do you insist on meddling in things you do not, cannot, and will not ever understand?"

"But, Malcolm, surely you believe that slavery is wrong!"

He had whirled around, facing her. "Yes, I believe it is wrong. If I could, I would have nothing to do with it. But don't you realize Montclair is run by slave labor? There would be no crops, no property, no profit, no life as we know it without slavery. These people are the offspring of slaves brought here when my great-great-grandfather first came here. We have bought very few additional slaves. We would not perpetuate an institution that we had not been born into, and now must maintain."

Then he softened his voice and spoke more gently. "We are responsible for these people, don't you understand, Rose? Clothing, feeding, caring for them when they are ill, just like children. It is a burden, not the luxury the North would have people believe. . . . Montclair is surrounded by what amounts to a Negro village, and every person out there is our charge. We never break up families. Sergus was a young, unmarried man, strong, capable, and willing to go —"

"But what about that poor woman?" Rose asked weakly.

"There are other young men here. She'll probably find one she likes as well and marry him." Malcolm was now as patient as if he were explaining something to a child.

He came over to the bed, sat on the edge, and touched her cheek. "Rose, don't worry yourself about such things. It isn't good for you to get upset, especially now."

"Was your father very angry with me?"

"Father isn't used to young ladies having such strong opinions. I'm sure he attributed it to your Yankee upbringing and has forgiven you. By tomorrow he will have forgotten the entire incident," Malcolm assured her.

But Rose was not so sure. She knew it would be impossible — at least for *her* — to forget the matter so easily.

It seemed particularly ironic to Rose that she was teaching Tilda and Carrie to read from the Scriptures and they were now in the book of Lamentations, where the Hebrews were taken into slavery by the Babylonians.

The following afternoon Rose discussed the "tempest" with Kate Cameron when she came to call. Asked her opinion of what had happened, Kate's answer was slow in coming, and then surprising.

"I have often pondered the question of slavery — it distorts the basic moral tenets by which we have been taught to live. We do not judge Negroes as we do white people. They are sometimes punished by brutal masters, but not for doing wrong. We look the other way when white men look lustfully at Negro women and ignore the little children who bear strong resemblance to their masters. It is a loathsome system and I know deep in my heart that most white women would love to be rid of it."

"Why, then, can't something be done about it . . . and such things as Sergus?"

Kate shook her head sadly, her lovely gray eyes darkening with infinite sadness.

"Of course it must go. But *when* is the question. We cannot just let these poor creatures fend for themselves without proper preparation." She kept shaking her head. "It will take time — or something quite beyond our own doing."

It seemed very strange to hear these words from one who was born and reared with slave servants, one who managed a plantation larger than Montclair. It was the kind of comment Rose had heard dozens of times in discussions on the subject of slavery between her father and his friends in her own home. But it was certainly not the kind of logic one expected to hear from a Southerner.

Of course, Mrs. Cameron would never have voiced such an opinion in mixed company. It would have been considered unseemly for a woman to do so, as Rose now knew.

June 1858

We have moved up to the main house for my confinement. Since all Montrose babies are born under the roof at Montclair, nothing would do but to move into the downstairs wing where a staircase leads to a nursery on the floor above. A bright girl, Linny, Carrie's younger sister, will be our baby's nurse.

As she was helping me one day, I made a strange discovery. I had sent Linny down to Eden Cottage to bring back some of the layette I have been making to place in the new cedar chest for our dear little one, and I was alone in the upstairs nursery.

While looking at some of the lovely watercolors that are framed and hanging along the walls, I accidentally leaned against a section of panel to get a closer look. Suddenly the whole partition slid back, revealing a small inner room.

I was startled at first, then curious. I peered in. The ceiling sloped back for some distance. As I stepped inside, I saw that there was quite a bit of floor space, but the farther in I ventured, the darker it was. Not being able to see very well, I withdrew.

Determined to investigate, I went back into the nursery and found a candle. With the lighted candle illuminating the way, I reentered the hidden room and looked around. Farther back there was a door with a wooden bolt. Sure that it must lead somewhere, I proceeded to shove it back, lift the latch, and push. It stuck, the wood probably warped from long disuse, so I had to lean my weight against it. Finally it gave way and the door creaked open. Cautiously I thrust it wider and then saw a narrow flight of steps going downward.

I might have had the courage or curiosity to see where it led, but I heard Tilda's voice calling to someone, and for some reason I hurried back, shutting the secret door behind me. Leaving the passageway and stepping back into the nursery, I touched the same part of the panel, and the partition slid back, leaving no trace of what lay behind that wall. My discovery both excited and mystified me until I remembered Mr. Montrose's telling about the network of underground tunnels and storage rooms, providing a safe hiding place from possible Indian raids for the first generation of the Montrose family. What a history this house has — what a heritage for my child!

September 1858

Malcolm and I have a son! He is nearly a month old and the most beautiful baby in the world! At least I think so. He is round and rosy, with dark fluff that will undoubtedly be thick, silky ringlets like Malcolm's when he was a little boy, for he looks so much like his proud papa. Everyone is elated and happy about the baby, who will be heir to Montclair.

Scripture describes my experience better than I ever could. "A woman when she is in travail hath sorrow, because her hour is come, but as soon as she is delivered of the child, she remembereth no more the anguish, for joy that a man is born into the world" (John 16:21).

When the longest night of my life was over and they placed that tiny creature in my arms, the tremendous feeling that came over me can only be fully understood by those who have known it.

Tilda, who stayed with me throughout

my ordeal and helped Dr. Connett and the midwife, Mrs. Thomkins, told me that my dear Malcolm suffered in his own way throughout the hours of my labor. He paced endlessly, unable to take refreshment, while his father calmly read the Richmond *Times*. Just as dawn was breaking, they came to tell him I was delivered, and that he had a son.

I scarcely recall his coming into the darkened room, leaning over my bed, putting his cheek against mine. He took my hand, which was too limp to lift, kissed it, then turning it over, kissed the palm and held it to his own cheek. I remember his whispering, "Rose, Rose! My poor darling."

I managed to murmur, "But I'm your *happy* darling."

chapter

13

With the birth of her son, Rose seemed to gain a new beauty. To Malcolm, Rose had never seemed so lovely. A serenity and softness had replaced the intensity and too-frequent emotionalism she had displayed before. Now her devotion to her child filled her days, and she no longer took the solitary walks nor had time for the long hours of reading that had marked her pregnancy.

Another unexpected result of little Jonathan's arrival was a change in the relationship between Rose and her mother-in-law. The baby's birth seemed to revitalize the part of Sara that her own children's births had brought into existence, that primal instinct of motherhood. She quite adored the baby, and whenever Rose brought him in to her, she would gaze at him. "He is so like Malcolm. Such a handsome, unusual baby."

Jonathan soon became the center of attention at Montclair, with everyone from his proud Grandfather Clay to Linny, his nurse, marveling at his perfection, noting each new development with awe, praising his strength and the intelligence in his wide, dark eyes. Everyone, that is, but Garnet who evidenced an aloof indifference. She had been away most of the summer and, after she and Bryce returned to Montclair in the fall, she still spent most of her days at her former home, Cameron Hall.

When Jonathan was six weeks old and Rose fully recovered from the birth, she asked Malcolm one night as they were dressing for dinner, "When can we move back to Eden Cottage?"

He seemed surprised. "Don't you like it here?"

"It's just that I miss our own little place, our privacy, our times together —"

"But we're together *here*." He turned to her, smiling indulgently. "And what about the nursery and Linny and the baby? Eden is a honeymoon cottage, darling. We're a family now," he reminded her with a smile. Placing his hands on her shoulders, he bent toward her and kissed her lightly. "There's no room for Jonathan there."

Rose sighed. "I suppose you're right."

But she felt an overwhelming sense of loss. She had not realized their move to Montclair's big house would be a permanent arrangement. She had never, in fact, thought of their spacious rooms as anything but temporary quarters until after the baby's birth. She felt another small twinge of sadness. Those days alone in Eden Cottage had been so fleeting. Now, it seemed, they were gone forever . . . as was that special closeness she and Malcolm had known there.

"Besides," Malcolm said, "from what I gather, there will soon be new occupants for Eden Cottage."

Rose whirled around from the mirror, her wide skirts swaying. "What do you mean? Who?"

"Why, Leighton — and Dove Arundell, the Camerons' cousin," he replied.

"How do you know?"

"Garnet told me."

"Garnet?" echoed Rose. *Why hasn't she said anything to the rest of us?* she wondered.

"Yes. I met her the other day when she was trying out her new horse on the bridle path along the river where Cameron and Montrose lands join." Malcolm spoke casually, adjusting his satin cravat in the mirror over Rose's head. "From what Garnet says, the romance started at Christmas, and Leighton has been going to see her every chance he gets." Malcolm chuckled as he turned to pick up his broadcloth coat. "I thought it rather strange that Lee pleaded extra studying for his examinations last spring instead of coming home. It seems he went to Savannah instead. At any rate, Miss Dove will be here at Christmas again and the happy news, I suspect, will be announced then. And perhaps in June, when Leighton is graduated, they will be married."

Rose did not reply at once. It was not that she was so surprised at the news of Leighton's love for the adorable Dove. That he was smitten by her was evident at the Camerons' Christmas party last year. It was Malcolm's casual remark about riding with Garnet that made her thoughtful. She had been so preoccupied with the baby that some days she did not see Malcolm until evening. Garnet, she knew, went out riding every afternoon and Malcolm, making the plantation rounds each day, was bound to run into her sooner or later. If not by chance, then by clever planning. *Garnet's, not Malcolm's, of course,* she thought loyally.

The fox-hunting season had hardly passed when preparations began for the Christmas holidays once again. The house took on a festive air, with Mrs. Montrose directing the decorating from her bedroom, and her maid Lizzie relaying the instructions to the rest of the house servants. Galax leaves and crimson ribbon were intertwined in the balustrades of the staircase. Fresh holly, red with berries, filled large vases in the hall. Wreaths adorned the windows, and glowing pine-scented candles brightened the mantels in all the rooms.

The house was filled to overflowing, people coming and going, carriages arriving at all hours, every extra room occupied with guests who stayed overnight or a week at a time.

A dozen or more people gathered around the dinner table almost every evening. Of course Rose knew that Montclair had always been known for its gracious hospitality, and its master as a genial and generous host whose guests were drawn from the gentry of the surrounding countryside — wealthy, cultured, elegantly dressed.

That is why Rose was amazed at the superficiality of the conversation. Most of these guests, certainly the gentlemen, were well-educated, yet the table talk was uniformly mundane. At least so Rose thought, until one evening after dinner, when the ladies had retired to the parlor and music room, leaving the men at the table.

Rose had hesitated for a moment after leaving the dining room, trying to decide whether to go into the parlor with Mrs. Cameron and some of the older ladies, or to the music room where the younger women, mostly Garnet's friends, were assembling. Before she did either, however, she would run upstairs to the nursery and check on the sleeping Jonathan, even though the faithful Linny was probably close by.

After caressing his round little head and tucking the silken quilt more firmly around him, Rose came back downstairs. As she passed the dining room, she heard the men's voices raised in argument from behind the closed door. Rose paused to listen — and then, to regret listening.

"Those Northern papers print nothing but lies," one man said indignantly. "To read them, you'd believe we whip our slaves every day."

Rose would have moved on, but she heard Malcolm's calm voice. "Surely no one, no *reasonable* person, would believe that kind of scurrilous yellow journalism."

"Well, Malcolm —" this was Mr. Montrose interjecting — "if a lie is repeated often enough, people tend to believe it's true."

"Some of our Southern papers are just as bad," countered another.

"All these lies are going to lead this country into a situation nobody can predict and nobody can get out of . . . It's a self-destructive path. No matter *what* is said, it's *where* it's said that counts. We're just as ready to believe what our papers say about the North." That was Malcolm again.

"They've been baiting us for thirty years about our slaves. But they don't turn down the cotton we send them for their mills. They're getting rich enough on it themselves."

"Yankee shrewdness," came a sarcastic comment.

There was general laughter.

"A Yankee would as soon cheat his grandmother as pinch a penny!"

Another roar of laughter.

"But, gentlemen, let's not sell them short

when it comes to convictions. They've bought the Abolitionist package and we best not shrug off their intentions."

"But slavery itself is not the issue."

"You think not? How would any of us run our plantations without slave labor? It's important, all right."

"Not all that many men in the South own slaves."

"But to the ones who do, it's important."

"What troubles me is if the Abolitionists get their way and elect a Republican next year. If so, we're in for real problems. South Carolina's talking secession."

Another round of laughter, then Rose heard Malcolm again.

"Virginia would certainly never leave the Union over slavery, of that I'm very sure. Look at our Virginia Presidents, all of them — Washington, Jefferson, and Madison, too — all freed their own slaves. I think most slave owners eventually would come to that conclusion, if the North would stop insisting and acting so righteous."

"Feelings run pretty high, Malcolm. We just won't stand for their telling us what we must do."

"You're right, we won't. The South, Virginia included, is not going to take orders from the Yankees."

There was the sound of clinking glasses and, through the slats of the louvers, Rose could see that Mr. Montrose had risen to get another decanter from the massive mahogany sideboard and was refilling glasses.

Her heart pounding, Rose slipped past, apprehensive that someone might come along and see her standing there. The conversation she had just overheard distressed her deeply.

She also realized that it was probably in deference to her that none of this type of discussion was carried on in her presence. Mentally she apologized for her judgment of the quality of conversation that had prevailed. She had underestimated the polite sensitivity, mainly her father-in-law's, which made them hesitate to raise such controversial issues while she was seated among the diners.

That was not the only bitter lesson Rose was to learn about eavesdropping that night. As she proceeded down the hall, she heard the sound of feminine voices and high-pitched laughter coming from the music room where Garnet and her friends had gathered.

Garnet had a gift for mimicry and a flair for the dramatic. Rose had often witnessed her caricature of some recent visitor at Montclair. She had even inwardly sympathized with the poor, unfortunate subject of the most recent hilarity. Inexplainably, Rose thought, Mr. Montrose was Garnet's most vocal supporter and heartily endorsed her performances. Even when the object of ridicule happened to be a good friend of his, he would laugh at her merciless rendition.

Now as Rose stood uncertainly, not knowing which room to enter, she heard Garnet's voice in a perfect imitation of *her own* New England accent. She halted, feeling her cheeks flame with humiliation, as Garnet's words reached her amid peals of derisive laughter.

"Now, Linny, *dear,* take the baby *very carefully* —"

"*Dear?* Does she actually call her baby's nurse *dear?*"

"Oh, my, yes!" retorted Garnet. "She's a regular little 'Mrs. Stowe'."

"Calls a darky *dear!* I do declare! I never heard of such a thing!" squealed someone else.

"Oh, all her servants are pampered pets," retorted Garnet.

Hot stinging tears rushed into Rose's eyes. She turned as if to run; her only thought, escape. How could she? How could Garnet who should, as her sister-in-law, befriend and defend her, hold her up to such cruel ridicule?

As Rose stood there immobilized, she heard the scraping of chairs and the sounds of movement coming from the dining room. Apparently the gentlemen were preparing to join the ladies. For a moment she was locked in mindless panic. Then, taking a long, shaky breath, she straightened her shoulders and went to the door of the parlor. Forcing a smile, she entered.

Kate Cameron, sitting on one of the twin sofas, beckoned to her, patting the cushion beside her. Gratefully Rose made her way forward and sank down.

Somehow Rose managed to get through the rest of the evening, even to exchanging pleasantries with Garnet's friends, who, merely out of politeness, Rose felt sure, complimented her on her gown or inquired about Jonathan. Her face felt strained with the effort of smiling without betraying her inner turmoil. She even managed to stand alongside Garnet as they all bade their guests good night.

Neither did Rose allow herself the relief of telling Malcolm about it later. He would have been angry with Garnet, but would have also chastised Rose for listening. Wearily she decided it was not worth the telling. Her hurt was something with which she alone must deal.

But sleep did not come easily for Rose that night. She lay awake long after Malcolm's even breathing told her he had fallen asleep. She heard the clock strike midnight, then one, and still her troubled thoughts would not allow her to rest.

All the voices, all the comments came hauntingly back to her as she lay there, staring into the darkness.

The talk of tension between North and South, the question of slavery, all reactivated past impassioned arguments. Garnet's sneering reference to Rose as "a regular Mrs. Stowe," recalled to her mind the famous writer's novel *Uncle Tom's Cabin*. Rose had been at boarding school when it was published, and everyone was talking about it. Many of the girls reacted violently as they read the one copy of the book that was passed around.

Rose, too, had wept when she read about little Eva and her cruel mother, recoiled from the evil Simon Legree, held her breath in suspense as Eliza traversed the ice-clogged river, sobbed when Uncle Tom died. She had never imagined that one day she would live in the South or, in fact, be married to a "slave owner." But then she could not think of Malcolm as a slave owner; neither could she hide from the truth. As his wife, she too, was one of that despised breed. Weren't Tilda, Carrie, and Linny her slaves? What would her Northern friends think if they knew it took twenty-two house servants to maintain a place like Montclair?

Rose moved restlessly, trying not to disturb the sleeping Malcolm as her tortured thoughts circled endlessly.

Much as Rose tried to lull her conscience and comfort her disquieted heart, the gray light of dawn was seeping through the shuttered windows before she finally drifted off into a shallow slumber.

chapter
14

With baby Jonathan's birth, Garnet found more and more excuses to be away from Montclair. It became increasingly difficult for her to be around the shining happiness of Rose and Malcolm's unabashed pride in their son.

An incident that occurred a few months after Jonathan was born precipitated a flaming row with Bryce. It happened the day the photographer came to take pictures of Rose and the baby to send to her family in Massachusetts.

The family had gathered in Sara's sitting room so she could observe the procedure. The photographer was busy arranging the pose, while the others formed an admiring circle about the adorable infant and his lovely mother.

It was Rose who noticed Garnet standing to one side, largely ignored.

Sweetly she asked, "Would you like to hold Jonathan, Garnet?"

Startled, Garnet quickly put her hands behind her back as if afraid Rose might thrust him into her arms. "Good heavens, no!" she exclaimed. "I wouldn't know the first thing about holding a baby!"

"No better way to learn," chuckled Mr. Montrose, giving Bryce a sly wink.

But Garnet turned away furiously. She didn't want a baby, she thought angrily. Certainly not *Bryce's* baby. In fact, she didn't want any child at all if it couldn't be Malcolm's.

If Rose had been hurt by Garnet's refusal, or the others puzzled by her attitude, it was because no one knew Garnet was sick with envy. Her secret anguish drove her frustration to an unbearable pitch and afterward she provoked an unnecessary quarrel with Bryce.

The result was that she packed again and went off for another lengthy stay with some cousins. Since one of them was about to be married, the wedding was a convenient explanation for her abrupt departure.

During the next two years their marriage followed this unpredictable pattern, with Garnet's impulsive comings and goings. Sometimes Bryce accompanied her, but he was never content for long away from the life of riding and hunting the land he loved. Because Bryce loved Garnet devotedly, he allowed her to come and go at will even if he did not understand her need to do so.

At times Garnet had bouts of conscience about Bryce. She knew she was withholding the generous love due him, was denying him the rapturous fulfillment that was his right, imprisoning them both in a marriage so limited that love's ideal joys and triumphs had not been attained. She also knew he loved her with all her shortcomings, her whims, and weaknesses.

Most of the time they got on well, for they had much in common. Their roots were the same, and these were deeply grounded in their families and the land. Even their sudden quarrels were quickly over and, like children or sunshine after a summer storm, they were soon laughing and teasing each other again.

In the spring it was decided that Rose should accompany her mother-in-law on her annual pilgrimage to White Sulphur Springs. Never yet having regained all her former zest after Jonathan's birth, Rose looked forward to bathing in the strengthening waters as well as to the change of air and scenery. Jonathan's nurse, Linny, and Lizzie would also make the trip to attend to their needs.

Rose's delight in the new surroundings, along with her profound sadness in being away from Malcolm, was quickly recorded in the diary he had given her. Knowing that she would return to her husband a much healthier, happier companion, however, eased the pangs of homesickness.

White Sulphur Springs, 1859

The magnificent hotel and grounds are approached by a winding road, through manicured lawns planted with flower beds. The main building is circled by a tiered veranda with hanging baskets of purple and red fuschias. Dozens of comfortable rustic rockers line the porch on which guests can sit to watch the new arrivals. The spectators all look so rosy and relaxed that upon arrival, the poor, weary traveler may take heart that the regimen here does one a world of good!

Each cottage has its own porch where invalids can rest in the open air, yet are secluded by a protective screen of trees. Mama was quite fatigued by the long journey and went immediately to the cottage reserved for her, where Lizzie put her to bed.

Before going inside to inspect my own quarters, I stood on the little porch and looked back across the smooth lawn to the hills beyond. A lovely passage of Scripture came to me then: "I look unto the hills from whence cometh my strength," and I whispered a little prayer of gratitude for the privilege of resting in this beautiful place and regaining both physical and spiritual strength. I have felt, in the last several months, a kind of ennui, a drifting from my long-held convictions, brought about perhaps by the atmosphere of luxury and leisure that abounds at Montclair. I have a feeling in this tranquil place I will once again find my true source of contentment and peace.

April 15, 1859

Although the food is healthy, it is hearty indeed, and the conversation at the table, stimulating. It is enjoyable to be in the company of such interesting, intelligent women as those at my assigned table, and to hold conversations of more substance than those at Montclair where the chief topics among the ladies are gowns, gardens, and gossip. I am like a starving person suddenly offered a feast — and I fear I shall be surfeited by intellectual gluttony!

One of the ladies, Natalie Harding, is remarkable in every respect — in appearance, tall and willowy with chestnut hair and glorious eyes; in personality, gracious; in intellect, keen and discerning. A rare woman.

We never seem to run out of topics to discuss. Books are her weakness, as they are mine, and we both thoroughly enjoy the evening musicales presented by the very talented quartet after supper in the lounge.

Natalie is interested in everything about me. She draws me out on every subject and, under her warm interest, I feel some of the reticence to express myself that I have felt over the past year disappearing. I have told her all about Montclair as she is particularly interested in customs and the lifestyle there. She was fascinated by my description of the secret door in the staircase leading from Jonathan's nursery that was once an escape route and hiding place from Indian raids when the house was built.

We did, at length, talk about slavery. I have been, it seems, under much criticism among the Northern ladies here, for having brought my baby's black nurse with me.

"Not criticism of you, dear Rose," Natalie said one day in her soft, well-modulated voice, "for you are much liked and well thought of among the ladies. It is just that perhaps you are not aware how sore a subject it is with most of us in the other states."

Rose tried to explain how Linny had been with Jonathan from the day of his birth, how the girl doted on him, seeing to his every need with loving attention.

"No one disputes that, my dear. It is the principle of the thing," she went on. "Does it not strike the very heart of one as sensitive as yourself that this poor girl is not free?"

It did strike Rose to the very heart. By her words Natalie had sprinkled the proverbial salt into the wound already opened within, a wound that she had tried to cover with acceptance because she was alone in a world that considered black people as property. What else could she do?

"You know, there are people who are helping slaves to escape, to move North, find homes, jobs, a place where they can live, work, and earn their own way, not be dependent on white owners for their very lives," Natalie began cautiously, then ventured on. "There are well-organized groups who are arranging such passages, who at the peril of their own lives, at times regularly, guide these poor unfortunates out of bondage. In the eyes of the world it seems to me the only way any white person can amend this terrible scourge on our whole country.

"It is called the Underground Railroad, and there are 'stations' along the way where the escaping slaves are housed, fed, and sheltered until another 'conductor' meets them and guides them to the next station and eventually to a place of freedom." Natalie paused. "It is all very secret, of course, because the penalties for such activity are dire, indeed, and the danger is great. It takes people of conscience, courage, and compassion to join such a movement."

Natalie's impassioned speech haunted Rose. Although the young woman never criticized her or in any manner made her feel guilty about Linny, she had brought to the surface again all Rose's original uneasiness. She determined to discuss her feelings with Malcolm when she returned to Montclair. At least, she wanted his assurance that if and when he became master of Montclair, the slaves would be freed.

Strangely enough, even with Natalie, Rose felt defensive and wanted to protest this view of slavery against what she had witnessed at Montclair — childlike people living in apparent contentment with no sign of restlessness or agitation for freedom. But the words were checked when she remembered the incident over Sergus, the plantation carpenter. She could not deny the lack of consideration for human feelings that episode implied and she felt a resurgence of horror at the system.

Rose recalled how her headmistress at boarding school reported an appeal made by Angela Grimke to "all Christian women of the Southern states," how she had passionately called upon them to persuade all the men they knew that slavery was "a crime against God and man." She urged immediate action. Women who owned slaves should free them at once, begin to pay them for their work, and educate them, whether it was against the law or not.

A sense of relief swept over Rose. At least she had done that! She had continued to teach Tilda, Carrie, and now Linny to read from the Scriptures. Almost every day they gathered around her, reading for themselves the simple, saving message. Of course, they had some difficulty deciphering the language of the Bible written in Old English. But they were all eager learners and far brighter than she had been led to believe.

Rose resolved to renew her efforts in teaching the three young black women when she returned to Montclair and she would again broach the subject with Malcolm. *We cannot be separated on this,* she told herself, determined to speak out boldly on what she was now convinced was a terrible evil.

It is the last night we will be here at the Springs. It has been a delightful time, perhaps self-indulgent to an extent, but, I firmly believe, an ordained time. I feel so much stronger in every way, and especially blessed to have made such a friend as Natalie. We agree it was a divine coincidence that we were both at the Springs at the same time.

Before I forget, I want to record our

conversation after dinner as I think it will have special significance for me in the days ahead. Natalie walked back with me to my cottage in the soft spring twilight.

As she left me to go on to her own cottage, she looked at me with those deep-set eyes and said, "Rose I think you have a special destiny. I think the Lord has placed you where you are, with all the qualities of mind and heart necessary for the work you are to do for Him. Are you — do you think — equal to the task?"

My heart began to pound and even my scalp tingled at her words. "I don't know. I'm not sure," I replied timidly.

"Remember Isaiah 6:8, Rose," she said quietly. "You, too, may be called upon to do something you feel inadequate to carry out. Sometimes there is no one else, Rose. Sometimes we are in circumstances that demand we be uniquely fitted for what needs to be done."

She put both hands on my shoulders and kissed my cheek. "Good-bye, Rose. God be with you in all you do."

We had already promised to write to each other and suddenly my throat was thick with a sorrow that welled up inside me at parting with this woman I had known such a short time but who had influenced me so profoundly.

As she disappeared into the gathering dusk, I went inside immediately and got out my Bible to look up the reference she had given me.

I repeated the words over and over, puzzled by their meaning as it applied to me.

I write the words here because I feel someday I shall understand why they were given to me: "Also I heard the voice of the Lord saying: Whom shall I send, and who will go for us? Then said I, Here am I; send me."

chapter
15

When the train pulled into the station at Richmond, Rose saw Malcolm's tall figure pacing impatiently on the platform.

Upon disembarking, she was lifted off her feet in an exuberant embrace, and her heart swelled with happiness.

"Oh, darling, darling! I'm so glad to see you!" she murmured over and over, tears filling her eyes.

"Welcome home!" Malcolm exclaimed.

Home! The word echoed in Rose's mind. Was Virginia now her home? Wherever Malcolm was had become home to her now, she realized.

Jonathan had to be admired, held, tossed, and tickled by Malcolm, with Rose pointing out all the changes and progress their little son had made in their absence. Linny stood by, beaming at the attention her cherished charge was receiving from his proud papa.

"Well, Linny, and how have you borne up under all this travel?" Malcolm challenged her.

"Jes' fine, Marse Malcolm, but sure 'nuf glad to be home." Linny grinned.

Rose's reunion with Malcolm was so sweetly tender, so joyously passionate that, as she lay in his arms that night under the lacy canopy of their great four-poster bed at Montclair, she resolved never to be separated from him this long again. She sighed with contentment as he pulled her close, and she snuggled into the curve of his arm.

The first few weeks after her return, Rose lived in a kind of euphoria. She and Malcolm seemed to have regained the precious intimacy of their European honeymoon and the sojourn in the woodland cottage. Malcolm reveled in being with Jonathan as well. He carried the child about on his shoulders as he and Rose strolled in the garden, and rejoiced at each new word the toddler lisped.

If only it could always be this way, Rose thought dreamily, watching them. *If it could only be just the three of us.*

But, of course, that was not possible.

Gradually the natural flow of life resumed to interrupt these idyllic times together. There were visitors, the demands of plantation management, family and social events. Increasingly, the turbulence of the political strife rampant in the country penetrated the peace and serenity of the remote, leisurely life of Montclair.

The talk Rose heard around the dinner table was disturbing. Could Southern men, many of whom had been educated in the great schools of the North, differ so drastically on principle with their Northern brothers who read the same books, the same newspapers, frequented the same libraries and museums of the world, enjoyed the music and art of the great European masters, generally professed the Christian faith, read the same Bible? Could they really believe the others to be liars and blackguards — despicable in habit, lifestyle, hopes, dreams, ideals? It seemed so.

Rose tried to discuss it with Malcolm, to share with him some of the sentiments expressed by her father and his friends. These, too, were thoughtful, patriotic men of intelligence and experience. Yet, in the North the sentiment was that slavery must be abolished if democracy as America represented it to the rest of the world was to be preserved.

Malcolm heard her out without comment. Then, using the methods of philosophic discussion he had learned at Harvard, he posed his theory for her to question.

"How, then, is the North any different from the South? We have made it a crime to teach Negroes to read and write for fear they will want to be free. In the North they keep the poor enslaved in factories and mills, uneducated, because the owners are afraid education will inspire them to demand better working conditions and higher wages. It is always the ruling class, the moneyed people, who keep others down, clutching greedily at what they have. But what does Scripture say about that sort? 'Even what they have will be taken away. . . .'

"You're fond of quoting Scripture, Rose. In marriage, two people become one. So if this is true, then my wealth derived from slave labor is yours as well, and your fortune, derived from underpaid workers in the mills your family owns, is mine. So I share your guilt as well as your responsibilities. Is that not so?"

Rose bit her lip and could think of no reply.

As she pondered all this, Rose's sensitive spirit was troubled. Now that she was once more living the life-style so deplored by the people in the North, she was caught in a terrible conflict of conscience. The words Natalie Harding had spoken to her burned like fire into her mind, smoldering there.

"Rose, you are in a position to help those poor unfortunate creatures," she had said. "Consider well what you can do."

Rose had determined in her heart she must do something. But what? It all seemed so impossible. The servants did not look unhappy as they went about their work. In fact, they seemed outwardly content, she rationalized. What could she possibly do? At least she could continue the Bible instruction she had begun earlier, she reminded herself.

So Rose resumed her teaching of Tilda, Carrie, and Linny; but now that they lived in the main house, the lessons were shorter and often irregular. Carrie had other chores now that Eden Cottage was not her only responsibility; and, as Jonathan grew and was more active, Linny had less time when he was napping to spend with her studies.

Then, unexpectedly, one day something

happened that was to change Rose's life irrevocably.

She and Malcolm and the baby had spent the afternoon together, walking along the riverbank, picnicking on the grassy knoll above, and wandering through the shady woods. It would, ever afterward, remain etched upon her memory as one perfect time they had shared.

It was late when they came back to the house. There would be company for dinner, and Malcolm stopped at the plantation office to check on something while Rose took Jonathan up to Linny for a bath.

When she came into her room to bathe and change, she found her mail on her dressing table. There was a letter from her aunt, one from her brother John, and another envelope, addressed in an unfamiliar handwriting.

When she opened it, she discovered it was unsigned. "It has been brought to our attention that you might be willing to help us in the transport of some merchandise," the letter began, and as Rose read on, she began to tremble. In veiled terms and ambiguous words, the writer mentioned that her name had been given as a person who would assist the illegal movement of slaves to freedom in the North.

After rereading the letter a dozen times, holding it in shaking hands, Rose felt a pressing weight that made it difficult to breathe. She took a shallow breath, almost regretting now her emotional discussions with Natalie on the inhumanity and oppression of the black people in the South. After all, she had never personally witnessed any ill treatment, nor had she heard of any cruelty inflicted upon the people owned by the Camerons or by any of the friends of the Montroses on the neighboring plantations. Maybe, as *they* all contended, Mrs. Stowe's heartrending story was mostly her own imagination with no particle of truth in the telling.

Shaken, she folded the letter into squares; then, on second thought, tore it into tiny pieces. The last paragraph of the letter, written in a bold, slanting hand, stayed with her as though engraved indelibly: "You will be contacted with further instructions at a future date." Not, "If you agree." It was already assumed she would be willing to do whatever was required.

Rose's heart thundered. It was her impulsive response to Natalie Harding's persuasive suggestions when they were at the Springs that had put her in this untenable position, she was sure. Rose never dreamed that their fervent discussion of slavery would have such far-reaching results. Now she had become, unknowingly, a link in a chain of events over which she had no control, involuntarily a "station" of the Underground Railway. It was her revelations about the secret passageway at Montclair that had brought this about. Now she recalled how intently Natalie had questioned her about the underground tunnel through the woods to the river — all for the purpose of investigating its possible use as an escape route for runaway slaves.

For days Rose walked on the knife's edge of fear. Suppose someone in the household found out? Suppose someone approached her openly? Suppose Malcolm were to discover her connection with this group? Or worse still, her father-in-law? Rose's nerves grew taut. Then, when weeks passed and she heard nothing further, she pushed her fearful thoughts to the back of her mind.

Rose was grateful when the news of Leighton's engagement to the Camerons' cousin, Dove Arundell, was announced. Plans for a gala party to be held at Montclair gave her something else to occupy her thoughts.

For all her fragility, Sara Montrose was adept at planning elegant parties. Her talent for entertaining had made Montclair famous, and she began at once, enlisting Rose and Garnet in carrying out her plans.

For once Garnet seemed all smiles and sweetness as she assisted in addressing invitations, suggesting a tableau to make guests aware of the engagement. She was so full of life and excitement that Rose felt for the first time a thawing of the coolness between them. They spent hours together in Mrs. Montrose's sitting room and Garnet was so amusing, making frivolous comments to make Sara laugh, that what might have been a tedious chore turned into a pleasant experience.

All three of them pored over the latest Godey's Ladies' Book, selecting patterns for gowns to wear for the party, and a seamstress from Williamsburg, who had made many of Sara's beautiful dresses, came out to fit, cut, and sew.

"It is said she could be employed by some of the most famous fashion houses in New York," Mrs. Montrose informed Rose. "But she seems content to stay here, live simply, and sew for the ladies of the county."

Henrietta Colby was a quiet, gray-haired lady. Widowed when very young and left with a small child to support, she had turned to needlework and fast became known for her skill.

The final fitting for Rose's gown went quickly, with Mrs. Colby making few comments from a mouthful of pins as she measured and pinned the hem.

Standing in front of the full-length mirror, Rose mused that Mrs. Colby was, indeed, a superb seamstress. She had created the most extravagant gown Rose had ever owned. Fashioned of rose velvet, its pleated, off-shoulder neckline was edged with lace. The skirt, which would be worn over a wide hoop, was of moiré shadowed silk, caught at draped intervals with small velvet roses.

After the fitting, when Rose got back to her own room and put her hand into the pocket of her pinafore, she discovered a piece of folded paper. Puzzled, she drew it out and opened it.

The words were printed in block letters and, as Rose read them, they seemed to rise up off the page and dance dizzily in front of her eyes.

EXPECT A PACKAGE OF THREE, DELIVERED TO THE SIDE ENTRANCE. HOLD SECURE UNTIL MIDNIGHT, THEN TAKE TO THE RIVER WHERE

IT WILL BE PICKED UP AND
TRANSPORTED NORTH.

But it was the date that brought Rose's
heart into her throat. The "package" was
due the night of Dove's engagement party!

Rose began to tremble uncontrollably.
Her knees felt so weak she had to sit down.
The night of the engagement party! How
could she ever manage to secrete three
people — for that was what the "package
of three" meant, she felt sure — and guide
them safely through the tunnel out to
Eden Cottage and then through the woods
to the river?

Of course, she had walked the path often
enough, both by daylight and in the evening with Malcolm, to know the way. But
how would it be possible to slip three
strangers — three Negro escapees with a
price on their heads — as well as hers if
they were caught! — past a houseful of
guests?

Rose's mind churned with confusion and
fear. How had she ever allowed herself to
be drawn into such a dangerous enter-
prise?

Evidently Natalie was deeply involved in
the Underground Railroad herself and had
been seeking new contacts, new "stations,"

new avenues of escape for slaves seeking liberation.

Rose put clammy hands to her throbbing temples. She had been so naïve! She had not imagined Natalie was pumping her for information as to the location of Montclair — right on the river! And then the priceless information about the underground tunnels leading to the spot where the "travelers" could be easily picked up by boat under cover of darkness.

Of course, by her very openness, she had been an obvious selection. It was her own fault. She had admitted her revulsion of slavery and her eagerness to help had been expressed voluntarily.

Rose closed her eyes. If she could only take back all those brave words, erase the image she had planted in Natalie's mind of a committed opponent of slavery, willing and ready to aid in any way.

Well, they had taken her up on it. Now she was involved. And she had no one but herself to blame.

As she sat there in a kind of trance, it began to dawn on her that Henrietta Colby was also a part of this chain. Mousy little Mrs. Colby? It must have been she who slipped the note into Rose's pocket while she was being fitted for the ball gown!

Well, there's no way out of it now, Rose thought hopelessly. The time, places, directions had by now been sent to all the links along the line of the Underground Railroad. She would have to go through with it, whatever the outcome.

"Luke 9:62," Rose whispered to herself. " 'No man, having put his hand to the plough, and looking back, is fit for the kingdom of God.' "

I must be brave. Rose clenched her teeth, never having felt more frightened in her life.

Rose knew one thing was imperative. Before the night on which the "package of three" was to be delivered, she must force herself to test the escape route.

Everything within her recoiled at the thought of entering that unknown underground passageway alone, with no idea of what might be lurking there after all the years of disuse. Her stomach lurched at her own imaginings. Still, she knew she had to do it. But what if part of the tunnel were blocked or had caved in? Then what would she do? There was no other way. She had to take the chance and, in case the plan was not feasible, somehow get word to her contact, Mrs. Colby.

She waited until one afternoon when the

house was practically empty. Mrs. Montrose was napping; Garnet was making social calls; the men were out. Sending Tilda away on the pretext that she had sewing to do in the nursery, Rose locked the door, then located the spring that activated the hidden lock of the wall panel. It slid back silently and Rose lit her candle and stepped inside.

She hesitated, not knowing whether to slide the door shut behind her. But the possibility of getting trapped inside made her shudder, so she risked leaving it open, reminding herself that the nursery door was locked. Heart pounding in her throat, she entered.

The stairway was very steep, spiraling downward between narrow walls, the steps uneven and the treads worn hollow in the middle.

It was dark and, even though she put her hands against the clammy earthen walls, she feared that she might fall.

The steps must have first been dug out of the earth, she thought, then the wood set into them, making them both irregular in height and in length, so that no even pace could be set. It was necessary to step carefully on each one as the stairway coiled deeper and deeper into the tunnel.

Rose counted the steps under her breath to remember how many there were. The light cast by the single wavering candle she held did not give much illumination to the tricky, turning stairway, though her eyes were gradually growing accustomed to the darkness, so she must rely on her quick mind and good memory. There would probably not be another chance to make a trial journey before she had to bring fugitives through it. The very thought filled her with a choking dread.

She heard a rapid, scuttling sound and a high, screeching noise that made her blood turn to ice, and her stomach cramp. *Rats!* She had disturbed them in their previously private domain, and she felt a cold sweat break out all over her body at the thought of them — perhaps waiting to dart out from some hole and bite her. She fought back a scream, clutched her skirts tightly about her, and hurried forward, slipping and sliding on the slimy earthen pathway. *O God!* she appealed, heart banging against her ribs as she ran, tears of fright and terror streaming down her cheeks.

As she tripped on her dampened skirt, her hands flailing wildly to catch herself before she plunged headlong onto the slick ground, she saw a strip of light in the distance. With a gasp of relief she steadied herself and proceeded. A slatted wooden trapdoor could be seen overhead and a few scooped-out indentations served as steps at the end of the tunnel.

Her arms shaky with nerves and fatigue, Rose reached up, searching for some kind of latch. She found a sliding bolt and tugged it, feeling the sharp pain of a splinter and a breaking fingernail in the process. With a final thrust she was able to move the wood covering, then give it a last hard push. It clattered back, and bright sunlight flooded the cavelike hollow where she stood. Almost sobbing now, Rose tucked her skirts about her waist, knotting the ends loosely, and heaved herself slowly, laboriously through the opening. For a few minutes she lay gasping for breath on the mossy grass of the woods into which the underground tunnel led.

Her entire body ached and throbbed with strain. She was chilled to the bone and numb with cold.

It would be difficult, but at least she knew now how to do it. She had done it once and she could do it again — God helping her.

chapter
16

The minute Rose opened her eyes on the morning of the party, she felt the beginnings of panic. As she sat up in bed, the first wave of nausea washed over her, a cold perspiration dampening her brow and the palms of her hands. Her only thought was that tonight was the night when she must somehow —

Tilda came into the room, bearing a tray with breakfast. But Rose could barely eat. She nibbled on a biscuit and managed to get down a few sips of strong coffee.

The black woman frowned, eyeing her sharply. "You sick, Miss Rose?"

Rose shook her head.

"You sure lookin' peaked," Tilda persisted, then, head cocked to one side, she fixed her mistress with a suspicious eye. "Is you pregger?"

"No, Tilda, I'm fine!" Rose snapped. "Now just leave me be."

Tilda, miffed, turned away and began straightening the room, casting anxious glances in Rose's direction. It was not like her mistress to be either cross or unwell.

After a bit, Rose spoke. "I'm sorry. Maybe I'm just a little tired from all the excitement about the party tonight."

The maid was all smiles again. "Yes'm, that's prob'ly so! Sho' goin' to be a fine party. Mighty pretty day for a party," she remarked as she went over to the windows and folded back the shutters.

From the bed, Rose looked out. The day was brilliant with sunshine, promising a perfect evening for the guests to be out on the veranda and garden during the early part of the evening.

After her maid left, Rose put her face in her hands. The enormity of what she had to do that evening was overwhelming. She slipped out of bed and onto her knees.

"Dear God, help me!" was the only prayer she could utter. Even as she knelt there wordless, help came in the form of a verse of Scripture that sprang to mind from the book of Philippians, fourth chapter, thirteenth verse: "I can do all things through Christ which strengtheneth me."

Rose repeated the words to herself

throughout the day, a day she wished desperately were over. Yet, at the same time, she was begging the hands of the clock to move more slowly to delay the hour of testing.

By late afternoon Rose's nerves were stretched to the breaking point. It was only sheer will power that enabled her to endure Tilda's chatter as she helped her dress for the party.

Rose was too preoccupied with what lay ahead of her this night to take any joy in her maid's extravagant praise as she hooked up the bodice.

"Umm humm, Miss Rose, you is goin' to be de bell of de ball tonight, fo' sho'!" Tilda declared with satisfaction.

Mrs. Colby's skill had produced a creation worthy of a Parisian salon. The finished dress was a dream, Rose had to admit, as Tilda dropped the skirt over her three-tiered hoop. The decolletage was flattering to Rose's shoulders, and the color perfect for her dark eyes and hair. If Rose looked pale and her eyes unusually bright, it would only be attributed to excited anticipation, not dread of the evening ahead, she sincerely hoped.

"Jes' wait till Marse Malcolm see yo', Miss Rose. He goin' to be some proud,"

Tilda observed, stepping back to survey her mistress.

Rose could only wish desperately that the entire evening were ending instead of only beginning.

The last thing before joining the others, Rose took from her jewel box the diamond snowflake pendant Malcolm had given her the first Christmas after they were married. Her hands trembled as she fastened the clasp. What would Malcolm think if he knew what she was about to do?

An involuntary shudder shook her slender frame. Then, lifting her head bravely, she murmured the Bible phrase she had used throughout the day for encouragement, and resolutely went to join Malcolm and Mr. Montrose in the front hall to receive the guests.

Sara had been carried downstairs and was seated in the parlor like a queen ready to hold court. Indeed, she looked very regal in her Colby creation of claret satin, lavishly trimmed in cording and lace. Rose noted with particular interest that she was wearing the legendary Montrose rubies.

By this time Leighton had left for Cameron Hall to escort Dove back to Montclair; the Camerons were to follow in their own carriage.

The guests, all friends from neighboring plantations, began arriving around five. Bevies of beautifully gowned ladies, escorted by their gentlemen, were met and greeted on the veranda by Mr. Montrose, then led in to pay their respects to Sara. Music was provided by a small orchestra brought from Richmond for the occasion. A sumptuous buffet supper was served on one side of the veranda, presented with all the elegance and artistry that over a hundred years of wealth and gracious living could bring. If Rose appeared distracted, it went unnoticed in the midst of the festivities.

Sometime after supper Joshua, the Montrose's head butler, approached Rose.

"Missus," he began in a low tone, "dar's someone outside say he got to see yo'." Joshua looked disapproving. He lowered his voice again. "Doan' look lak a gennelmun, missus, but he tole me he hab somethin' important to deliver to you pussenally."

Rose felt a clutching sensation in her chest. She tried to steady her own voice, not change her expression.

"Where is he?"

"He be waitin' out the side do', missus. I wuz sho' he weren't no invited gues',"

Joshua said disdainfully.

Her heart beat erratically, thumping so hard she could hardly breathe as she made her way through the party guests, smiling, nodding, stopping here and there to say a word to one acquaintance or another, to accept a compliment. All the time inwardly quivering so much that she wondered that it was not visible.

At the side door, she stepped outside, carefully closing the door behind her.

"I'm Rose Montrose," she said huskily to the man leaning against the house.

The man tipped his hat, straightened, but did not give his name in return. In a hushed voice, he said, "The merchandise is here. Behind those bushes at the end of the driveway. That's as far as I could drive my wagon. Shall I bring . . . it . . . up here?"

Though the man's voice was rough, it was not common. Who could he be? Who were these people who were willing to risk their lives like this? Were they people like herself, who had inadvertently become involved? No, she thought guiltily, there were probably many brave souls who believed in this cause so completely that life had come to mean nothing in itself.

"Wait. I'll have to see if the back stairway is clear," Rose whispered. Suddenly all that mattered was helping these poor slaves.

Although Rose had rehearsed this moment mentally for days, and even though she had made the trip through the tunnel twice, she was racked with fear. Anything could go wrong.

" 'I can do anything through Christ which strengtheneth me,' " she said over and over through numbed lips.

She went back into the house and walked cautiously along the hallway to the door leading to the back staircase used by the servants to bring hot water, meal trays, and laundry baskets to the upstairs rooms. Turning the knob, she opened it, looking over her shoulder as she did, and then peering up the darkened steps. From the front of the house floated the sounds of music, the murmur of conversation, the echoes of someone's hearty laughter. All the house servants were occupied, it seemed, serving the front parlors, dining room, and veranda. The time had come!

She ran outside again and was startled to see no trace of the man in the slouch hat — only three pitiful creatures huddled together in a crouching position next to the wall of the house.

"Come!" she said, beckoning, and the

three moved slowly toward her, two adults and a child.

"Hurry!" she hissed.

A small figure was thrust forward, and she saw it was a little boy of about four, his large eyes peeking out from the blanket he held around him. Rose grabbed him by the shoulders and, pushing him ahead of her, yanked open the door leading upstairs, then held it for the other two, a man and woman, both clasping tattered blankets.

They stood rooted to the spot. Rose realized they were afraid to go farther. Holding her wide skirts, she brushed by them and ran up the steps in front of them. Halfway up, she turned and saw them still standing at the bottom. Frantically she motioned them to follow her, but they seemed unable to move. She ran back down and picked up the child, feeling his skinny frame quivering like a frightened little animal. The thought struck her that he was not much older than Jonathan — nor much larger. To his parents she whispered an urgent plea, "You *must* hurry!" and they obeyed, scrambling up behind her.

At the top she held out her hand to halt them while she paused to look up and down the hall. It was empty. "Hurry!" she whispered again, then dashed across the hall and into Jonathan's nursery.

Without more than a glance at her sleeping baby, she moved over to the wall and pressed the panel. The secret door slid slowly open. Rose turned. The couple stood motionless; their fear, almost palpable. She set the black child down. As his blanket fell to the floor, she could see him in the dim light from Jonathan's flickering night lamp. He looked frightened to death, and Rose's heart lurched with sympathy. How far had he come on this perilous journey, sensing as a child must, his parents' fear? But there was no time to comfort him. She must secure them all, then return to the party before anyone missed her.

"You must wait here until I come at midnight to take you through the tunnel that leads down to the river. There you'll meet the boat that will take you on —" She paused, short of breath. "Do you understand?" The man nodded. "Have you food?"

The woman held up a calico bundle. "Yes'm."

"There's a lantern." Rose pointed to the one she had placed there the day before. "You know how to light it? Now be careful. You're safe here until I come.

There is a pallet on the floor where you can sleep. I must go now. I'll be back when it's time."

Rose waved them into the little room and they went in silently, their faces tragic masks of suffering.

"If you hear anything, it will probably be my baby's nurse coming up to check on him. Don't be frightened. I will tap three times on the wall before I open this door," she assured them.

"Thankee, ma'am," the man mumbled in a hoarse whisper.

Rose slid the door shut then leaned on it with a heavy sigh. That part was over. Now all she had to do was get through the rest of the evening until midnight, and then the real danger would have to be faced.

She had timed the trip through the tunnel out to Eden Cottage and on to the river to take about twenty minutes. Then, if the boat was there waiting, she would have to make her way back to the house — another twenty minutes. She prayed fervently that there would be no delay and that she could find her way without incident. Most of all, that no one would miss her in her long absence and come looking for her!

Rose took a few minutes to look at the

sleeping Jonathan, to touch his rosy, round cheek, caress the soft curls, smooth the silken blanket. *How precious he is to me,* she thought with infinite tenderness. *How terrible it would be to be forced to carry my child through the night, fraught with all kinds of dangers. My child lies here sleeping peacefully, safely, simply because he happened to be born white.* Rose shook her head, newly aware of the inequity of life.

She glided down the curved front stairway, her hand on the wide banister, her skirt rustling on the polished steps. She saw with surprise and a tiny start of apprehension that Malcolm was standing there, looking up as if he had been waiting for her.

As she reached the bottom, he held out his hands.

"I've been looking for you, darling. Now that I have dutifully asked all the ladies for one dance, I'd like to escort my favorite lady out to the veranda for a breath of fresh air." He smiled as he offered Rose his arm.

On another occasion Rose would have welcomed the beauty of the spring evening and the opportunity to be with her husband, unobserved. On this night an almost full moon was rising slowly above the trees, shedding a lovely, luminous glow. It would be far safer to travel under cover of darkness, she reasoned, terror striking her heart.

Tonight, moonlight meant danger!

chapter
17

At midnight, supper was to be served. Rose, chatting with Stewart Cameron, pretending an amused interest in the humorous experience he was recounting, was tensely aware of the time. Over the music she heard the grandfather clock begin to strike the hour of twelve.

Forcing a smile, she said with an air of gaiety, "Excuse me, Stewart, but I must run upstairs to check on baby Jonathan before supper. Forgive a doting new mama!"

Stewart bowed, smiling, and released her.

She started toward the stairway with no apparent haste. But as soon as she rounded the bend of the balcony on the second floor, she broke into a run. In the darkened nursery she lifted her skirts and unfastened the waistband that held the three tapered circles of her hoop, letting her crinoline petticoat drop to the floor. Quickly she stepped out of them and kicked them aside. She knew the widened skirt of her dress would have only hampered her progress through the narrow tunnel.

Unconsciously looking over her shoulder, she gave three light taps before running a trembling hand along the wall until she found the ridge where the hidden spring released the secret panel and opened the entrance to the slanted space.

The light from the lantern gave little illumination to the interior, and the first thing Rose could see was the whites of three pairs of eyes staring at her. As she stepped inside, the smell of lantern oil, the odor of bodies, damp wool, and the airless closeness of the hiding place assaulted her nostrils.

Rose fought back a threatening sensation of nausea.

"Ready?" she whispered to the three black people who were watching her fearfully. They nodded.

"Follow me very closely," she told them. "The steps down are very short and steep. It would be best to carry the child," she directed the woman. "I'll hold the lantern high so you won't miss your footing."

Steeling herself against the sickening

memories of her other trips through the dank passageway, calling upon all the inner courage she could muster and repeating over and over her constant prayer, "I can do all things through Christ which strengtheneth me," Rose began the tortuous descent.

She could hear the rasping breathing behind her, could almost hear the frantic beating of those hearts so near to gaining their freedom.

O dear Lord, let everything go right! Rose prayed. *Let the boat be there! Let them get away . . . safely, safely.*

Her foot slipped on one of the slimy steps and she stumbled, but caught herself with one arm and without dropping the lantern. It swung wildly, casting weird shapes and shadows, and she heard the others' quick intake of breath behind her.

It seemed to take longer than she remembered, and she felt cold perspiration roll down her back, even in the murky dampness of the cavern.

On and on they went. Then, through the thin soles of her satin dancing slippers, Rose felt the change from packed earth to stone, and knew they were nearing the storage room where the trapdoor in the ceiling opened up to the latticed breezeway of Eden Cottage. She breathed a long, shaky sigh. When they climbed out here, there was only a distance of about twenty yards to the river. Beyond the clearing of the small walled garden of Eden Cottage, Rose could see the water shimmering in the moonlight, but there was plenty of foliage where they could hide until they saw the flat boat that was supposed to meet them there.

Rose stepped aside, and, motioning to the man, had him slide back the wooden bolt that held the trapdoor shut. When he pushed it, a welcome, fresh woodsy scent rushed into her starving lungs and Rose turned and picked up the little boy and handed him up to his father. Then she drew the woman forward and pointed out the rungs of the wooden ladder to her. After she was up, Rose gathered her gown about her and carefully followed.

"From here, you will be safe. I'll wait until we see the boat, then I must go back to the house before I'm missed," she told them.

Even as she spoke there came the unmistakable plop and swish of an oar being lifted, the slap of water against the side of a boat. As they stood there waiting in the darkness, a long, flat skiff slid into view, with a figure hunched over the helm.

"That's it!" Rose exclaimed. "There's your boat. Go!"

The two made an abortive movement, then the woman fell on her knees, sobbing. She took up the hem of Rose's skirt and kissed it, saying in a low moan, "Thankee, ma'am! Thankee kindly!"

"Go on! Hurry!" Rose whispered, a surge of emotion taxing her already over-wrought nervous system. She pulled the woman up and gave her a gentle shove in the direction in which the man, with the child in his arms, had already started.

Rose watched their shadowy figures, then waited until the boat began to move. It glided slowly away, only the slightest sound of lapping water disturbed the stillness of the night.

When it disappeared, Rose dared not think what time it was, or how long she had been away from the house, or if she had been missed.

Only one thing she knew with certainty. She could not bring herself to go back through that dark tunnel again. She would have to make her way through the woods on the familiar path to Montclair. It would take longer, but she could not face the horrors of the tunnel twice in one night.

The moon must have slipped behind a cloud because, as she started back, the woods were full of shadows.

The wind felt chill, sending a shiver through her very bones, tightening the skin on her scalp. Its sighing in the trees above her whispered a message of eerie foreboding. Now, as she made her way along the path, there was an unearthly silence. Once, breath short and heart pounding, she thought she heard footsteps behind her. She halted, afraid to draw a breath.

Could someone have possibly come looking for her? Followed her to Eden Cottage and seen the escape?

She steadied herself and moved on.

Then as she neared the house, seeing the lights from all the windows along the veranda shining out onto the terrace, Rose started to run.

She went around the side of the house, up the steps and in through the side door, along the servant's hall and up the back stairway. Reaching the second floor undetected, she hurried along the hallway and dashed into the nursery.

Picking up her hoop where she had dropped it, Rose bunched up her skirt, stepped into it, and pulled it up. With hands that shook, she fastened it on her crinoline, then draped her skirt over it.

Rose knew she had to do something about her hair before she went back downstairs. Her side combs had fallen out, and her curls now tumbled about her bare shoulders in wild disarray. She picked up Jonathan's soft baby hairbrush and tried to smooth out some of the tangles.

Her frustration mounted, for she knew she had to get back to the party, or there would be no end of explaining to do.

She was leaning over to examine the wet hem of her gown and to brush off some of the mud and twigs that had clung to it, when she suddenly became aware of another presence in the room.

Slowly she raised her head and saw to her utter dismay, Lizzie, Mrs. Montrose's personal maid, standing in the doorway.

Rose's blood chilled.

Lizzie had always treated Rose with a kind of aloofness that bordered on disdain. Hidden beneath an exaggerated politeness, it could not be called to account nor corrected. Rose thought Lizzie always seemed fiercely jealous of anyone Sara seemed fond of, even members of the Montrose family. Malcolm, too, had noticed this trait and dismissed it as a kind of protective loyalty to his mother.

But now as Rose withered under her penetrating gaze, she thought she saw something new in Lizzie's eyes — suspicion, vindictiveness. Did she *know?* Rose wondered, with trepidation.

"Is anything wrong, ma'am?" Lizzie asked her with a cold wariness.

Trying not to sound flustered, Rose replied coolly, "No, nothing's wrong, Lizzie. Everything's fine. I was just looking in on Jonathan."

"You sure, ma'am? I came upstairs to get my mistress her shawl, and I thought I heard something. Should I find Linny and send her up to stay with the baby?"

"No, no, that won't be necessary. He's sound asleep now," Rose replied evenly, knowing full well Lizzie was suspicious.

Head spinning, nerves jumping, Rose waited until Lizzie went away before opening the door and flying down the short flight of steps to hers and Malcolm's bedroom below the nursery.

She had to change her slippers, at least; their thin soles and satin uppers were soaked and ruined. Her combs were gone, so she replaced them with her everyday ones. Peering into the mirror, she saw that she looked pale, agitated. Leaning closer to the glass, she pinched both cheeks, bringing color to them. With a final, frantic glance and a prayer that neither her long absence nor anything about her appearance would betray her, Rose took a long, shaky breath and returned to the party.

Rose never knew how she endured the rest of the evening until she was standing on the veranda with Malcolm, seeing the last carriage full of guests disappearing around the bend of the drive.

There were faint pink streaks in the pale dawn sky when, at last, Rose was in her own bedroom in front of her dressing table. With hands that fumbled, she began unfastening the tiny hooks of her bodice.

"Need some help?" Malcolm asked softly, coming up behind her. "I've not had much experience as a lady's maid, but I'm willing to learn." He laughed teasingly, lifted her lustrous curls, and kissed her bare shoulder.

In spite of her weariness Rose felt herself responding to the feel of his warm lips on her skin. She sighed, leaning back against him as his arms wound around her slender waist.

"You were the most beautiful lady at the party tonight," he told her, his lips moving along the side of her cheek, touching the tip of her ear.

She shivered delightedly, put her hands over his, tightening his embrace.

"Then we were a splendid couple, for you were by far the handsomest man." She sighed happily, looking at their reflection.

As she did, she experienced a jolting shock. Her diamond pendant was gone! Involuntarily she started to put her hand to her throat, then stopped herself, not wanting to call Malcolm's attention to the fact it was missing. A horrifying certainty struck her. Somewhere along the underground passageway or out in the woods, she had lost the beautiful jeweled snowflake Malcolm had given her for Christmas!

Again Rose summoned the acting skills she had practiced all evening. Her expression did not change; the dreadful panic she felt did not register on her face; only inside, where tension knotted itself, was her terrible discovery evident. She could not tell Malcolm of the loss nor go look for it tonight. The thought that she might have to take that awful journey through the underground tunnel once more filled her with horror. But if she had to, she would. First thing tomorrow though, she would comb the woods along the path from Eden Cottage and the area beyond it to the river where she had watched the slaves escape.

"Come along to bed, Rose," Malcolm whispered, spinning her around gently and drawing her close. With one hand he tilted her chin and kissed her. "I was very proud of you tonight. You were so poised, so gracious. Everyone spoke admiringly of you. You have such an air of grace, an indefinable quality that is so rare. . . . Did I tell you how much I love you today?"

"I don't think so. There really hasn't been much time for the two of us —"

"Then I'll just have to show you."

In the warm intimacy of the deep, downy bed, Rose nested her head on Malcolm's shoulder. By the evenness of his breathing, she knew when he had dropped off to sleep. Rose was always amazed that even after nearly two years of marriage, the act of love was still thrilling.

If only she did not have to keep secret from Malcolm her terrifying errand tonight. It destroyed the perfect unity she longed to have with him. But she knew he would have been appalled at her involvement in such an undertaking. No, she and Malcolm would never be in agreement on the subject of slavery.

She shifted her body slightly, winding her arms over Malcolm's chest and fitting herself more deeply into the curve of his long, lean frame. She sighed.

Well, the ordeal was over, and she had managed to get through it. Tomorrow she would search the woods for her pendant. It must be there. Or in the tunnel. She would go there, too, if necessary. Malcolm must not know it was ever missing. She hoped this would be her last secret from him. Nothing must come between her and Malcolm. Nothing to jeopardize this precious oneness —

But in the morning Rose awoke with a splitting headache. Feverish, she alternated between shivers and washes of perspiration. When she attempted to sit up, she was gripped with nausea.

With a groan she fell back upon the pillows, calling weakly for Tilda.

She felt so ill she could neither raise her head nor take but a few sips of water. Tilda nursed her skillfully while Malcolm hovered nearby.

"Jes' wore out!" clucked Tilda, shaking her head. "Jes' too much of everythin'. Too much fussin', too much preparin', too much partyin'. Miss Rose need her res',

Marse Malcolm. Jes' let her be. Tilda will take keer of her."

So Malcolm tiptoed out of the room, leaving Rose to Tilda's ministrations.

For the rest of the day Rose lay in the darkened room, feeling sick and helpless. She knew her illness was the result of all the nervous strain she had been under, but she could not share that with anyone. Let them think what they liked, she felt too numb to care. What bothered her most was the lost pendant. If only she could get up and search for it.

Late that afternoon she heard her bedroom door quietly open, but was too weary to turn her head to see who it was. Then she heard someone standing beside her bed. "Miss Rose?"

It was not Tilda's familiar voice and, when Rose lifted her heavy eyelids to look, to her surprise she saw it was Lizzie.

Rose felt far too ill to wonder why Lizzie was here holding a cup in her hand. The night before seemed like a nightmare now and she vaguely recalled that Lizzie had something to do with it.

"I've brought you some camomile tea, Miss Rose. I always make it for Miss Sara when she's po'ly."

"Thank you, Lizzie. I'm not sure I can

swallow it, but —" she paused, gesturing weakly to the bedside table — "put it down and I'll try."

"Would you want me to help you sit up?" Lizzie asked.

"Not just now, but thank you, Lizzie." Rose closed her eyes wearily. Perhaps Mrs. Montrose had sent the woman to inquire how she was feeling. But Lizzie did not leave after she set down the cup. Rose opened her eyes and saw her hesitating. "Is there something else, Lizzie?"

Lizzie drew herself up and Rose thought again what a handsome woman she was. She held her tall, erect figure proudly, almost haughtily. Her coffee-colored skin was smooth; her features even, in her high-cheekboned face. As she hesitated, Lizzie put one hand in the pocket of her apron, drew something out, then stretched out her hand to Rose. Something glittered brightly in her palm.

"Did you lose this, Miss Rose?"

"My snowflake pendant!" Rose gasped. "Why, Lizzie, where —" Rose started, then stopped mid-sentence and gazed wide-eyed at Lizzie.

Lizzie took a step closer, leaning over Rose. She spoke very low, but distinctly.

"I know about last night, Miss Rose. I

was comin' out of Miss Sara's room when I seen you bring them folks up. I knew there was a passageway in this house somewheres, 'cause I heard the old folks talk about it. But none of us people knew where it was or how to get to it. 'Course we knew about how folks get led up No'th to freedom. We jes' never guessed it was from Montclair."

Lizzie paused for a long time, then she bent close to Rose and looked at her unblinkingly. "Miss Rose, *I* wants to go nex' time."

Rose stared back at her. Sara's devoted maid! Lizzie was the last person Rose would have ever suspected of being unhappy. Tilda was always complaining about Lizzie's privileges, telling Rose that many of the other house servants grumbled about her special position in the household.

Trying to disguise her amazement at this revelation, Rose murmured, "Well, Lizzie, I don't know if there will be a next time. I don't know if they'll ever contact me again."

"But if they do, Miss Rose," Lizzie persisted, "I's got to go."

"You would leave Miss Sara?" Rose asked, bewildered.

"There's lots of slaves Miss Sara could have as her maid." Rose noticed the slight contempt in Lizzie's voice, the emphasis on the word *slave*. Lizzie held her head up and said distinctly, "My man Sergus, what ole Marse sold some months ago, is up No'th now. I wants to be with him."

So that was it. That explained everything. Lizzie was the woman who mourned Sergus's departure; she was the one Tilda had said would make someone pay for it.

"You will let me know the nex' time, Miss Rose?"

It was more a statement than a question, and in it Rose sensed a kind of threat. Would Lizzie betray the movement if Rose did not enter into a conspiracy to help her escape? Rose could not be sure. Lizzie was unpredictable, just as her handling of this volatile situation had been. Rose had hoped she would never again be called upon to make that dreadful journey through the tunnel.

"Shall I put your necklace away, Miss Rose?"

"Where did you find it, Lizzie?"

"It was on the floor of the nursery right beside the secret door, ma'am. It must have come loose and fallen off there."

"Thank you, Lizzie." Rose closed her eyes.

Suddenly everything was too much. The entire nightmare she had experienced, the complete physical exhaustion, emotional depletion — and now Lizzie's outrageous request.

As for the black woman — an accomplished seamstress, a skilled nurse, a matchless ladies' maid — she would have no trouble finding employment in the North, would, in fact, be in demand and discover the new experience of being well paid for her work.

It was only fair, Rose told herself, only simply justice. And yet she felt an inner shrinking at Sara's reaction, the storm that would follow Lizzie's departure, and shuddered.

What would Malcolm's mother do if she knew she harbored a traitor under her own roof, and that the traitor was her own son's wife?

PART V

Beloved Enemy

Mayfield and Richmond
1860–1862

chapter
18

The tension fermenting throughout the South was felt strongly among the planters in Virginia. Talk of following South Carolina's lead was heard at almost every dinner hour at Montclair, and with strong feelings being expressed all around her and having learned her own lesson in discretion, Rose again took to her diary. Because of the nature of her subject, however, she kept it hidden. She had inadvertently discovered a secret drawer in the bottom of a small applewood chest in her bedroom. She would take the book out whenever she was alone and jot down the rapidly changing events and her own private thoughts.

August 1860

Lizzie is gone. Determined to leave once I showed her the secret passage, she made her way alone through it and out to the river where she joined others whom Mrs. Colby had secreted in her house until the connection North was assured. I still tremble to think what would happen if anyone at Montclair knew of my part in this "underground movement."

November 1860

Abraham Lincoln, against all odds, has been elected the sixteenth president of the United States. In Virginia he is an unpopular choice. Reaction is strong against him, talk of secession runs high.

Christmas 1860

In spite of everything, a happy day. Jonathan — our beautiful son — so healthy, happy, and handsome, wildly pleased with his rocking horse. Adults subdued under surface holiday gaiety.

January 1861

I write this date with a grim foreboding, remembering other beginning years of such happiness and hope, not knowing nor daring to think what this year will bring to our country, both North and South.

March 1861

The talk now is of two separate nations, North and South . . . yet here in the Virginia spring, all is lovely and peaceful. Out my window I see acres of jonquils, their bell-like fluted heads nodding in a gentle breeze; a quiet, golden hush lies over everything.

Yet, amid all this beauty, like brushfire ravaging everything in its path, are rumors of war and secession. The furor over slavery continues unabated.

Rose did not write in her diary again after March. Her thoughts seemed too dark, too dismal to record for posterity.

The question on everyone's mind was whether Virginia would go the way of South Carolina and secede. Rose had to know how Malcolm felt and, although they had avoided all discussion of this subject for months, she finally broke their un-spoken truce and asked him.

His reply chilled her. "It is not always what a man wants to do, but what is his duty," he said in a manner that closed the subject.

Would he consider it his duty to go with his state?

"If it were a matter of protecting her from Northern invasion."

Rose responded immediately and indig-nantly. "The North would never invade! We are all one country!"

Malcolm shook his head. "Not for long, Rose, I'm afraid."

"But surely there are reasonable men who don't want a war!" Rose exclaimed, a secret terror clutching her heart.

"Yes, but they are being vilified and called traitors by the hotheads on both sides."

Rose's passion for the truth paralyzed her with fear.

That night, when Malcolm had blown out their lamp and they lay together under the canopy of their bed, Rose wound her arms around his neck, her head nestled into his shoulder. She clung to him, not daring to say all that was in her heart to say. And he held her, not speaking, gently brushing her hair away from her smooth brow. Gradually she felt his arms relax, heard the even sound of his breathing. She knew he slept. But she could not.

Her mind was turbulent with uneasy thoughts of the conversations she had overheard. If war came, where would Malcolm stand? Her heart raced, a pall of anxiety suffocating her. She stirred restlessly. Malcolm's arms tightened and he murmured her name in his sleep, his lips brushing her temple. *Dear God, don't let anything happen to separate us,* Rose prayed, not sure her prayer would be heeded. Not because God could not or would not answer it, but because man's free will, that dangerous gift, might prevent it.

Not long after Rose breathed that desperate prayer, the day arrived that she had dreaded, yet knew was inevitable. Sick at heart, she made this entry.

April 1861

News from Charleston brings the dire report of the surrender of Fort Sumter. There is no way out. War is inevitable.

Malcolm says Virginia must now decide. She stands on the dividing line between North and South and must choose which way she will go.

Within days after the fall of Fort Sumter, Virginia threw in her lot with the newly formed Confederacy of Southern States.

The news was greeted with enthusiastic support. Rose was unable to bear the elation, the toasts offered, the hum of activity as men came and went on various errands to Montclair.

As for Montclair, it became the center of discussion, debate, and grandiose plans. Talk went on endlessly at every meal as men from the surrounding plantations gathered there each day. Rose was horrified at the relentless vindictiveness of their words, and even when she and Malcolm were in their private wing an uneasy silence hung between them.

At last the fateful day came.

Rose was in her room trying to distract herself with needlepoint when Malcolm came in, closing the door firmly behind. "Rose, there is something I have to tell you, and you must try to accept. I've decided to sign up. I can do no less than the others. Our state is in grave danger of being invaded, our honor violated. I *must* stand with my fellow Virginians to defend our homes."

The fear that rose up in her was translated into fury. Fury at the senselessness of Malcolm's going to fight for a cause she knew he hated. Whatever the fine and noble rhetoric being tossed around about homeland, a defenseless Southland threatened with violent aggression from the North, Rose deeply felt they were denying the truth. She rose, dropping her frame and yarn, fists clenched.

"Oh, Malcolm, that doesn't sound a bit like you," Rose lashed out at him. "The *real* issue is slavery, isn't it? The economics of the South depends on these thousands of miserable human beings called slaves! A way of life is at stake . . . nothing honorable or noble —"

"Now you are quoting the rhetoric of your Abolitionist friends," Malcolm objected mildly.

But Rose was not to be put off. She had to remind Malcolm how much he had changed.

"I am recalling some of the things you and I discussed not so long ago!" she retorted. "How can you fight for something you believe is wrong as much as I do?" she demanded. "And no matter what anyone says, the real issue *is* slavery."

Malcolm turned away as if to leave, to end what his attitude conveyed was a pointless argument.

"I thought I married a Christian," Rose said scathingly, halting him. "You give your slaves biblical names and yet won't allow them to read the Bible to find out about the men they've been named for. What are you afraid of? That they might learn that men's souls are free, that before their Creator all men are equal?"

"Rose, you're wrong. You don't understand —" Malcolm began wearily, as if he dreaded retracing the same path they had been over a dozen times before.

"Then you *want* to go, don't you?"

Malcolm turned on her furiously. "I didn't say I *wanted* to go! I said I *had* to go!"

"Against your beliefs? Against everything you hold sacred? Against your country? Against my wishes? Against *me? Why?* I don't understand."

"Because I'm a Southerner . . . because I'm a Virginian!"

"Because your brothers have shamed you into it!" Rose heard her own voice and barely recognized it. It was harsh, laced with sarcasm. "Why don't you admit the

250

real reason? You're not man enough to stand up to them. All the bugles blowing, the flags flying, all those wild boys jumping fences, giving the Rebel yell, playing at soldiers . . . playing at war! It's gone to your head. Oh, Malcolm, listen to me . . . listen to your heart!"

"You don't understand, Rose. You'll never understand. It's in my blood . . . I'm a Montrose . . . before anything else. This is *my* land. They're going to invade us! I have to defend that!"

Rose felt the panic rising, the certainty that all her arguments were in vain. She felt helpless and fearful and yet at the same time, something stubborn, something tenacious demanded she make one last attempt to change what was being forced on her. She knew Malcolm, knew his gentleness, his inability to see anything but good in people or circumstances.

A kind of swift compassion for his weakness softened her voice. Malcolm, Rose knew, had convinced himself that it was right, noble, and honorable that he should go, that the cause was just.

For a moment her spirit rallied. Perhaps, just perhaps, she could still reach him by appealing to the old values to which they had both once had allegiance.

"Oh, Malcolm, I beg you, as I've asked you before, let's take Jonathan and go away, live somewhere in peace and happiness. You don't share your father's or your brothers' beliefs. I *know* you don't. *Please,* while there's still a chance for us."

He sighed. An expression of sorrow and resignation passed over his face.

"I'm sorry, Rose. Not even for you. I must do what I feel is right. I could not look my son in the eyes if I did not go to the defense of our land — Virginia. That's what it is about, Rose. The land that will one day be Jonathan's. I cannot do less."

She looked at him in disbelief. He could not mean what he was saying. Not after all they had discussed.

His eyes pleaded for her understanding.

Rose met that glance. "You are my husband, and I love you but — I don't believe you. I don't believe in your cause."

She broke into wild sobbing. What Malcolm did not know was that just that morning she had received a letter from Aunt Vanessa, telling her John had applied for a commission in the Union Army. If Malcolm joined the Confederates, her brother and husband would be fighting against each other.

Malcolm went over to comfort her, knelt

beside her. He tried to pull her hands away from her face, but she turned away.

"No, don't touch me! Leave me alone!"

Malcolm got up silently. At the door he paused, his hand on the knob, and spoke softly. "Rose, don't do this to us."

"You're the one who is doing something to us!" she flung back at him.

Malcolm shrugged. There was something hopelessly final about the gesture. Then he went out and shut the door. After he closed it, Rose threw herself on the bed, crying hysterically.

That night and the next, Malcolm slept on the couch in his dressing room. Rose lay sleepless in the big four-poster bed in the next room.

Two days later Leighton announced that he and Dove wanted to be married at once in case his company was called up immediately. They had planned a June wedding, but since Dove's gown was ready and she was already ensconced at Cameron Hall, there was no reason for further delay. For Sara's sake the ceremony would be held at Montclair.

Everyone who attended the wedding declared Dove to be a beautiful bride. Her petite frame was perfectly complemented by the flatteringly cut gown of creamy satin, its square neckline bordered with heirloom lace in a deep bertha. Her dark hair was covered with a veil of rose pointe lace seeded with tiny pearls. Lee, looking inordinately proud and happy, handsome in his new Confederate uniform, stood beside her to greet the guests after the ceremony.

Rose, who had watched the couple take their vows, her eyes bright with unshed tears, had silently repeated her own, glancing up hopefully to catch Malcolm's glance. Memory of that day nearly four years ago when they had stood together joining hands, hearts and lives before God, seemed a long time ago.

"Until death do us part" had a terrible new meaning in these uncertain times, Rose thought, and longed to experience once again that precious closeness she had once known with Malcolm.

She reached for his hand, but he had moved away to answer a whispered question from one of the ladies. Rose drew back her hand, feeling an aching hollowness.

A moment later the small band struck up the recessional, then spontaneously broke into "Dixie," and immediately the whole assembly took up the song, ending in wild applause and a few "hurrahs." Rose found herself standing quite alone, experiencing a sense of loneliness and isolation.

She alone did not share the others' happiness. Although she kept a brave smile on her face as she went about her duties, her spirit was crushed within her. Her heart felt bruised from the terrible scene with Malcolm. A scene she deeply regretted. Something had ended with the hurtful words they had exchanged.

chapter

19

The call to arms echoed through the Southland, its reverberations felt in every individual heart.

Fort Sumter was the spur that activated
all the dormant independence of the other
states, some impulsively, some reluctantly,
yet all were stirred by the insistent, oft-re-
peated cry of state sovereignty and resistance to compulsion.

The Cassandra-like voices that had been
raised, both North and South, urgently
warning the consequences of secession,
were lost in the furious, self-righteous
clamor.

War fever raged and, once afire, nothing
could halt the spread of the conflagration.
For Rose, the war had already left her be-
reaved. A pall had fallen on the bright and
shining joy that had been their love.

In her heartbreak Rose got out her diary

and wrote: "I cannot believe that what began with such hope of happiness has come to this. If I could only open up my heart to Malcolm as I used to — but this is no longer possible. He has stepped behind an impenetrable wall, and I cannot reach him."

Her words were smudged by the tears that fell upon the page as she wrote.

The night before Malcolm was to leave for Richmond to join the company Leighton was heading up, Rose lay sleepless, alone in their big bed. Malcolm had lingered after dinner, talking with his father, Bryce, and some other guests.

Would he come to her tonight? They had not slept together since the day of their awful quarrel. *If only I could take back some of the things I said,* Rose wept bitterly. Or if Malcolm could have seen his way clear to do what she had begged him to do. To take her and Jonathan away — perhaps to Europe, where they had been so happy! Why did he have to fight a war he did not believe the South could win, a war he had no heart for?

Rose remembered hearing a visitor say to the group of men gathered around the table at Montclair one day, a month or so before Sumter fell: "It is foolish to doubt the courage of the Yankees or their will to fight. All this Southern hotheaded rush into the fray, I fear, will soon be put to the hard test. I think it will be a long, bitter conflict . . . not easily won by either side."

Rose agreed, knowing the Yankee spirit of pride and patriotism. She had no doubt of the courage and resolve in her own heritage.

And John would go. John, her adored older brother. *Oh,* Rose moaned into her pillow, *it is madness. Sheer madness.* She lay awake in the dark and heard the slow, resonant strokes of the clock in the downstairs hall strike four.

And still Malcolm did not come. She had wounded his pride, insulted his integrity, doubted his purpose, accused him of perfidy. He would never forgive her! Never!

In the morning, heavy-eyed from crying and lack of sleep, she awoke early and found the bed beside her still empty. His last night and he had not come to her! How cold and cruel Malcolm had become, Rose thought, with a hard shell forming about her easily bruised heart. *So that is the way he will have it,* she decided with a kind of weary pride.

After a silent Tilda served her breakfast

and helped her dress, Rose went up the small flight of stairs that led from the bedroom to the nursery for her time with Jonathan.

When Linny took the child down to the kitchen for his breakfast, Rose descended to her bedroom just as the door of the dressing room opened. Malcolm, attired in a gray uniform trimmed in gold braid and sashed with a yellow fringed scarf, stood there. Rose's heart froze.

"I've come to say good-bye, Rose," he said quietly.

She could not answer. He came over to where she stood and leaned down to kiss her, but she turned her head so that his lips only brushed her cheek.

She whirled around, her back to him. She heard Malcolm's sigh, then, "I'll go say good-bye to my son."

Rose was aware of his footsteps as he crossed the room, and that he was standing at the door hopefully, waiting for her to say something. When she neither turned nor spoke, the door opened and closed softly.

She wrapped her arms tightly around herself as if to contain her grief. In her ears lingered the words she heard him say before he left, not sure whether she had only imagined them. "Good-bye, sweet Rose."

Less than an hour later, Rose, standing at the window of the bedroom, saw Josh bring Malcolm's horse to the front of the house.

As she saw him mount into the saddle, Rose was gripped with panic. Her anguish tore the word "Wait!" from her throat. She could not let him go without begging his forgiveness. The urgent need to be in his arms once more overcame all else. Before he left, she had to wipe away the memory of all the terrible words that had passed between them.

She tried to open the window, but the latch was stuck. As she struggled to loose it, she saw to her surprise a figure coming from behind the high privet hedge at the end of the driveway down which Malcolm walked his horse.

Rose's hands dropped from the window's lock and hung limply at her sides as she watched, an unwilling spectator to the scene that next unfolded —

Not wishing to tell Malcolm good-bye in front of the others, Garnet had gone into the garden where she could watch from behind the high privet hedge until she saw his man bringing the horses around to the front of the veranda.

Her heart thudded heavily when Malcolm finally appeared, looking dignified and splendid in his new Confederate uniform. He seemed to hesitate as if considering reentering the house. Then he smoothed his dark hair in a characteristic gesture, donned his wide-brimmed hat, and walked slowly down the steps. Josh held Crusader's head while Malcolm mounted, then started.

As he neared the place where Garnet was secreted behind the hedge, she dashed out. "Malcolm! Malcolm!" she called.

He turned his head and, seeing her, smiled and reined in Crusader. Josh, on the other horse, halted at a respectful distance.

"Garnet! I missed saying good-bye to you. Wondered where you were. I thought maybe you'd gone over to Cameron Hall."

"No!" She reached up to stroke Crusader's neck. "I just didn't want to tell you good-bye in front of everybody."

She looked up at him, memorizing every feature of that well-loved face, all at once aware it might be a long time before she saw him again. All the old aching anxiety she used to feel each fall when he left for Harvard returned. "The worst thing is I don't have anything . . . I mean, I didn't

know what to give you as a farewell gift —"
she broke off, feeling the sting of tears in
her eyes. She blinked and turned away so
Malcolm wouldn't see them.

He leaned down and touched her damp
cheek. "Look, Garnet," he said gently, and
unfastened the two top buttons of his
tunic, opening it to show her the jade
stickpin she had given him for Christmas
four years before. "My good-luck talisman."

Overcome, Garnet tried to speak, but
her throat was too tight. A blazing joy
rushed through her at the thought that
Malcolm would be keeping that small
"part of herself" with him, perhaps carrying it into battle. But her joy was short-
lived, for his next words reminded her
poignantly of the reality of their situation.

"I must go, Garnet. Comfort Rose if you
can. And be kind to her and little Jonathan."

Nearly blinded by tears and speechless
with the wounding impact of his words,
all Garnet could do was nod. Malcolm
clicked to his horse, and Crusader moved
forward.

At the gate she saw him turn in his
saddle, look back and lift his hat in a sa-

lute. Then he cantered through the gates and was gone.

For some reason at just that moment, Garnet glanced up at the house and thought she saw a figure standing at the window of the downstairs master bedroom in the wing Malcolm shared with Rose. With a little pang of guilt, Garnet wondered if Rose had seen her talking with Malcolm and if she minded that Garnet's had been the last farewell.

Garnet shrugged and walked back into the garden. What difference did it make one way or the other? Malcolm belonged to Rose in a way he could never belong to her. All she had of Malcolm were memories of bygone days.

Suddenly she remembered Malcolm's parting words: "Comfort Rose if you can, and be kind to her and little Jonathan."

Garnet gave her head a careless toss as if casting off such tiresome requests. Rose and Jonathan were not *her* responsibility! And she had no intention of taking them on, in spite of what Malcolm had asked. Besides, there were plenty of servants to care for Jonathan, and Rose seemed content enough with her endless Bible reading and piano playing and walks in the woods. *It is not any concern of mine,*

Garnet assured herself.

"I have enough to do just taking care of myself!"

How strange, thought Rose, observing the encounter with Garnet and Malcolm on the afternoon he left to join his regiment. *What terrible irony that Garnet should give Malcolm his last good-bye, instead of me.*

Garnet had gloried in the excitement of the last month, as if going off to fight a war were something romantic and heroic. She did not seem to mind when Bryce joined up one day after Virginia declared itself for the Confederacy. In fact, she had accompanied him to Richmond and become caught up in the carnival atmosphere of that city. She had even stayed to help her Cousin Nellie entertain the new soldiers at her gracious home on Franklin Street while Bryce was in training.

But then Garnet was a Southerner, too, and a slave owner as well. Her whole life of leisure and luxury had been fashioned by the institution; she knew no other way of life, would not have understood nor cared about Rose's convictions. Both her brothers were heading up companies of volunteers. *It is to all of them a grand and heroic undertaking,* Rose thought with a sense of helplessness.

What made Malcolm's going so horrible was that Rose was sure he had no such illusions about war.

After a last parting word to Garnet — what had he said to her? — Malcolm kissed his hand to her, Rose recalled with a sinking heart, and she backed away as he guided his horse forward and began cantering down the drive.

Seeing them together, a sword-sharp pain had plunged into Rose's heart. Then for some reason, almost as if he somehow sensed her watching from the window, he had turned in his saddle, touched his hat brim with one gauntleted hand in a farewell wave, then whirled and galloped around the bend, out of sight.

Turning back into the empty room, Rose pressed both hands to her mouth as a convulsive sob escaped. Malcolm was gone!

How could she stay here? How could she go on?

And what of Malcolm? Out there waited the "enemy." He had never known an enemy, nor fought a battle, nor been close to death. Now surely two of them lay ahead of him, and perhaps the other. Once he passed through those gates, his life, everything, would change forever.

chapter
20

Back in Richmond, Garnet was again caught
up in the social whirl at Cousin Nellie's.
There was open house everyday, and her relative's house soon became a mecca for the
popular young people now in the city. The
house rang with the sound of young voices
and laughter and running feet up and down
the polished circular staircase.

Garnet circulated freely, making the
rounds of parties, balls, theater, and late
suppers. She had never been happier.
Sometimes, in rare moments of reflection,
she would suddenly think how odd that all
this was going on while, just a few miles
away, men were preparing for war. But
these were only fleeting thoughts, for the
war was still unreal and Garnet lived for
the moment.

Leave was easy to obtain that summer,
and Bryce was often at the house on

Franklin Street, enjoying seeing Garnet surrounded by admiring fellow officers, realizing that they envied him his vivacious wife. But though he often mentioned the possibility of a quick visit home to Montclair, Garnet always found a reason to put it off.

As it turned out, they did not find time to go home that summer, and then quite suddenly Bryce did not come nor was he heard from for days. Even Garnet sensed a creeping anxiety as rumors of a tremendous battle to be waged at Manassas spread throughout Richmond. She knew Bryce's regiment, attached to General Beauregard, was there.

During the battle special prayer services were held in all the Richmond churches. Because everyone else was going, and because it was expected of the wife of an officer, Garnet went, too. But she was most uncomfortable, feeling herself strangely detached from the kneeling, prayerful women around her.

The deep, melodious voice of the minister called the people to pray with David from the Psalms. There was a rustle all about her as desperate wives and children of the men even now engaged in battle flipped through their Bibles to find the right place. Garnet, who did not own a Bible, sighed impatiently until Cousin Nellie held hers so Garnet could read along with her: "God is our refuge and strength, a very present help in trouble. Therefore we will not fear —"

But suddenly Garnet was seized with fear, real and quivering through her whole body.

The church seemed unbearably close as the service proceeded. Garnet moved, shifting her position, but she was wedged in between Cousin Nellie's voluminous skirt and another lady who, head bowed devoutly, sat stiffly immobile.

With one finger Garnet loosened the ribbons of her bonnet, for she was finding it difficult to breathe easily. Then her bodice seemed too tight, her stays cutting sharply into her waist. Her mouth felt dry, and she could not swallow. When her heart began to flutter, and she felt suddenly faint, she sought out the possible exits, her eyes darting nervously from side to side. If only she had found a seat in the back of the church instead of marching up front to the Perrys' pew! Panic gripped her at the realization that she was trapped here until the end of the interminable service.

She would have stood up, in spite of everything, and rushed out right then, except that the minister began to address the congregation, and she could not go without causing a commotion. She clenched her hands tightly in her lap and tried to listen.

"There is not one here who does not have a son, brother, husband, or friend in the fray —"

The names flashed like fire across her mind: *Malcolm! Rod and Stewart! Bryce! Maybe even Leighton!* All the men in her life, and those she had met so casually in the last few weeks. All of them were there, in danger — killing, or perhaps, being killed!

Garnet's throat tightened, and she felt as though she were being strangled. How could she sit here another minute and be reminded of all she could lose. Hadn't she lost quite enough already?

Then everyone was standing to sing the final hymn, "The Lord is my light and my salvation, whom shall I fear?"

The words rang in her ears: "To sing praises unto Thy name and of Thy truth in the night season —"

The night season! Surely this was the darkest moment she had experienced in her life thus far. What if Malcolm should be killed? Or her brothers, or Bryce?

Now everyone was kneeling again and Garnet slipped to her knees, too. She was trembling. Again the voice of the minister flowed over her — as if he were speaking directly to her.

"For God hath not given us a spirit of fear, but of power and of love and of a sound mind —"

As the words penetrated Garnet's clouded mind, she felt calmer. Slowly her breathing returned to normal, and the panic subsided. *Of course,* she thought, *there is nothing to fear. They'll be all right. How silly of me to be frightened!*

She did not realize, because she was unfamiliar with spiritual things, that she had been touched by the Word of God, and something within her had responded to that touch. The assurance came, startling her with its intensity, that Bryce was all right. He was safe!

Without being conscious of its significance, Garnet slipped to her knees and breathed an inner "thank you." Then she took a long breath and rose to join her clear, strong voice to the final hymn, "Now Thank We All Our God."

Two days later came the news of the Confederate victory at Manassas, and the city celebrated.

A victory party was in full swing at Cousin Nellie's house when Bryce appeared, his arm in a sling from a slight flesh wound. He was hailed as a conquering hero; for once, Garnet preened with pride in her husband, content to relinquish center stage and bask in the reflected glow of his glory.

The days after Malcolm left seemed all gray to Rose, although it was still only early summer.

The big house was strangely empty with all the men away. Mr. Montrose had gone to Montgomery, Alabama, where the first convention of the Confederacy was taking place. Leighton and Malcolm were training with their company. Bryce had left for Richmond, and Garnet soon after.

With Lizzie gone, too, Rose soon found her time filled with chores. Since no other maid had been suitably trained to meet her mother-in-law's demands, Rose tried to fill in the gap.

Although she soon discovered Sara was almost impossible to please, Rose was determined to be patient with her. Apparently Lizzie had carried out her mistress's management duties as well. Here Rose stepped in quite satisfactorily. Her Aunt

Vanessa's training had prepared her well, and she was anxious to make amends for her part in Lizzie's defection, and to keep Sara's fretting from making her condition worse.

Rose never knew there was so much to running a plantation household. She soon learned, however, that unless she gave specific directions, the well-trained house servants tended to waste time. Besides meeting with the cook each morning to plan the day's menus, Rose found she had to go to the smokehouse, granary, and storage cupboards to measure out the supplies of butter, flour, and meal necessary for the preparation of each day's meals. Montclair did not run by magic as she might have imagined when she first came — so effortlessly and smoothly had things seemed to get done.

Rose's days were long and full of decisions to be made, orders to be given, servants to oversee. Time spent with Jonathan was unalloyed joy, but most of his care had to be turned over to Linny.

Even though they were difficult, Rose could handle the days. It was the long, lonely nights that were hardest to bear. At least during the day her thoughts were diverted. But at night all she could do was think about her broken communion with Malcolm.

She relived those last few days before he left, going over the conversation, word for word, that had severed their relationship. Why had it happened? If their love was as strong and true and real as she had believed it to be, why had this broken the cord that bound them so completely? She longed to recall those words, spoken in anger.

As she tossed and turned half the night, Rose questioned herself relentlessly. Whose fault was it that they had let something so splendid slip away? Malcolm's? Hers?

Night after night, she lay in the big four-poster alone, alternately weeping and pounding her fists into the pillow. At last she came to the sad conclusion that their love had been an illusion. They had been so young, so bedazzled by emotion, that they had mistaken these feelings for the kind of tenacious love that is needed to survive the storm that now had swept them in its path.

Rose's tragedy, she felt, was that she loved a man who no longer existed — or who may have existed only in her imagination. She yearned for the adoring suitor of their romantic courtship; she could not understand the stubborn stranger he had become.

Even his letters were addressed to the entire family, and were read aloud by Mr. Montrose. He ended them with the words, "Love to each of you, special hugs to my little son, and a howdy to the servants." Each word — so cold, so casual, so impersonal — fell on Rose's spirit like a hammer blow. How unlike the young man who had written such impassioned lines to her from Harvard, when he was only a few miles away and would often be seeing her the next day.

Jonathan was Rose's chief consolation. He was merry, handsome, loving — the pet of the whole household. His nurse and the other house servants adored him, and Rose was hard put to keep him from being completely spoiled. She was determined that he would not grow up thinking himself superior to anyone, ordering people about, expecting to be served. Of course, who knew into what kind of a world Jonathan would grow up?

So Rose kept her hurt to herself. She wept in secret and hid her pain, taking a kind of pride in not showing her feelings, flowing with the life of the house and the countryside as it swirled about her, while she wondered how it would be when Malcolm came home.

Rose could not help resenting a little that Garnet, sparkling with gaiety, came and went like a will-o'-the-wisp, bringing with her all the gossip and amusing tales told in the parlors of Richmond. She never stayed long and no one ever knew where she would be, for she rode back and forth between Montclair and Cameron Hall constantly.

Bryce was still in Richmond, deciding which regiment would see the fighting first.

"I declare that man wants to be the first one to kill a Yankee!" Garnet said lightly, tossing her curls without a glance or a thought that her remark might wound Rose.

John Meredith was already in the blue uniform of a Union lieutenant, and Rose asked herself if the situation were reversed, if she would have been more considerate, knowing that Garnet's brothers had already joined the Confederate Army.

Rose's only comfort was that she was not the only person suffering from the sorrow of a divided family, split loyalties. Even

Mrs. Lincoln, it was said, had sisters who married Confederate officers and were loyal to the South. The sword of division slicing through the country cut a wide swath; virtually no one was left untouched.

Rose's thoughts often turned with longing to those days of the past filled with small joys, ordinary pleasures, spun out in unrippled serenity. Days when nothing much seemed to happen. Now she wished those days back with a fierce yearning. Did anyone ever imagine that a time would come when the most uneventful day would seem something to treasure?

Rose got out her diary again. She had not written in it since before the fateful day of her disagreement with Malcolm. But now she needed to pour out the feelings that were impossible for her to express elsewhere.

Everything is happening so quickly. The pleasant, quiet days of last summer seem like a dream, for everything here is changing even from day to day.

Garnet, home from Richmond, is bursting with enthusiasm for the Confederate cause. She wears a palmetto cockade a friend from South Carolina gave her, and you would think she was personally advising President Davis, so positive are her opinions on how the war should be conducted.

I should make allowances and not be so easily offended. Garnet is so childish in many ways, so careless in her remarks, yet I can understand. Malcolm explained her to me once: "She has always been so pretty, so amusing, that she is forgiven everything." He is right — Garnet has never grown up. She is still her papa's spoiled little girl. Father Montrose perpetuates the same attitude toward her outrageous behavior, calling her "that little scamp" when she ridicules one of his friends. And Bryce merely shrugs it off. He has no influence over her whatsoever. Yet I wonder what will happen to all that surface gaiety so like spun sugar, in the face of the reality that must someday come into her life?

I shouldn't judge Garnet when I have so many unchristian feelings toward her myself. In a way I envy her lightheartedness, her total confidence that she will always be on the winning side, that everyone will always love her, give in to her, pardon her. It must be reassuring to go through life on such a cloud of universal approbation.

I think I most envy her having known Malcolm since childhood. I wish Malcolm and I could have had all those lovely, leisurely years to remember. Our time together now seems so heart-breakingly brief. I hold onto it like a drowning person grasps at straws, and each day I lose a little of it as though it never really existed at all.

Rose set down her pen, thinking of Garnet's last visit. She had run lightly up the stair-case, her taffeta skirts swishing on the pol-ished steps, gold-red curls flying, and down the hallway to Sara's suite. Rose had been there, settling Sara for her afternoon nap when they were both startled by Garnet's ar-rival.

With a passing glance at Rose, Garnet had perched on the end of Sara's bed and handed her a box, ornately bowed and wrapped.

"It's from Pinzinni's, Mama — chocolate strawberry creams!" she announced with a little bounce of satisfaction, dimples winking. "Oh, it is the loveliest place in Richmond. Everyone seems to end up there after making calls, and it is like an impromptu party every afternoon." She gave a laugh and pulled off her kid gloves, finger by finger.

Rose watched Sara's languor fade into eager interest as Garnet rattled off story after story of Richmond's social life.

After Garnet had danced off to prepare for a visit to Cameron Hall, Rose recalled with some surprise that throughout the long conversation with her mother-in-law, Garnet had not once mentioned Bryce or his plans.

When she had gone, Sara was quite agitated and irritable. No arrangement of pillows or choice of shawl suited. Finally Sara snapped, "That wretched Lizzie. Ungrateful girl! After all I've done for her, to run off to the Yankees that way! And worse are the blackguards who help these poor ignorant people to leave the good life they have here for who knows what up North. I hear the Yankees don't want them, and they end up living in horrible conditions. I hope she's good-and-sorry!"

Rose said nothing. Her own duplicity kept her silent. There was nothing she could say that would lessen Sara's feeling of betrayal and animosity toward those she believed responsible for Lizzie's running away.

"When I think of it —" Sara began with irritation. "Rose, fix me my medicine."

Reluctantly Rose took the bottle of laudanum Sara always kept on her bedside table and, using a dropper, put five drops into a glass of water.

"Ten, at least, Rose," Mrs. Montrose corrected. "My nerves are frazzled. I need to rest." She passed a fragile hand across her eyes in a weary gesture.

Rose hesitated, then added another five drops. She was concerned about the older woman's use of the opiate, far more than her condition required.

But if Rose mildly demurred when Sara asked for a dose, she became very annoyed. Certainly Lizzie had never countered the least of Sara's requests, so Rose finally gave up. All she could do was comply and try to keep Sara as calm and comfortable as possible, considering the trying circumstances under which they were all living.

Then, unexpectedly, Malcolm appeared. He looked lean, but tanned and fit, splendid in his uniform with two lateral bars on his collar and a loop of braid on his sleeve, indicating his new rank of lieutenant. Leighton, who had come with him, caught the wildly ecstatic Dove in a swinging embrace, then bragged on

Malcolm's popularity. When their original leader was promoted to General Longstreet's staff, he explained, the men of their regiment unanimously elected Malcolm.

Rose had been in the nursery with Jonathan when she heard the shouts, the sound of running feet as the house servants gathered, the noise of general confusion downstairs. She hurried out into the hall and leaned over the balcony to see what was happening.

When she saw who was there, her heart began to race and she started slowly down the stairs. Mr. Montrose, alerted to the excitement, came out of the library to greet his sons at that moment, and over his father's head, Malcolm looked up and saw Rose.

When she reached the bottom of the steps, Malcolm started toward her. Within an arm's reach he stopped suddenly, not touching her. Was he waiting for her to move toward him? Rose searched his face for some sign of acceptance. Both seemed frozen to the spot, unable to make that first gesture of reconciliation.

Something curious flickered in Malcolm's eyes, then his expression grew inscrutable.

"Where is Jonathan, Rose?" he asked. "We can only stay a few hours. We have orders to report back tonight. We came to get fresh horses."

At the news that Malcolm would leave again right away, something melted inside Rose. What did anything matter but that they forgive each other all those cruel words, forget their terrible parting, and at least find what joy and happiness they could in this short time that had unexpectedly been granted them?

But before Rose could move or speak, she heard the light patter of slippers on the steps behind her and a rustle of crinoline as Garnet rushed past her, crying, "Malcolm!" and flung herself into his arms.

Rose grew rigid. A cold resentment washed over her that Garnet could so freely show her gladness at seeing him while Rose was locked in all the misunderstanding and misery of their last encounter.

Throughout Malcolm's short, unsatisfactory visit, Rose had to keep her emotions closely in check. Only after he and Lee were gone could Rose pour out all her anguish once again in the pages of her secret diary.

Malcolm has come and gone, and we had not a minute alone at all. I cannot believe that two people, whose only joy was to be together with the rest of the world forgotten, have come to this. When I remember how it used to be with Malcolm and me, my heart is broken.

Little did we realize when Malcolm and Lee departed that they would be going into immediate battle. Now comes news of a great Confederate victory at Manassas. It is said that the Union forces panicked, broke their lines, and all fled in wild disarray. Everyone here is claiming the war will soon be over. If it is true, many lives, both North and South, will be spared. I pray to God for the safety of my beloved husband, his brother, and my own dear brother John as well.

August 1861

Jonathan's third birthday. What a happy day that was, perhaps the happiest day of my life, when our son was born. If only Malcolm were here to celebrate it with us.

Instead, we go to Cameron Hall for a

great victory party. The tactful Camerons invited us for their thirtieth anniversary celebration; however, it is understood that we celebrate the undisputed victory. My own heart will be heavy until I know that all my dear ones are safe. I do not know if John was involved in this battle, since mail from the North is slow, and, some say it is opened and censored because anything coming across the lines is suspect.

September 1861

At last a letter from John, part of which I quote herein, then will destroy. He writes:

"A week after Manassas, or what we call the Battle of Bull Run, they [meaning the Confederates] could have walked into Washington, so great was the confusion, consternation, and feelings of defeat." And he finished by using the words of Shakespeare in *Julius Caesar*: " 'There is a tide in the affairs of men/Which, taken at the flood, leads on to fortune;/Omitted, all the voyage of their life/Is bound and in shallows and in miseries . . .' If anything, this defeat has brought us to the realization that this may be a long and bitter conflict and that we must be better prepared for a foe that was underestimated."

October 1861

My faith sustains me through these long, lonely days. The fall weather is so beautiful it makes me think of other such days spent with Malcolm. Now we are separated in more ways than miles, war, and circumstances. In spite of that, I continue to "trust in the Lord," knowing He will "give me the desires of my heart," mostly that once more Malcolm and I will be together in loving harmony.

November 1861

Malcolm's letters are brief, mainly to be read to Jonathan about the horses, the marching, songs around the campfire, and what they will do together when Malcolm comes home.

I am worried about his mother. Mr. Montrose is away on business for President Davis, some kind of procurement, and I am alone here with Mama. She is so fretful at night and cannot sleep unless given large doses of laudanum. I have begun staying with her until she falls asleep, reading to her from the Bible. I believe there is healing in the Word, and that reading to her plants a seed of faith. "Faith comes by hearing and hearing by the Word of God."

December 1, 1861

Every evening, on the pretext of helping me get Jonathan ready for bed, Tilda, Linny, and most of the time, Carrie, too, slip in with their little Bibles for our lesson. It is then I realize even more that God's Word stands and truly is "a lamp unto my feet, and a light unto my path" (Ps. 119:105).

As I continue teaching these three, I see that it is not my efforts but the Word itself that sheds the true light. I can see it in their eyes as it comes alive for them, becomes real that God loves them. It is a comfort to me to know that in some small way I am bringing that assurance into these lives that before were so barren of the knowledge of a heavenly Father who cares for them individually. Last night I was reading from Matthew 10 and came to verse 29: "Are not two sparrows sold for a farthing? And one of them shall not fall on the ground without your Father. But the very hairs of your head are all numbered. Fear ye not, therefore, ye are of more value than many sparrows."

I looked up into three pairs of wide eyes staring back at me. Then Tilda breathed, "Fo' sho', Miss Rose?" she asked, touching her turbaned head.

They take everything literally, as accepting as little children. Isn't that what He asked us to do? "Except ye . . . become as little children, ye shall not enter into the kingdom of heaven."

This was always a stumbling block for Malcolm when we discussed the Scriptures. His fine mind, his analytical, skeptical intellect was always questioning, examining. Even when he attended church with me, I used to glance over at him during the sermon and see that intelligent expression, those deep-set eyes, that attentive, yet reserved attitude.

As long as he had one doubt, he often told me, he would not be able to make a full surrender.

If only Malcolm could come to know the Lord as simply and with the childlike faith of these three!

chapter
21

The first days of December, 1861, were like Indian summer. Warm, sunny afternoons lingered. Over everything shimmered a lovely golden haze.

Yet, along with this aura of peace, a kind of restless wind moved through the countryside, an unsettling sense of foreboding.

Stories of small bands of Yankee marauders making foraging missions for horses, cattle, and other livestock, spread among the plantations. In fact, some had already been visited by these unexpected raiders. Groups of six to ten riders would suddenly swoop into a place, round up all the booty they could carry, then ride out again in a matter of minutes. There were more disturbing stories of Negroes, who looked upon the soldiers as liberators, going along with them or even helping them steal their masters' property.

Perhaps because Montclair was set so far back from the main road and partially hidden by the deep woods between the gates and the house, nothing of that kind had happened. Yet the threat was very real and added to the general anxiety that lay like a pall over the household.

Early in the second week of December, Bryce came home on a brief furlough to see his mother and bring Garnet from Richmond.

Rose, who had taken Jonathan out to the orchard to gather some late pears, was just coming back up to the house when they saw Simmy, the little black boy posted near the gates, come running toward them, waving both his skinny arms. "Yankees! Yankees comin' down de road!" he hollered, his eyes wide with fright.

Reacting instinctively, Rose gathered up her skirts, grabbed Jonathan's arm and began running toward the front porch. The little boy's chubby legs were pumping hard to keep up with her, and at the steps, Rose swung him up in her arms, basket and all, and rushed into the house.

Inside the front door she set him down and called for Linny. The other house servants who at the sound of her voice had left chores, came into the hall. Rose began issuing directions.

"Joshua," she said, "send word to the stable that the grooms are to take the horses to the woods and wait there until we tell them it's safe to come back. Hurry! There are Yankee soldiers on their way here."

The startled servants stared at her dumbly. Rose spoke as calmly as she could manage, "Don't be afraid. Just do as I tell you and everything will be all right."

Standing in the middle of the front hall, she saw Garnet bending over the second-floor balcony, and Rose ran halfway up the stairway. "Garnet," she said in a low, steady voice, "get Bryce out of Mama's room, quickly! Yankee soldiers will be here any minute. We'll have to hide him or he'll be taken prisoner. Try not to upset Mama. Get him out some way or other first."

Garnet nodded, her face drained of color, her eyes wide and frightened.

Rose went rapidly up the remaining steps, thinking hard. She met Linny coming out of the nursery. "Quickly! Get Jonathan!" she ordered, pointing to the little boy who was still standing where Rose had left him, holding his basket of pears.

Linny scuttled past her and Rose

reached the top of the steps just as Bryce came out of his mother's suite.

"What is it, Rose?"

"Yankees. They're coming here, Bryce. We've got to hide you. There's no time for you to make it to the woods."

"But where . . . how? They'll probably search the house."

"Come with me." She grabbed Bryce's arm and pulled him along the hall toward the nursery.

She went right to the secret panel, feeling along the wall for the ridge beneath. She pressed the spot, and the door to the storage room and tunnel swung open.

"How did you know about this?" Bryce demanded, aghast.

"Never mind that now. Just get in there and stay until we come to get you," Rose said frantically as through the open window they could hear the pounding of horses' hooves on the crushed shell drive, and the distant shouts of the soldiers.

She gave the big man a gentle push. As he crouched forward and went in, she pressed the spring again and the panel began to slide shut. She turned to see Garnet standing at the doorway, mouth partly open, looking on in amazement.

"Garnet, gather up any clothing or belongings of Bryce's that may be lying around and get them out of sight. Those soldiers just might have heard that one of Jackson's men is here and, if they find any evidence, they'll not give up till they find him." She spoke sharply and for once Garnet did not pause to question, but whirled and ran down the hall.

In a moment she was back as Rose, poised at the top of the staircase, stood ready to descend.

"What now?" Garnet asked.

"Mama?"

"She's dozing, has taken her laudanum. I really don't think she is aware —" Garnet broke off. "Rose, that secret door — how did you know?"

Rose shook her head impatiently. "There isn't time to explain now." She took Garnet's hand, squeezed it tightly. "Stay up here until I need you. We must keep Mama calm," she whispered intently. "Let's say a prayer." She closed her eyes, felt Garnet's soft little hand clutching hers. "Dear Lord, give us courage!" was all Rose could pray. Then she hurried down the steps, her wide skirts sweeping behind her.

As she moved toward the front door she had a moment of utter panic. Carrie was standing to one side, and Rose motioned her to open it. The girl hesitated as if either she did not understand Rose's order or was afraid to obey, so Rose said quietly, but with definite authority, "Open it at once."

Carrie did so, and Rose walked steadily out onto the front porch just in time to see eight or nine blue uniformed cavalrymen rounding the bend of the driveway and galloping up to the house. The officer in front raised his arm to signal a halt as they reined their mounts behind him.

Rose's heart was beating so fast and hard she was afraid she might faint. She steadied herself, then locked her hands tightly in front of her and stood at the door, watching the officer dismount.

His face, shaded by his broad-brimmed hat, was bearded. He was tall with a soldierly bearing, and his dark blue tunic was double-breasted, its brass buttons blazing, the gold insignia on his sleeves indicating the rank of major.

As he started toward the porch, Rose stepped out of the shadows cast by the columns and walked steadily to the top of the steps.

When he saw her, the officer swept off his hat and bowed.

"Good day, madam, my men and I —"
he began, then stopped short. "Is it possible?" he gasped, then, "Rose! Rose
Meredith!"

Just as startled, Rose stared back, then
slowly recognized the familiar face behind
the beard. Unmistakably, it was Kendall
Carpenter.

"Rose!" His voice faltered as he came
nearer, then stood, one booted foot on
the first step; he could barely speak.
"Rose *Meredith!* Of all places — of all
times, *you* . . . here!" He seemed to be
struggling. "What in heaven's name are
you doing here —" Again he seemed at a
loss for words.

"It is Rose *Montrose* now, Kendall, and
this is Montclair, my husband's family
home," she replied quietly.

Kendall shook his head. "I can't believe
that after all this time, we should meet
here and now —"

"I hope you and your men have not
come to do us any harm." Rose spoke with
cool dignity.

Kendall gave her a long measured look,
and said evenly, "Harm? Do *you* harm,
Rose? When I have never felt any but the
kindest, most affectionate feelings for
you?"

"But you are in enemy territory now. You come as an enemy."

"You and I — *enemies?* Never!"

His gaze lingered, taking in the still lovely young woman, the dark, glowing beauty, the pale oval face. Despite their deep serenity, he saw that her eyes held, too, a certain defiance, and smiling slightly, he drew an immaculate linen handkerchief from his pocket and waved it toward her.

"Truce, Rose? May I approach under a flag of truce?"

The terrible tension of the last few minutes eased as myriad thoughts flashed through Rose's mind. Then she allowed the corners of her mouth to relax and the enchanting dimple to show as she stepped back and made a welcoming gesture. "Perhaps you would like to come in and we could have a visit — for old time's sake?"

"With pleasure, Rose. With great pleasure." Kendall spoke with a note of excitement in his voice. "But may I ask a favor? Could my men refresh themselves at your well? We've ridden a long way in this heat."

Rose called to Josh, who had been standing right inside the entrance, concealed by the half-open front door. In a low voice she instructed him to show the soldiers around the side of the house, where they could draw water for themselves and their horses. Then she led the way into the house, with Kendall following.

To the dumbstruck Carrie, Rose said, "Bring a tray of refreshments into the parlor. Tea, some of the scuppernong wine, some cake."

In the parlor Kendall looked around him curiously, not missing a detail of the luxuriously appointed room, the crystal-prismed candlesticks on the marble mantle, the fine furnishings, the velvet upholstery, the damask draperies.

Rose motioned him to one of the twin sofas, and took a seat on the one opposite him. Then a silence fell between them, each momentarily struck by the irony of the events that had led them to this strange meeting.

"Well, Rose," Kendall sighed after a long pause.

"Well, Kendall —" She smiled.

Carrie came in with the tray, set it down on the table by Rose, giving Kendall a sly, hurried glance. She left quickly.

Rose poured the wine into two small crystal glasses and handed one to him. Their fingers brushed slightly and Rose blushed under his penetrating gaze.

"So, Rose, how have you been? How is it to live in a rebel state?" There was a sarcastic tone underlying Kendall's bantering question.

"I think we should observe the truce, Kendall, and not speak of controversial matters." Rose replied smoothly then began to ask questions about Milford, about mutual friends and the family she had left behind. He told her he had seen John recently as well as her aunt and father when John had been home on leave.

"They all miss you very much, Rose, are concerned about you, grieve that you are where you are — surrounded by enemies."

Rose sat up straighter and admonished him gently. "Kendall, you forget that I'm married to a Virginian," she admonished him gently.

"No!" he retorted harshly. "I've not forgotten you're married, Rose, nor that you are married to a *Virginian.* But *that,* I profoundly hope, has not changed you, nor made you a traitor!"

Rose held up both hands. "Please, Kendall!"

"I'm sorry. I apologize. We'll change the subject. It's just that — it did something to me just now to see you giving orders to that slave. I never thought —" He broke off, his face flushed.

"This is my husband's home, his people, Kendall," Rose replied, her hands clenched tightly in her lap, hidden in the folds of her dress. She warned herself that she must not get angry, must not blurt out the truth — that she had worked in the Underground Railroad, had taught her servants to read, was living for the day when they would all be set free. For now, she must keep her composure. Kendall must not suspect that there was, within his grasp, a Confederate officer, a prize prisoner that he could take easily, along with a stable of fine horses, a storehouse of hams, venison, valuable foodstuffs for his men who were probably camped with meager provisions just across the river.

"My apologies." Kendall lifted his glass in a salute to Rose, then said,

"You have often been in my thoughts, Rose, and I have wondered about you, especially in the unfortunate turn of events that has forced the lines between North and South to be drawn so irrevocably. Knowing you and how you felt when I knew you, it seems very strange to see you" — he made a sweeping movement with one hand — "in these surroundings."

"Where would you think I should be?"

"Certainly not here, served by slaves. I would imagine you rather to be fighting for what you believe in."

"And what do you imagine that to be?"

"Justice. Equality. Freedom. The things we used to discuss with such passion at your home in Milford."

Rose touched her glass to her lips before answering. "That seems a long time ago, Kendall. Another time, another world."

"Yes — another world. I believe here you are insulated by luxury and leisure. You have no idea what the rest of the world is thinking, doing. . . . Rose, you have lost touch with reality. You have been lulled into complacency about the things you used to care about deeply."

Rose set down her glass and smiled sweetly at him. "I would like you to see something I *do* care deeply about. My son." She rose, went to the tapestry bell-pull by the fireplace, and tugged it lightly. Carrie appeared so quickly Rose knew she must have been waiting in the hall nearby. She gave a little curtsy.

"Yes'm?"

"Carrie, ask Linny to bring Jonathan in here, please."

Within minutes, Jonathan, face

scrubbed, hair brushed, appeared in the doorway. He glanced at Kendall curiously, then ran across the room, then buried his face in Rose's skirt. Not usually shy, Jonathan's behavior momentarily startled Rose. She put her hands on either side of his face and tried to turn it up. "Why, Jonathan, whatever is the matter? This is an old friend of mine, Major Carpenter."

Jonathan ducked his head again, mumbling something Rose did not catch at first. Then, when she realized what he had said, she flushed hotly. Leaning down to him, she whispered, "Where did you ever hear such a naughty word?"

"That's what Uncle Bryce calls them," the little boy lisped.

Of course he was right. The only time the word *Yankee* was spoken in this house, it was preceded by the word *damn*. Rose could not blame Jonathan for having learned it. But now he also had to behave properly. Kendall had already come forward and held out his hand to Jonathan, who backed away and demanded,

"Would you shoot my papa?"

"Jonathan!" exclaimed Rose.

But Kendall only laughed. "Well, Rose, I see you've got a true 'Johnny Reb' here!"

Rose gathered her wits together and

laughed, too, as she shook her head and shrugged.

"Go along, Jonathan," she told the child, who ran from the room into Linny's waiting arms. To Kendall, she said, "He's only three."

Kendall held up his hand, dismissing Rose's implied apology. "He's a fine, handsome boy, Rose. You must be very proud of him. And I'm sure his father is, too." He reseated himself, then smiled as he looked over at her. "He has *your* eyes, Rose, your beautiful eyes."

Uncomfortable under his gaze, Rose quickly changed the subject to mutual acquaintances, some shared reminiscences of happier years. Inwardly wondering how Bryce was faring in his cramped, dusty hiding place, Rose poured Kendall another glass of wine, and kept the conversation far from current events.

Finally Kendall rose, saying reluctantly, "I must go. This was an unexpected pleasure, one I certainly never could have foreseen, but who is to question fate?"

He picked up his hat, his fine beige leather gloves and stood for a moment in concentration, as if deciding whether or not to say something more. At last he fixed Rose with a riveting look and said, "Rose, why not let me arrange safe conduct north for you and your son? It would mean so much to your father and your aunt. They're not getting any younger, you know, and this may be a long war."

Rose shook her head slowly. "No, Kendall. I know you mean well — but no."

"This is not your country, not your fight, Rose. I know you don't believe in their cause." Harshness crept into Kendall's voice.

"*This* is my home now, Kendall," Rose said quietly. Her dignified response precluded further argument.

Kendall slapped his open palm with his gloves. Rising abruptly, he strode toward the parlor door. When he was almost there, he whirled around and took a few long strides back to where Rose was still seated.

"Rose, before I leave, I must say something." He pushed aside her wide skirt so that he could sit down on the love seat beside her. Then, taking her fragile wrists in both hands, he raised her hands to his lips, turned them over and pressed a kiss into each dainty palm.

"I have never felt about another woman the way I feel about you, Rose. I never thought I'd have another chance to tell you . . . the things I always intended to say when the time was right. I wanted to wait until I had something to offer you. . . . But Malcolm managed to get to you first. . . . He did not need to come to you empty-handed as I would have had to then. He had all this —" Kendall said contemptuously. "How could I — poor, in debt to my relatives for my education, without any sure means of supporting a wife — how could I hope to compete? All I had was my love. And that I still have, Rose. I've never stopped loving you. Are you happy? Really happy?"

"Kendall, don't, please don't say any more." Rose tried to withdraw her hands, but Kendall held them fast.

"I had to tell you, Rose. Forgive me if I have offended you. But fate has brought us together, and it will just as swiftly part us. In these uncertain days, who knows if we shall ever meet again. I wanted you to know that I loved you, will always love you, no matter what happens. I only hope Malcolm Montrose realizes what a fortunate man he is." Kendall sighed, then released Rose's hands, got up and without looking back, left the room.

Rose sat very still until she heard a shouted command from outside. Then she stood, listening, then ran over to the parlor window and looked out.

Kendall was going down the porch steps. There was an almost arrogant swagger in his walk as he approached the aide holding the reins of his horse. He swung into his saddle and whirled his horse around, then raising his arm in a command, started at a gallop down the drive from Montclair.

Rose, her hands clasped against her breast, watched him go — with him went her past, she thought, and her chance to escape.

When the last blue-uniformed horseman had rounded the far bend of the drive, Rose rushed into the hall and up the stairs. She met Garnet at the landing.

For a moment they stared at each other in disbelief, then clinging to each other, dissolved in laughter while tears of relief rolled down their cheeks. Then, as if struck by the same thought at exactly the same time, they turned and, stumbling on their skirts, hurried up the rest of the stairway and into the nursery.

Garnet watched as Rose found the spring that released the secret panel. At the sight of Bryce crouched inside and covered with dust they burst into giggles of laughter, finally collapsing on the nearest chairs as he emerged, smiling sheepishly, while pulling cobwebs out of his hair.

That night at dinner there was an atmosphere of mild hilarity. Bryce had raided his father's wine cellar and had reappeared with a fine old bottle of champagne. There were many toasts raised during the course of the evening — not the least to Kendall Carpenter.

"To Rose's old beau!" Bryce announced, lifting his glass, to Rose's combined amusement and embarrassment.

When she murmured a disclaimer, Bryce insisted. "Now, Rose, don't be modest. If you had not been the belle of Milford, who knows? I might be in chains now, being led into some Yankee prison dungeon."

In spite of the merriment that was in part the release of enormous tension, there was an undercurrent of foreboding. Today's incident had been deflected by the remarkable coincidence of Rose and Kendall's past friendship. But it had left its mark. Now they knew Montclair was not invulnerable to the fate of some of the neighboring plantations, victims of Yankee foraging thrusts. Now they had seen the edge of the sword.

chapter

22

"Fancy Rose being so clever," Garnet remarked to Bryce one night a few weeks later at Cousin Nell's Richmond home while they got dressed for a holiday party.

"Yes, she was the cool one, I'll say that!" Bryce agreed. "I would have spent Christmas in some Yankee prison if she hadn't used her wits."

"Or her *wiles*," murmured Garnet under her breath, unwilling to give Rose too much credit, even if she had practically saved Bryce's life. "I wonder just how well she knew that Yankee officer."

"Well, Rose is beautiful as well as intelligent. I would say any man, Northerner or Southerner, could well be smitten by her charms."

"Yes, I'm sure." Garnet cut him off. Rose was not her favorite subject, even though she had begun to have a grudging admiration for the girl. Curiosity, as well. Unknown to anyone else, Garnet had slipped back downstairs that day and listened outside the parlor door while Rose was playing hostess to her Yankee friend, and had overheard a surprising declaration of love from him.

Garnet was slightly ashamed that she had eavesdropped on such an intimate conversation. Her original purpose in listening had been to catch any hint that the house might be searched, but that tender scene remained etched in her memory. *Fate,* the Yankee officer had called it. Probably considered it an *unkind* fate that Rose and Malcolm had ever met! In that, she and the Yankee major had something in common, Garnet thought with a resigned sigh.

"Are you ready?" Bryce's question startled Garnet out of her thoughts. He was holding her cape for her, eager to be off. It would be a gala evening, for even though the reality of the war and its probable length had finally set in, Richmond was still humming with festive activity.

"Wait 'til I get my hood and muff," Garnet replied, then peered out the window. "What wretched weather! Will this rain never stop?"

"As long as it keeps McClellan bogged down on the other side of the river, it's fine with me!" Bryce gave a wry laugh.

After the disastrous defeat of the Northern troops at Manassas, the South had braced itself for a retaliatory attack all through the fall. It had not come, but winter rains had turned Virginia roads into quagmires. With what the North considered discretion and the South called cowardice, the Union forces under General McClellan were encamped across the Potomac, preparing a spring offensive. In the meantime Richmond relaxed and enjoyed the reprieve granted by inclement conditions.

Garnet and Bryce were on their way to the kind of party that had become *tres chic* in wartime Richmond. "Contribution Suppers" were gay, lighthearted affairs to which each guest brought whatever he or she could contribute to the meal, masking the fact that food was becoming a costly commodity. But these days under the surface a trace of sadness ran like a dark thread, for many had already suffered loss. Virtually no family had been left untouched. No matter how they tried to forget, everyone knew that less than a hundred miles from the city lay the enemy, poised to strike.

Garnet fought the melancholy with animation, making even more effort to sparkle and shine in the company of others. And everywhere she and Bryce went that season, she was a refreshing reminder of life.

Tonight had been no exception. In fact, Garnet had been more devastating than ever. Later in their bedroom at Cousin Nell's, she had tried to hold on to the lightheartedness of the evening. Pirouetting in the center of the room, she whirled her wide skirts gaily.

"Oh, Bryce, wasn't that fun? It doesn't seem as if there's a war going on at all, does it? I love it here in Richmond. Do you think we could live here after the war's over? Or maybe have a small house in town where we could give parties and such?"

Bryce shrugged. "I don't know, honey. That's a long way off. I'm beginning to agree with Malcolm that this might be a long war."

"Oh, we'll send those Yankees packing for good before long, won't we?"

Bryce looked at her for a long moment, sighed. Under his scrutiny, Garnet felt a small twinge of fear.

"But we're winning, aren't we?" she demanded, willing him to reassure her.

"I'm afraid we're outnumbered, honey," he replied laconically.

"Oh, fiddle! One Confederate soldier's worth a dozen Yankees!" Garnet used the flippant retort Southerners were fond of saying.

But Bryce looked serious. "We have to be realistic, Garnet. The Union forces have more of everything — men, guns, supplies."

"Let's not talk about things like that tonight, Bryce," Garnet interrupted petulantly. "Let's try to be happy while we can."

Bryce crossed the room, drew her close to him in the circle of his arms, then suggested with a smile, "Let's not talk at all."

There was only a moment's hesitation before Garnet wound her arms around his neck and returned his embrace.

"I missed you," he whispered.

"I missed you, too," Garnet replied, realizing with some astonishment that it was true. Of all the attention, the admiring glances she had received lately, only Bryce knew her beyond the pretty face, the spritely manner. Except for her parents, only Bryce loved her just the way she was. With him she never had to pretend to be nicer, kinder, or anything more than she was.

His mouth on hers beseeched her to love him, its pressure awakening an ardor she had almost forgotten, and she responded with surprising warmth. Maybe she didn't love Bryce with the girlish passion she had lavished on her dream of Malcolm, but there was something deep, true, and real in what she felt for him.

And that night they found a tenderness in their relationship that was new, enhanced perhaps by the drama, the uncertainty, the urgency of time running out.

Afterward, held securely in Bryce's strong arms, Garnet fell asleep, her earlier fears stilled for the moment.

In the cold gray dawn of the next morning Bryce made his preparations to return to camp. When he could get leave again or be able to come to her, neither of them knew as they said good-bye.

Bryce held Garnet close, kissed her again, and before he left, asked, "You will go down to Montclair soon, won't you, darlin'? I hate to think of Mama and Rose alone so much of the time with Father away on government assignment. It would cheer them up to see you. Promise?"

"Yes, yes, I promise!" Garnet tried to hide her impatience. The last thing she wanted to do was go to Montclair, hear Sara's dreary complaints, see Rose's bravery in spite of the fact her brother was now in the Union Army fighting against her husband. "I will. I'll go right after President Davis's inauguration. And the ball, of course! You wouldn't want me to miss that, would you? Then I can tell your mother and Rose all about it. That should cheer them up!" she finished complacently.

On a blustery, wind-swept March day Garnet took the train from Richmond to Mayfield. The scene at the depot depressed her dreadfully. Clumps of Confederate troops waiting for transport were standing in the drizzle in shabby, ill-fitting uniforms. They looked gaunt, cold, and miserable. It was a far cry from scenes in this same place last spring and summer, when throngs of pretty girls and cheering crowds had seen their sons, husbands, and fiancés off to battles they were confident of winning.

Garnet huddled in the corner of the seat in the dirty, smelly car and pressed her face against the window. She looked out at the bleak landscape, trying to forget the

312

haunted looks in the eyes of those soldiers. Shivering, she drew her cloak closer, then tucked her hands deeper into her fur muff. What lay behind was gloomy, but she dreaded more what lay ahead of her — at Montclair!

The Montrose carriage met her at the Mayfield station. Mordecai, the head coachman, was there to greet her and despite the abysmal weather, managed to look dignified as he swept a bow that bared his grizzled gray head to the pouring rain. But Garnet noticed that even his swallow-tailed blue livery looked shiny and worn. After Garnet was settled in the carriage, they started the trip to Montclair.

The winter rains had done their damage, and the ride was bumpy and slow as the carriage wheels stuck and slid in the muddy ruts.

As they turned up the long, winding drive from the gate to the house, Garnet was reminded of all the times she had ridden her horse or been driven by carriage along this same route — sometimes with happy anticipation; at other times, with a leaden heart. It seemed impossible that so much time had passed since she had come here as a bride. With a strange sense of irony, Garnet recalled the bitter-sweetness of that day. She had won Bryce and become the future mistress of Montclair only to realize how empty that victory seemed now.

As they rounded the last bend, Montclair came into view. In the gray veil of rain that almost obscured it, the great house still had an austere beauty, the slanted roof outlined majestically against the dark, clouded sky. The welcoming arms, steps that had been added when Sara came here a bride, seemed less welcoming today, Garnet thought, and she noticed that all the windows were shuttered. It gave her a strange feeling of foreboding.

chapter
23

"Oh, Garnet, how wonderful to see you!" Rose exclaimed, greeting Garnet at the door. "Mama has been so anxious to learn when you would be arriving that I could hardly get her to take a rest. Come into the parlor first and warm yourself. You must be chilled to the bone from your long ride."

Rose seemed thinner than Garnet remembered, but her eyes were luminous, her face radiant as if from some inner joy.

Garnet handed her rain-dampened cape to Bessie who came scurrying to fetch it, then she followed Rose into the parlor, kicked off her wet slippers, and sank down on the rug in front of the fireplace, holding out her hands to its warmth. To cover her sudden awkwardness in finding Rose in such distressed circumstances, she began to chatter mindlessly. Garnet felt guilty she had stayed away so long, leaving all the responsibilities they should have shared, to Rose.

"Have you heard from Malcolm lately?" she blurted and was surprised to see Rose blush.

"Yes, as a matter of fact, just today." A smile lighted Rose's face. "He's with General Lee in western Virginia. He wasn't able to get leave for Christmas. Jonathan was terribly disappointed, of course."

Garnet turned away, unable to look at Rose. Didn't Rose know that General Lee's men were suffering severely in the bitter mountain cold, where supplies were not able to reach them due to heavy snows? She bit her lip. Maybe, isolated here at Montclair, Rose had not heard all the news.

Garnet was saved from the necessity of making more conversation by the sound of a child's voice, and a minute later, Jonathan, accompanied by Linny, came to the doorway. At once he broke away and ran into the room, plunging himself into Rose's arms. From that haven he peeked at Garnet mischievously.

"Say hello to your Aunt Garnet, Jonathan," Rose instructed softly, cuddling her small son.

" 'Lo, Auntie 'Net," Jonathan lisped.

How like Malcolm he was! Garnet thought. The same dark, silky curls, the same high coloring.

" 'Scuse me, Miss Rose," Linny interrupted, "but Miss Sara's awake and axin' who's downstairs. I done tole her it wuz Miss Garnet, an' she wants her to come upstairs."

"We better go right up, Garnet. Mama's been waiting to hear all the Richmond gossip!" Rose gathered up her skirts and took Jonathan's hand.

Garnet stood, too, and started out of the room. At the stairway, Jonathan held out his other chubby little hand to her, and, as she took it, Garnet felt a curious sense of belonging.

"Did you know Dove is expecting?" Rose asked as they made their way up the stairs.

"No!" Garnet exclaimed, inwardly wincing.

Rose had a child — now Dove and Leighton would have one. She knew Bryce would love to have a son. She had seen him playing with Jonathan, carrying him on his shoulders, tossing him into the air.

Garnet resisted the thought. She couldn't imagine herself a mother!

When they reached the top of the stairs and turned toward Sara's suite, Garnet whispered to Rose, "However is *she* managing without Lizzie? And where in the world do you think Lizzie disappeared to? Gone over to the Yankees, most probably! Lots of Richmond families have had their slaves slip across the line to the North." She shrugged. "They say even Mrs. Jefferson Davis has had trouble keeping help."

"Well, your Bessie is helping out, and Carrie, too," Rose replied, staring straight ahead.

For some reason Garnet felt she should ask no further questions. She knew Sara was difficult and that Rose probably had had her hands full trying to keep her pacified.

Garnet spent the next hour regaling Sara with tidbits of gossip, humorous recitals of social events, and descriptive personality profiles of some of the people now in the upper echelon of government and society in Richmond who gathered at Cousin Nell's. She deliberately skipped the dreary details that Richmond society could not avoid seeing, as grim witness to the real cost of war. But the truth lay behind her bright words.

Sara, who before her accident had once been a social butterfly herself, leaned forward, listening to each word, her lethargy temporarily suspended.

"And what is Mrs. Davis like?" she asked eagerly.

"Very handsome," Garnet replied. "Tall, graceful, strong features, yet there is a softness about her. I think it's her eyes, which are dark and rather almond-shaped. You would have loved her gown for the Inaugural Ball, Mama! It was white with a deep lace bertha, and she wore a jade brooch — leaf-shaped, with a large pearl in the center. She has dark hair and usually wears a flower tucked into her chignon. That night it was a white rose."

Mrs. Montrose insisted Garnet have dinner on a tray upstairs with her while Rose went to the nursery to eat with Jonathan. Garnet was grateful when at last Sara finally lay back on her pillows, looking wan and exhausted from all the vicarious excitement and said reluctantly, "Perhaps you best wait 'til tomorrow to tell me more."

Rose came in with Carrie to administer Sara's nightly dose of laudanum, then both of them left while Carrie settled Mrs. Montrose for the night.

Garnet herself felt fatigued. The dismal train trip, the jolting carriage ride over the rutted country roads to Montclair combined with the long draining visit with Sara left her weary.

She stifled a yawn, asked Rose's pardon, and said she thought she would go to bed early. Rose said she understood. Telling Garnet she still had to read to Jonathan and ready him for bed, they said goodnight.

On her way up the lovely winding stairway to her room on the second floor, Garnet passed all the portraits of former brides of Montclair. The three current ones — herself, Rose, and Dove — were not yet among them. Rose's portrait was completed, but not framed and hung. Although arrangements had been made for Garnet's portrait to be painted, she had never had the patience to sit, and kept breaking her appointments with the Richmond artist commissioned to do the work. Dove, the newest bride, had not even made plans for her sitting. The war, thought Garnet sadly, had changed everything!

Even Montclair had not escaped change. Garnet was glad she would be leaving within the next day or two. Montclair was no longer the way she remembered it — the once-beautiful house now seemed empty, lonely, full of shadows.

She would be relieved to get back to Richmond where things were lively, happy, and bright in spite of everything! In Richmond, there was no time to brood or worry or feel afraid, for there were always handsome officers to cheer up, flirt with, talk to. Yes, thank goodness, she would soon be leaving!

As Garnet prepared for bed she felt a strange restlessness, despite her physical weariness. She drew the curtains against the night and the eerie shadows cast by huge trees bowing in a macabre dance from the winter wind outside her bedroom window.

She called for Bessie to put fresh logs on the fire in her fireplace, yet still felt chilled. Downstairs, the house was quiet, but filled with unsettling noises. Garnet could not help thinking how isolated Montclair seemed after the frenetic activity of Richmond.

"This place is like a tomb!" she said aloud. "How can Rose stand it?" And she huddled, shivering, under the feather quilt.

But Garnet could not go to sleep right away and lay there, listening to the wind moaning at the windows and whistling down the chimney. When she finally drifted off, her sleep was shallow and filled with troubling dreams.

With Garnet's retiring early, Rose made her way quickly to her own bedroom where she longed for a few moments alone to savor the momentous thing that had happened that very day.

Going to the little applewood desk, she pulled out an envelope and withdrew its contents. A letter from Malcolm! By its condition, it must have made many detours, met many delays before reaching her for whom it was intended.

That morning, half-dreading what she would find, she had opened it with shaking hands and heart-catching breath. But when her eyes raced over the first few lines, a sob of joy caught in her throat. Her hands, holding the pages, shook so that she finally spread them on the counterpane to read.

My beloved Rose,

As I write these words very late at night, all is still, except for the even breathing of my fellow officer asleep on his cot. No campfires are burning except for the one in front of the guard tent, ever vigilant, we hope. I can see out into the darkness through the flap of my tent as the wind blows, and again I am struck by the strangeness of being here so far from all I love and hold dear.

I have orders with my company to join General Lee's forces in western Virginia. It may be a long time before I am able to get home to Montclair. So there may not be any time soon that I can say what is in my heart to say to you except on these pages. It may seem inadequate, but I must try.

At Manassas I saw men die and saw the wounded piled into carts and taken to hospitals and I ask myself, For what? In the thick of battle, with ear-splitting shriek of bullets bursting all around you, the noise, the smell of smoke and blood, the cries of men injured and suffering, the scream of terrified horses, life is reduced to the absolute fundamentals.

I read somewhere that the three great essentials of happiness are something to do, someone to love, and something to hope for. Once all three were mine, before all clarity was blurred by rhetoric and our country was torn apart.

That you and I — who had the rare privilege of knowing a union so complete, an intimacy so precious, a harmony so special — could be separated by divided loyalties, false pride, and outside pressures, seems to me, now, a tragic loss. And one for which I take my rightful share of blame.

I realize that it is too late to remedy except to beg your forgiveness.

So many memories sweep over me tonight that I am weakened by longing — the satiny feel of your skin, the scent of meadow clover in your hair, the sweet fragrance of your kiss, the joy, ecstasy, and peace I've known in your arms.

I think of Jonathan, our son, and I remember the warm weight of his head on my shoulders as I carried him, his chubby little arms around my neck, his high sweet voice calling to me, "Look, Papa! Look at me!" when he tried to turn somersaults on the grass that day last spring.

On the eve of leaving for where I am not sure, for what I do not know, my lack of appreciation for those moments assails me. Do any of us ever appreciate the ordinariness of uneventful days until the storm comes?

This question burdens me now, Rose. And I want to say what I may not have a chance to say later.

I could not do what you asked me to do, even though I hate slavery as fiercely, perhaps, as any Stowe, Greely, Thoreau, Emerson, or Sumner. Not two men in a hundred own slaves in the South, and most feel as I do. Slavery must go, and none will hail its going more than I.

We stand together on this issue, Rose, closer than I was willing to admit when we parted in anger.

I have always had great contempt for so-called deathbed conversions or last-minute confessions, but I must now place myself with those who see clearly with hindsight.

You may be surprised to learn that of late, I have taken to reading from the small New Testament you gave me before we married and which, for some reason, I packed to bring with me to camp. I quote from it now, dearest heart, because it says what is my deepest desire for us:

"But from the beginning of creation God made them male and female. For this cause shall a man leave his father and mother, and cleave to his wife. And they twain shall be one flesh: so then they are no more twain, but one flesh. What therefore God hath joined together, let not man put asunder" (Mark 10:6–9).

Dear Rose, as you read what I have copied down, let us take our marriage vows again, for this is what I truly feel I want us to be "from this day forward."

I have no way of knowing when I shall see you again, beloved, or clasp you to my heart, or what we two must pass through before we can begin a life together once more with our little son. I ask you to pray God it will not be too long and that this cruel conflict that has so divided our nation and caused so much sorrow on both sides will not leave a heritage of bitterness to our children for years to come.

And now, I will close, hoping that when you read all I have written, you will find it in your heart to give me a full pardon for the grief I have caused you. Good night, my darling, and farewell, sweet Rose.

> Always your loving husband,
> Malcolm Montrose

Rose reread the precious words for the dozenth time since its arrival, weeping with joy that all her prayers had been answered.

God is faithful, she thought. He had promised her the desires of her heart and now He was giving them to her. "My cup runneth over!" she whispered to herself, sending up loving little prayers of gratitude.

When Malcolm came home, things would be so different for them. The faint hope she had clung to for so long now soared within her. She thought Malcolm had stopped loving her. But he hadn't, after all! Joy surged within and she almost laughed aloud.

Buoyed by these new sensations, Rose's feet fairly skimmed the floor as she left the bedroom to go in search of Jonathan. Since Malcolm's departure, the child had declared himself too old for the crib in the nursery and had moved down with Rose. It comforted her to look over at him at night and see his dark, curly head snuggled into the pillows so close to her.

She found Jonathan looking at a picture book with Linny. Readying him for bed, she tucked him into the trundle bed beside her own and sang to him all his favorite songs until he fell asleep.

Tonight, when Tilda, Linny, and Carrie came to her room for their reading lesson and Bible study, Rose knew she would be sharing with them her new joy and assurance. As they gathered in the lamplight with their Bibles and bowed for prayer, there was always so much to pray for. Tonight, Rose knew, there would be new hope in the forthcoming answers!

The three girls came one at a time to rap softly on her bedroom door. When they were all seated on the floor beside her bed, open Bibles in their laps, Rose took an added precaution and tilted a side chair under the doorknob to secure it.

Lately on the rare occasions when Garnet was at Montclair, she had sought Rose's company unexpectedly. Tapping at her door one night, Garnet had asked, "Can I come in? I can't sleep. I hate it here now with everyone gone!" And, flouncing onto the end of Rose's bed, she had given a small shiver. "It's so spooky and still! I used to love it here, but that's when there were people and parties and fun!"

Not that any interruption was likely tonight. Sara was already sleeping when Rose left her earlier in the evening, Garnet had pleaded weariness right after supper and gone to bed and Dove was with relatives.

Still, Rose could not chance discovery.

"I think we'll start with a psalm tonight," Rose announced, setting the oil lamp on the little bed stepladder and settling herself on the floor alongside the three servants.

"Turn to 118:24," she directed them. " 'This is the day which the Lord hath made; we will rejoice and be glad in it!' "

Rose usually allowed each girl to read verses in turn and, even though she was pleased at the progress they had made since she first began teaching them, it was sometimes slow going. Regrettably, she had noticed there was rivalry among them, each one competing with the other two to excel. She tried to balance this competition by equally praising the individual efforts.

As one or the other struggled with line after line, following with her index finger and sounding out the words, Rose sometimes found her own mind wandering. *Where is Malcolm tonight?* She must write him right away. If he was with Lee in western Virginia, she knew they were experiencing terrible hardships. *O Lord, keep him safe,* she prayed. She could not wait to tell him how much his letter had meant to her, how much she loved him, too.

After the psalm had been laboriously read, Rose turned to one of her very favorite passages, strongly inclined to it tonight. In her soft, clear voice, she began to read:

" 'To every thing there is a season, and a time to every purpose under the heaven: A time to be born, and a time to die; a time to plant, and a time to pluck up that which is planted; A time to kill, and a time to heal; a time to break down, and a time to build up; A time to weep, and a time to laugh; a time to mourn, and a time to dance. A time to cast away stones, and a time to gather stones together; a time to embrace, and a time to refrain from embracing; A time to get, and a time to lose; a time to keep, and a time to cast away; A time to rend, and a time to sew; a time to keep silent, and a time to speak; A time to love, and a time to hate; a time of war, and a time of peace.' "

As she read, Jonathan stirred and made a small moaning sound from his bed. Automatically, Rose paused, turned, and started to raise herself to look across her own wide bed to his trundle on the far side. At the same time, his nurse Linny also scrambled to her feet to check on her charge. In the resultant movement, the oil lamp that had been rather precariously balanced on the top step of the bed ladder tipped, toppling its glass chimney and spilling oil on the bedspread along with a ripple of fire.

There was instant pandemonium as all four women jumped up and lunged for the lamp. Before anyone could reach it, the fire caught the lacy loops of the crocheted bedspread.

"Linny! Get Jonathan!" Rose ordered

frantically. "Get him out of here! Tilda, help me! Carrie, run for help!"

The flames climbed like some wild living thing, grabbing, tearing, devouring bedcurtains and canopy, until the entire bed was a monstrous inferno. Her heart was pumping, her head bursting. Choking and gasping, Rose pulled at the blankets, flapping them vainly as the intensity of the heat made her feel as if her bones were melting. The hot breath of the fire rushed at her, leaping furiously. She could hear the sound of crackling wood as the flames spiraled up the bedposts, and the curls of smoke sent her into a paroxysm of coughing. As she backed blindly away, the red-bright darts of fire spouted sparks onto her skirt. Before she realized it, her whole voluminous ruffled hem was ablaze.

The last thing Rose remembered was Linny's running past her with Jonathan wrapped in a blanket in her arms, the sound of Carrie's shouts, and Tilda's desperate voice screaming, "Miss Rose, you is on *fire!*"

Garnet woke up with a violent start. She did not know how long she had slept nor what had awakened her. She sat up, tensed, stiffly alert, straining to listen.

331

From somewhere in another part of the house, she heard noises, disturbing ones that sent little fingers of fear rippling throughout her body.

Then she heard the screams, terrifying cries penetrating the thick walls of the house, reaching up into her secluded wing. She threw back the covers. Her bare feet scarcely touched the carpeted floor as she rushed in her nightgown out from her bedroom through the adjoining sitting room and flung open the door leading to the upstairs hallway.

At once her nostrils flared with the unmistakable acrid smell of smoke. The sound of running footsteps along the polished floors downstairs mingled with the shrieks and frantic cries.

Garnet ran to the balcony that encircled the first floor and leaned over in time to see billows of smoke and the red-orange flames leaping from Rose's wing of the house.

The house was on fire! Montclair was burning!

chapter
24

Contrary to Dr. Connett's grave pronouncement that Rose would not last the night, she was still breathing when morning broke on the third day after the fire.

Garnet had been sitting, stiff-spined, in a chair placed at an angle, halfway between the window and the bed. Hour after hour she remained unmoving, every muscle tensed, every nerve in fixed awareness of the slightest movement from the still figure swathed in bandages. The devoted Tilda was there, too, having tended the unconscious Rose like a baby, changing the linens, soothing her when she moaned in her delirium.

Now Rose opened her eyes, stripped of the long lashes that had enhanced their beauty. Her lovely, luxuriant hair was scorched all around her blistered face, and her lips were parched and cracked.

Garnet jumped to her feet, bending near to catch Rose's faint words.

"Jonathan —" she croaked, her eyes moving to the ambrotype of Malcolm on the bedside table. "If Malcolm . . . if anything happens . . . take Jonathan . . . promise?"

"But Rose —" began Garnet anxiously.

Wearily Rose closed her eyes as if to shut out Garnet's useless protest. She knew she could not hold on much longer, that there was only time for the essentials. The effort to talk was exhausting, and Rose sank back into the pillows, seemingly beyond reach. After what seemed a very long time, she opened her eyes again, glimpsed her Bible lying on the bedside table, then turned to Garnet.

"Read." Her voice was raspy with the strain of speaking.

Garnet picked up the book. Its well-worn cover was singed; the edges of the pages, scorched. By some miracle, Tilda had carried it out of the burning room and later handed it to Garnet, saying, "Dis is Miss Rose's Bible. She'll be wantin' it."

Garnet was uncomfortably aware of her unfamiliarity with its contents, as she took up the Bible, feeling convicted by that knowledge. She had often secretly scorned

Rose's reliance on Scripture, even openly mocked what she labeled "pious utterances" as a substitute for wit.

She had never felt the need of much prayer. Life had been such a golden path for Garnet Cameron that she had trod as if all belonged to her, and had grabbed at its treasures with greedy hands. What she had not been given, she had taken.

She felt none of that assurance now, only a gnawing fear that somehow she had missed something precious and important — that if she were lying where Rose lay now, she would be lost and hopelessly frightened.

Garnet lowered her eyes to the well-marked page and began to read in a voice that trembled.

" 'I am the resurrection and the life: he that believeth in me, though he were dead, yet shall he live. And whosoever liveth and believeth in me shall never die.' "

A slight smile passed over Rose's mouth as if she had been comforted, and she seemed to drift back to sleep. Garnet closed the book, feeling terrified and empty.

Outside, rain pebbled against the windowpanes. The sigh of tree boughs scraping the side of the house and the keening of the wind increased the loneliness of her vigil. Mesmerized by the staccato sound and her own fatigue, Garnet's eyes grew heavy. She fell asleep, awakening with a jerk when the Bible slid from her lap with a soft plop. She sat erect, glancing fearfully at the bed. Suddenly bathed in cold sweat, she leaned over to check Rose's shallow breathing. She was still alive, thank God!

Then she became aware of movement, muffled voices from downstairs. Garnet moved quickly to the door and went out into the hall. At the head of the staircase she looked down into the lower hall and saw a man's tall figure, water dripping from the brim of his hat onto his broad shoulders, his cape making puddles on the floor. Joshua was helping him off with his things. Malcolm! His name caught in her throat. He started up the stairs and saw her.

His eyes, beseeching, sought hers. "Rose?"

"Still alive — but barely. Come quickly!"

Malcolm mounted the steps heavily, almost like a man bound for the gallows.

Wrapped in oiled linen, Rose slowly regained consciousness. She heard the steady beat of the rain, the slight creak of the bedroom door as it opened. The light from a lamp held high threw a tall shadow against the wall and across the bed. She tried to focus her fuzzy vision on a figure moving toward her to bring it into recognizable form. But it was not until she heard her name spoken in that deep, familiar voice that her heart leaped.

"Rose, dearest," came the hoarse whisper ragged with emotion.

She must be dreaming. It couldn't be . . . not possible. Malcolm was far away. Then as he fell to his knees beside the bed and she felt his weight leaning against the mattress, saying her name over and over like a sob, she squinted at the heavily bearded face. The voice was Malcolm's and those eyes looking at her with such love — it *had* to be! Malcolm! Come home to her!

God is so good, she thought gratefully and longed to tell Malcolm what she had come to understand almost too late. He looked so terribly sad. If she could only make him see that earthly love is so limited, but divine love can transform — can restore, heal misunderstanding, set one free to forgive. That death is not the end — for whatever we have once loved, we can never lose —

But there were tears streaming down the

face of Malcolm, who never cried. Rose tried to move or smile, reach out to comfort him, but the attempt sent shooting arrows of pain through her and she moaned involuntarily.

Malcolm's head went down on the bed beside her, his shoulders shaking convulsively.

"What can I do, Rose?" came his broken cry.

Rose knew she had to do something to comfort him. Struggling, she finally managed to bring words from her raw, damaged throat. "You've made me so happy."

"Not happy enough, Rose, my darling. I meant to do so much more." Malcolm lifted his head, shaking it sadly. He longed to take this woman he loved into his arms, hold her, help her, but he had been told the slightest touch was agony for her. Feeling helpless and desperate, he wanted to say something that might give her strength and hope to live. "Listen, my dearest, we'll begin again when this is all over. You and Jonathan and I will go away somewhere, be happy again."

But even as Malcolm spoke he felt her slipping away. Rose's eyes closed, her parched lips twisted in a travesty of a smile.

338

Behind him he heard movement, the rustle of skirts, felt the presence of others. He did not know how long before he saw Tilda on the other side of Rose's bed, bending over the motionless figure. Garnet came and stood beside Malcolm; he felt her hand on his shoulder. Slowly Malcolm reluctantly met Tilda's gaze and saw that the black woman's face was wet with tears.

"She's gone, Marse Malcolm. Miss Rose is wid de Lawd now. Miss Garnet, Miss Rose is *daid*." Then Tilda threw her apron over her face and moved over to the window, her body shaking with sobs.

Garnet, with Malcolm's harsh sobs in her ears, groped her way out of the darkened bedroom into the hall, over to the balcony. She clutched the banister for support.

Rose was dead. Through her numbed senses, the stunning reality of what had happened and what it meant suddenly struck her. What it meant to *her!*

How often she had dreamed of being mistress of this great plantation, envied Rose, *coveted* her husband. She had believed that Rose had spoiled all her dreams, stood in the way of her true happiness, kept her from the man she adored.

But now Rose was dead. Now all these

things were a possibility.

Garnet swayed and steadied herself, feeling lightheaded, almost ill. Out of the past the dire warnings of her old mammy-nurse taunted Garnet: "Be keerful what you wish for, child, you jes' might git it!"

But *not* like this! she silently screamed. Not like *this!* She sagged against the railing as rising panic overtook her. With Rose gone, who would take over here? What about Sara and Jonathan and the servants? *Who?* Fear gripped her and rebellion coursed through her as the inevitable truth dawned.

"I don't have to stay here! I have my own mother, my own family, my own home — where I can be taken care of, where I can be safe!" The childish words rushed up even as she knew the pointlessness of such protests against fate.

Garnet knew she must stay. There was Sara, helpless, locked in her self-imposed prison of invalidism, to be told about Rose. And Jonathan! Dear God, that little boy without his mother would be inconsolable.

"Oh, God! It's too hard, all too hard!" Tears rolled down her cheeks, unchecked.

As if from a long distance, against the background of the dirge-like sound of the rain, she heard Malcolm telling Joshua that they must have the burial the following day, that he had to rejoin his regiment without delay.

Garnet knew then there was no one else. After Malcolm left tomorrow, she would be alone here at Montclair with only the tears of self-pity. She brushed them away now, quickly, almost impatiently. She thought of all the other foolish tears of her life. Tears over a dress that didn't suit, a dish that didn't appeal, a beau who didn't call when she expected him . . . so many wasted tears! And now that there were really important things to weep about, Garnet had no time for tears.

Determinedly she lifted her head. As she turned, she saw Rose's charred Bible on the hall table where she had distractedly placed it. Should it be buried with Rose or perhaps saved and given to Jonathan? Garnet picked up the volume, leafing through its well-marked pages. Strange, how Rose had seemed to find such comfort, such strength within its pages —

Presently she heard footsteps coming along the hall and put the book down. She would decide what to do about it — later. Right now there were other necessary things to do, and only she was left to do them. She replaced the Bible on the table,

341

her hand lingering for a moment on its blistered cover. Yes, later, when there was time —

In the meantime somewhere in the house a child was crying. And she must go to him.

PART VI

To Everything There Is a Season — A Time of War —

Montclair
1862-1865

chapter
25

Garnet pushed open the gate of the spiked black iron fence encircling the Montrose family burial grounds. It gave a protesting creak as she stepped inside and closed it behind her. A brisk wind, rising suddenly, sent a flutter of golden leaves from the branches of slender maple trees surrounding the graveyard, scattering a profusion of color over the newest granite marker. A banner of September sunlight slanted across its surface, illuminating the finely cut inscription:

ROSE MEREDITH MONTROSE
1839–1862
Beloved Wife of Malcolm
Mother of Jonathan
"Love Is As Strong As Death"

Malcolm had arranged with a stonecutter in Richmond for Rose's memorial headstone, but it had taken months for his order to be filled, the stone placed according to his express directions. It was Garnet who had to see to its placement only a few weeks ago — long after Malcolm returned to his regiment.

So much had happened in the five months since Rose had lost her life in the tragic fire that destroyed one wing of Montclair. Yet, standing in the warm fall sunshine, it still seemed impossible that Rose could be dead. She was so young! Only a year older than Garnet herself!

Placing the bouquet of late roses from the Montclair gardens on Rose's tomb, Garnet turned and left the little enclosure. Rose was dead, Malcolm gone back to his Army duties, and Garnet left with the responsibility of their little son.

She walked over to where she had tethered her horse, Trojan Lady, and mounted. Today she was riding over to Cameron Hall to see her parents, a visit she had both anticipated and dreaded. It was always a shock to see her father. Since his stroke, Judge Cameron was pitifully changed.

Garnet started down the familiar bridle path along the creek, her heart heavy with all the newly acquired sadness. Seeing Rose's gravestone brought back all the trauma of the tragedy — a multiple tragedy, as it turned out. On the very night of the fire at Montclair, Garnet's brother Stewart lay dying of typhoid in a Richmond hospital, and, following his death, her father had been stricken.

"Love is as strong as death. . . ." The words of Rose's epitaph, chosen by Malcolm, had surprised Garnet, taken as they were from Scripture. What had Malcolm meant by these words? She knew that he was not a declared Christian even if Rose was. Garnet frowned. She hoped he had not gone all religious with some kind of imagined guilt over Rose's death.

Garnet's old fear of God had come back with fierce intensity, compounded by Stewart's death and her father's illness. How could an all-loving, all-caring God such as Rose had believed in so fervently, do such things to people?

Garnet gave Trojan Lady a little kick and, with a flick of the reins, gave the mare her head. Then she leaned into the forward surge of the horse's gait, feeling the rush of wind in her face. She did not want to think of things like death or dying — certainly not on a gorgeous day like this! Such carefree moments were too rare for her now.

It seemed that every day brought some

new responsibility — like the arrival of a Montrose cousin, Harmony Chance and her little girl, refugees from a Yankee occupation of Winchester. It appeared the two would be guests at Montclair for the duration of the war.

Characteristically, Garnet felt the hot surge of rebellion against the fate that had suddenly thrust all these people, all these odious tasks upon her. Her life of leisure and gaiety were over.

Leaving the woods, Garnet followed the low stone wall into the meadow that bordered the drive leading up to Cameron Hall. She took the fence easily then slowed to an easy canter.

As the gracious white-columned house came into view, Garnet gazed on it with a fondness one sometimes feels for childhood things. Cameron Hall did seem like that to her now. Something of that long-ago time when her life had been all sunshine and no shadows.

As she neared the house, she saw her mother in the side yard where part of the formal gardens had been converted into a vegetable garden. Garnet reined to a stop, dismounted, and led her horse over to graze under the shade of one of the giant elms.

Seeing her daughter, Kate Cameron waved, adjusted the wide-brimmed straw hat she wore to shield her delicate complexion from the sun, picked up an oak chip basket of carrots, and paused to pluck a late-blooming yellow rose to tuck into her belt.

The two women embraced, then stood a moment looking into each other's eyes. The unspoken message passing between them was too deep for words. A moment later, her mother's pale, compressed lips curved into a smile and she slipped her arm through Garnet's and they walked up to the house together.

"How's Papa?" Garnet asked.

"Some better today, I do believe," her mother answered. "He's resting just now. Mawdee's sitting with him. Before you go, you can look in on him. If he's awake, he'll want to see you. In the meantime we can have tea out on the porch. It's so nice and sunny — real Indian summer. I'll go tell Minna."

While her mother was inside, Garnet thought about how different life was for Kate Cameron now. With her husband's stroke and her son's death, Kate's previously sheltered life had taken a tragic twist. In spite of it she had somehow maintained her quiet dignity, her graceful bearing. And now, Garnet noticed, a new, finely honed strength had emerged.

Rose had possessed something elusive, too. What was it? Garnet puzzled. And how did one go about getting it?

A sullen-faced black woman came out on the porch just then, carrying a tea tray. Garnet remembered her as a kitchen helper to their cook. She mumbled something inaudible and went back in the house.

Kate shook her head slightly and sighed. "I declare, the servants are getting so difficult these days. The news of Abraham Lincoln's Emancipation Proclamation must have got through to them somehow —" Her voice trailed off wearily as she dragged the rocker into the sun and sat down, a thoughtful expression on her face. "Not that I wouldn't be glad to see the end of slavery," she said, her gray eyes darkening. "I was raised with slaves, married a slave-owner, and my own father gave me ten slaves to bring with me to Virginia as part of my dowry. But my earliest recollection of its evil came when I was a child of five or six, perhaps. And the powerful impression was one of pity for the Negroes and a deep desire to do all I could to help them."

"But, Mama, you do!" exclaimed Garnet, disturbed by her mother's sad countenance. "There are no people better treated than ours here at Cameron Hall!"

"Yes, I know, but I have ever felt the guilt of it as a moral burden — lain awake nights wondering if it were impossible for a slave-owner to win heaven. I believe, if the truth were known, all Southern women are, at heart, abolitionists."

Then, as if with an effort, Mrs. Cameron changed the subject. "Well, how are things at Montclair?" she asked brightly.

Garnet made a wry face. "I guess they could be worse, but I don't see how. I would have welcomed some help and support from any number of women, but Harmony is such a ninny! No help at all!" Garnet complained.

Kate gave her daughter a look of silent reproach and said quietly, "Harmony is bearing up as well as she can under the strain. After all, she is without husband, home, and all she's been used to. We cannot expect others always to be as brave or strong as we ourselves try to be."

Garnet accepted her mother's gentle rebuke without further comment.

"And have you heard from Malcolm?" Kate asked with concern. "I think so often of that dear little orphan boy."

"Jonathan is *not* an orphan, Mama. Malcolm's not dead!"

"I should have said *motherless.* Such a tragedy!" Kate shook her head. "And Bryce? What news is there from Bryce, dear?"

"Not much. Bryce never was much of a letter writer. But I expect he'll get home when he can. It's Leighton we're wondering about."

Kate's face brightened. "Why, yes, I almost forgot. We got a letter from Dove and she plans to come and bring the baby soon. Here, let me read you part of her letter . . ." and Kate drew an envelope from her pocket.

"Dear Cousin Kate," she began and although Garnet listened with half an ear to the rambling description of Dove's baby girl's growth and progress, her mind wandered back to the wedding day of Dove and Leighton at Montclair in the first month of the war they all thought would be short and victorious for the South. Young men like Lee and Bryce had gone off as if on a kind of gallant adventure surrounded by an aura of romance. And no more were all those elements present than at the magical wedding at Montclair.

Garnet recalled the romantic atmosphere that day: how she had been caught up in its magic, secretly envying the mutual love she saw in Dove's radiant face uplifted to Lee's rapt adoration. For a moment she was stabbed with the stunning truth that she had never experienced that kind of love.

"So, they should be here within the month," Kate concluded, and Garnet returned to the present, knowing that she had missed most of the content of Dove's letter. "I think she should probably stay at Montclair, don't you, Garnet? I'm not sure it would be good for your father to have an infant here. Everything . . . even small things . . . seem to upset him now."

The shadows on the lawn were lengthening and Garnet stood reluctantly to leave. So much awaited her at Montclair — so much to be done. "I really must go now, Mama. But I'd like to see Papa first."

Standing at the doorway of the downstairs parlor that had been converted into a bedroom, Garnet felt the familiar constriction in her chest. How drastically changed her father appeared. The shrunken figure in the bed bore scant resemblance to the man who had once stood proudly erect, overseeing the affairs of his world with authority and vigor.

Seeing Garnet, Mawdee left her post at his bedside and lumbered over to hug her "Little Missy." Garnet leaned against the comforting bosom, wishing she could turn back time and become a child again — smothered by the love and pampering that had always been her lot until now.

When she hugged her mother good-bye, Garnet blinked back tears and left quickly, running down the veranda steps to where she had tied Trojan Lady. She swung gracefully into the saddle and turned the horse's head in the direction of Montclair, to where her new life, her new responsibilities lay. She turned several times as she moved slowly down the drive to wave back at the slim figure of Kate standing on the shadowed porch.

With a shake of her head, as if to clear it of its shroud of memories, Garnet snapped the reins. Her carefree childhood was in the past. She must face with courage whatever lay ahead.

chapter
26

Afterward, when Garnet thought of the year 1863, all the memories blurred mercifully into a parade of passing impressions. The winter was bitterly cold, but what was suffered at Montclair seemed insignificant when they heard of the cruel conditions under which most of the Confederate soldiers were fighting. With all their men in daily danger, the women could scarcely complain. They knew it was the same all over the South and so learned to cope with their reduced circumstances.

With shortages of all kinds Garnet and her little family became ingenious at finding substitutes for ordinary staples. Candles were in short supply, so they burned wood knots, split into manageable lengths and stored in baskets by the hearth. The fire kindled by the knots gave too flickering a light for reading or sewing, but cast a cheerful glow throughout the high-ceilinged rooms.

In matters of cooking, they were hard-pressed to discover adequate substitutes. Soda for use in baking bread was made from corncobs, burned in a clean-swept place, and the ash gathered into jugs, then doled out a teaspoonful at a time. Tea was made from dried berries of all kinds; okra seeds, roasted and brewed, were the best and came nearer the flavor of coffee than anything else. Berries and weeds were used for dyeing cloth.

Garnet found it was easy enough to be cheerful about shortages and substitutes. Those things seemed simple in comparison to her other heavy obligations. Never patient, Garnet chafed in the role of head of the household. A household of women, unaccustomed to hardship. A household of small children as well as childlike servants who never did anything unless specifically told to do so — and who often had to be shown how!

Sara was left to the tender ministrations of Dove, who was sweetness itself. Dove read to her by the hour or played cribbage with her to divert the older woman from her constant worrying.

Garnet had come to rely on Dove and to

see in her cousin some of the same strengths and sweetness of character Rose had possessed. Loving Rose had come late, but now Garnet cherished and valued her memory. Harmony was a different matter — Harmony, of the mournful sighs and dire predictions.

Harmony just missed being beautiful, and one never knew exactly why. She had ivory skin, light blue eyes, hair like golden wheat. Perhaps it was the vacuity of her smile, the emptiness in her eyes, which sparkled only when they rested on Alair, her fairylike daughter.

But even Harmony could have been endured if Garnet had not begun to feel a horrible depression. She covered it well. No one would have guessed that as the days wore on, she felt helpless and fearful much of the time. Yet something within her stubbornly refused to submit to defeat, and she continued as the leader on whom they all depended.

Garnet, who rarely in her healthy, young life had suffered from insomnia, now knew sleepless nights. One night after lying awake for hours, counting the strokes of the grandfather clock downstairs, she got up. Shivering with cold, she wrapped herself in a shawl and huddled near the fireplace, stirring the embers of the dying fire.

She knew why she couldn't sleep to-night. Thoughts of the Montrose men, all in the front lines of duty, marched through her head — Bryce, attached to General Stonewall Jackson's cavalry; Malcolm, still with Lee; Leighton, with Johnson. What if they were all killed? What if none of them came home to Montclair? What then?

She shuddered and could not stop shaking. The dark room filled her with terror. Shortage or no, she would light candles, chase away the frightening darkness.

Rising, she groped along the shelf beside the fireplace for the box of candles she had kept there to use sparingly. As she did, she knocked something to the floor, and stooped to pick it up. It was a book of some kind. Her hand felt the roughness of the leather. When Garnet returned to the light of the fire, she could see that its cover was blistered and charred.

Rose's Bible! Tilda had rescued it on the night of the fire, and later given it to Garnet. It was from this very Bible that Garnet had read to Rose the last day of her life.

Garnet lit a candle with shaky hands, then slowly examined the book. Almost re-luctantly Garnet opened the pages, leaning closer to the firelight to better see the words. Unconsciously Garnet's eyes roamed the passages as if searching for something. Ah, there it was — the Twenty-third Psalm. Even she recognized that one. She had heard it often enough at church services in Richmond. The minister had read it at Rose's funeral, as well: "Yea, though I walk through the valley of the shadow of death, I will fear no evil: for thou art with me; thy rod and thy staff, they comfort me —"

I wish I believed that, Garnet anguished. *I wish I were not afraid.* But there is so much to be afraid of, so much to fear, so much evil. The safe, secure world Garnet had always known had become a frightening place.

So many people were depending on her to be strong — and she knew she wasn't! She continued to read, stopping here and there to examine passages that Rose had underlined. One passage caught her attention — "I can do all things through Christ which strengtheneth me."

Her lips moved, forming the words, murmuring them out loud, the sound of her own voice comforting. Maybe she had stumbled on Rose's secret, her inner strength. *Through Christ* — not on her own, but *through Christ, I can do all things.*

Without fully understanding what she was doing, Garnet knelt beside the chair and began to pray haltingly to a God she had always feared. Unexpectedly a soothing warmth that had nothing to do with the sputtering fire spread through her, enclosing her in peace.

Every day after that, Garnet began to find comfort in repeating that simple phrase, especially in times of frustration or stress. And at night she began to read regularly from Rose's Bible until she fell asleep. At length she was able to sleep more soundly, wake more rested, feel better able to handle the crises that arose daily.

Although Garnet was unaware of the change, the others noticed a new patience in her.

chapter
27

War or no war, spring came to Montclair in its usual blaze of beauty. The children became as frisky as the new lambs in the pasture and the small heifers leaping through the high meadow grass. Acres of yellow jonquils and purple iris spread a tapestry of color around the house.

After the fierce winter the balmy weather of 1863 was welcome. Even the adults spent more and more time outside after the long months of confinement. Spring slid into summer, almost unnoticed. If it had not been for letters from Cousin Nellie and the regular, if sometimes tardy, delivery of newspapers, those at Montclair might never have known a war was being waged.

Garnet would never forget the day they had all gone out to the peach orchard to pick fruit for canning. The July sun was hot, and the children were running barefoot under the trees while the others stood on ladders, plucking the fruit from the heavily laden branches.

Alair and Jonathan were playing hide-and-seek, with Druscilla toddling after the older children on her fat little legs, laughing her gurgly baby laugh as she tried in vain to catch up with them. The sight of them sitting in the grass, eating the ripe, juicy fruit, their chubby hands stained, their moist smiling mouths, the sunshine creating little auras of light around each small head, would often come to her afterward. Garnet would see it clearly, vividly, as a treasured picture of the last day they had all been so happy.

Later when they went into the house, Garnet found one of the Negro men from Cameron Hall with a message from her mother. Its contents sent a shiver of fear like an icy finger down her spine.

Kate had sent word of a huge battle raging near a small town in Pennsylvania called Gettysburg.

The Battle of Gettysburg was like a saber, slashing into the heart of the nation, North and South. Casualties on both sides had run into the thousands. Montclair was struck by a series of devastating blows as news trickled in. Malcolm had been captured, taken prisoner, as General Lee's forces were thrust back; Leighton was missing, believed killed; Bryce had escaped, but the Confederacy had sustained an agonizing loss in the death of General Stonewall Jackson. A horrifying rumor was later confirmed that he had been fired on by his own men.

Bryce, who had been in the honor guard for the general's funeral in Richmond, arrived at Montclair for a few days' leave. He was depressed, saddened by the fate of his two brothers, and by the loss of his commander. Although he tried nobly to present a great show of bravado and optimism for the others, when he and Garnet were alone in their wing of the house, he confided to her.

"I've applied to join Mosby's scouts."

"What is that?" Garnet asked.

"It's a special unit authorized by General Lee to combat some of the Yankee raiding parties. It's made up of men who know the countryside, the woods, and rivers. It will be undercover operations mostly, scouting out enemy positions, then making surprise attacks and routing them."

"Sounds dangerous," Garnet murmured.

"Hah!" Bryce made a derisive sound.

"All war is dangerous. *This* kind I understand. Far better than lining men up and mowing them down, row after row —" His voice took on a bitter edge.

Garnet looked at the face on which the firelight shone, and realized how haggard it was. Bryce was far different now from the high-spirited, handsome young man who had ridden off to fight a knight's crusade nearly three years ago.

Garnet remembered having met Mosby in Richmond before he headed up his unit, and once Bryce had brought him home to Montclair on their way back from some adventure.

For a "legend" John Mosby's appearance was wholly undistinguished. He was thin and wiry, sharp-featured, with a kind of nervous energy that kept him from being still for ten minutes at a time. But it was his eyes that Garnet had noticed particularly, for they were keen, sparkling, alert as if they missed nothing.

Mosby's Raiders, like their leader himself, John Singleton Mosby, were a unique breed — planters' sons, for the most part, of whom Bryce was a perfect example. Bryce had cared little for education, never worked with his hands, loved horses and rode them superbly well, was an excellent hunter and a crack shot. In addition, he possessed the gracious manners of a born gentleman who followed the rigid, unwritten code of the South's elite class. His daring made him a prime volunteer for the Raiders.

Each man kept a horse or two and all were daredevil, reckless riders with a deep-seated loyalty to the Confederate cause and a wild streak that made them indispensable in the risky assignment they had been given.

Thereafter, as a member of the roving band of Mosby's Raiders, Bryce often made unexpected, brief visits to Montclair. They never knew when he might suddenly appear — usually at nightfall with a few of his comrades.

The very qualities that made them superior soldiers also made them wonderful company and welcome guests, and their coming was heralded as occasion for a spontaneous celebration. It was always a boost to the flagging morale of the small band of women to have these high-spirited young men in the house, and Garnet was relieved to see that Bryce had gradually recovered his old spirit and flair.

It was Dove who announced that in spite

of all that had happened, Christmas, 1864, must be observed. For the children's sake, at least, everyone pitched in to make it a happy occasion.

Bryce had sent word that he would be coming for Christmas and bringing some of his fellow scouts whose homes were too distant for them to spend the holiday with family. So the preparations were especially joyful.

With sugar so scarce, the baking of the cakes and other traditional holiday treats was a problem, but they used their few supplies with prodigal abandon. The children entered into the mixing and stirring with great enthusiasm. Afterward, they were allowed to lick the spoons and the bowl when the batter was poured into baking pans.

Garnet set Jonathan and Alair to the task of grinding the sugar cones into powder for the Christmas cake. The two worked with a will, using a little white stone mortar with a stone pestle until they were both flushed with the effort. Then, with Dove and Harmony each holding an end of a muslin cloth, Garnet poured the sugar through until it was pronounced fine and smooth enough for the recipe.

For the first time in a very long while,

the kitchen hummed with the sound of happy voices and cheerful activity and was fragrant with warm, delicious aromas. The store of delicacies began to mount in the pie-safe. Montclair had no lack of fruits from the orchards, and, as the women — black and white — and the children sat around the round oak table cracking nuts, seeding raisins, cutting orange peel it would have been hard to imagine that a savage war was being fought not too far distant.

When Bryce and his three companions arrived, they were greeted with happy excitement. The piano was opened and soon the beautiful old Christmas carols rang through the house, filling it with joyous melody. Suddenly Garnet was reminded of Christmases past when Montclair had been bursting with guests, song, laughter, and the sounds of dancing feet.

Even Sara responded to the gaiety and asked to be carried down on Christmas Eve to see the lighted Christmas cedar and to watch the children open their home-made gifts — cornhusk dolls for the girls, with pretty wardrobes made for them from Dove's and Harmony's scrapboxes, and a wooden stick horse for Jonathan, carved for him by Joshua. There were pincushions, "housewife's sewing kits" for the men, scarves and socks, knitted from wool grown, carded, and spun from sheep raised at Montclair. Whatever the gift, large or small, the exchange was wonderfully merry.

As they gathered about the dinner table the next day it, too, was reminiscent of pre-war Montclair. Days before, the servants had dug up the silver buried the summer before in fear of a Yankee raid, and had washed and polished it to a glowing sheen. Lovely English bone china dinnerware graced the table, covered with a fine drawn-work linen cloth, and set with crystal goblets.

Bryce and his fellow scouts had brought their contributions to the festivities, also, and the feast boasted fresh-brewed coffee, a roasted turkey, a ham, cornbread, sweet potatoes, plum jelly, and a variety of desserts that were "fit for a king," as Bryce later declared.

When at last the children were settled for the night, Bryce confessed that he and his men must leave at daybreak. There was always the chance that a roving Yankee patrol would be ready to ambush, and they wanted to be away before first light.

"But there haven't been any Yankees

sighted around here since the earliest part of the war," protested Garnet, hating the thought of another parting. "We're so far back from the road, and besides, Mayfield isn't near anything important."

"Still, it's best we go," Bryce said firmly and Garnet knew there was no use in arguing.

She went to check on Jonathan then. Standing over him as he lay sleeping, she felt an indefinable sadness. *Poor little boy*, she thought, mother dead; father — who knew where? But at least Malcolm had gone away knowing he had a son, and Rose lived on in their child.

Returning to their bedroom, Garnet observed Bryce from the doorway. He was slumped wearily in the wing chair, his long legs stretched out before him, staring thoughtfully into the fire.

There was something touchingly pensive about his expression, and Garnet longed to comfort him. Tomorrow when he left, Bryce would be riding into certain danger. With a wrenching sensation, Garnet realized that she was the only thing Bryce had left to love. His mother had never made any secret of her preference for Malcolm, and Lee held a special place as her youngest. All Bryce would leave behind, should anything happen to him, was a wife who had never really loved him the way she should have.

Garnet felt a moment of self-accusation along with the deep, abiding fear that always lurked in her wayward heart that she would someday reap what she had sown. The way she had wooed Bryce by wile, won him by false pretenses, treated his love with a careless indifference, longed for another man's love . . . all these were seeds of her own destruction. Every once in a while Garnet would be frozen with fear of her possible, probable retribution.

Was it possible at this late hour to make up for all she had withheld from Bryce? All that was rightfully his? Garnet was torn between the risk she might be taking and the fear of eternal punishment. What if she were sending Bryce back to war, back to his death without his ever knowing the fulfillment of being loved for himself? Always in her mind Malcolm had stood between them.

Now, she saw Bryce for the fine, loving person he was, and she was ashamed. For the first time Garnet thought about the vows she had taken . . . "to love, honor, cherish, obey." She had taken them without real understanding or commitment.

Drawn by something indefinable, Garnet walked over to Bryce and lay her hand on his shoulder. When he looked up into her face, his clear, blue eyes, as lacking in guile as a child's, sent a sharp thrust of guilt through her.

He reached up and took her hand, brought it to his lips, and kissed it, then looked at her again and smiled.

"Come sit down for a while and watch the fire with me," he invited and drew the hassock alongside his chair.

Garnet sat down, her skirts billowing about her, and held out her hands to the warmth of the blaze. The curtains were drawn against the night and the room had a cozy, intimate atmosphere.

She felt Bryce's hand upon her hair, stroking it, and she lay her head against his knee. Only the crackling and hissing of the fire broke the stillness of the room.

Perhaps Bryce remembered, in the tranquility of the quiet fire-lit room, discussions by men gathered around a campfire at night — the poignant dreams of the warm sweetness of domestic bliss he himself had never known. Maybe in this moment he was tasting it for the first time.

For these two who had always had so much to say, the silence was strange but not threatening. Words uttered merely to fill the silence would be hollow and empty. They who had chatted aimlessly, carried on social banter, argued and exchanged heated words, now rested in the quiet. Now that there were so many important things to say, neither could find the words to say them.

At the striking of the grandfather clock downstairs, they each thought of the hours flung away carelessly in the years past. Now it reminded them that only a few hours remained for them to be together.

They turned to look at each other reading within the other's eyes a longing, a need for love they had not recognized before.

Bryce lifted Garnet onto his lap, cradling her head against his shoulder, rocking her gently as he whispered, "Darlin', darlin', I *do* love you so much. I never knew how much until —"

"I know, I know," she murmured, tilting her head back to answer him.

He stopped whatever else she might have said with his lips — a long, infinitely tender kiss to which she responded as she had not done before.

The room seemed to recede as they clung to each other, murmuring endearments interspersed with kisses — each one deeper, more demanding, possessively passionate.

Bryce gathered up Garnet and carried her over to the same bed where their married life had begun. But this night the love they shared was far different than either of them could have imagined in another lifetime.

It was still dark when Garnet was startled awake by the sound of screaming coming from downstairs — high-pitched, terror-stricken. Without losing a minute, she threw back the quilt and ran out to the hall without slippers or robe. Leaning over the balcony, she saw the front hall swarming with blue uniforms.

She turned and ran back to the bedroom where Bryce was flinging on his clothes.

"Yankees!" she gasped, slamming the door behind her and trying to move the heavy chest in front of it.

"Look, darlin', I'll try to make a break for it out the window!" he told her. "If I don't make it —" He grabbed her by her shoulders and spoke low and intensely, "Open that mattress! Do what you can!" Then he kissed her, a quick, hard, ardent kiss, and dashed to the window, throwing one leg over the sill and disappearing from sight.

There was no time to do anything. The sound of stomping boots just outside the bedroom door signaled imminent danger. In another minute the door was crashed open, shoving the bureau out of the way, and the room was full of Yankees.

"Out the window!" shouted one.

"He won't get far! We posted men below!" another yelled back and, after taking a hurried look around, taking special note of Garnet who had pressed herself against the wall, they dashed out.

As soon as they had left, she ran to the window and looked out. Her heart sank as she spotted a circle of Yankee soldiers right under the window. Bryce was surrounded, his hands tied behind him. A moment later she saw the other three men coming out of the house between armed guards.

She watched, stricken, as the Yankees hoisted Bryce and his friends onto horses. Then they all galloped down the drive and out of sight.

Garnet stood rooted to the spot where she had last seen Bryce, until her common sense returned. She must rally her strength. The others would be depending on her — as always.

The whole household was awake by now — the servants, frightened; the children, crying. She dressed hurriedly. Then, composing herself, she descended the stairs to the kitchen to help with the children's breakfasts.

"What will happen to Bryce and the others?" wailed Harmony.

"They'll probably be taken to prison," Garnet answered flatly.

It wasn't until she had gone back upstairs that she remembered Bryce's strange last words. "If I don't make it, open the mattress." What in the world had he meant? But she knew it must be important somehow. At such times people don't use unnecessary words.

Curious, Garnet looked at the bed, still rumpled from her hasty departure. With both hands, she felt along the mattress under the feather puff. As she searched, she felt a ridge at the very end of the mattress, near the headboard. Taking out her sewing scissors from the basket on her bureau, she ripped at the heavy ticking material, struggling to penetrate it. When at last her scissors punctured the fabric, she tore it open to find a package of papers tied with string.

How clever of Bryce, she thought, wondering when he had concealed them there. Picking up the packet, she saw written on the top:

REPORT TO GENERAL R. E. LEE. EXPEDITE. URGENT!

Hands shaking, knees suddenly weak, Garnet sank down on the bed. Did Bryce really expect her to deliver these papers to General Lee? Her heart began to race. How could she possibly manage that? *Expedite. Urgent!*

However she managed to do it, it had to be done at once!

chapter
28

It was soon apparent why the Yankee patrol had been scouting in the vicinity of Montclair. A sneak attack on Christmas Day had placed the town of Mayfield in Union hands. Mayfield, the "unimportant" place Garnet had imagined would have no possible interest for the Yankees, was a part of a strategic plan to control all the railroad stations on the route to Richmond. With spies in the area, Montclair had been watched for weeks, along with other homes along the road.

This, of course, complicated Garnet's plan to deliver the packet of information addressed to General Lee. It must contain vital information, Garnet thought, or certainly Bryce would never have sent her on such a perilous mission.

She would need a pass to Richmond now that Mayfield was in the hands of the Yankees, Garnet knew. And to obtain one, she would have to go to City Hall, which they had commandeered for headquarters.

Extremely conscious of the papers she had sewn into the shirred satin lining of her bonnet, Garnet walked up the steps of the Mayfield City Hall, inwardly enraged to see the building guarded by blue-uniformed soldiers. As requested, she gave the guard at the door her name and the nature of her errand. Explaining that she must see the officer in charge, he opened the door for her courteously. But Garnet lifted her head high and swept past him, indignant at the thought of engaging in more than the necessary conversation with anyone wearing that hated uniform.

As Garnet entered, she saw another soldier seated at a table just inside. At her approach he looked up, giving her a swift, appraising glance. Something curious flickered in his eyes, and she could not be sure whether it was scorn or admiration. She had dressed very carefully in a green plaid traveling suit, trimmed with narrow velvet cording, and wore her most becoming bonnet. She stated her request once again. This time the soldier was less polite and brusquely motioned her to a seat where she must wait to be questioned by the commanding officer.

Garnet seated herself warily on the edge of a straight-backed chair and looked around her speculatively. She had never been in the Mayfield City Hall before, and she had certainly never expected to be here under these strange circumstances.

At that moment a tall, smartly uniformed Union officer, bearing a lieutenant's stripes, entered and glanced in her direction.

As he did so, Garnet's hand went to her mouth in a quickly suppressed gasp of surprise. In the look that passed between them, there was a flash of recognition then a warning, indicated by the merest drop of his eyelids and swiftly averted head. He seated himself at a corner desk.

Francis Maynard! Garnet's mind struggled to grasp the fact that he was wearing a *Yankee* uniform! *Francis a spy for the Confederates?* That was the only possible explanation.

Composing her face and consciously erasing any telltale expression, Garnet concentrated on her gloved hands folded tightly in her lap, tense with anxiety that she might by some inadvertent gesture give him away. If only she could get Bryce's message to *him*, it would probably reach its destination much faster than by the circuitous route she was still devising, Garnet thought.

But there was not a chance of the slightest sign of communication. The soldier who had gone to check on the availability of his commander returned, and politely asked her to follow him into an inner office.

It took all Garnet's willpower not to look at Francis again as she passed him.

Inside she waited impatiently to be acknowledged by the Union officer behind a massive desk. She recognized the insignia of a colonel. He was quite distinguished looking, with sandy-gray hair, and a well-trimmed mustache. Lifting her eyes to a spot above his head, she saw to her horror, the United States flag. She had not seen one flying hereabouts for nearly three years. The colonel looked up with a brief, indifferent glance before bending his head once again over the papers on his desk.

"What is the purpose of your trip to Richmond?" he barked gruffly.

"To see relatives, one who has been ill," she replied, her voice sounding whispery to her ears. She cleared her throat, hoping to make her next answer firmer.

The colonel looked up again, gave her a penetrating stare.

"How long do you intend to remain in Richmond?"

"Only a few days. Long enough to satisfy myself that my relative is recovering."

"With whom will you be staying?"

"My cousin, Mrs. Nell Perry."

"You are carrying no contraband?"

Garnet's throat constricted; her heart thundered. What should she say now? She was not quite sure what constituted contraband, but she felt sure Bryce's notes would be considered hostile to the enemy.

Noting her hesitance, the colonel glowered at her under his bushy eyebrows.

If they suspected her of lying, the colonel might order her searched. Reports of such things were numerous. The Yankees were on the alert for any rebellious activities among civilians, she knew. She drew a long shaky breath, but before she could answer, a knock came at the door.

"Come in!" the colonel called, and Francis Maynard entered.

Salutes were exchanged, then he placed a sheaf of papers before the colonel. "These require your signature at once, sir."

The colonel accepted them and began riffling through them. Then, as if remembering Garnet's presence, quickly took an ink stamp, pounded a slip of paper authoritatively, and handed it to her.

"Madam, your pass."

Weak with relief, and not daring to meet Francis's eyes again, Garnet quickly took the paper. Holding herself stiffly, she left the room and found her way out of the building. Yet she could not truly relax for the danger had not passed — not until she was safely behind Confederate lines once more.

Settled on the train bound for Richmond at last, Garnet thought about Francis Maynard, whom she had rejected as a beau because he had no spirit, no daring! Now he was playing a dangerous game indeed. The penalty for losing — a firing squad! How wrong she had been about him — about so many things.

There was no one to meet Garnet at the station. Cousin Nell's carriage and horses had long since been contributed to the war effort. Since there were also no hacks for hire, she picked up her valise. With Bessie, who had accompanied her mistress, carrying the other bundles, Garnet started out on foot in the direction of Franklin Street.

She was acutely and distressingly aware that Richmond had changed drastically since her last visit. The sidewalks were crowded with people, some of a type she had never before seen in the charming town she had once known.

Suddenly their progress was halted and Garnet felt her heart wrung with sadness as she heard the familiar sound of the funeral dirge played by a military band coming down the street. She edged to the curb and watched as the sorrowful pageant passed — the coffin, draped with black crepe and crowned with cap, sword, gloves; the riderless horse following, with empty boots fixed in the stirrups of an army saddle; the honor guard marching behind with arms reversed and folded banners.

This, then, was how some of the young men she had flirted with and kissed good-bye came home, Garnet thought, her throat raw with anguish. Here at last the war was seen in all its stark reality, and no one watching the grim procession could miss its fatal message.

She was greeted with loving cries of welcome by Cousin Nell. "Oh, my dear, I'm just now on my way to hospital duty. All Richmond ladies are needed to nurse the wounded." Her eyes moistened and she gave her head a sorrowful shake. "So many, so young. But I shall be home this evening."

She hugged Garnet warmly. "I am so very happy to see you, child. How you will brighten the place. Some young people are coming tonight and your cousin Jessie is here from Savannah. Perhaps you won't mind sharing your room with her. It's the one you and Bryce had. And how is the dear boy? Oh, dear, I do believe I'm late!" and without waiting for a reply, she bustled off.

When Garnet was at last safe behind the closed bedroom door upstairs, she carefully ripped out the tiny stitches along the inner edge of her bonnet. When the slit was wide enough, she drew out the small flattened sheets of paper, trying not to tear them. Glancing at the jumbled series of words and figures written hastily with the stub of a pencil, she assumed this was information about the enemy, written in code, they were some kind of code, probably gleaned in an intelligence-seeking mission.

Smoothing them out, she then slipped them into an envelope. As soon as possible she must get them to President Davis's office. Surely someone there would know how to get them to General Lee. Pray God, it was not too late!

Suddenly feeling the exhaustion of her recent ordeal, Garnet stretched out across the bed, reliving her part of Bryce's dangerous assignment. It seemed abundantly clear that she had been divinely protected. Certainly it had not been by chance that she had been interrupted at the precise moment the colonel was interrogating her about contraband. That she had received a pass so quickly, so easily was surely a miracle. She knew of others who had waited for weeks for such clearance.

She had heard of other incidents where women had been searched. The Yankees knew there were too many information leaks, too many maneuvers precipitated, too many battles lost due to skillful, surreptitious spying. It was a miracle she had not been even requested to drop her hoop from under her starched petticoats, an experience reported by a Mayfield lady only recently. It seems there had been a document discovered, sewed into the circling bands, on its way to the Confederate capital.

Garnet closed her eyes and whispered a prayer of gratitude. Angels must have gone before her to make a way, just as she had read recently in Scripture: "If ye have faith — even faith as small as a grain of mustard seed, nothing shall be impossible." She had found it in Matthew 17:20.

That passage Garnet had tried to memorize, convinced that her own faith was very small, but trusting His promise: "If thou canst believe . . . all things are possible." Even the *impossible!* Her eyes grew heavy and she felt herself drifting into an exhausted sleep. As she did so, she murmured, "Lord, I believe. Help Thou mine unbelief."

That evening it was like old times in Cousin Nellie's parlor, although there were many new faces and everyone seemed so much younger. Among the guests were quite a few refugees, people who had fled Yankee occupation of their homes. But tonight discussion of the War was curiously absent. It seemed that all wanted to forget for at least a few fleeting hours the reality of the Confederate plight.

In spite of her secret anxiety Garnet soon was caught up in the spirit of gaiety and fun. There was much merriment as they played a game of "Similes" and afterward, gathered around the piano for a songfest.

Earlier in the evening Garnet had been introduced to some newcomers — the lovely Marylander, Constance Cary, and her escort Burton Harrison, the young secretary to President Jefferson. As Garnet glanced across the piano, she saw him standing there, and an idea flashed through her mind. Who better than *he* to deliver her packet? But how could she pass it to him without being obvious?

Jessie had whispered that he was engaged to Constance and wasn't likely to leave her side all evening. Furthermore, Garnet wasn't eager to chance any malicious rumors by employing her old flirtatious wiles to take him aside.

The solution came shortly. As some of the guests were leaving, Cousin Nell tucked her arm through Garnet's and whispered, "We have been invited to Mrs. Davis's reception tomorrow!" She dimpled delightedly. "It is to be a musicale for the benefit of the hospital. Burton especially asked that you be included."

A perfect opportunity! Garnet decided. Surely at a large reception with people milling about, there would be a chance to seek out Burton Harrison and give him the papers.

There were light snow flurries the next afternoon as they set out for the Presidential mansion. The house purchased for the First Family of the Confederacy was elegant with spacious rooms, high ceilings, and a lovely curving stairway leading from the front hall to the upper stories.

As Garnet, Cousin Nell, Jessie and her escort, Captain Alec Hunter, a physician assigned to the Wayside Hospital, entered the foyer, Garnet saw Burton Harrison standing beside Mrs. Davis in the receiving line.

"I don't see the President," said Cousin Nell in a low tone. "He has been quite unwell of late. Migraine. Suffers dreadfully for days, they say. Then some sort of neuralgia, as well."

If circumstances had been different, perhaps, Garnet would have been disappointed not to see President Davis himself. She had often seen him riding, sometimes alone, sometimes with an aide, but had never been formally presented to him. Like all Southern women, Jefferson Davis epitomized for Garnet the Southern gentleman — tall, aristocratic features, impeccable manners, gracious demeanor. But today Garnet's eyes were focused on his secretary, Burton Harrison.

They stood in the slow-moving line of guests and when at last they reached Mr. Harrison, he greeted Garnet cordially, mentioning a humorous incident at the party the night before and expressing hope that she planned to remain for the musical program to follow.

"Oh, yes, indeed!" Garnet replied, giving him her most winning smile and thereby incurring the disapproving stare of Cousin Nell. "Shall we see you later?"

"Perhaps you could save me a seat beside you?" he suggested.

"With pleasure!" she responded.

In the adjoining room, chairs had been placed in a semicircle in front of the elevated platform on which a piano, a harp, and chairs for two violinists were arranged.

Garnet, who had secreted the small packet in her muff, sent up a silent prayer that somehow during the concert she could easily hand it to Burton with a whispered explanation.

After they had partaken of the refreshments set out for the guests, Garnet and Cousin Nell found seats, and Garnet casually placed her cloak and muff on the one next to her to keep it unoccupied until Burton Harrison could extricate himself from his receiving line duties.

Garnet smiled apologetically to several persons seeking a seat, murmuring sweetly that it was taken.

After several such incidents Cousin Nell

asked, "Whom are you saving it for? Jessie and her beau have already found seats."

"Burton Harrison." Garnet whispered back, and Cousin Nell raised an eyebrow.

Garnet mentally shrugged. She could not risk explaining. If Cousin Nell took the wrong implication, it could not be helped. Besides, her reputation as a flirt was well-established, and even now she was probably being discussed behind certain ladies' fans as running true to form — "And her husband a prisoner of war, too!"

In the end it all worked out perfectly. Just as the musicians took their places, Burton Harrison slipped into the chair beside Garnet. The program began and there was no chance to speak to him until the intermission. Then Garnet turned to him quickly. Putting her hand over her mouth so that no one else could possibly hear, she leaned close and whispered her message.

"I realize I am taking advantage of our slight acquaintance, Mr. Harrison, but I have in my possession a packet of papers designated for the President's or General Lee's immediate attention. May I ask you to deliver them?"

Burton's eyes widened and a look of incredulity passed over his face. But there was no time for further enlightenment.

He gave a quick nod.

Garnet put her hand inside her muff, felt the edges of the small bundle, and grasped it, drawing it out of its hiding place. Then, under the cover of their printed programs held at an angle, she passed the packet to Burton, who skillfully inserted it into an inside pocket of his jacket.

While the musicians were tuning their instruments, he excused himself and quietly left the room. Garnet felt the release of tension that had kept her in a viselike grip for days. She gave a deep sigh. Cousin Nell shot her a sharp look and, completely misinterpreting the entire episode, bent over and hissed into Garnet's ear, "The beautiful Miss Cary must have just arrived! Burton has made a hasty exit."

Garnet only smiled. Let Cousin Nell think what she liked. It was over at last! She had successfully fulfilled the trust Bryce had given her.

chapter

29

It turned bitterly cold in mid-January, and for the next two months the weather alternated between freezing rain, snow, and sleet. Throughout the South the common suffering endured seemed to strengthen an indomitable spirit. The belief that their cause was noble and no sacrifice was in vain did not diminish a heartfelt longing for peace. But that winter, peace was still far away.

At Montclair the outer storms mirrored the turmoil of mind and emotions of the three young women. Garnet, on whom the burden rested most heavily, tried to meet each day with courage and her newfound faith.

Not a single word had come from Bryce since his capture. Rumors were rampant that Mosby men had arranged a daring raid on a prison camp and that the captives had been hiding in the woods, waging guerrilla warfare. But Garnet knew nothing.

In her heart she was determined when Bryce came home — *if he came home* — it would be to a different kind of wife. Meanwhile Montclair waited in a kind of wary suspense for the return of the Montrose men.

It was, however, an immediate crisis that took their minds off the constant, insidious anxiety that permeated every moment of every day.

One evening as they gathered for supper, Garnet noticed that all the children looked unusually flushed. Both Alair and Jonathan were cross, and Alair gave the little boy a shove as they took their places at the table. He pushed her back, and a squabble ensued.

Dove quickly stepped between them, took a hand in each of her own, and began their mealtime prayer: "Bless, we beseech Thee, those from whom we are now separated. Grant that they may be kept from all harm, and restore them to us in Thine own good time. Amen."

Momentary quiet prevailed as Tilda came in with a tureen of stew, and Garnet began to fill the plates Harmony passed to her. But then little Dru started fussing, rubbed her eyes, pushed away her food, then climbed up on Dove's lap, sucking her thumb and lying limply against Dove's shoulder during the rest of the meal.

"What's the matter with you two?" Garnet asked Alair finally when another little tussle of wills erupted.

Alair gave her golden head a stubborn little toss and lifted her chin. Jonathan turned his large dark eyes upon her accusingly, and Garnet noticed they were glazed and heavy-lidded.

Tilda, who was serving biscuits and passing behind Jonathan, placed her hand on his forehead. "Why, dis here chile is burnin' up wid de fever, Miz Garnet!"

"Oh, dear!" sighed Harmony. "If Jonathan's coming down with something, the others are sure to get it, too. Come over here, Alair, baby, this minute. Come away from Jonathan. He's got something that's catchin'."

Garnet had to bite her tongue not to snap at Harmony. As though keeping Alair at the opposite end of the table would protect her if Jonathan did, indeed, have something contagious. After all, they played together constantly, lived in the same house!

Garnet rose from her place and went

over to Jonathan. Bending down beside his chair, she asked anxiously, "You feel bad, honey?"

He nodded, his little head drooped and he leaned against Garnet heavily.

"Tilda, I think we best get this boy to bed right away," Garnet said, lifting him and passing him into Tilda's waiting arms. "I better go get the Remedy Book and see what we can find to help us."

Dove followed with Druscilla as Garnet went into the library and looked for the book. With Dove peering over her shoulder, she skimmed the contents until she came to "Children's Fevers." They both read silently, then Garnet raised her head and met Dove's worried gaze.

"The first and most important thing, I guess, is to get their fevers down. It could be any of a number of things — scarlet fever, or . . .," and they both looked panic-stricken, "or worse, diphtheria or typhoid."

A forty-eight-hour nightmare followed. All three children were very sick. Head-aches, chills, then high fevers had them tossing restlessly and mumbling deliri-ously.

So that the children could receive con-stant nursing care, they were placed in the same room. Only Harmony was not any real help, hovering over Alair most of the time, getting in the way of the others as they changed damp nightgowns and bed-clothes, or tried to administer remedies. Harmony cried when Dove suggested cutting off some of Alair's curls, which were becoming tangled from her delirious movement and her refusal to be touched with brush or comb.

The nursing was constant as were the work and chores associated with three children so desperately ill. All the bed linens and garments had to be changed daily, then boiled and hung out to dry. In the uncertain March weather this meant sheets were spread before every fireplace, then often had to be ironed dry to be used again.

Each child had to be bathed three times daily, their dry, burning skin soothed with oil, poultices of hot towels soaked in soda water, mixed with a teaspoonful of dry mustard, and wrapped in flannel to relieve some of the pain, while compresses of tepid water were regularly renewed to alleviate the raging headaches.

The three women, Garnet, Tilda, and Dove, were running up and down the stairs dozens of times a day, while Linny and Carrie took over the laundry and cooking.

The three little patients could eat nothing due to the soreness of their throats and their upset stomachs, but Sara, complaining as ever, required her meals strictly on time and prepared delicately as always.

Three dreadful weeks of anxiety crawled by before the three children showed any signs of recovery. By then their aunts and mothers were ready to fall into their own beds from exhaustion and worry.

Garnet found continuous employment for the very first Scripture verse she had ever learned. Some days it was all she had time to pray, during those weeks: "I can do all things through Christ which strengtheneth me."

Little by little each child began to come out of the long period of illness, sat up in bed, and, finding the other children similarly confined, thought it something of a lark. To be read to and brought up trays of fresh soft-boiled eggs and dainty custards began to be fun after all the weeks of boiled tea and broth.

To Harmony's dismay Alair's hair began to fall out in huge clumps. The result was an angelic halo of close-cropped pale gold curls that gave her a cherubic appearance far different from the little girl's true mischievous personality.

Garnet could only thank God for His profound mercy in sparing all three children the dangerous complications that were possible with such a serious illness. She found she cherished even more the wonderful treasure she had been given in Malcolm's little son.

The dark days and dread under which the whole household had functioned suddenly lifted, and, to their surprise, they discovered that while they had all been preoccupied with the children, spring had come to Montclair in all its glory.

That year the season seemed especially beautiful to Garnet. The blooming flowers, the sunny days, the singing of the birds like some lovely symphony seemed to say that the war had been just a dreadful dream and not real at all. And yet, the cold of winter lingered in her heart.

When she allowed herself to think about it, her faith faltered. The loneliness, the weariness, the waiting for word that Bryce or Malcolm might have somehow escaped or been exchanged wore heavily. Now the Yankees had stopped exchanging prisoners, knowing how the South needed all able-bodied men to shore up their depleted forces.

Because of Montclair's isolated location, communication from the outside world had virtually stopped. Although they had heard of the terrible Bread Riots in Richmond, when hungry, desperate women with starving children had stormed the capital and broken into the storage depots, those at Montclair had not felt the acute plight of the poor city-dwellers.

From occasional letters Garnet knew Cousin Nell saw first-hand the bitter hardships the war had brought to Richmond, the drastic way the city had been transformed from the quiet charming place it had been.

Sadly "war profiteers" abounded. Gunmakers, contractors, wholesalers plied their trade aggressively and grew wealthy. Corruption, black marketing, greed, and indifference to the suffering of others caused by the very goods they manufactured and created and hoarded was rife.

If there was anything to worry about at Montclair, it was whether or not there would be sufficient fieldhands to harvest the crops come fall. Mr. Montrose had come and taken nearly eighty of his ablest workers to work on the fortifications at the southern harbors where it was feared a Yankee attack might be forthcoming. As wagonload after wagonload left, he promised they would be back in time.

Neither he nor anyone else discussed what was often a haunting horror in the backs of the minds of most Southerners.

Rumors of a possible slave uprising had run the gamut among the white people when the Emancipation Proclamation became effective in January, two years previously. Hatred of Lincoln was at a fever pitch throughout the South, and tales of Yankees infiltrating and stirring up trouble ran rampant. However, at Montclair and at Cameron Hall as well, the slaves still seemed unaware of what had taken place. At least on the surface everything was just as before, with the servants going about their tasks and chores quietly and as usual. If there were whisperings or news circulating of imminent liberation for their people, it was only in the privacy of their own quarters.

Certainly Garnet had no reason to doubt the loyalty of the house servants who had risen to every new challenge with surprising ease and had shown themselves unexpectedly adaptable to the added responsibilities. Tilda had been particularly dependable, willing, and able to help Garnet in everything. Linny had full charge of the three children. Carrie had become Sara's maid-nurse-companion; Bessie, formerly Garnet's personal maid, had become a fair cook.

There was so much to be done every day — the gardening, canning, preserving, and drying of food for next winter — that there was no time to dwell long on the shadow of uncertainty about the outcome of the war. But since Gettysburg, discouragement and disillusionment hung over the entire South like smoke over a battlefield.

It was the children who made life at Montclair bearable. They were allowed almost total freedom because the adults were so busy and preoccupied. They spent most of the day running barefoot to save shoe leather now too scarce to waste. Because of the clothing shortages they wore as little as the black children used to wear, growing tanned and healthy under the summer sun. It was a joy to watch them play together under the shade of the leafy trees near the house.

One day Garnet had just stepped out on to the veranda for a breath of fresh air, seeking a brief respite from the heat of the kitchen where they had been boiling a mixture of berries for jam.

As she stood there watching the children

at play, Garnet saw one of the menservants from Cameron Hall coming up the driveway on horseback, and a cold premonition gripped her. No one ever came from Cameron Hall these days; no one could be spared. Her mother's servants were as busy as those at Montclair. As the man came closer she saw it was Nemo, a younger servant who had helped old Porter in the care of Garnet's father since his stroke.

He dismounted and, wide-brimmed straw hat in hand, advanced toward the porch. It was then that Garnet saw his face contorted in grief and tears running down his cheeks.

Her heart lodged in her throat, Garnet moved to the top of the porch steps and asked through numb lips, "Is it my father, Nemo?"

The man bowed his head, nodding, "Yes, ma'm, Miz Garnet. I's sorry to be the one to tell yo'."

Garnet went to Cameron Hall at once. Kate held her as Garnet wept in her mother's arms, and tried to comfort her saying, "It's over for him, darling," Kate said softly. "He doesn't have to see any more of the tragic things that are happening to the South he loved, the people he cared for so deeply, the way of life he knew. We can't feel sad about that, Garnet."

Two days later, sitting beside her mother, pale, tearless, composed, Garnet looked out the open French doors through which she could hear faint birdsong, smell the fragrance of garden flowers on the soft summer breeze billowing the curtains inward. How could birds still sing, lilacs nod their lavender plumes to the gentle wind, when part of her world had ended?

The minister's voice was reading with the infinite sadness of one who had often, and many times recently, read these same words: "Blessed are they that die in the Lord . . ."

Had her father died in the Lord? Garnet wondered. Had he come to accept Jesus as his Savior before he was struck down with that lightning blow of paralytic stroke? She knew something had happened to change his former agnostic attitude, but when or how it had happened she could not be sure. She remembered his saying sometimes to her mother, "I wish I could believe as whole-heartedly as you do, my dear Kate! That is not to say I don't believe, I just wish I could be *convinced.* . . ."

Had he been convinced? He looked so wonderfully at peace when she had looked down into that beloved face yesterday. Garnet felt the constriction in her throat, the need to cry as stinging tears sprang into her eyes. She felt her mother's soft hand cover hers in gentle pressure, heard the minister's voice again, . . . "And God will wipe away every tear from their eyes; and there shall be no more death, nor sorrow, nor crying: and there shall be no more pain, for the former things have passed away."

Yes, the former things had passed away. That much was true. But what of the rest? Had her father found that those blessed promises are fulfilled?

Garnet fervently hoped so, prayed so.

chapter
30

Now Garnet knew that there would be no son for Bryce, no strong, young boy to ride his father's land, to learn to hunt in his woods or fish in its streams, to grow up and inherit Montclair.

The hope she had wanted to offer Bryce, a reason to go on fighting, to come home to, all vanished and Garnet felt a sense of purposelessness and futility.

It became harder and harder for her to drag herself through each day's duties. She felt helpless and fearful much of the time and yet something stubborn within her refused to give in to her circumstances. Ironically, she thought, since Abraham Lincoln had issued the Emancipation Proclamation, the slaves were free but she wasn't. She was tied to a house that wasn't hers, and had responsibility for three small children and an invalid. Dove and Harmony depended on her, too.

But with the coming of summer, Garnet rallied. The gardens and orchards at Montclair produced an abundance that year, and all of them spent much of every day outside — picking berries, gathering fruit. The children again grew rosy and healthy playing in the fresh air and sunshine, and some days Garnet almost felt happy.

Summer slid away and one dry, warm September day Garnet left the house and walked up along the hillside above the meadows. From there she could look down and see the ribbon of the river in the distance, the wooded area now here and there slashed with the crimson of a maple or red-berry tree against the dark green pines.

At the crest of the hill she turned and sank down on the grass. From where she sat she could see Montclair and the blackened wing with its windows boarded up where the fire had been — the fire that had changed so much for so many.

For her the change had been as sudden as the flames that had swept through that part of the house. For years she had dreamed of being Mistress of Montclair. Now she was, and with that role had come all the unexpected burdens and responsibilities unknown in that childhood dream!

A kind of numbed desolation seized her and she felt a desperate hunger to bring back her yesterdays. She saw them now as she saw Montclair — from a distance, with none of the inevitable flaws, and knew they were just as much a dream as her childish ones.

The idealistic view she had held of her father as invincible, of Malcolm as perfection itself, of her desires as attainable — she now saw as unrealistic fantasy.

She thought of that passage she had recently read in Rose's Bible and now began to understand. "When I was a child, I spake as a child, I understood as a child, I thought as a child." Now it was time "to put away childish things" — but it was hard. Garnet closed her eyes and a parade of all the lovely things that had been part of her youth passed before her — the gentle pattern of days at home, the sound of laughter and soft voices, the sense of comforting security, the low hum of singing from the quarters in summer twilight.

The happiness she had taken so carelessly, never realizing it could not last.

Gone, all gone.

Garnet turned and lay face down on the

grass. Grabbing handfuls of it, she buried her head in the meadow fragrance, spreading out her arms on either side. *Like a cross,* she thought pensively.

That's the way she felt sometimes, stretched to the utmost, broken. She heard that word so much. Especially lately. Sara was "brokenhearted" over Malcolm's imprisonment, over the sad loss of the way of life she once knew.

Brokenness? What do they mean by brokenness? Whenever Garnet had heard that topic preached, she had dismissed it just as she did any other thing she did not understand. This one or that one was "broken" — by bereavement, by sorrow, by losses of all sorts. Even her mother had used the word, saying that her father was "broken in spirit."

But there was another meaning, deeper and more subtle, Garnet was beginning to believe. It was a feeling she was experiencing more and more. That of being spent, devoid of her own strength, relying more and more on God. Almost without her knowing it, it had happened. The weariness, the heartache and, just when she thought she could not bear one more thing, something else always happened.

Yet somehow she had managed to go on,

taking care of the children, Sara and the servants. But as though she had some kind of invisible support. They all kept taking from her, drawing their courage, strength and ability to keep going from her, and still she was able to give it. It was as though their need supplied her giving.

It was strange. Again and again she turned to the mystery of it. She had heard once that Jesus had become "broken bread and poured out wine" for the salvation of men to nourish and sustain them.

In a way He was squeezing her by circumstances, by the burden of helpless adults and little children, by privation and loss — squeezing her like grapes into wine. Before all this had happened, before the war, before Rose's death and all they had to contend with here at Montclair, she had not been "ripe" to be squeezed. She had resisted, railed against her lot, been angry with God, hard. Anything that had come from her then would have been bitter, not fit to nourish or sustain anyone.

But gradually, God had done something in her. She was not even sure what it was, but she had slowly and gradually softened. She had stopped fighting the way things were. She had tried to make the best of what came along. She had tried . . . to love!

Loving the children wasn't hard, especially Jonathan, and baby Dru. Alair was a bit difficult sometimes and Harmony impossible . . . unless you laughed at her ineptness. Dove was a darling and not a problem. The servants were, after all, her responsibility, and like children, more easily led by love than harshness. Whatever had happened, God was using her, in spite of herself, to be the kind of "bread and wine" that would benefit others.

Garnet knew she had not completely changed. But she knew she was changing for the better. As the outer things of her life had been stripped away, she had discovered a tiny spark within herself that she was fanning into flame. As her self-interest diminished, her compassion, tolerance, and understanding for others grew.

She no longer had any illusions about herself. She saw herself for what she had been, what she still was. The word "brokenness" again came to mind — this time in a different context.

The more she had read God's Word, the more convicted Garnet had become. The commandments she had learned by rote as a child she now realized she had broken, all of them. Or nearly all.

But as she slowly got to her feet that day

and started back to the house, Garnet said
with David in his Psalm:

Thou delightest not in burnt offerings. . . .
The sacrifices of God are a *broken* spirit
A broken and contrite heart,
O God, you will not despise.

chapter
31

It was just before midday the second week in December. The weather all month had been unusually mild. The rains had ceased and, although the mornings were frosty, by noon each day the sun was bright and warm. The children, released from the confinement of the house during the dreary, gray days of November, were playing happily outside.

In the pantry Garnet was helping Tilda store freshly baked pies in the pie-safe when they both heard something, stopped suddenly and stood listening. Then their eyes met, Tilda's widening and Garnet's narrowing, as simultaneously the same thought struck each woman.

"Oh, Lawdee, Miss Garnet —" whispered Tilda in a voice that held the terror that gripped Garnet. The dread word neither of them could utter rose in both throats.

And then Linny, in a high-pitched wail, voiced the word. "Yankees! Yankees!"

Mingled with the terrified cries of the children was the thundering sound of horses' hooves and, as Garnet and Tilda looked out of the windows, they saw the blue-coated men on horseback literally surrounding the house.

Garnet went rigid as the noise and clash of arms rose to a frightening crescendo. Then her brain reacted, activating her muscles, and she rushed out toward the front of the house.

There she found Linny squatting just inside the front door, with baby Druscilla clinging to her. Dove and Harmony were huddled at the foot of the staircase with the two other children, their faces blanched with fear.

When he saw Garnet, Jonathan ran over to her and she lifted him up. From the long windows across the front of the house they could see the driveway, and the sight sent shock waves of horror over them.

The crescent in front of the house was a sea of blue uniforms — at least thirty or more galloping down the road and into the yard, running their horses over garden, bush, shrubs, and lawn. They came like a rushing wind, with loud shouts, blood-chilling yells, rifles lifted, bayonets glinting in the sun. Each new group arrived in the same way, their horses careening, sliding as their riders yanked their reins, sending them into dust-raising spins, their slipping hooves spitting gravel. Some reared, adding their whinnying to the men's strident cheers, shattering the quiet of the afternoon with the piercing noise.

Yankees! The word screamed in Garnet's mind, splintering her courage. Yankees here at Montclair. Her knees wobbled and she swayed, putting out her hand to steady herself on the stairpost.

A series of bangs of the brass knocker crashing against the front door made delay dangerous. Garnet set Jonathan on his feet, and, hoping the sight of this appealing little boy might soften the hearts of whoever was demanding entrance, she took his hand, saying to him in a quick, clear voice, "Now, Jonathan, you come with me. They're nothing but some mean old Yankees, and we're not to be afraid, hear? Your Papa and Uncle Bryce could lick 'em all singlehanded, but they're not here right now to protect us. So you've got to be the man of the house, and we're just going out there and stare 'em in the eye."

Jonathan nodded solemnly.

"Well, come on then," she said, and taking him by the hand, Garnet hurried out to the hall and unlocked the door and opened it.

A noncommissioned Union officer with a sergeant's chevrons on his sleeves, stood there. He had a broad, weatherbeaten face and looked hardened, battleworn. He gave Garnet a swift, appraising look and no greeting.

"We have come for horses and provisions," he said gruffly. "But we also have orders to search the premises. We've been told this house has harbored *rebels*."

"There is no one here but defenseless women and children and an invalid, sir. I would hope your men would have the decency not to disturb her further, for her health is very delicate and has probably already suffered great distress at your arrival." Garnet was astonished at how steady her voice was, for her heart was slamming so hard, her knees like water.

"Well, ma'am, as I said, we came for horses and provisions only, not to frighten women and children. So, we'll just be about our business, which should be profitable —" he added with a slight sneer. "We've heard Montclair keeps a full stable of fine-blooded horses and well-stocked storehouses."

Garnet felt indignation arise in her. What right had these invaders to come on private property and take whatever they wanted? She lifted her chin and took a few steps forward.

"You are mistaken. Most of our horses went with *our* men into battle. What is left are mainly farm animals, work horses that are needed to work the land and harvest our crops so that we will not be without food."

Again the man's mouth slid sideways, and he gave a scornful, mirthless laugh.

"It's a matter of indifference to us, ma'am, whether you rebels go hungry or starve. We need *work* horses as well as riding horses, to pull our supply wagons. We'll take whatever we need. But before we do, we have orders to enter this dwelling and search it."

"On whose authority?" Garnet countered, her hand tightening on Jonathan's. "I told you there was no one here but women and children."

"Ma'am, I mean you no personal harm. Just stand aside so my men can enter and search." He turned and waved a squad of five soldiers forward. Five more followed and five after that. They pushed past Garnet and within minutes the house seemed to be swarming with blue-clad soldiers.

"Where do you keep your arms?" the sergeant shouted above the rattle of clanking sabers and spurs as some of the soldiers started upstairs.

"Arms? We have no arms! I told you we are only defenseless women and children here." Garnet started toward the staircase in a futile attempt to stop the never-ending tide of blue coats. "My mother-in-law is a helpless invalid confined to her bed! I beg you, do not allow your men to frighten her by intruding upon her!" Garnet pleaded. Frantically she looked up to the balcony and saw Dove with Dru in her arms run down the hallway toward Sara's suite. Thank God! Garnet thought. Maybe Dove could keep them from entering Sara's room and terrifying her.

The sergeant was paying no attention. He stood at the archway leading into the parlor and was directing his men in their search. Garnet saw them lift the lid of the grand piano, poking down through the strings ruthlessly with rifle butts. She heard the cacophony of strings being broken, the crack of fine wood splintering.

They were everywhere, knocking against the delicate end tables, overturning the fragile lyre-backed chairs, yanking open drawers of the French chests flanking the fireplace.

A teakwood chest in the hall was flung open, its contents of linens, tea napkins, and embroidered cloths tossed out carelessly onto the floor, then trampled underfoot as the muddy boots of the men moved on into the dining room.

Garnet followed them in a kind of horrified trance. She saw one soldier try to open the glass-fronted china cabinet and, when it would not open, he took his rifle butt and broke the glass. She spun around and, facing the sergeant who stood in the middle of the hall, his hands on his hips, she implored with flaming eyes.

"Do your men have to do that? How would you like *your* home to be ransacked, your furniture broken and destroyed?"

"We are only doing our duty, ma'am, following orders," he replied without a change of his stony expression. "We were informed there were weapons stored in this house, and possibly fugitives from the United States government in rebellion." Then he stretched out his huge hand, palm up and demanded harshly, "If you'll give

418

me the keys to any other locked cupboards, chests, trunks or closets in which such might be hidden, then my men wouldn't have to use force."

Garnet looked at the shattered priceless china cups, Sara's prized Sevres and Spode, all heirlooms. She felt sick. How could these men do this? They weren't human, she thought with disgust. She gave the sergeant a scathing look and said through clenched teeth, "I'll get what keys I have. But from the sound of smashing upstairs, I'm sure I'm too late."

Still holding Jonathan's clammy little hand, she pulled him with her as she walked into the library to Mr. Montrose's desk where a ring of household keys was kept. There she saw more wanton damage. All his fine books had been swept off the shelves, scattered on the floor, kicked aside as the men continued their pointless search.

The sergeant was right behind her and she asked in a voice that shook with fury, "Is this really necessary?" She flung out her arm in a despairing gesture.

Ignoring her question, he said, tight-lipped, "Your keys, ma'am."

Garnet went over to her father-in-law's massive mahogany desk and drew the keys from the pigeonhole behind its small door. The sergeant was practically stepping on her skirt as she turned to hand them to him. He grabbed them out of her hand, raking the edges along the soft skin of her palm.

Unable to endure what was happening in there, Garnet left just as some of the soldiers had shouldered open the locked door into Mr. Montrose's plantation office off the library. As she went into the hall, she could hear more breakage and stomping behind her.

At the foot of the staircase Garnet was halted by a high-pierced wail from the kitchen area. She whirled around and, dragging Jonathan behind her, ran in that direction. Before she could reach the entryway, she heard the crash of clattering dishes. When she reached the door of the pantry, she saw Carrie cowering against the wall while a hulking soldier shook her by the shoulders so vigorously the girl's head struck the wall.

"Where's the liquor? Speak up, you little —" He called her a terrible name and shouted, "Where does your master keep his spirits?"

"Leave her alone!" rasped Garnet, bending over Carrie.

Suddenly another soldier called out, "Here it is!"

Garnet heard the sound of shattering glass, the splintering of wood, and knew they had broken open the inlaid and beveled glass cabinet in which Mr. Montrose kept his table wines.

Carrie sobbed, "Gawd hep us, Miz Garnet! Dey is takin' ebrything! Robbin' us ob all de food. I done tole 'em what little we had was mostly fo' de chillun."

"Never mind, Carrie. You take Jonathan. I'll try to stop them," Garnet said, her voice choked with anger. Her blood was pounding in her head, her breath shallow. She picked up her skirts and ran back into the kitchen. There she met a sight that defied description.

Soldiers were flinging sacks of potatoes, onions, and yams over their shoulders and disappearing with them out the back door and through the breezeway, tossing them across the saddles of their horses they had tethered to the posts. Then back they rushed, heaving sacks of cornmeal and flour in the same way.

Another group of soldiers was piling pots and pans into an empty flour sack from which they had emptied its former contents onto the floor. The sight of all this waste overwhelmed Garnet, knowing as she did the diminished state of their supplies. Now, their larder would surely be bare.

"Please! You're taking food out of the mouths of children, and an invalid!"

The soldier growled, "We have our orders. All stores found on rebel property is to be confiscated by the government."

Helplessly, Garnet turned at ominous sounds in the dining room.

There she saw two soldiers emptying out the drawers of the Sheraton sideboard in the dining room, throwing the ornate Montrose silverware helter-skelter into pillowcases they must have stripped from the beds upstairs. Enraged, she tried to make herself heard over the noise.

"Haven't you done enough damage?"

The sergeant simply glowered at her and snarled, "We're just doing our duty."

"Is it the duty of Union soldiers to enter private homes, to rob and steal everything in sight?" Garnet asked scornfully.

"Have you no honor, no decency that you would threaten a household of defenseless women with no man to protect them?" she demanded.

"Have your damn Rebel husband come home and protect you!" he retorted, his narrowed eyes cold as steel.

Garnet drew in her breath at the insult and saw in an instant flash of discernment that his mean-spirited nature was a mixture of envy, hatred, and revenge. Something in this man's life had formed him into this mold. She saw in his expression that, woman or not, Garnet was his enemy and should be treated as such.

The men went about their despicable tasks. One man looked over his shoulder at her and shouted an obscenity. Feeling nauseated, Garnet averted her eyes and with a great effort pulled herself away. She staggered back through the pantry and out into the hall. Carrie with Jonathan was crouched under the curve of the stairwell. She stopped there for a moment, murmuring some words of comfort or encouragement, hardly aware of what she was doing. Then she mounted the steps, dreading what must be taking place on the second floor as she heard the heavy clump of bootsteps on the floorboards.

To her utter despair when she reached the top of the stairs, she saw the spoilers had done their work as thoroughly there as well.

They had entered every bedroom, pulling covers and linens off every bed.

Nothing had been left untouched, bureau drawers yanked out, the contents overturned on the floor and tromped underfoot as the mad search went on. Curtains had been dragged down, draperies torn, armoires opened, and clothes indiscriminately scattered in every direction — dresses, bonnets, cloaks, and shoes tossed everywhere.

Garnet, standing in the middle of the hall, glanced down toward Sara's wing and saw Dove with Dru in her arms, bravely guarding the door.

She heard Dove's soft, sweet voice raised as two of the soldiers advanced. "Sirs, in the name of God, I entreat you. My mother-in-law is a very sick woman. The sight of you in her private rooms could kill her! I beg you to think of your own mothers and how you would feel if they were being treated thus."

To her amazement Garnet saw the two men, even as they mumbled oaths, turn away with shamed faces and start in another direction. This time Garnet realized it was her own wing of the house to which they were heading.

With a heart-clutching sensation, she thought of that apartment she had come to as a bride, all newly decorated and furnished, with the beautiful cabbage rose wallpaper, the velvet draperies, the marble-topped tables, the bedroom with its satin quilt and lacy pillows. All her jewelry and the little gold ormulu clock and her Staffordshire dogs on the mantlepiece, the globed wax flower arrangements. . . .

She closed her eyes and drew a long, ragged breath as she heard the sound of porcelain breaking, the tinkling sound of shattering glass.

Heartsick, she turned and started back down the stairs, her knees shaking so that she had to cling to the banister. The front door had been flung open and suddenly she heard the increased sound of pounding horses' hooves. She hurried down the last few steps and ran out to the porch just in time to see soldiers coming from the stables with the six carriage horses, the four chestnuts that belonged to Mr. Montrose, the two bays for Sara's landau. But it was when she saw a trooper on horseback with *her* Trojan Lady on a lead and with Jonathan's pony behind it that she threw caution to the wind. She ran across the porch, down the steps and across the lawn and made a grab at the soldier's reins shouting, "You can't take that pony! It belongs to a little boy! I won't let you!"

The trooper looked startled at first, then a mean, vindictive expression came over his face. "Let go my reins, woman!"

"Not the pony! You can't take it!" Garnet said dragging on the reins until the horse, tossing his head wildly, came to a stop.

Jonathan, who had followed her out to the porch, now stood at the top of the steps, sobbing and calling, "Aunt 'Net, don't let them take Bugle Boy!"

"I won't, honey!" Garnet screamed back and moved to untie the lead when all of a sudden a slicing pain snapped her head back and brought scalding tears to her eyes. The soldier had brought his crop down to hit her hands, missed, and in his swinging thrust had slashed her face. Garnet dropped the rope knotted onto Trojan Lady's lead and put a trembling hand to her cheek. It came away bloody.

"That'll teach you, you —" The trooper called her a name Garnet had never heard used in her presence. She only knew of its crude vulgarity by the way it was hurled at her. With the vicious attack the trooper spurred his horse, jerking its reins and rode off, pulling Jonathan's fat pony after him.

Another soldier riding nearby gave a

harsh laugh and shouted at Garnet, "I'd be careful if I was you, lady! This house is marked for burning! We know you've been harboring rebels! I wouldn't take no chance going to sleep too soundly tonight!"

Garnet stood there momentarily stunned, feeling the blood trickling through the fingers of the hand she held to her cheek as the noise and loud voices of the soldiers pounding by her reverberated in her ears.

Garnet, who had never been touched except in tenderness, gentleness, and love, felt the excruciating pain of the lash quiver from the side of her face all down her arm. Suddenly she felt the bitter taste of nausea rise up in her and she doubled over and slowly sank onto the dusty ground.

Everything blurred before her as the pain exploded in her brain and she fought the blackness of vertigo come upon her. She lowered her head and saw her blue skirt spotted with crimson.

Then Garnet felt a hard thud on her back and knew that Jonathan had run from the porch and flung himself upon her. His little arms went around her neck in a stranglehold and he was sobbing hysterically, the hot tears dampening the collar of her dress.

chapter
32

"Those brutes!" Dove said over and over as she and Tilda fussed over Garnet, applying cloths wrung out in cool water to her face, which was already beginning to swell. It was so painful that Garnet could barely bear the gentle pressure of their ministrations.

Harmony stood a little apart, looking on, wringing her hands and shaking her head, making small, sympathetic noises as the other two hovered over Garnet.

"Is anyone with Mama?" Garnet asked.

"Carrie's with her," Dove replied.

"Well, don't tell her about this," Garnet said, closing her eyes and wincing as the pad Tilda was pressing against her cheek sent pain searing through her. "I'll not go up. Seeing me like this would only upset her more." She sighed, then looked at Dove and said, "But we should probably give her a double dose of laudanum tonight if what that man said is true. If they're really going to come back tonight and . . . torch the house. Perhaps that was just meant to terrorize us."

"Her supply of laudanum is getting low . . . just like everything else." Dove shook her head.

"Well, we still have camomile tea," Garnet said wearily. "Whatever else, we don't need her in hysterics."

"What about tonight?" Dove asked. "What are we going to do?"

"I don't know what we can do but be ready to leave at a minute's notice." Garnet's head ached so furiously it was difficult to think. But she knew she had to try, help Dove plan. She could count on Dove to carry out any suggestion.

Every nerve in her body seemed to be twitching. Deep within her burned a fiery anger at the outrage of the morning, but she knew she had to keep it under control, to think clearly what would be best for all the lives under her charge.

"Oh, God, what now?" she heard herself moan.

"Garnet, you need to rest for a bit now. I'll come back later and we can talk . . . decide —" Dove said softly. "I'll go see Mama and check on the children. Linny is with them so they are all right for now. Except Jonathan — he's very upset about his pony."

Dove covered Garnet lightly with an afghan and tiptoed out of the room, leaving her alone.

It was impossible for Garnet to rest. She felt so helpless. What were they going to do? Without food? Without horses for transportation or for the farm work? But then what was left of the farm? The animals had been taken or killed. The fury of her hopeless dilemma swept over her and her muscles reacted, jerking spasmodically.

Unable to lie still, Garnet pulled herself up stiffly. She saw Rose's Bible that she now kept by her bedside for those sleepless nights. She groped for it, brought it up to her breast, clutching it with both hands, feeling the roughness of its blistered cover. Holding it against her, she rocked back and forth in a kind of agony. She remembered Rose saying once, "There is an answer for everything in the Bible. It wasn't just written for people living in those times — it has meaning for our lives now." Was there any meaning for what had happened to her that morning? Garnet wondered bitterly.

She placed the Bible on her lap and

prayed silently: *O Father, you know I'm having a hard time believing that You really care about me, about what's going on here. I want to believe, with all my heart, I really do! I want to trust You like Rose did, only somehow, it's harder for me. I thank You for what You've done for me before now. I know You helped me that time I had to go to Richmond, take those papers for Bryce. I know You are helping me manage things here. But, O God, I don't know what to do now! I am so scared, Lord. Show me in your Word what this is all about, what I should do!*

She opened the Bible, turning the pages one by one, until she came to Psalm 91. There her eyes rested and she began to read.

"Oh God!" Garnet pleaded aloud. "Give me *courage!* Whatever is ahead, whatever lies in store, don't let me give way!"

Garnet did not realize it, but in that heart's cry, in that act of flinging herself on His mercy and protection, she had come the closest yet to believing God is real.

That evening as it grew dark and night approached, struggling to mask their own fear for the sake of the children, the women went about shuttering the windows, bolting the doors, shoving furniture in front of them, leaving only one avenue of escape if the threat of burning was carried out. This was through the pantry, out to the breezeway that connected the kitchen to the main house. They decided that they would bed down in the dining room all together. The women would take turns keeping watch while the others slept if they could.

They fed the children, dressed them in warm, outer clothing over their nightdresses, made them beds of quilts and pillows in the center of the room. Childlike, Alair and Jonathan thought it an adventure and, since the adults did not betray their own apprehensions, they were allowed to make a game of it.

Carrie was stationed outside Sara's room in the upper hall so that she could be alerted at a minute's notice to help Sara out. Since she was the strongest and stoutest of the Negro women, she could easily carry the fragile invalid, if it came to that.

Everything was done now that could be done. To her own surprise Garnet heard herself say, "There is nothing more to do now but pray."

The other women nodded. They formed a circle around the children, who, with the innocence of childhood, were cuddled down and drowsy in spite of the peril that surrounded them.

"How shall we pray?" quavered Harmony.

"We'll pray the Psalms," Garnet answered with assurance unknown to her before. She got out Rose's Bible and in the flickering light from the stub of a single candle she began to read the Ninety-first Psalm, heavily marked by Rose's hand:

> I will say of the Lord,
> The Lord is my refuge
>   and my *fortress:* . . .
> My God, *in Him* will I *trust.* . . .

As she continued her voice grew stronger:

> Surely He shall *deliver* thee
> from the snare of the fowler. . . .
> He shall cover thee . . .
> Under His wings shalt thou trust. . . .

There was more assurance now in Garnet's reading:

> *Thou shall not be afraid*
> *for the terror by night,*

she read with great emphasis.

Nor for the arrow that flieth by day.
Nor for the pestilence
    that walketh in darkness.
Nor for the destruction
    that wasteth at noonday.

Her voice broke a little at this point, and there were soft sighs, low sobs from the women kneeling with her in the shadows.

A thousand may fall at thy side,
Ten thousand at thy right hand;
But *it shall not come nigh thee.*
Only with thine eyes shalt thou behold
And see the reward of the wicked.

Garnet swallowed, thinking of what had happened to them. It certainly looked as if the victors had walked away with the spoils. She went on steadily:

Because thou hast made the Lord,
    which is my refuge,
Even the Most High, thy habitation;
There shall *no evil befall thee,*
Neither shall any plague
    come nigh thy dwelling.
For He shall give His angels
    charge over thee.

A hush fell on the little group.

Suddenly a loud knocking shattered the stillness. All the women jumped. Garnet scrambled to her feet. There was a frightened moan from Harmony. The others stirred anxiously.

Garnet thought, *Oh, dear God, they've come to burn the house, to give us five minutes to get out!*

Her mind raced to Carrie keeping watch outside Sara's room. Should she send one of them to help her with Sara and have Linny get the children ready to run outside? Before she could decide what to do first, another knock came at the front door.

"Wait! Hush!" Garnet commanded the others. "Why would they just knock if they'd come to burn the house? We would have heard the horses! Maybe it's someone sent from Cameron Hall to see if we're all right, to help us. I'll go. Everyone stay just as you are. Don't wake the children. Not yet."

She took the candle and started down the dark hall toward the front door, not knowing what awaited her on the other side.

"Who is it?" she asked in a voice louder and steadier than she felt.

"Major Jeremy Devlin," came a deep, masculine voice.

435

Garnet held the candle higher and peered out through the glass panels on either side of the door. All she could make out was the dark outline of a tall uniformed figure. The voice came again reassuringly.

"I am alone, ma'am. There is nothing to fear, I assure you. I just want to speak with you. On my honor, ma'am."

"What do you want?" Garnet asked cautiously.

"I have come on a mission of my own as an officer and a gentleman, ma'am," was the reply.

Garnet hesitated only a minute longer, then dragged away the chest they had pulled across the door, slipped the bolt back and opened the door. In the wavering light of the candle she could see a man strongly built, wearing a Union officer's well-cut uniform. He bared his head and bowed politely.

"I have come to deeply apologize for the trouble, for the discourtesy with which you have been treated. The men who vandalized your home came here before I arrived at the garrison. I do not know on whose orders. However, I am here to tell you I will personally guard these premises so that your household can rest secure." At this he saluted, turned, and marched down the porch steps. Garnet watched, amazed, as he untethered his horse, then took a place on one of the lower steps.

She closed the door, overcome with a feeling of relief and gratitude. Surely it was an answer to their prayers, a confirmation of the words David had written long ago in the Psalms they had just been reading: *My God, a constant help in time of trouble. I called to you in my distress and you heard and answered me. Blessed is the name of the Lord,* she whispered.

In the gray light of dawn Garnet got up from the floor where she had been resting and went to the window just in time to see Major Devlin mount his horse and ride off in the morning mist.

For the next two days there were no Yankee visitations. But each evening at dusk a lone rider would appear at the bend of the driveway and take his post at the front of the house.

The household slept peacefully.

Two days later Garnet was in the pantry helping Tilda re-sack some of the flour they had swept up from the Yankees' wanton pillage when she heard Jonathan shouting at the top of his voice.

"Aunt 'Net! Aunt 'Net! It's Bugle Boy! Some Yankee's brought him back!"

Jonathan, who had been trying to help them, dropped the small bucket he was filling with cornmeal and ran into the yard.

Garnet followed him. A blue-uniformed officer on horseback was coming up the drive, leading the trotting butterscotch colored Shetland pony toward the house. He stopped as Jonathan reached him and watched as the small boy threw his arms around the pony's neck, hugging him and saying over and over, "Bugle Boy! Oh, Bugle Boy! You're back! You've come home!"

She recognized the officer. It was Major Devlin.

Garnet picked up her skirts and hurried forward, then she stopped. Her hand automatically went to her cheek where the welt from the trooper's whip had left an ugly, red mark. It had not been visible in the dark when he had come to guard Montclair. She wondered if he had also heard of that incident.

The Major again bared his head and said quietly, "I want to apologize again for what happened. It was a shameful deed."

"Their excuse was — they said we were known to be harboring Confederate soldiers," Garnet said scornfully. "It wasn't true."

Major Devlin frowned, shook his head slightly, "An inexcusable episode. Totally without cause." He paused, then said, "Strange, but we had entirely opposite counter-intelligence that this place was a station on the Underground Railroad, assisting blacks to freedom in the North."

Bewildered by his statement, Garnet did not reply.

"This pony was brought in along with other horses conscripted for army use, but I had not had an opportunity to inspect them until this morning. When I saw him . . . I knew there was no need for him and no use to us in his acquisition. I understand he belongs to this boy."

Garnet nodded. "Thank you for returning him," she said stiffly. She felt an urge to burst out with all the other things *conscripted* by his men, but thought better of it. The less said to the enemy, the better.

It was he who seemed to linger, openly enjoying the reunion of boy and pony. His eyes resting on the two seemed to soften, "My sister has a boy about your boy's age," he remarked thoughtfully.

Garnet drew herself up in her old defiant stance and lifted her chin proudly. "I hope he and his family have not been subjected to suffering such as we have known." Then she shrugged and added, "But then you are the victors and we the vanquished, and the fortunes of war are always weighed in the balance of the invader," she said coldly.

Major Devlin glanced away from Jonathan and regarded Garnet with a steady, direct gaze. She was taken aback by the expression of genuine regret, almost sadness, in his clear, gray eyes.

When he spoke his voice was edged with melancholy, "This war will leave no man the victor. It is a cruel travesty on the dreams our mutual forefathers envisioned for this nation. American against American, state against state, brother against brother. The wounds, both North and South, have been deep and will not soon nor easily be healed. I pray to God that this child and all the children of this land will eventually build something stronger and better over the scar."

Major Devlin bowed slightly from the waist, gave Garnet a salute at the brim of his hat, then turned his horse and cantered back down the driveway.

Garnet stood watching him until he was out of sight.

Afterward Garnet kept thinking about

what Major Devlin had said. She had not known much more than rumors about the so-called Underground Railroad. Before the War she had been too self-centered to think of anything else. Now she wondered. Could Rose have been in any way involved? One by one, random thoughts began to fall into place, forming a tapestry of understanding. Rose's sympathy with the slaves: She had been secretly teaching her own servants to read and write. That had come out when the three, Tilda, Carrie and Linny, had confessed why they were all in Rose's bedroom the night of the fatal fire.

Then, how did Rose alone know about the hidden room in Jonathan's nursery? Had she held black people there and somehow sneaked them out to freedom?

Lizzie! Garnet gasped. Had Rose even helped Lizzie escape?

Slowly the probable truth gripped Garnet, followed by a kind of awed admiration. How daring of her! How brave to have risked so much for her convictions that slavery was wrong!

Garnet thought of those heavily underlined passages in Rose's Bible: "I can do all things through Christ which strengtheneth me." How much fragile, gentle Rose must

441

have relied on the Word of God to give her the courage to carry out such dangerous tasks.

Regretfully, Garnet wished she had known Rose better, allowed herself to love her sooner.

chapter
33

The first week of April the weather was beautiful. The trees wore pale green halos as the delicate first foliage began to appear. The orchards blossomed into canopies of pink and white fairy lace. Walking through the sweet-scented paths, Garnet breathed in the perfumed air, relishing the beauty as if for the first time, realizing she had often taken happiness for granted in the past, never knowing each day should be treasured.

That spring, bad news followed bad news. The crumbling of the Confederacy came as hammer blows of heartbreak as one after the other of the strongholds fell before the sheer numbers of the enemy that now seemed invincible. Vicksburg, then Atlanta, taken over by the Federal forces. At Montclair, infrequent letters from friends and relatives related the dire disasters that had befallen those in the path of Sherman's ruthless drive to the sea.

Although all seemed entirely lost, Cousin Nell's notes relayed that Richmond was still putting up a gallant front. President Davis was maintaining morale in spite of the tragedy of the death of his small son "little Joe" in an accident.

Then like the proverbial last straw — when the word came that Charleston had surrendered, the soul of the Confederacy was broken. Where it all began, it ended.

Within days the pretense that the remnants of the Confederate army would fight on was discarded. Lee surrendered his weary, hungry troops to Grant and the hopes of the South were finally shattered. President Davis and his cabinet evacuated Richmond, and within forty-eight hours Richmond was occupied by federal troops. The war was over after four endless years. On top of the dreadful defeat they suffered, the South was stunned by the shocking tidings of Lincoln's assassination. Now they girded themselves for a personal apocalypse believing the vengeance of the North would be terrible.

Finally word reached Montclair that Leighton had died of wounds and illness in a Yankee prison hospital. Dove's brave resignation was an inspiration even as they mourned him with her.

As summer approached, Garnet worried not only about Bryce but about what they would do about the acres of unplowed, unplanted fields. The fieldhands who had come back after being recruited by the Army showed no inclination to work, and Garnet hoped desperately Mr. Montrose would soon come home and take over some of these responsibilities. The last letter they had from him was posted in Georgia, where he had gone to oversee some of the fortification building. They knew that no one who had been connected with the Confederate government, as he had been, would now be allowed to travel through "occupied territory" without taking an oath of allegiance to the United States. Garnet was not sure the proud, stubborn Clay Montrose would ever bow to that demand.

For those at Montclair the day to day effort for survival seemed overshadowed by the new fears that sharpened their ordinary daily life. The Negroes, informed of their freedom, began to slip away, leaving work undone, fields unplowed, wandering the countryside in search of their liberators and the new life promised them. The Yankee raid that had depleted their stores had not been replenished, and the gardens were still unplanted.

Men began to straggle home. Harmony got word her husband was coming and they all went to the Mayfield depot to meet him. The scene this time was a far cry from the days when they had seen their eager, youthful soldiers off to battle. Then the air had been filled with gaiety and gallant promise.

When Clint Chance stepped off the train, Garnet hardly recognized him as the strong, young man she had known. Harmony burst into tears at the sight of his worn, hollowed face, his shoulders sagging under the once-trim gray uniform, now torn and stained. He gathered his wife into his arms silently. As his eyes met Garnet's over her head, only she saw the utter weariness and defeat in them.

Clint and his little family left soon to go to his parents' plantation outside of Winchester, though they were uncertain as to how it had survived its Yankee occupation. Guiltily, Garnet felt no real regret at seeing them go. It meant fewer mouths to feed, and besides, Harmony had never been any great help.

One morning soon after, they came

down for breakfast and found Bessie had departed. Tilda informed them that she had packed all her things the day before and left at dawn. It was only one more incident in all the other changes of the postwar South. The same thing was happening in the households of most of the people they knew. A whole new order was being established, and no one knew exactly how it would evolve.

Then one night toward the end of April, Garnet went to bed after a particularly wearying day. It had started raining early in the evening and it rained all night. The wind rose and the rain and wind beat upon windows, sending the boughs of the trees scraping against the house. Garnet had fallen asleep to the sound and did not know why she awakened.

Wide awake she sat up in bed listening — for what she did not know. It was then she heard hoofbeats on the crushed shell drive below. Her heart thumped in alarm. There had been bands of renegades, stragglers, deserters from both armies seen in the vicinity over the weeks since the surrender, and she was frightened.

She got out of bed, moved cautiously over to the window and, concealing herself behind the curtain, peered out into the misty night. She saw a single horseman coming slowly up the drive. She went out into the hallway, then padded barefoot down the stairway across the lower hall and to the front door. She looked out one of the glass panels, holding her breath.

As the figure on horseback came nearer, Garnet stiffened. As she watched, she saw the shadow of Josh, the faithful groom who had taken to sleeping on the veranda at night to protect the household. Instantly he was on his feet, rushing down the steps toward the stranger. Garnet stood frozen as Josh took hold of the horse's bridle with one hand, then used the other to support the rider's body that was slumping forward.

In the same instant she realized who it was and flung open the door, she heard Josh nearly sobbing, "Lawdy, lawdy, Miz Garnet! It's Marse Bryce!" He was staggering under the burden of the taller, heavier man. Garnet rushed to help, hardly aware of the gravel cutting into the soles of her bare feet.

Bryce gave a groan as they half-carried, half-dragged him down from the horse. Garnet saw that one arm hung useless, and his torn uniform was stiff with blood.

"Go get somebody to help!" Garnet ordered Josh. "Quick!"

The rain was soaking her, her unbound hair streamed into her face, her nightgown was clinging to her. She knelt beside Bryce, knowing they must get him into the house, tend to his wound.

Josh was back with one of the younger men, and together they picked Bryce up and carried him into the house. By this time Dove had awakened and was standing at the top of the stairs.

"It's Bryce!" Garnet told her hoarsely. "He's been hurt."

Dove ran down the steps. She took in Garnet's condition and said, "You're wet through, Garnet. Go get changed. I'll help Bryce."

Her teeth chattering from the chill, Garnet threw on her clothes and was back downstairs in a flash. The men had laid Bryce on a sofa in the parlor, and Dove had cut away the sleeve of his coat, revealing a bullet wound in his upper arm that had splintered the bone. It had been primitively treated, for it was festering.

Dove's and Garnet's eyes met in alarm.

"We'll have to go for the doctor in Mayfield tomorrow," Garnet said through stiff lips. Blood poisoning could have already started, she realized. "We'll clean it as best we can tonight and . . . pray!"

Bryce was out of his head with fever. Garnet wasn't sure whether he knew he had somehow made it home. She leaned over him to hear what he was mumbling, then straightened and nodded to Josh.

"It's his horse he's worried about. Take him out to the barn, Josh. Rub him down, see he gets some oats."

Together Garnet and Dove cleansed and wrapped Bryce's arm, made him as comfortable as they could. They were afraid to move him until the doctor had seen the arm, afraid they might start the bleeding again, that a piece of shattered bone might pierce an artery.

Tilda, aroused by the stir, had come out from the room near the kitchen where she slept, and helped the other two women. When Dove went back to bed, Tilda remained beside Garnet in her vigil.

Josh left early the next morning and brought back a young doctor recently paroled, who had served as an Army surgeon in Richmond. He examined Bryce immediately.

Garnet took one look at Dr. Myles's face and a cold certainty wrenched her heart. He had dressed Bryce's wound, left powders for the fever, but there was something in his eyes that betrayed the professional cheerfulness of his voice.

When he said gravely, "It's a matter of time," she was not exactly sure whether he meant "until he's well" or "until he dies."

"I've seen many men in worse condition recover, Mrs. Montrose," he told her. "Your husband has suffered from exposure and the wound has gone untended who knows how long . . . but with good care —"

Dr. Myles repacked his bag with a sigh. Something in his voice chilled Garnet's heart, something in his eyes betrayed a cold certainty when he added, "Only time will tell —"

She thrust back the fear that rushed up inside her. In its place came a fierce determination. She would not let Bryce die. He couldn't die! Not before she had a chance to show him how much she had changed, how much she regretted her selfishness. Please God, not before she had a chance to make up to him for all that she had not done that might have made him happier.

Garnet knew it was wrong to bargain with God, but in spite of that, her prayers took on a desperate quality as she vowed to do everything in her power to nurse Bryce back to health.

There was something redemptive in each

task Garnet set herself to, as if in a way she was doing penance for all the wrongs she had done Bryce. The first and worst was marrying him when she had not really loved him, depriving him of a wife who would have loved him more completely. She hoped somehow she would be forgiven for that sin even though she found it hard to forgive it in herself.

She found a kind of exaltation in the very menial nature of all she did, serving him in the necessities without which he would not have been comfortable, nor be healed and eventually recover — as if in doing these things, she was compensating for all the times she had not treated him with kindness or consideration.

"Thank God, he did not die!" she whispered to herself as she hovered over his bed, washing his wasted frame, turning the hot fever-warmed pillow, gently combing his thick, wavy hair.

Whenever he opened his eyes, hazy and drugged with fever, he seemed surprised to see her. He murmured something unintelligible and weakly held her hand. She had to bend low to hear the words of gratitude he whispered.

She felt ashamed. She deserved no gratitude. She only wanted him to live. But as the days passed and there was no improvement, Garnet grew frantic.

Word had gone out to the quarters, and the few remaining Negroes gathered in little clusters under the bedroom window each morning to see if Marse Bryce had lived through the night. Garnet would go to the window and raise her hand and nod, and they would move away slowly, murmuring among themselves, shaking their heads. Bryce was well-loved among the Montrose people. She had never heard him say an unkind word to any of them.

Mom Becca, Bryce's old nurse, long crippled with arthritis, had not worked for years. She spent her days sitting either by the fire in her little cabin or in the sun in front of it. Now she daily shuffled laboriously up the stairway of the big house and took a place outside the bedroom door, where "ma baby" lay nearly unconscious most of the time.

One day late in the afternoon, Garnet was sitting alone beside the bed and Bryce opened his eyes, for once seeming clear and lucid. He moistened his cracked lips, raised one hand weakly and motioned her closer. She leaned down to hear what he wanted to say.

"We're two of a kind, darlin'." His fingers curled around her hand. "We thought our world was the only one." He shook his head, his sad gaze upon her. "It isn't, you know. You're finding that out, too, my poor little Garnet." His eyes widened, grew bright with tears.

"People like us are a dying breed. Nobody out in the real world gives a tinker's dam about us. They call us the idle rich. Only a handful of us are left even in the South. We lived in a dream. Even thought war was some kind of glorious game. But it wasn't." His eyes grew wild, his grasp on her hand tightened painfully. "It was *hell!*"

"I saw it . . . it was hell! I believe in hell, Garnet. I didn't always before, but now I know what it must be like —"

"Please, Bryce, save your strength, honey," she pleaded.

"I just want to know it was worth it," he groaned.

"Yes, it was worth it," she said, frightened that she might not be able to control him. "Lie back now, honey." She smoothed the sheet soothingly.

"Life is precious, Garnet. I've seen so much wasted."

Garnet began to stroke his hand. She wished Tilda would come in so they could give him one of those powders the doctor had left.

His head moved restlessly on the pillow, then his eyes closed wearily. "You don't understand . . . but how could you?"

"Please, Bryce, don't get so excited, honey, it's bad for you."

Bryce struck the mattress weakly with a clenched fist. Two tears rolled down from under his closed eyelids over the hollowed cheeks.

He seemed to fall into an agitated slumber after a while and Garnet, looking down at him, tried to recall the dashing young officer in his slouch hat, his fresh uniform and shiny boots who had ridden away through the gates of Montclair four years ago accompanied by his black body servant and two fine horses. The picture faded as she tried to bring it back, much as if it had never been.

She couldn't think about the past. She must think of the future. *That's the only way I can keep from falling apart,* Garnet told herself, willing the weak, grieving part of herself into iron.

The only way I can stand what's happened is to believe that things will be better. I will be better, too. I'm better than I used to be. She looked down at the gray, thin face on the pillow. When Bryce was well, he would see how she had changed.

Not that she didn't still have a temper or get easily annoyed by stupidity or slowness. But that was mostly because she had discovered she had a brain and could often see better ways to get things done. She'd had to change these last years. But she wanted Bryce to benefit from those changes. More than anything else, she wanted the chance to be a better wife to him, better than the old Garnet would have even chosen to be.

But soon Garnet realized she would never have that chance. The doctor's next visit confirmed her worst fears. "No need for me to come any more unless there is some crisis." By that she knew he was telling her there was no hope.

Bryce slept more and more, waking for brief intervals. Garnet left him only to bathe, rest, or eat something to keep up her strength. Always the bulky black figure at the door remained. Every once in a while, Mom Becca would give a heavy sigh and say mournfully, "Glory, glory, sweet Jesus."

One evening Garnet was alone with Bryce, Tilda having gone for a little rest and Mom Becca persuaded to lie down.

Sitting in the shadows with only the dim light of one lamp, Garnet became conscious Bryce was stirring. She went at once to him, bending near.

He opened his eyes, tried to smile. She leaned down, took his hand, pressed it to her breast, trying to hear the hoarse, whispered words.

"Thank you," he said.

Garnet's heart contracted.

"There's nothing to thank me for, Bryce," she protested. Inside she grieved, inside she confessed, *I never loved you the way I should have, or appreciated you. I loved another man most of our marriage.*

But Garnet knew better than to ease her own conscience by unburdening her guilty secret to a dying man. It was too late to do anything but give him comfort as he slipped away. His voice was weak, but she bent close and heard him say, "Rose was right, you know. About life — and after. I'm sure of it now —" His voice faded away.

At first Garnet did not understand what he meant about Rose. Then she remembered Rose had believed in "a place of beauty, light, and peace" after death, and she reached for the little book and asked, "Would you like me to read something for you, honey?"

Garnet turned her head and saw lying on the bedside table the small worn black leather New Testament and Psalms Rose had given Bryce before he went to war. She recalled the day she had seen it lying near a pile of freshly ironed shirts he was packing and questioned him about it.

"What in the world is *this?*" she had asked, for Bryce was not a reader.

"Rose's going-away gift to me." Bryce had grinned disarmingly. "Said I should carry it in the pocket right over my heart. Maybe she thinks it will protect me from a stray Yankee bullet. I hear they can't shoot worth a hang."

"Surely Rose doesn't think *you're* a true believer like *she* is!" Garnet winced, remembering the sarcasm in her words.

Somehow the small volume had survived the months of battle, the weather, the rough riding Bryce had been through. They had found it in the inside pocket of his uniform jacket when they had cut it off him. A sob pressed against Garnet's throat as she thought of how she had read to Rose from her Bible the last day of her life.

His eyes were closed. *He's sinking fast,* something warned her. Still holding Bryce's hand, Garnet fumbled through the pages of the book with the other and found

a well-marked passage in Psalms. She wondered how often Bryce must have read this
by the light of a campfire to have underlined it so many times.

Slowly, haltingly she began to read:

The Lord is my strength and song,
And is become my salvation. . . .
The Lord has chastened me sorely:
But He has not given me
    over unto death.

Open to me the gates of righteousness:
I will go into them,
And I will praise the Lord:
This is the gate of the Lord,
Into which the righteous shall enter.

I will praise thee:
For thou hast heard me,
And art my salvation.

There was a sound from Bryce. Garnet
stopped reading, sank to her knees beside
the bed. Bryce was trying to tell her something.

"You've been so good to me."

"Not half good enough," she said brokenly. "Not what you deserved."

"You've been all I've ever wanted," he said.

She held him in her arms until his head dropped to one side and she knew with a sudden sense of abandonment that he was gone.

Garnet did not know how long she knelt there, feeling the weight of Bryce against her shoulder. After a while she laid his head gently on the pillow and got up.

She moved slowly, stiffly, over to the window and looked down into the garden where the rose bushes were in full bloom, so heavy they drooped their heads and fell in a flutter of petals onto the ground. No one had bothered to pick them, for the whole household had been suspended during the last few days as "Marse Bryce" lay dying.

Now he was gone, and so was Leighton, and her father, her brother Stewart, and Rose, gone *where?* The tears she had held back so long began to flow now as she thought in anguish what Bryce had said . . . "I'm sure of it now —" Garnet leaned against the window frame. She felt a bittersweet pain. Bryce had gone, left her and now he knew, and she did not.

He had spoken of "wasted lives" that day his mind was so clear. Their life together had been wasted. She knew it was true even as she knew it was useless to regret. He had also said, "We're two of a kind." That also was true. Headstrong, reckless, spoiled — but they had both grown and they might have become more, much more together, given time. They might have one day had children together, Garnet mourned, and she put her head into her hands and sobbed out her remorse.

But Garnet had not yet shed all her tears.

chapter
34

Only his son's death and funeral would have ever induced Clay Montrose to take the despised oath of allegiance in order to come home in time to bury Bryce.

War had taken its toll on the sturdy, youthful looking man. The twinkle was gone from his eyes, the spring from his step. The uprightness of his proud carriage was bowed now beneath the weight of the years of suffering.

Garnet watched his approach from the parlor windows, saw him mount the veranda steps with a kind of leaden weariness. She saw him stop short at seeing the crêpe-hung front door, throwing one arm up in front of him as if warding off a blow. She turned away and walked into the hall to meet him.

A small band of neighbors and friends gathered in the other parlor to mourn the second Montrose son to fall in the service of the Confederacy. Only the year before, they had been present at her father's funeral at Cameron Hall.

Garnet stood with her father-in-law to receive their condolences, to hear people remark in amazement at her calm and strength.

In truth, Garnet herself was awed by the deep peace she felt. Maybe the full impact of Bryce's death and the grief would come later, but now she was in a state of transcendent thankfulness. Bryce was beyond pain and the bitterness she saw in some of the other eyes that gazed into her own. It seemed to her in these last weeks that she and Bryce had been closer than they had ever been, that she had been given a priceless gift.

In the past two days her mind had been cleared into a startling truth that stunned her. She knew now that what she had imagined love to be did not exist. It had all been an illusion. Like her love for Malcolm. It seemed to her now some kind of sickness, a shallow hope without foundation that had bred within her jealousy and bitterness, near hatred for someone innocent — Rose! More than that, it had led her into a loveless marriage. Another sin against an innocent person — Bryce!

Now she knew with a knowledge born of grief and loss what love really was. She had learned it in the days she had nursed Bryce, praying for forgiveness. The old Garnet would never have imagined that one day she would sit beside a man, broken in body, mind and spirit, and know the true, full meaning of love.

For weeks after Bryce's death, Garnet could not sleep at night. She paced the floor restlessly, her mind as wide awake as if it were morning. Sometimes she slept for a few hours toward dawn on the chaise lounge in her dressing room. Somehow she could not bring herself to sleep in the bed Bryce had died in, the one they had shared through their tempestuous marriage.

She did not know what to do. The future loomed ahead in bleak uncertainty. In a prostrate South few knew how to face the changed order.

One of those was Clay Montrose. His whole world had disappeared, and he did not know how to put the pieces back together. Once authoritative and decisive, he was now totally frustrated. Only a remnant of blacks remained from his hundreds of slaves, too few to restore the farmlands to complete productivity. There were new laws that had to be observed dealing with former servants, papers to fill out, forms to be filed.

Observing her father-in-law's changed personality, Garnet gradually came out of her own grief-stricken cocoon and tried to comfort him. "When Malcolm comes home, things will be different, Father Montrose. He'll help you sort things out, get started again —"

Clay swore, scowled, walked over to his desk, the one that had been battered and vandalized by the Yankee invasion of Montclair, took out a letter and shook it at her.

"Malcolm won't be coming home, Garnet. We got this letter from Illinois a few days ago. I didn't want to tell you right away because I knew you thought any day. . . . Well, he won't. He's going west. Here — you can read it for yourself." He handed her the two sheets of thin paper, bearing Malcolm's familiar handwriting.

The first few paragraphs told them sparingly of the horrors of the place where he had been imprisoned since his capture at Gettysburg; of having to sleep on blankets in which some poor soul had just died of smallpox and how, by some miracle, he had escaped the illness.

At first he had hoped to be exchanged, but then they moved him to another prison. There he had tried to smuggle out letters, but never knew if they had been received or not. They had not. His hopes of being exchanged were dashed when the new ruling came through that only men too weakened by illness or injury again would be released.

Garnet's eyes flew over the pages until she came to this part. "I have become friends with a fellow prisoner. He is from Texas — no wife or family — and we have become close companions. It is his plan that has caught my imagination, given me the hope I had almost lost in these dreadful years. We are going together to California.

"I cannot bear the thought of returning to a devastated land, a defeated South, everything I loved laid waste, destroyed. It is not impossible, I am told, that in the gold fields of California there are limitless veins of gold and other precious metals and ore running through the hills, riches to make a man wealthy, there for the taking. Any man with enough determination, strength, and courage can make his fortune in a matter of months. If this is true, I can come back to Virginia a rich man, able to restore Montclair to its original splendor, restock our stables, replant, and reap the harvest. I will not come back until I can do this. I will not come back a beaten man.

"I trust, until that happy day, my little son Jonathan will understand. That he will be proud of his father. It was Rose's wish that, after the war, he would go to see his Meredith relatives in Massachusetts. This request should be honored. I give my permission. I will let you know where I am and where you can write me as soon as Jack and I are settled somewhere. With dearest love to you, my parents, to the others at Montclair. . . ."

Silently Garnet handed the letter back to Mr. Montrose.

"We Southern men were not prepared for ruin," he said morosely.

How ironic, Garnet mused, another lingering hope shattered. For she had to admit that it had occurred to her that now that both she and Malcolm were free, there might have been a chance for them in the future. But now that had dissolved like all her other childish dreams. Even what gratitude Malcolm might feel for her in caring for his mother, his child, his home during these years, was a poor substitute for the love she had longed for —

Instinctively Garnet straightened her shoulders as if steeling herself for yet another loss. She had lost in such quick succession so many whom she loved. This little boy was all she had left to lose.

Within weeks the letter from John Meredith came. Having anticipated yet dreaded it, Garnet opened it reluctantly. As she did, she could hear the sound of children's laughter outside — Jonathan and little Druscilla playing tag under the trees. She dragged her eyes back to the finely-scripted letter and read:

It was my dead sister's earnest request and deepest wish that in the event of her or her husband's death, their son should be sent to us to raise as our own child. In her letter written to both my father and me shortly after she received word that Captain Montrose was missing, presumed dead, she told us she had made her wishes clear in a letter, witnessed and signed and placed in an envelope to be opened after her passing, if such a sad event were to occur. Which, in spite of her youth, the tragedy of fate brought to pass — to all our sorrow.

Now that the calamitous war that has divided our country these past four years is at last over, I am able to communicate with you, my dear Mrs. Montrose, and convey my intention to carry out my dead sister's wishes. Rose spoke of you so lovingly in her letters to us, and I trust you returned her sisterly regard for you and are as anxious as we are to fulfill her last wishes.

I will soon be relieved of my duties here in Washington, and will be returning to civilian life shortly. If you could arrange to bring young Jonathan to Richmond, I can meet you there.

His grandfather Meredith, his great-aunt Vanessa, my wife Frances and I are all looking forward to meeting our nephew whom we have not seen since he was an infant, and to welcoming him into our home and hearts.

> Yours most sincerely,
> John Meredith,
> Major, U.S.A.

Reading it over, Garnet tried to imagine the haughty bearing of the cold New Englander, the arrogant Army officer who was Rose's brother. The handwriting was of an educated man, a Harvard man like Malcolm, she thought bitterly . . . if Malcolm had never gone north to college, he would never have met Rose Meredith, and she would never be facing the dreadful parting before her.

Garnet folded up the letter and put it in her apron pocket, then looked out the window again.

Every time she looked at Jonathan, she saw Malcolm. He was a handsome little boy, small and quick, perfectly coordinated.

He had dark hair like his father's but his eyes were rich brown like Rose's. His skin was tanned to a golden brown after running barefoot in as few clothes as possible all through the spring, which had been early and hot this year.

Sometimes when he came running in for a drink of water, out of breath, laughing with his small, white teeth showing, his head back, his dark curls damp and tousled, Garnet could not resist snatching him up for a quick hug.

Garnet fought back the rush of anger, the resentment that flooded her, the renewal of heartbreak that cut like broken glass inside her. Biting her lip, she turned abruptly away from the window, the sight and sound of the laughing children.

It wouldn't hurt to wait a while before telling Jonathan, Garnet decided. A few days' delay — what would it matter? They would have him the rest of his life. Why shouldn't she hold on a little longer to what should have been hers?

Two weeks later Garnet, with Jonathan, waited tensely in the lobby of the Richmond Hotel where she had arranged to meet John Meredith. When a tall, dark-haired man approached them, Garnet's first thought was, *Thank goodness he's not wearing a Yankee uniform!* That would have scared Jonathan right away and started them off on the wrong foot.

John Meredith was an impressive-looking man, well-dressed, serious of expression. The only resemblance he bore to Rose was his eyes — deep brown, heavily lashed for a man. And as they rested on Jonathan, they softened noticeably.

Garnet felt Jonathan's little hand tighten in her own as the man approached them. She leaned down and whispered, "This is your Uncle John, honey, your mama's brother."

John Meredith halted in front of them, then bent down so that his face was on the level of the child's, his eyes looking directly into the boy's.

"Hello, Jonathan." John Meredith's voice was deep, but gentle. He held out one large hand and offered it to him. Jonathan waited a full minute then hesitantly put his small, chubby hand out and let John Meredith cover it with his as he began to speak very gently to Jonathan.

"Jonathan, your mother was my little sister and I loved her very much and I love you, too. Not just because you're part of her, but because you're *you*. We're going to get to know each other. I'm going to take you to all the places your mama knew when she was growing up. We'll go fishing and when it snows and the river freezes, I'll teach you to iceskate. You'd like that, wouldn't you?"

Jonathan nodded, his eyes beginning to shine.

"There are two other people who loved your mama very much too. Her father, your grandfather Meredith, and your mama's Aunt Vanessa. They've been waiting so long to meet you. Wouldn't you like to go with me to see them? They live where your mama lived when she was a little girl."

Again Jonathan nodded eagerly.

472

John Meredith continued to talk to Jonathan in a low, gentle voice. The little boy seemed fascinated that this big, grown-up man was giving him all this attention. He had not been around many men in his short lifetime. His memory of his own father was dim, fading more and more with every day that passed. The men who had been in and out of Montclair during the war, had played with him, teased him and tossed him into the air, tousled his head, and called him a "good little soldier." But they, too, had come and gone quickly and left no more than a fleeting impression. Now all Jonathan's focus was concentrated on this tall, gentle-voiced man, his eyes riveted on John Meredith's face, nodding every once in a while as his uncle continued to talk. There seemed to be a total acceptance of this person who only minutes before had been a stranger.

Then, without a word to her or a look back, Jonathan went with John Meredith a little apart from Garnet, to sit together on the bench across from her.

Jonathan seemed completely absorbed in all John Meredith was telling him.

Garnet watched in resentful surprise. How quickly John Meredith had gained the child's confidence. Her immediate reaction was a kind of stunned realization that the man and boy had become friends within a few minutes. The saying "blood is thicker than water" flashed through Garnet's mind, and she thought perhaps there was some truth to that. Maybe there was an invisible bond that flowed as soon as it was activated by such a meeting.

As she watched from a distance, another emotion took the place of that first sting of hurt. It was joy not unmixed with sorrow. She had seen the man reach out to the child with tenderness and love and the special affection given to those who are particularly dear by kinship. Garnet felt a surge of gratitude for Jonathan's sake, that he was to have a new family who cared deeply for him, who could give him all the things neither the Montroses nor she could give him now — a comfortable home, material security, a good education. All the things Jonathan would need to grow up into a fine, outstanding, educated man and take his rightful place in life. In a defeated, impoverished South, orphaned and with an inheritance now ravished beyond restoration, Jonathan could have none of this if he remained in Virginia.

But even though her mind confirmed this truth, deep within her was resentment.

Through the pure weight of force of the North's victory, the Merediths were in a position to do more for this dearly beloved child so much a part of her he might have been born to her.

John Meredith led Jonathan back, and they stood before her, hand-in-hand.

"Well, I think it's time to go now," John Meredith said. "We have a train to catch. Say good-bye to your Aunt Garnet now, Jonathan."

Garnet folded Jonathan into her arms, struggling against the dreadful ache in her throat as she nestled her face into the thick dark curls, feeling the warmth of his small, sturdy body against her breast, the scent of his fresh-washed hair, the starchy smell of his shirt collar, and newness of his cotton suit. She kissed his cheek, then cupping his rosy little face in both her hands, she looked long into those beautiful brown eyes now dancing with excitement.

"We're going on the *cars*, Auntie 'Net!" he exclaimed.

"I know, Jonathan!" Garnet replied, holding herself rigidly so as not to give way to the crowding tears.

She stood watching them, the tall man and the little boy, as they walked away from her, her hands clenched so tightly she felt her nails bite into the soft flesh of her palms. Just before they went down the steps, Jonathan turned and waved once — then he was gone.

Garnet had been back at Montclair less than a week when she faced another parting. Dove was taking Druscilla and going to Savannah.

"Maybe I'll be back, Garnet," Dove told her. "It's just that I haven't seen my relatives there since . . . since I lost Leighton . . . since the war," she sighed. "Montclair doesn't really seem my home any more. It never really did. Mr. Montrose had promised Lee property of our own, you know, but now —" She shrugged. "The only real family I have is in Savannah, although there's not much there, either."

"There's my mother here," Garnet reminded her. She had come to love her cousin who was also her sister-in-law dearly, and little Dru.

"Cousin Kate is wonderful and I love her, but she has all she can manage herself now with Rod still recovering from his wounds and sickness, and that big place —" Dove paused and her delicate face took on a look of determination as she said, "I've got to find my own way, learn to support myself and my daughter." She turned to Garnet and in her eyes Garnet saw a new strength. "We women of the South are survivors, Garnet. We've come through all this with more courage than anyone ever gave us credit for, but we have to find new ways of dealing with things as they are now."

Before Dove left, she hugged Garnet and said tremulously with tears brightening her eyes, "I may be back, Garnet. Let's not say good-bye!" She smiled.

After they were gone, Montclair seemed achingly empty, filled with the ghosts of the children who used to make the house ring with happy voices, laughter, and the sound of running feet.

With Dove's going, Garnet had to fight a paralyzing apathy. She knew what Dove had said about their being survivors was true and she felt she should be getting on with her own life. But what could she do? The Montroses depended on her more and more. There was no one else to take over the responsibility of the house, the few remaining servants, to try to direct what little farming was being done now.

It seemed ironic that she should be the one who at long last was Mistress of Montclair. But how different from the way she had once dreamed it would be.

Then she received another unexpected jolt, another parting.

Garnet was sitting at the window of her room, staring vacantly out past the orchards to the river, when a tap at her half-open door made her turn to see Tilda standing there.

She was neatly dressed in gray cotton, a shawl around her shoulders. Instead of a bandana tied around her head, she wore a broad-brimmed straw hat. In one hand she had a large cloth-covered bundle, tied and knotted; in the other, a lidded split-oak basket.

"What is it, Tilda?" Garnet asked.

"Miss Garnet, I jes' — kin I speak to you fo' a minute, ma'am?" The tone of voice was hesitant.

"Of course, Tilda, come on in." A queer little tingle of awareness tensed Garnet for the encounter.

Tilda set down her bundle and basket, advancing into the room, both her hands twisted nervously in front of her.

"I jes' came to say I wuz goin'."

"Going where, Tilda?"

"Goin' No'th, ma'am. My Jeems is in Philadelphia since he went dere afta de war, and he done sent fo' me to come. Sent

478

me the carfare to take the train." Tilda lifted her head proudly.

"To *Philadelphia!*" exclaimed Garnet. "You don't want to go way up there where you don't know anybody, do you? Philadelphia's a big city. Does Jeems have a place for you to live? What will you do there?"

Tilda shook her head. "I doan' know fo' sho', Miss Garnet. I jes' knows I has to go. We is free now, Miss Garnet. I neber been nowhere 'cepn on dis here plantation. I wuz born here, lived here all my life. I gots to have ma chanct. My chillen has got to hab deres. I mean fo' them to grow up free."

Garnet stared at the black woman she had come to know, come to depend on through all that had happened in the last four years. She felt compassion, knowing Tilda did not realize what might lie ahead of her once she left Montclair. At the same time she had to admit she felt a stirring of resentment as well. Tilda was leaving, and that meant she would not be here when Garnet needed her. *But who could blame her? I'd leave if I could,* Garnet sighed.

"Well, Tilda, all I can say is I hope you know what you're doing. I'd like to give you something to help you on your way, but I don't have any money." She threw out her hands, palms up.

"I knows, Miz Garnet. Jeems sent me 'nuf fo' the trip." She did not add it was United States Government money. All the paper money the Montroses had now was the worthless Confederate issue.

Suddenly Garnet felt a desolate sensation to realize she might never see this strong, kind woman again, another link in the old life.

"I hate to see you leave, Tilda," she said at last.

"Well, Miss Garnet, Miss Rose taught us dat we is all equal in de Lawd's sight and now de *law* sez we free jes' lak ebryone else. 'Sides that, she taught me that iffen the Bible is right and we seek it, we shall know de truf and de truf shall set us free. I gotta seek it. Truf and freedom. Gotta find out if what de Yankees promised is de truf and black folks is free up No'th."

Garnet felt a tightness in her throat and chest. Tilda had been so faithful — like a rock when the children were so ill.

When Bryce had come home to die, she nursed him as tenderly as if he had been her own. Impulsively Garnet got to her feet and went over to where Tilda stood and embraced her.

As the two women clung to each other,

black and white, their tears poured unchecked. They knew that neither time nor distance could sever the bond that united them. They had both been born and reared in Virginia, their roots went deep in the same soil; they had been through the desert of the war together, shared its suffering and its sorrows. Though mistress and slave, they were both women and they knew that in Jesus *there is neither slave nor freeman,* but only God's beloved children.

PART VII

— there will streams in the desert. . . .

They shall obtain joy and gladness,
and sorrow and sighing will flee away —
from Isaiah 35

Cameron Hall and Montclair
1868-1870

chapter
35

The months after Jonathan's departure with his uncle John Meredith, were drab and monotonous for Garnet. She missed the little boy dreadfully. He had been her joy and comfort. Now the pressure and responsibilities that were hers at Montclair became heavy indeed without the happiness his presence had provided.

That first winter after the war, hard times were widespread in the South, and Montclair did not escape any of them. Both the Cameron family and the Montroses struggled to adjust to how much life had changed. The once beautifully maintained houses and land were stark witnesses to the lack of money and labor to keep things up.

No place showed more the ravages of time and lack of help than Montclair. Everything looked run-down, it needed painting, the shutters sagged, mildew gathered around the base of the columns on the front porch, the roof leaked, the chimneys, glutted with resin and choked with rain-soaked leaves, caused the fireplaces to smoke, and winter set in. The black people who had remained were all older, and having been trained as house servants, were unwilling to do work relegated to field hands in the past.

Garnet had all this to cope with and Sara, too, who grew more difficult and dependent every day. She had never become accustomed to the loss of luxury and complained constantly. Mr. Montrose, since his return, seemed to live in a world of his own, struggling to accept the drastic alteration that defeat had brought to his personal life.

Fighting her own battle against depression and hopelessness, Garnet was relieved and delighted when Dove returned to Mayfield, bringing with her not only her welcome optimism to lift everyone's spirits but an idea as well.

Dove suggested that they open a school for young girls at Cameron Hall. Because it had been used briefly as Union headquarters when the Yankees temporarily occupied Mayfield, the mansion had not suffered the vandalism that so many other plantation homes in the area had sustained. With its spacious rooms and a half-dozen double bedrooms it would make a perfect boarding school.

Many wealthy Northerners, after the surrender, drawn by the milder Virginia climate, began flooding into the county to spend the winter. Most were families with children.

Dove pointed out that by combining their talents, the three of them could teach a variety of subjects, offering Yankee mothers a "finishing school" for their daughters in a refined Southern atmosphere.

Rod Cameron could be the equestrian instructor supplying horseback riding as an added incentive for socially ambitious mamas.

Kate immediately responded to the idea with enthusiasm, as did Garnet. They put a small advertisement in the local paper and then were amazed how quickly they began to receive applications. Within a year the school was thriving beyond their expectations — there was even a waiting list for admission.

On a bright day in June 1867 Garnet was getting dressed to ride over to Cameron Hall Academy's first graduation day program. In all the excitement of the school's success only *she* remembered that the date they had set also happened to be that of her tenth wedding anniversary.

Garnet still had lingering feelings of guilt about her marriage to Bryce, considering herself a failure as a wife. She hoped she had changed since then, and become a better person. She had tried, but she was well aware of her own faults. They seemed the same ones she had always had, only now she recognized them. She saw her own impatience and selfishness reflected in her mother-in-law, and frequently bit her tongue when dealing with Sara, where once she might have exploded in a fit of temper.

If not her character, her appearance had certainly changed, Garnet thought ruefully, looking at herself in the mirror. At twenty-eight, she was thin where she had once been slenderly curved; her burnished gold hair had darkened, but at least she had no gray hair yet, unlike poor Dove. And no wrinkles yet, either, she saw with some satisfaction.

She wished she had something better to wear to the ceremonies this afternoon than her twice-turned blue poplin. But there was hardly enough money for necessities let alone luxuries, like new dresses. But she needed something to give a touch of elegance, she decided. Maybe a lace collar or her grandmother's cameo brooch? She opened the bureau drawer to take out her small jewelry box. As she did, she saw under the pile of handkerchiefs, the edge of a small picture frame. It was a daguerreotype of Malcolm that she had had for years and kept hidden there. She had not looked at it in a long time.

"Oh, Malcolm," she sighed, shaking her head. "Where are you? What has happened to you? Why don't you write?"

Studying the handsome face, it was as though she was gazing at a stranger, someone she had known ages ago. This must have been taken when he was still at Harvard. He seemed heartbreakingly young with clear, bright eyes, filled with ideals and dreams, a smile hovering at the corners of his mouth. It had been so long since she had seen him — Garnet could hardly remember how he moved or spoke or how he used to laugh at the things she said. He was part of the past of the passionate, foolish girl she had been. She remembered how sick with rage she had been when she first heard of his engagement to Rose Meredith, and how that rage had poisoned her life for so long. Now she felt another kind of rage as she gazed at Malcolm's picture. Why didn't he let them know where he was? She thought of Sara, slowly sinking into premature senility, mourning her two dead sons, grieving the loss of her favorite one, Malcolm. A cold dread overlapped Garnet's frustrated anger. Maybe Malcolm was dead, too. They had heard of the violence in the gold fields, of claim jumping or murders of miners who struck it rich then were never heard of again. Malcolm had gone to recoup his family's fortunes. But had he lost his life in the pursuit of such a far-fetched hope?

Garnet put the little picture back and shoved the drawer shut. Whatever had happened to Malcolm, she could not think about it now. Living in the past was a terrible trap. Garnet had seen too many people around here do that.

A soft tap came at the bedroom door, followed by Carrie's voice,

"You has company downstairs, Miss Garnet."

Garnet went over and opened the door, and Carrie handed her a small calling card on which was printed JEREMY DEVLIN. As she read the name, Garnet was puzzled. She knew no one with that name. He couldn't be from Mayfield, so who could this caller be?

Curious, she went down the curving

stairway, her hand on the balustrade still scarred by Yankee saber marks from the day of that terrible raid on Montclair.

Through the open front door she saw the tall figure of a man, his back to her, standing at the edge of the veranda. There was something vaguely familiar about the set of his shoulders, the shape of his head, she thought, as she walked forward. Standing in the doorway, she asked,

"You wished to see me?"

At the sound of her voice the man turned around.

"Mrs. Montrose?" he bowed courteously. "Jeremy Devlin," he introduced himself although she was still holding his card in her hand. "I have taken the liberty of calling without first sending a note requesting permission. I hope you will forgive my presumption. However . . . I had to come."

Still mystified, Garnet asked, "I do not believe we have ever met, have we? Perhaps it is my mother-in-law or my sister-in-law you wished to see?" His identity was annoyingly elusive. Perhaps he was one of the high-spirited young officers she had danced with or flirted with in Richmond during that first winter of the War, in that brief season of gaiety and optimism and frivolity. And yet this man had a northern

491

accent. Who could he be?

Suddenly memory assailed Garnet. Surely this mild-spoken, graciously mannered gentleman could not have been one of those rude invaders who had terrorized them during that ruthless raid! Then, *in an instant, she knew who he was.* The gallant officer who had volunteered to guard their house and property, who had returned Jonathan's pony! Of course, *Major Jeremy Devlin.*

Garnet shook her head. "It is *you* who must forgive *me.* We have never forgotten your kindness. It's just that —"

He held up one hand to halt her apology. "Please! My coming like this might even have revived painful memories. For that I am truly sorry." He gestured with one hand to the flower-strewn yard. Spring had come late and so in June, Montclair was in full bloom, yellow daffodils and iris in a variety of blues, purples, and pale lavender spread a magnificent carpet of color, as well as the rhododendrons and azaleas. "I always remembered this place as being so beautiful. I had to come back and assure myself that it was still here, that it had not been destroyed —" An expression of concern cast a shadow on his handsome face, a catch in his voice made it falter.

"Somehow Montclair has managed to survive . . . even the Yankee army," Garnet replied, with an edge of bitterness in her tone. But her inborn good manners caused her to make a quick change of subject diverting it from that dangerous trend. "— although not too well, I'm afraid."

"So much needs doing but there's no —" she stopped herself before she had said *there's no money, no help, and no way to pay them if you could get help.* She certainly did not want to flaunt their poverty in front of this obviously wealthy Yankee stranger. She asked quickly, "What brings you to Virginia now, Mr. Devlin? Not just curiosity surely?"

"Besides being haunted by a lovely Southern mansion? Yes, Mrs. Montrose, I confess there were extenuating reasons for my being in this part of the country just now. I accompanied my sister who has come to collect her daughter attending Cameron Hall Academy."

Garnet gave a little gasp. "Your niece attends Cameron Hall? What is her name?"

"Malissa Bennett."

"Malissa! A really delightful girl!" smiled Garnet.

It was Devlin's turn to look surprised.

"You know Malissa?" he asked.

Garnet nodded.

"In fact, she is one of my favorite students."

"Students?"

Garnet could not help laughing at Devlin's expression.

"Yes. You see, Mr. Devlin, my sister-in-law and I along with my mother, Mrs. Cameron, run the school at Cameron Hall, which was my childhood home."

"But I thought this . . . Montclair . . . was your home."

"It was, after my marriage and during the war. My husband's parents still live here."

"And your son . . . your little boy?" Devlin asked.

"My son?" Garnet shook her head. Then, with sudden awareness, she explained, "Oh, Jonathan is not mine. He is my nephew. My husband's brother's child."

"I see." Devlin hesitated a moment. "Your husband —"

"Is dead. Captured. Wounded. Killed." The words came out in staccato.

"I'm sorry." Devlin looked truly distressed.

As if he had been too abruptly brought back to the present, Jeremy Devlin took a second to reply. "Yes, indeed, I wouldn't miss it. Again, I beg your forgiveness for my intrusion today . . . perhaps it was wrong of me to come, to stir up unpleasant memories —"

"Not at all, Mr. Devlin. It gave me the opportunity to thank you again for the service you rendered us during a very . . . difficult time. I remember especially your extraordinary kindness in bringing Bugle Boy back to Jonathan."

"How is Jonathan? I imagine he has grown into quite a lad."

Garnet's voice was tinged with sadness caused by the long separation from the child she loved so much.

"He is with his mother's family in Massachusetts now. I haven't seen him in nearly three years," she said, and in spite of herself, her voice shook.

"I'm sorry," Devlin said, shaking his head. "Again I seem to have brought up a painful subject. Dare I ask your forgiveness once more?"

Not trusting herself to answer, Garnet merely bowed slightly.

The conversation shifted and to her surprise Garnet found Jeremy Devlin to be delightful company, intelligent, interesting and an amusing raconteur as well. She discovered there was often a mischievous twinkle in those usually serious eyes. At one point she heard herself laugh at something he said, and realized with amazement that it had been a very long time since she had laughed.

He worked for a New York publishing firm and would be going to England in the fall to make contacts with some writers and publishers there.

"How wonderful," Garnet sighed. "I'm green with envy! I've never been to Europe — or anywhere but to visit relatives in Charleston and Savannah. Nowhere exciting or foreign, for that matter."

"But you're still so young! You have your whole life ahead of you — to travel, go places, do many things —"

"Young? I feel a hundred years old." Garnet made a comic face, then laughed a little self-consciously. "And I suppose I'll spend the rest of my life right here, traveling back and forth between Montclair and Cameron Hall!"

"Not necessarily," Jeremy paused. "Is there any reason you should remain here instead of living with your mother at Cameron Hall?"

"My mother-in-law is an invalid and my father-in-law . . . Well, he just never has quite readjusted since the war . . . They both depend on me," she told him, wondering why she was confiding so much to this virtual stranger. But it seemed comfortable and natural.

"Things change, you know. Nothing ever stays exactly the same. The time may come when you feel you can leave," he said.

"If Malcolm came back —" Garnet began, then flushed. Jeremy looked puzzled, so she went on. "Malcolm is the oldest son, the heir. He was expected to take over the plantation, but — the war, and personal tragedies —" She hesitated. "Afterward, he went West to California and until . . . I mean, my *obligation* is *here*."

Jeremy Devlin called twice more before leaving Mayfield with his sister and niece, but not before he had asked Garnet if he could correspond with her during the summer.

When he rose to leave, she had given him her hand to say good-bye and he continued to hold it as he said, "If I should be able to come back to Virginia before sailing for England in September, may I call again? And may I write to you?"

Although Garnet was tall, he towered over her and the pressure of his hand was firm on hers as she tried to withdraw it.

"Why yes, of course, Mr. Devlin, I should be pleased —"

chapter

36

Even without the classes she taught at Cameron Hall Academy, the summer was a busy one for Garnet, supervising the house, Sara's care, the produce from the gardens of vegetables and fruit from the orchards to be canned or made into jams and preserves.

Gradually summer became early autumn. A lovely haze hung over the hills and the sun turned the yellow maples to gold. Along the drive the giant elms formed an arch of russet and bronze and the Virginia creeper blazed crimson as it clung to the sunny side of the house.

On a beautiful September afternoon two letters were delivered to Garnet at Montclair, and she took them out to read them in the walled garden known as the English bride's garden.

The first was written in a bold, angular hand and she knew almost before she opened it that it was from Jeremy Devlin.

They had spent most of two delightful days together in June after school closed. His sister had taken Malissa to the Springs, but Jeremy had remained in Mayfield. He had driven out each day to Montclair to visit Garnet.

Thinking of him now, Garnet read his letter with a ripple of anticipation. He would be returning from England within a few weeks and wanted to come to Montclair if she could receive him.

Garnet felt her cheeks grow warm with pleasure as her eyes skimmed again the line he had written: "I can assure you it will be the high point of my trip, something I have been looking forward to since June."

As she read the letter through a second time, a mental picture of Jeremy Devlin came vividly to life. He was different from any man she had ever known. He had a quality of gentle strength combined with keen intelligence and an amusing wit. Although his manner was reserved, there was a special quality of warmth. She would be glad to see him again, she thought, as she refolded the letter and put it back in the envelope.

The second letter was a mystery. The envelope was of cheap paper written in a laboriously childish handwriting. When she opened it, she was surprised and touched.

"Dear Missy Garnet. Many times I been wishing to rite to you but did not have the oppertunity. I have got two little chilren, a boy I named after Miss Rose's fine boy Jonathan James. James is after my husbin. Now a baby girl I named Lorena Rose. Lorena from the pretty song Miss Dove used to sing on the piano, do you remember? My husbin Jeems is working in the Mill here. I do laundry for some folks. We all doin well and in good health. Praise God. I larned to read more and now rite when my boy started school. We send our best love to you all. We hope all there is fine, too. TILDA"

For some reason tears came into Garnet's eyes as she finished reading this letter. How proud Rose would have been to see the results of all her efforts with Tilda. Obviously Tilda was still bettering herself, growing and learning.

One crisp fall morning not long afterward, Garnet was working in the garden.

She was cutting the last of the chrysanthemums, tying up the stems, when a shadow fell across the ground from behind her and she sat back on her heels, looked up into Jeremy's smiling face.

"I didn't expect you so soon!" she gasped. "I never heard your carriage drive up!"

"I couldn't wait any longer to see you!" He held out his hands and helped her to her feet.

"But I'm hardly suitably dressed to receive company!" she said, looking down at the rough cotton pinafore she had on over an old calico dress with turned-up hem, and putting her hand to the battered straw hat tied under her chin with faded ribbons.

"You look beautiful to me!" Jeremy laughed but his eyes were serious.

Although flattered, Garnet retorted lightly, "They say 'beauty is in the eye of the beholder.' Mr. Devlin, I suggest you have your eyes checked!"

"I've been told I have perfect vision," he replied with a straight face even as his eyes were amused. He held out his hand to her and together they strolled toward the veranda, where they sat down on the steps shaded by the leafy elms.

Feeling his eyes still upon her, Garnet brushed back the strands of hair that curled in tendrils around her forehead.

"I declare, I must look a sight —" she

said rather self-consciously.

"Not at all," Jeremy said quickly. "I meant what I said. You *are* beautiful. I just want to look at you, the way you are — I've thought of nothing else since June."

Amazed at his frankness, Garnet stared at him.

"I'm sorry. Maybe I shouldn't have said that. But it's true. I came especially to tell you — to ask you —" He halted then rushed on, "I suppose I should have led up to this with traditional etiquette, written it in a formal letter first, but I couldn't — I *had* to come, see you again, tell you in person." He reached for Garnet's hand and said simply, "I love you, Garnet. I think I have from the first time I saw you."

"But . . . we hardly know each other!" she exclaimed.

"I feel as if I've known you forever. You've been in my heart and mind for a long time. I've carried an unforgettable picture of that beautiful, brave Southern lady for years. I could not get you out of my mind. You've haunted my waking hours and been in my dreams ever since the first time I saw you." He closed his eyes for a moment. "I can still see you standing in the doorway in the moonlight.

The porch was shadowy, and you held a candle in one hand, your hair all about your face . . . your lovely face with the light on it —" He stopped. "Do I sound like a fool?"

She shook her head.

"I don't know what to say."

"You don't have to say anything unless you want to. I guess I just had to tell you. I couldn't leave without telling you. Perhaps I rushed into this, perhaps I should have waited. . . . It hardly seems the right way but . . ." Another pause. "I had no real hope of ever seeing you again. Then I did not know you were free."

He reached over and took her hand, gently removed her gardening glove, and raised it to his lips, kissed it.

"I would like to do so much for you, Garnet. I would like to love you, care for you, take you traveling, show you the world . . . give you the world. Do you think you could care for me . . . in time?"

Garnet was breathless, stunned by all Jeremy was saying. She jumped to her feet, his hand still holding hers. He stood, too.

"I've frightened you, haven't I? I'm sorry." He sounded upset. "I've blundered when I wanted to be so careful. Have I ruined everything?"

Garnet shook her head, glad that the wide-brimmed hat hid her face. When at last she found her voice, the words tumbled out.

"Yes, I suppose I was frightened. I never thought, never guessed."

Long ago Garnet had lost her assurance that any man was hers for the application of a few flirtatious wiles. Life had been too difficult, too full of responsibilities during the last few years, to think anything would ever be different. Now this stranger, this man of strength, intelligence, vigor, had come into a life she had come to accept and offered her a chance, a choice . . . the world!

"Then, you will think about what I've said? I may hope? . . . Oh, Garnet, there is so much more I want to say —"

Her voice was so low he had to bend to hear her reply.

"Yes, Jeremy."

"May I come again this evening?" he asked. "May we talk more later?"

She nodded.

"I do love you, Garnet," he said earnestly.

She stood motionless as he left. She heard his boots crunching on the shell drive and she watched his tall figure mount and disappear down the drive.

He came earlier than expected and sheepishly apologized. "I found myself too restless."

Garnet, who had been ready and watching the drive for his arrival, smiled and led him into one of the two smaller parlors. There was a fire glowing in the marble fireplace. They sat on either side of the twin loveseats and for a long moment neither said anything, just watched the flames rising in red, blue, gold pyramids while the applewood logs snapped, scenting the room with pungent fragrance.

Finally it was Jeremy who spoke. He was watching the play of firelight on Garnet's face when he said, "Forgive me for staring."

"You'll make me uneasy," she said but she smiled and handed him his tea.

The room was still, with only the sound of the crackling fire on the hearth and the wind rising outside in the autumn evening to accompany the cadence of their beating hearts.

"Have you thought about what I said this morning, Garnet?" Jeremy asked gently after a while.

"Yes, I have. And I should have told you

right away, Jeremy. I am not *free*."

He sat forward in his chair, set down the teacup, clasped both hands in front of him, leaned toward her anxiously.

"You mean, there's someone else?"

Immediately Garnet thought of Malcolm. Had she really given up all hope of him? She was sure she had. Yet, should he suddenly come home, what then? But that was not what she meant when she had told Jeremy she wasn't free. How could she leave Montclair, abandon Sara and Clayton Montrose? They were so helpless, living out their days in a kind of relentless despair, reliving the days of glory that were gone and would never return. They were pitiable, but Garnet was bound by her pity for them.

Jeremy's intent gaze drew her and she had to look into his truth-probing eyes searching her very soul, delving into the secrets of her heart.

"Not in that way," she replied slowly, then tried to explain to him about the Montroses.

"I understand. But if you should marry, they would have to make the necessary adjustments, wouldn't they? Surely, they did not expect a young, vibrant, beautiful woman to remain a widow forever . . . to stay here with them?" Jeremy frowned.

"Five years ago I would never have imagined something like this happening. I never thought of marrying again —" *except to Malcolm,* Garnet had to add silently and truthfully.

"Five years ago we did not even know each other," Jeremy reminded her. "Now, everything is different."

Impulsively Garnet asked him, "Have you ever been in love?"

Jeremy smiled slightly. "Before *now,* you mean?"

She nodded.

"Yes. I was engaged to a lovely girl before the war. We'd known each other most of our lives. I did not think it fair to her to marry her, not knowing if I'd come back, or worse still, how I might come back. But she died. Consumption. She had always been delicate." His eyes were leveled at Garnet as he said, "We were both very young." He repeated, "Very young."

"I'm sorry. I did not mean to make you sad."

"You didn't. It's all part of my life just as your marriage, your loss is part of yours. Everything we go through becomes part of what we are. Sorrow either strengthens us or embitters us, don't you think?"

Garnet looked at him and felt his strong faith, his courage and optimism flowing through her. For the first time in years she felt the stirring of hope. Maybe, after all, there was a new beginning possible. Before she could explore it further, Jeremy got up, came over, and knelt beside her. Their eyes were level. They were only inches apart, and then he kissed her very tenderly.

She closed her eyes as he kissed her again, this time responding instinctively to the gentle insistence of his lips. Then, slowly the kiss ended and she opened her eyes again and dazedly looked into those deep-set loving ones.

In a strange way Garnet felt she had waited all her life for such a moment.

Later, they walked to the door, hand-in-hand. The time for parting had come.

"I will write as often as I can," Jeremy told her. "When I come back, perhaps you will know how you feel and whatever we need to do, we can do."

There was still so much unsettled, so much unresolved. This had all happened with such amazing swiftness Garnet's head reeled with it.

"I do love you. I know we can be happy together," Jeremy assured her.

Happy? Is happiness really attainable, to

me, to anyone? Once she might have believed in the "happily ever after" of fairy tales. But she had been stripped of romantic illusions by the reality of her life. She wasn't sure she believed in happiness any more.

That night after Jeremy left, Garnet stood at her bedroom window and gazed out at a scene she had looked at a thousand times. But this night had a dreamlike quality. Montclair and its surroundings were wrapped in a kind of magical light, the moon shimmering down through the trees, enveloping everything in an unbroken peace.

She knew a life with someone like Jeremy would be entirely different from anything she had known before. He was northern born, bred, educated. He was cultured, well-traveled, worldly, urbane, sophisticated. He was also mature, considerate, gentle. A different kind of man from her experience.

She had been married to a boy — Bryce of the boyish charm, the sweet, easygoing manner. He had loved her in his fashion and, in the end, she had cared deeply for him.

She had hero-worshiped Malcolm, dreamed about him, imagined, and fantasized a romance. But now she realized she had never really loved nor been loved by any man.

Jeremy Devlin was offering her just that, a second chance at life, a second chance for love, the possibility of a new kind of happiness. And now that he had returned from England, he would demand her answer.

Garnet turned away from the window, took off her robe, and got into bed. But an hour later, by the striking of the big grandfather clock downstairs, she was still wide awake.

Maybe it was the moonlight streaming in the window that was keeping her awake . . . maybe. She moved restlessly, shifting her body so that the milky glow of moonlight would not be in her eyes. Why was she sleepless after such a long, eventful day? Was it just the moonlight? Or was it the disturbing thoughts of Jeremy Devlin?

He loved her, she thought in some wonder. Perhaps he had first fallen in love with an imaginary woman, a vision held in a romantic, misty dream. But now he must see something in her that attracted, compelled.

But did she love him? Enough to marry him? Garnet knew she would have to find the answer in her own heart.

chapter
37

That winter seemed especially long to Garnet, a parade of gray days brightened considerably by the flow of letters that arrived regularly from Jeremy Devlin in England. They became for her a window to a world she could only imagine. Jeremy wrote of the interesting people he met in the literary circles in which he traveled, of attending theater and lectures, dinner parties, and weekends at country manors. It all seemed a million miles from her own isolated existence at Montclair.

Jeremy never failed to close his letters without reminding her of the answer she had promised to give him the next time he came to Virginia.

Garnet spent much prayerful time thinking about the answer she knew Jeremy wanted. Over and over she asked herself the important question she knew she must answer for herself before she answered Jeremy's. Garnet admired Jeremy, had come to appreciate his intelligence, sensitivity, and strength — but did she love him?

Garnet understood so much more now about the real meaning of love; the kind of love a lifetime of devotion demanded. Was she capable of that kind of love for Jeremy? Garnet did not want to make the mistake, a second time, of marrying unless her love was as Paul defined it in 1 Corinthians.

Those last weeks as Bryce's wife, as he lay dying, Garnet had determined to become the wife he deserved, if he survived. But she had not had that chance.

Somehow, Garnet felt when she saw Jeremy again she would *know* what her answer should be. In the meantime, she read his letters, feeling both humble and thankful that such a fine man loved *her.*

Then at last, winter disappeared. In mid-March, almost overnight, spring came to Montclair. Pink and white dogwoods spread their lace over bare branches, and in the yard around the house suddenly were carpets of yellow daffodils.

One balmy, springlike day, Garnet gathered armfuls of the flowers and brought them into the house. She was in the pantry arranging them into bouquets to take up to Sara's room when she heard footsteps along the hall. She paused in her task for a moment and looked up just as a man's figure filled the doorway from the dining room. The flowers she was holding dropped from her numb hands even as he spoke her name.

"Garnet!"

Her heart sprang up like a wild thing, fluttering in her breast, choking off her breath. She felt faint and weak for a moment, then he spoke again in that old teasing manner she recognized instantly.

"You look like you've seen a ghost! It's just *me*, Garnet. I've come home."

At last she found her voice. "Malcolm! Malcolm, it really *is* you!"

As he took a step toward her, she rushed from around the table and flung herself into his outstretched arms, crying out, "Oh, Malcolm! I can hardly believe it!"

He caught her up and swung her around in his arms, hugging her tightly. She kept saying his name again and again, laughing and half-crying. It wasn't until he finally set her back down on her feet, his hands still on her waist, that she saw behind him, framed in the doorway, a stunningly beautiful young woman.

Garnet stared at her, then looked at Malcolm in bewilderment.

He swept off his hat with a flourish, made a short bow, and said,

"Garnet, may I present my wife, Blythe." To the girl he said, "This is my sister-in-law, Garnet — Cameron Montrose."

When Garnet tried to piece together the scene that followed, it all came in a jumble of impressions heightened by her exploding emotions, her struggle to contain the mixture of unbelief, shock, dismay, and finally, acceptance of the unacceptable.

Malcolm had come home. But he was *married*. For the second time, he had brought an unexpected bride to Montclair.

Garnet's relief at his return, the hopes she had clung to that once he came back Malcolm would take over the management, that he would share the burdens and responsibilities that she had shouldered so long, were smashed.

At his introduction to Blythe, Garnet felt dizzy but managed to make some kind of greeting while she absorbed the reality of the word *wife*.

The "new" Mrs. Montrose was as astonishingly attired as she was extraordinarily lovely. Her slim-waisted, full-breasted figure was clothed in a travel-stained violet suit with deep purple lapels and cuffs. The bonnet, from which red curls straggled, looked as if it had sustained irreparable damage. But even though her outfit was peculiar, her face was perfection — wide dark eyes, pink and porcelain complexion, full, rosy mouth.

The girl advanced into the room after glancing at Malcolm, as if for permission, held out her hand to Garnet, and said shyly, "I'm very pleased to meet you."

Garnet swallowed and murmured something, but it was Malcolm to whom she spoke in a voice that sounded harsh even to herself as she demanded,

"But why did you never write? Why didn't you let us know?"

Malcolm shrugged. "Too much happened. It was hard to explain, difficult to try to write. Where I was I didn't know even if any letters would get to you. Then, too much time went by and I —" He halted and asked abruptly, "How is my mother?"

Garnet bit her lip in frustration. Indignation at Malcolm's indifference to what *she* might have been feeling all this time, what she had been through *because* of *him* boiled up in her. But she managed to restrain the words her anger prompted her to say. She left unsaid that he had let them all worry and wonder whether he was alive or dead. That he had let *her* take on the care of *his* son, *his* mother, *his* ancestral home, expending all her strength and energy *here*, putting aside her own needs, her desires, delaying getting on with her own life —

The truth, Garnet knew, was that underneath it all, she had been waiting for him to come home — possibly to *her!* It had never crossed her mind that Malcolm might again choose another bride instead of *her.*

Suddenly Garnet felt as if she were smothering. Turning quickly to Malcolm, she said, "Malcolm, I'd best go prepare your mother — otherwise, the shock might be too much for her. If you'll excuse me —" she nodded her head briefly to Blythe, then brushing by her, Garnet made her escape and walked out of the kitchen into the hall. At the foot of the staircase she leaned on it for a moment, her breath coming shallowly. Praying for strength and with a valiant calling up of willpower, she mounted the steps. She held herself tightly, thin shoulders straight, until she reached the second balcony. Then she lifted her skirts and ran down the hall to her room. There she flung herself upon her knees beside her bed, pleading for help.

"God! My God!" was all she could utter as anguish flooded over her. Malcolm was home — and he had brought a bride — again! All the old pain of that long-ago day when he had brought Rose to Montclair assailed her, and yet — it was not the same.

Gradually Garnet stopped shaking. She became very still as if listening. In a few minutes a calm, almost a peace began to steal over her. What was it Tilda had said when she left Montclair to find a new life? She had repeated something learned from Rose:

"Ye shall know the truth and the truth shall set you free."

Garnet struggled with the truth. Malcolm had never loved her the way she wanted him to — she would have to finally accept that. Now he was forever out of reach. It was so final that she could feel the raw hurt of it.

The shock of Malcolm's homecoming, the fact that he had brought home a bride, was devastating. But with it there was also a feeling of relinquishment that was almost good, peaceful.

She could leave Montclair now. There would be a new mistress here and Malcolm would take over the care of his parents, the responsibilities that were now his.

Garnet could leave with no recriminations, no regrets. There was a future to think about. A future, perhaps, with Jeremy Devlin. At any rate, she could go freely, leaving the past behind.

Garnet gathered her pride around her like a ragged cloak, and got up from her knees. She would tell Sara of Malcolm's return, then she would go downstairs and welcome the new mistress properly.

chapter
38

Three months had passed since Malcolm returned to Montclair with his new bride. Within days of their arrival, Garnet left Montclair and came back to Cameron Hall. It had been over ten years since she had left her home to become Bryce Montrose's bride. She felt she had come full circle. It was now June and she was back in her girlhood room waiting for the arrival of a "suitor."

Upon his arrival in New York from England, Jeremy Devlin had written that after he completed his business there he would be on his way to Mayfield. Needless to say, he was coming for the answer Garnet had promised to give him.

In his last letter Jeremy told her that the publishing company for which he worked wanted him to divide his time between their New York and London offices, spending six months a year in England. Garnet read this information, knowing Jeremy meant her to consider that if she married him, they would be living part of the year a long way from her native Virginia. The idea both excited and frightened her. Of course, the first decision she had to make was whether she would accept Jeremy's proposal of marriage.

The day he was coming, Garnet felt as nervous as a young girl preparing for her first party. She did her hair at least three times, changed dresses twice, fretting about how her appearance might compare to the fashionable women Jeremy associated with at London gatherings. But by the time she heard the sound of carriage wheels coming up the drive, Garnet was too eager to see him to worry about how she looked.

As she started downstairs, her heart was beating so hard that she had to pause at the landing to draw a deep breath. From there Garnet could see into the drawing room, and Jeremy standing in front of the fireplace. He was turned away from her, looking out the French windows toward the garden. It was not until she reached the last few steps that he happened to glance into the mirror above the mantel and see her reflection in it.

Their eyes met in the mirror, and for an endless moment they looked at each other. Then Jeremy slowly turned around. Holding her breath, Garnet hesitated. Jeremy took one tentative step toward her. Then she moved swiftly across the hall. A few feet from him she halted.

"Well?" Jeremy asked.

Garnet looked up into the face regarding her so hopefully, into eyes gazing at her with infinite tenderness and love. At once all her doubts, her old sorrows, disappointments vanished. She felt young again and deliriously happy, and she knew what her answer would be.

"Yes!" she whispered huskily.

"Yes?" he repeated as if he had not quite heard correctly. "Yes, you will marry me?"

Garnet nodded solemnly. "Yes, Jeremy."

"Oh, my darling Garnet . . . I'm so . . ." for once the articulate, suave Jeremy seemed at a loss for words. Instead he opened his arms and Garnet walked into them. As they closed around her, Garnet felt serenely happy, sheltered, and at peace.

She heard him murmur her name and she sighed contentedly. The icy hardness that had formed around her heart to ward off hurt suddenly melted and she was flooded with joy.

> For, lo, the winter is past,
> The rain is over and gone;
> The flowers appear on the earth;
> The time of the singing of birds
> is come. . . .

Epilogue

The huge steamship moved slowly out of New York Harbor. Standing at its rail, a graceful woman in an amethyst velvet traveling suit and mink capelet turned and smiled at the tall, dark-haired man at her side.

"I can hardly believe it! It's like a fairytale. I'm really on my way to England!"

"And Paris! Then Italy and Switzerland!" The look he gave her was so tender and loving it made her feel undeserving. "I want to take you everywhere, show you everything!" He took her hand in his and asked her earnestly, "Did I tell you how enormously happy you've made me?"

Jeremy raised her hand to his lips, singling out the third finger of her left hand where beside the gold wedding band was the cluster of garnets and diamonds he had brought her from Austria for her engagement ring.

Garnet did not say anything, but the light in those beautiful amber eyes spoke volumes, expressing to Jeremy how much she loved him.

Garnet, thinking she would never know happiness, had decided if she could find contentment, that would be enough. She had never expected to know the thrilling sweetness of desire, the response to passion, or the fulfillment of complete love. But she had found them all in Jeremy.

Garnet, who thought she had lost everything, had been given her heart's desire, just as the prophet Joel had predicted: "I will restore the years the locusts have eaten."

They stood together watching the shoreline grow dimmer and more distant. Virginia, Montclair seemed very far away now. But Garnet knew a new life waited for her just beyond that far horizon.

"Come, darling, it's getting cold," Jeremy whispered. "Let's go in."

Garnet slipped her hand into his and they walked toward the opening door ahead.

Family Tree

In Scotland

Brothers GAVIN and ROWAN MONTROSE, descendants of the chieftan of the Clan Graham, came to Virginia to build on an original King's Grant of two thousand acres along the James River. They began to clear, plant, and build upon it.

In 1722, GAVIN's son, KENNETH MONTROSE, brought his bride, CLAIR FRASER, from Scotland, and they settled in Williamsburg while their plantation house — "Montclair" — was being planned and built. They had three children: sons KENNETH and DUNCAN, and daughter JANET.

In England

The Barnwell Family.

GEORGE BARNWELL first married WINIFRED AINSELY, and they had two sons: GEORGE and WILLIAM. BARNWELL later married a widow, ALICE CARY, who had a daughter, ELEANORA.

ELEANORA married NORBERT MARSH (widower with son, SIMON), and they had a daughter, NORAMARY.

In Virginia

Since the oldest son inherits, GEORGE BARNWELL's younger son, WILLIAM, came to Virginia, settled in Williamsburg, and started a shipping and importing business.

WILLIAM married ELIZABETH DEAN, and they had four daughters: WINNIE, LAURA, KATE, and SALLY. WILLIAM and ELIZABETH adopted NORAMARY when she was sent to Virginia at twelve years of age.

KENNETH MONTROSE married CLAIR FRASER. They had three children: KENNETH, JANET, and DUNCAN.

DUNCAN married NORAMARY MARSH, and they had three children: CAMERON, ROWAN, and ALAN.

CAMERON MONTROSE married LORABETH WHITAKER, and they had

one son, GRAHAM. Later CAMERON married ARDEN SHERWOOD, and they remained childless.

After the death of his first wife, LUELLE HAYES, GRAHAM MONTROSE married AVRIL DUMONT. Although they had no children of their own, they adopted his nephew, CLAYBORN MONTROSE.

The Montrose Family

CLAYBORN MONTROSE married SARA LEIGHTON, and they had three sons: MALCOLM, who married ROSE MEREDITH; BRYSON, who married GARNET CAMERON; and LEIGHTON (LEE), who married DOVE ARUNDELL.

The Cameron Family

DOUGLAS CAMERON married KATHERINE MAITLAND. They had twin sons, RODERICK and STEWART, and one daughter, GARNET.

About the Author

Jane Peart, award-winning novelist and short story writer, grew up in North Carolina and was educated in New England. Although she now lives in northern California, her heart has remained in her native South — its people, its history, and its traditions. With more than 20 novels and 250 short stories to her credit, Jane likes to emphasize in her writing the timeless and recurring themes of family, traditional values, and a sense of place.

Ten years in the writing, the *Brides of Montclair* series is a historical, family saga of enduring beauty. In each new book, another generation comes into its own at the beautiful Montclair estate, near Williamsburg, Virginia. These compelling, dramatic stories reaffirm the importance of committed love, loyalty, courage, strength of character, and abiding faith in times of triumph and tragedy, sorrow and joy.